THE MURDER OF PHILIP OAKES

Gavin Maynard-Wyatt

First published in paperback by
Michael Terence Publishing in 2022
www.mtp.agency

ISBN 9781800944176

Michael Terence
Publishing

Dedicated to

Liam Michael Maynard-Wyatt

I love you with all my heart and I'm so very proud of you

Acknowledgements
Liz Hudson
Charlotte Thomson

With thanks to
Tony Briant
Carol Kelleher
Janice Nash
Glenn Chaplin
Sarah Henderson

Characters

Philip Oakes: Victim

Ethan Oakes: Brother of Philip
Emma Oakes: Ethan's Wife
Children: Adam, Saul and Max

Jacob Spencer: Philip's Best Friend
Tanvi Spencer: Jacob's Wife
Children: Rory and Adrian

Rebecca Firth: Woman from the Pub and Hospital
Children: Amelia and Alice

Arjun Singh: Bartender
Brothers: Rajan and Rohit
Mrs Singh: Mother of above

Lewis Mayhew: Young Man
Janice Mayhew: Lewis' Mother

Stan and Hannah: Bartenders

Detectives -
Isaac Davidson: Detective Chief Inspector (Brother: Alan)
Emily Morgans: Detective Sergeant
Jian Wong: Detective Constable
Anne Michaels: Detective Constable
Hamish Potter: Detective Constable
Faisal Asher: Detective Constable
Alex: Forensic Lead

1:

4th January 2018

At the end...

7:00pm

Detective Chief Inspector Isaac Davidson paced quickly through the dark London streets in the heavy rain. His waterproof coat, which he had only bought three days ago from an expensive outdoor specialist shop, was not as waterproof as he had hoped. He was beginning to feel wet and cold and quite frankly, miserable at spending £200 on a garment that wasn't fit for purpose. The wind was fierce tonight and the dark clouds made it appear like a storm was brewing.

Isaac grimaced as he battled with the elements. As he walked, odd thoughts were running through his head, such as this being a perfect night to solve a murder. He was heading towards the police station in the hope of solving his latest case and putting a callous murderer behind bars.

Unfortunately for the DCI, his evening hadn't started out well. Halfway to the police station, his car, a blue Vauxhall Astra that he had owned for fifteen years, had finally packed up. It just cut out and refused to start again. This now left him with a three mile walk in awful weather.

Due to a bad night's sleep and waking at 4:00am, Isaac had left work early to go home and rest, eat and shower before going back again. In his eagerness to do this he had forgotten to bring his house keys and wallet and therefore public transport was out of the question. He supposed he could flash his badge at the bus driver, but he'd never been one for pulling rank. His brother, Alan who lived with him, was always telling him to do the three important checks before leaving the house: Keys, both house and car, phone and wallet. At this moment, he only had his car keys and phone.

'I've failed on house keys and wallet,' he berated himself.

Isaac knew that his suspected killer was already in police custody, but as he walked through the cold, wet night he mulled over the details of the crime. He enjoyed summarising things in his head and found walking was an effective way to achieve this, although in this weather his thoughts might get a bit distracted.

Philip Oakes was a thirty-six-year-old Caucasian male. On the evening of Friday 8th December 2017, he had been murdered. From all accounts he was not the nicest of men. However, in his vast experience, Isaac had found that there was frequently a reason, or reasons for someone not coming across as a nice person, of course this wasn't always the case. The DCI knew extremely well that there were some real, nasty pieces of work out there.

With the help of the victim's mobile phone records, his emails and interviews, five potential suspects had been identified, each with a different yet plausible motive. However, no murder case was ever as simple or as straight-forward as it might first appear at the onset of an investigation. The strangest aspect of this case had been the inclusion of a clown. Trying to work out how it had fitted in to the case and why.

Getting soaked as he continued through the rain the detective started to walk faster, matching his increasing heartbeat. He knew he was excited to find out why the murder had taken place. This was the part of the job he liked the most. If it were up to him, he'd gather all the suspects together in one place and solve the crime in front of them, exactly like an Agatha Christie novel. However, that was the stuff of fiction and real life wasn't like that.

It was busy in town this evening, with the usual type of drunks causing problems, but also with people just out having an enjoyable time. Isaac liked to see people having fun and wished his brother would have more. Since the accident, Alan had become isolated and had turned his back on most of his friends. Isaac was the only person he seemed to like spending time with.

The detective was now approaching the police station and felt excited to finally be able to confront the killer of Philip Oakes. As he pulled open the door to the building and walked in, his heart started to race even more. His breathing sped up and the exhilaration raced through his veins. He spied his Detective Sergeant, Emily Morgans who had worked on the case with him.

'Interview room one,' she said to her boss with a serious look upon her face.

'Coming with me Emily?' He asked.

'I am indeed sir, as I want to hear how and why this happened.'

The two detectives headed over to the lifts, stepped in and pressed level three. Each could hear the other breathing.

'You're soaked,' the DS said staring at her boss's hair and coat properly for the first time since he had arrived.

'Oh yes, I forgot I was so wet,' he said laughing, 'I'm too excited to get closure on this case.'

'Didn't you come by car?' She asked.

'Long story,' he said with a smile.

'You'd better take off your coat or you'll get really uncomfortable,' Emily said with concern.

'Good idea, thanks.'

Taking off his coat, he put it over his arm. As the lift door opened, they glanced at each other, walked into the central office, and saw the four Detective Constables who had also worked on this case. DCs Wong, Michaels, Potter and Asher.

Isaac dropped his coat over the back of a chair in the corner in the hope that it would dry out before he was heading home. He quickly grabbed a cup of coffee from the percolator in the office's kitchen and used a tea towel that he saw by the sink to try and dry off his wet hair.

'Sorry Emily, but I just need this drink to warm myself up, I won't be long.'

'No problem sir,' she replied.

The DCI took three large mouthfuls of the warming liquid and put his cup in the sink. With his coffee finished, they headed to the interview room. He looked at his DS.

'Ready?'

'Ready,' she replied.

Isaac opened the door and straight away saw the frightened figure sitting in the chair next to someone from legal aid. On the table sat a voice recorder. Isaac walked into the room in a commanding way and sat down in front of the shaking individual. DS Morgans sat next to her boss and turned on the recorder. This station was still very backwards when it came to technology. After announcing all those that were present in the room, the DCI glared directly into the eyes of the person sitting directly in front of him.

'So, let's start at the beginning, with you telling me what led to the murder of Philip Oakes!'

2:

8th December 2017

Philip: The morning of his death

06:30am

Philip lay on his king size bed in his immaculate bedroom, where everything had a place and everything was in its place. His room was always presented to the standard of a luxury hotel, including decoratively placed cushions and satin grey bed linen. Before he even opened his eyes, he knew the light, whatever the strength, would cause nothing but irritation and pain and so he refused to open them. His head was lying on his plump, expensive pillow and was not able to move. He knew any slight movement was going to cause a huge amount of discomfort and may even induce a vomiting frenzy and this was to be avoided at all costs. Philip started to deep breathe, to try to ward off any chance of being sick.

'What happened last night?' he thought to himself.

Something happened, but at this precise moment he couldn't remember. He slowly felt under his duvet, moving as little as possible, to feel what he was wearing. As was usual, nothing, so he had obviously not just fallen into bed straight away last night otherwise he would still have his clothes on.

Lying there, he tried to remember the events of the night before, but was struggling.

A vague memory went through his thoughts, 'Did I fall out with Arjun?'

He cautiously placed a hand under his duvet again, but this time to see if he could feel his mobile phone. He slowly moved his hand around the bed, without stretching in any way. Nothing came to hand. To be honest, it could be anywhere in the bed, or on the floor, or even in the Uber cab that he got home in last night.

'Did I get an Uber?' he thought to himself.

Although he had no memory of it, he felt sure he must have called a cab, as he had an account with them and usually came home that way when he knew he would be drinking. His memory was blank from about 10:30pm onwards, but he did remember that Arjun came around at 9:00pm and they went out straight away. Philip also vaguely remembered being in a foul mood. He had spoken on the phone to his brother, Ethan and also to his nephew Adam for about the millionth time about Ethan's health. Arjun, he remembered, even commented that if Philip would rather not go out, he'd be OK with that.

Lying in bed fighting back the nausea and trying not to open his eyes, Philip knew he needed to hydrate himself, but that would require movement. He endeavoured to open his eyes, a process he had been dreading and consequently failed. The first spec of light had made him tighten up his eyes again. He hadn't been in this state for as long as he could remember and it certainly did not feel good at all.

'Did I speak to Jacob? Or Rebecca?' he thought to himself, 'maybe, or maybe not.' No answers were coming to him, just a more intense throbbing in his head.

He lay there motionless and reflected that the worst part of not remembering what you did, or didn't do the night before, was suddenly remembering. He hated post-mortems the following day and usually made sure his phone was either switched off, or on silent. He did however have a strong feeling that when he eventually found his phone, it would be full of messages and voicemails.

It was obvious to Philip that if possible, he needed to drift back to sleep. He hoped with all that was good and holy, that when he next woke up, he'd be feeling a little better. He took a deep breath and tried hard not to think of anything, or more importantly, of anyone.

08:30am

Philip woke again and it was soon evident that his head was still throbbing. It didn't take any movement for him to know he was still in pain.

'Oh, my head!' he thought to himself. 'I'm such an idiot.'

As he lay there trying not to move, he was swiftly aware that he had an erection.

'It's probably the only part of me that had moved all night!' he inwardly smirked as he said this to himself.

Completely unaware of the time, he decided he was at least ready to open his eyes, but knew it wouldn't be easy. He wished he'd now bought one of those digital clocks that shines the time on the ceiling. With extreme caution and very slowly, Philip started to open his eyes. He started with a small squint and then slowly began to open them. As he thought, the glare of light caused discomfort and made him jerk his head, which caused pain. Now that his eyes were fully open, he hoped that by glancing to the side, at his bedside table, he'd see a glass of water. Hydrating himself was vital. His tongue was dry and tasted odd and his head was banging in pain. Philip really hoped he'd done the practical thing and placed a large glass of water on the table ready for when he woke up. Slowly turning his head, he saw a glass, but it was a large wine glass with a third of wine still in the bottom. He retched and knew that he had come home and carried on drinking.

'You bloody fool!' he thought to himself.

He knew he never just poured a small amount of wine. It was always poured to the very top of a large wine glass and the remnants were now staring at him. Just the sight of the wine in the glass caused him to feel nauseous. He started his deep breathing again. This usually stopped the feeling of sickness and he prayed it would work this time too. After about five minutes the feeling had passed, but he then became aware that he needed to go to the toilet. This was going to be quite a task. He lived in a semi-detached, three-bedroomed Victorian house. As with many Victorian homes, the bathroom was downstairs and through the large kitchen. He didn't believe that at this precise moment he was able to make it downstairs, but he needed to try. Slowly he manoeuvred himself to the side of the bed, but pushing the duvet off himself took some effort. He then swung his legs onto the floor and sat up. Straight away his head felt like it would explode. He sat there for a few minutes and then cautiously stood up. Still feeling dizzy, he looked down to help steady himself. He noticed his erection was still there and smiled. He felt proud of it. Not for its size as it was probably just below average, but for the fact that although his blood stream was full of alcohol, he was still managing to maintain it. This made him laugh a little, which in turn hurt his head. He often got what he had heard called the 'hangover horn' so no doubt he would be revisiting his erection later in the day. Standing there for a few minutes, he realised that he wasn't going anywhere. He wasn't even sure if he could put one foot in front of the other.

'Oh, my God!' he said aloud, his face showing pure anguish.

Philip peered around his room to see if there was anything that he could use to take a pee in, he saw there was nothing. At that moment, he thought that the Victorians had the right idea by having a chamber pot under the bed. The notion of using the wine glass did cross his mind, but he wasn't going anywhere near that. He was also sure that it wasn't going to be big enough for the volume he thought he might end up passing, even if he did try. Giving up, he sat back on the bed and put himself into a lying position and pulled the duvet back over his head. It was clear to him that he wasn't anywhere near ready to start the day and more sleep was needed.

'Go to sleep Philip,' he said to himself, 'and when you next wake, things will hopefully feel better.'

He could only hope this would be the case.

11:00am

Philip woke for the third time that morning and could immediately tell that his head felt better. He moved it from side to side and there was an improved range of movement. It still wasn't perfect, but it was at least going in the right direction. He opened his eyes and took a deep breath. Almost instantaneously he knew he needed to pass urine. Yawning and with a deep stretch that felt surprisingly good, he moved to the side of the bed and stood up. There was a slight dizzy feeling, but much improved from earlier. He headed for the stairs.

Philip was a naturist, so very rarely wore clothes when at home. He left a dressing gown by the front door amongst his coats in case he had to answer the door and then depending on who was there, the gown didn't always meet in the middle. An exhibitionist was also a word to describe Philip Oakes. Naked, he descended the stairs, turned left at the bottom and walked into the kitchen and through to the bathroom.

Philip, on this occasion, stood rather than sat which was his preferred method of peeing. He was afraid of feeling dizzy when he'd have to stand up again, so best not to put himself in that position. Philip soon comprehended that dehydration was an issue, as he didn't pee anywhere near as much as he thought he needed to. The dark, almost burnt orange colour of the stream also alerted him to the fact he needed lots of water and promptly.

He now walked back into the kitchen, scratching his bottom and pulling down on his scrotum. Philip filled the kettle to make coffee and at the same time poured himself a glass of water. Unfortunately, he started to drink this too fast and suddenly felt like he was going to throw up. He took some deep breaths and slowed his drinking to sips and this he found to be much better.

'Philip, learn to drink less when you go out and then mornings like this wouldn't happen,' he told himself aloud.

As he waited for the kettle to boil, he tried to recall other memories from last night. It hadn't been a great couple of weeks for him, so he had been really looking forward to last night. Two weeks ago, Rebecca, the drunk from the bar, had asked him around to her place for dinner. Stupidly he went with no idea why, as he really detested her. He'd had sex with her a few times, but only because he had been horny, not because he found her attractive in any way. The last and final time, if he remembered correctly, had been a quickie in the cellar at the pub at the end of September. Her cigarette breath had turned his stomach, so kissing her hadn't happened since the first time.

Philip reflected on Arjun and Stan, two of his bar staff. Both had asked for her to be banned from the pub due to her frequent drunken and vile behaviour. He had always told them that she spent a lot of money and therefore it wasn't good business sense to ban her. That evening at hers hadn't ended well and she hadn't returned to the bar since, so maybe the two barmen got what they wanted after all.

With the kettle boiled, the coffee was made. Two slices of toast were also ready. Not because he felt hungry, but because he knew he should try to eat something. He drank more water and took two painkillers. Today was going to be a very lazy day indeed. As he continued with his breakfast, Jacob was also playing on his mind. They had been friends since they were three years old. Then last week when they had met up, as far as Philip was concerned, that solid friendship had been destroyed and all down to money owed and broken trusts. That evening with Jacob had also been explosive and very upsetting.

'What the crap is going on in my life? Everybody seems to want a piece of me!' he thought to himself.

He then let out an exasperated sigh and finished his toast.

It was then that the clown featured in his mind. What the bloody hell was that all about? Had he seen it last night? The police certainly weren't interested, but it had truly spooked him over the past three months.

'Sod it!' he shouted.

Philip now put on his Spotify and chose light opera to listen to as he walked back into the bathroom to run a hot bath using his lavender bath gel. He made more coffee and took it into the bathroom with him, along with a pint of water. Once the bath water was hot and ready, he edged his way in and laid back and closed his eyes. His music app was now playing his favourite aria, O Mio Bambino Caro.

He was now determined to think of nothing and just relax and chill. However, upstairs, his mobile phone, which was somewhere in his bed, was showing twenty-four missed calls. Five were from Ethan, three from Jacob and the rest from Arjun.

3:

6th September 2017

Ethan

Ethan Oakes was a forty-two-year-old man with ginger hair, freckles and deep blue eyes. These were the same features shared by his younger brother Philip, however, the similarities ended there. Ethan was of athletic build and took great care of his sculptured body and Philip was overweight, sluggish and appeared to carry the weight of the world on his shoulders.

Lately Ethan had lost weight without trying and had felt very run down and lethargic and not at all like his usual self. Emma, his wife, had been the one to suggest he should get an appointment with the GP. That had been two days ago and now he was feeling extremely anxious as he was waiting for the doctor in the haematology out-patient's department to see him.

'Ethan Oakes,' a young man called out from one of the clinic rooms.

He was an exceptionally good looking, fit man and the muscles in his arms were stretching the material of his dark blue uniform and his straight teeth were as white as they could be.

Ethan stood up and walked towards the door. His wife and son went too. Liam, the young man opened the door as the trio walked in and took their chairs. Ethan felt sick! Sitting behind a large desk was a petite woman with long red hair, which was the same colour as Ethan's.

'Hello Mr Oakes, my name is Dr Sue Kelleher and I am a haematologist and this young man is Liam, he is a clinical nurse specialist who works alongside me. Who have you brought with you today?' she said with a kind, soft voice.

'This is Emma, my wife and this is Adam, my son.' Ethan's voice was shaking.

There was a surge of emotions in the room.

'I can see that you are very nervous, so I'll tell you straight away what we have found out so far.' She took a deep breath.

'I'm sorry to have to tell you this Mr Oakes, but it isn't the news I was hoping to tell you.'

'Why isn't it?' said Ethan quickly, 'I thought I just had the flu?'

'Flu like symptoms Mr Oakes, which were prolonged and hence you ended up being sent to A&E by your GP with a remarkably elevated temperature, bruising, lethargy and breathlessness,' said Dr Kelleher.

'So, what is wrong with me?' demanded Ethan. 'Tell me!' he was aware he was being rude, but he was scared now.

'You have Acute Lymphoblastic Leukaemia, known as A.L.L.,' answered Dr Kelleher. 'I'm sorry to have to tell you this Mr Oakes, but this is a type of blood cancer.'

Ethan just sat there staring at nothing. He felt numb and at the same time dizzy. His arm moved to the left and was searching for Emma and his right arm did the same seeking for Adam, his eighteen-year-old son. He felt both touch his hands and they squeezed tight.

'Mr Oakes,' said the haematologist, 'Is it OK if I carry on?'

Ethan nodded in a terribly slow and mechanical way.

'We need to finalise our results to get the complete picture,' she continued, 'we know for sure it is A.L.L, but we need to ascertain exactly which type of A.L.L it is.'

'What do you mean? Isn't there just one type of Leukaemia?' whispered Ethan, almost unable to find his voice.

'No, there are several types, four main types, but they then get broken down into different subtypes,' she stated. 'It is complicated Mr Oakes, but I promise you I will go slowly and answer any questions that you or your family may have.'

He turned to look at Emma, his wife of twenty years. He glanced at her slim, tall, defined figure, her liquorice black hair and her full red lips and knew that he worshipped her. She tightened her grip on his hand and smiled at him. It was the type of smile that said that she would be by his side throughout.

'We will get through this, I am with you and this won't beat us,' Emma said firmly, looking directly into her husband's eyes.

Emma had always been the stoic one, the composed one and the strong one. Ethan looked into her hazel eyes that were glistening with the first few tears and searched for hope that he knew he would see in his beautiful wife's eyes. He then turned to Adam. His son wasn't like his wife, Adam, a plain looking teenager with acne scars, bright red cheeks and a tall scrawny body, was crying hard, sniffing loudly and cuffing the mess coming from his nose. Ethan squeezed Adam's hand tight and leaned into him and touched his thigh and gently murmured,

'I love you Adam, we can do this together and all will be right again.'

Adam, using the hand not holding his dad's, brushed through his thick, wavy brown hair and smiled gently at his dad.

'Mr Oakes,' said Dr Kelleher, 'is it OK if I continue?'

'I'm sorry, please do,' he said.

'You don't need to be sorry,' she said. 'We should have all the results back in two days and then I can fully discuss the treatment plan with you, however,' she continued with compassion, 'you do need to be aware that it is going to be a long journey ahead of you.' She gazed for understanding. 'The treatment will be chemotherapy in the first instance and this will have many side effects.'

Ethan looked at her and said, 'I'm,' he hesitated, 'I'm scared.'

Compassion showed clearly on her face and she said in a soft caring voice,

'Ethan, you're allowed to be scared, that is a perfectly natural response,' she continued, 'I'd be surprised if you weren't. Please remember I am here to help you every step of the way.'

'Did I cause this to happen? Did I do something to make this happen? Am I a bad person? Why me?' All four questions left Ethan's mouth almost without breath.

'Why me?' This was the question that finally caused Ethan to start crying. Sobbing would be a better word.

Adam flung himself at his dad and held him tight. Both sobbing in unison. Emma looked on.

'No Ethan,' Dr Kelleher calmly said, 'you didn't cause this to happen, it is just one of those things.'

Ethan took some deep breaths and pulled himself out of the sobbing state that he was in. He took Adam's face in his hands and kissed his son. Adam sat back in his chair and like his dad, started to do some deep breathing to calm himself down. Ethan looked at Emma and smiled, albeit an extremely nervous smile.

Liam now fully introduced himself as a clinical nurse specialist for Leukaemia. He had sat in the corner of the room and watched all that had happened. The word Leukaemia was always omitted when he was first introduced at the beginning of a consultation, so as not to frighten the patient. His part in Ethan's journey was about to start.

'Ethan, when Dr Kelleher has finished with you, I am going to stay and discuss again anything from today that you would like me to. I will also answer any questions you may have,' he spoke in a very calming, soft way.

Ethan nodded.

'I will also provide you with my contact details.'

Ethan nodded again to let Liam know he had understood.

The doctor stood up and walked towards Ethan.

'I need to transfer you to the haematology ward and I am going to come back to that ward in two days at 10:00am and we can discuss the treatment plan,' Dr Kelleher said. 'I can confirm the exact subtype by then and you'll have a better understanding of what is to come.'

'Thank you,' Ethan said.

He then glanced at Liam, who gave a reassuring nod.

The doctor left the room and as she walked out of the department she frowned. She knew exactly where this was heading, as she had seen it so many times in adults with A.L.L.

8th September 7:30am

Ethan lay in his hospital bed listening to the routine sounds of the ward starting up again after a quiet night. The tea trolley was being taken round and curtains were being opened. The nursing staff who had tried during the night to be quiet were now waking their patients to do the morning observations and drug round.

'Good morning Ethan,' Nichola said, 'I need to do your blood pressure, temperature etc,'

Ethan just stared at his nurse and half smiled.

'That's better,' she said, 'but I am sorry I had to wake you, you can go back to sleep when I have finished giving you your antibiotics.'

09:30am

Ethan woke for the second time and quickly looked at his phone. It was 9:30am. He hadn't missed Dr Kelleher. He let out a huge sigh, noticed that he'd received a text from Emma.

'Morning my love, I am on the ward, but I have just nipped into the loo x'

'Hello Ethan,' came a voice that caused Ethan to jump.

'Hi Liam, how are you?' a sleepy voice responded.

'I am fine Ethan, but more importantly how are you feeling this morning?'

'I slept OK I think,' said Ethan. 'You get woken up so many times to have your observations taken and medications given to you that you lose track of your sleep.'

'Dr Kelleher is going to be here soon,' Liam told him. 'Ask as many questions as you want and remember, I am going to be with you the whole time.'

'Thanks Liam, I just want to get the treatment started,' Ethan sighed loudly.

'Are Emma and Adam coming in to hear what is said?'

'Emma is already here; she is in the loo. It is too much for Adam so I have told him to stay at work and I will tell him everything when he visits later.'

'What job does he do?' Asked Liam.

'He works for a painting and decorating company,' Ethan said with a smile on his face. 'They paint commercial buildings. He was so pleased when he got the job.'

'I can tell by the look on your face that you have a great relationship with him,' observed Liam.

'Yeah,' said Ethan, 'he is a great kid. First day he came home after he got the job, he was still wearing his white overalls and huge black boots that they make them wear, he was so excited.' Ethan laughed. 'The boots are not so new now, with the paint splotches all over them.'

'It must be nice to have such a close bond with your children,' Liam said with a smile on his face.

'Yes, it really is. Adam had just joined the gym where I go, to help turn his skinny body into a more defined one. We were going to be working out together, but I guess that has to be on hold for the foreseeable future.'

The two men just sat in silence for a few moments, each taking in the surroundings and the noises of a busy ward.

'Morning Liam,' said Emma as she approached Ethan's bed.

'Hey, morning Emma.'

There was a tension in the air that was unmistakable, but completely understandable. It became a waiting game as 10:00am came and went.

'How are the boys?' Asked Ethan.

'Missing their daddy of course,' smiled Emma.

Ethan and Emma had two other sons. Saul, who was eleven and Max, who was two. They hadn't been told what was happening yet, as their parents didn't want to scare them. Emma's mum, Suzanne was taking care of them.

10:30am arrived and there was still no sign of the haematology consultant. Ethan was getting increasingly anxious.

'Let me go and find out where she is,' Liam said, looking at the watch that was attached to his uniform.

Ethan looked at Emma, tears were now falling from his eyes and down his face.

'I'm so frightened Emma, all I keep thinking about are my beautiful boys and my darling wife.'

Lost for words, maybe for the first time, Emma reached out and took Ethan's hand in hers and squeezed it tightly. She lovingly gazed into his face and took a breath.

'Whatever we are told this morning, we are going to face it as a united family.' She took another deep breath, 'do you want me to talk to Philip?'

'No, not yet,' said Ethan, 'let us see what we are about to be told.' He indicated with his eyes that Dr Kelleher was approaching. He tried to read her face, but he couldn't.

'Morning Ethan, Emma,' the doctor nodded to both. 'Ethan, How are you feeling today?'

'I am OK but I just want to get on with the treatment.' Ethan glanced at Liam.

The emotion around the bed was stressful and nerve-wracking. Ethan looked at the doctor's face and knew he was about to get news that he really didn't want to hear, but knew that he had to. Emma picked up on this too and moved closer to her husband and took hold of his hand.

'Ethan,' the doctor now hesitated. 'Ethan, the type of Leukaemia that you have, as you know is Acute Lymphoblastic.' She hated this part of her job. 'The subtype has come back as B-Cell Philadelphia positive type.'

Ethan was bewildered, 'what does that all mean?' He asked.

'It means, that although we can treat this disease, it is more complicated. The fact that it is also Philadelphia positive, which is a chromosome abnormality, makes it even more difficult to treat.'

'Am I going to die?'

Ethan wasn't even sure why he asked this question, but it seemed to just blurt out. Emma's eyes were closed and she appeared to be taking in deep breaths as she squeezed tightly on Ethan's hand. He squeezed back.

'We can start today, which will be chemotherapy and called the induction phase. Our goal is to try to cure you Ethan.' Dr Kelleher did her best to smile at the worried couple in front of her.

Ethan nodded.

'The idea of this phase is to get you into a remission.' She observed Ethan's face to check for understanding. 'Remission means that the Leukaemic cells have gone. However, if we stopped treatment at remission, the Leukaemia would come back, therefore we need to keep treating it.'

'Do you understand Ethan?' Asked Liam.

Ethan nodded and glanced quickly at Emma, who also nodded.

'To get the best chance of a cure in this type of situation is to give you something called an allogeneic transplant as soon as you are in remission.' Dr Kelleher again observed for signs that Ethan was following what she had said.

'What is that?' he understandably asked.

'It means that we need to use stem cells from another person and then transplant, meaning, put them into you.'

'What is a stem cell?' Asked Emma.

'They are cells that provide new cells for the body. So, in Ethan's case, if we took someone else's stem cells and injected them into Ethan, they would divide and grow into new types of cells that were needed to help try to cure him.'

Ethan's eyes widened and he visibly started to shake and then he started to cry. Emma held him.

'Ethan, can I continue?' Dr Kelleher asked with consideration.

'Yes,' was all he said.

'The best result for this type of transplant is if we can use a sibling's stem cells.'

'Do you have any brothers or sisters?' Liam asked.

'He has one brother, who is six years younger than him.' Emma spoke for her husband.

'Is he a full or half sibling?' Asked the doctor.

'Full,' said Emma.

'We need to do something called Tissue Typing on him, it's various blood tests to check to see if he is a match and therefore can be your donor.'

'Match?' Ethan said confused.

'It means that your cells are as near the same as someone else's.' Liam volunteered.

Ethan nodded that he understood.

'We will also search on the European and if necessary, the International Donor Register, just in case your brother isn't a match. Just because you are brothers, that doesn't mean it is guaranteed that he will be a perfect donor,' said the doctor.

'Will your brother get tested?' Asked Liam. 'We have to ask as we can't assume that just because you are related that he will be willing.'

'Yeah, Philip will be happy to get tested for me, I know he will.'

'Do you want me to call him and explain?' Asked Liam.

'No, it is fine, I'll do it when you've all gone,' answered Ethan.

Same day: 2:00pm

Ethan stared at the trees through his hospital window and watched how they were blowing in the wind. They were still green from summer and not yet turning the reds and browns of Autumn. He looked at his mobile phone and picked it up and started scrolling through the names of all the people he would need to start telling about his illness. When he came to Philip's name, he paused and took in a deep breath. Their relationship had always been difficult, ever since they were kids. Memories floated in and out of Ethan's head, as he was remembering their childhood together. Sadly, not all of them were good, in fact very few were. Ethan now questioned why they hadn't been closer and whether it had been his fault.

'Of course it's your fault, you know damn well it is,' he said quietly to himself.

He looked again at Philip's name that was displayed on his phone and finally pushed the green phone symbol. The ringing started and Ethan felt sick.

'Hello Ethan,' Philip said as he answered the phone. There was an abruptness to his tone.

'Hey Philip, how are you?' he said in a nervous voice.

Philip moved the phone away from his ear and pulled a disinterested face. He then put it back to his ear and replied in a bemused tone.

'I am fine, what do you want?'

'I need to tell you something and it is going to be hard.' Ethan said.

Philip could sense the tension in Ethan's voice.

'I have Leukaemia Philip; it is a cancer of the blood.'

There was silence at the other end of the phone. After about twenty seconds, the conversation continued.

'Oh my God Ethan!' Philip said to his brother, 'I am so sorry to hear that.'

'I am so frightened Philip; I don't want to die.'

'Aren't they going to treat you?' Asked Philip, screwing up his face.

'Yes, they are, with chemotherapy, but they also need to do a stem cell transplant.'

Ethan took a deep breath and tried to explain to his brother everything he had been told earlier.

'I need you to get tested Philip, to see if you match my cells and can be my donor.'

'Oh, I see,' said Philip. 'Sounds complicated.'

'Will you get tested to see if you are a match?' Asked his brother.

Philip contemplated the question for a few moments.

'I don't fully understand what you are asking of me Ethan.'

Ethan felt slightly irritated, as he felt he had already made himself perfectly clear.

'My illness is exceedingly difficult to treat and cure. I have to start off with chemotherapy, but my only chance of survival is to have a transplant from somebody who has as near to 100% matching cells to me, once I am in remission.'

'What's 100% matching cells mean?'

'I don't overly get it yet, but they compare your blood cells with mine and we have to hope that they are the same,' Ethan said, trying to explain something still very difficult and alien to him.

'What is remission?' Philip asked next.

'It means that I don't have Leukaemia anymore, but without the transplant, it will definitely come back.' Ethan took yet another deep breath. 'They always test siblings first to see if they are a match. Will you get tested for me Philip?'

'Yes, of course I will, that goes without saying.' Philip said. 'What do I have to do?'

'Can you come in on Monday and have your blood taken?'

'Yes, I can, no problem.'

'I was told to tell you that the results can take about five weeks to come back,' said Ethan.

'So, what happens in the meantime then?'

'I continue with the chemotherapy.'

'Ah man, I am gutted for you,' replied Philip. 'How are Emma and the boys taking it?'

'Emma is being her usual tower of strength. Adam has fallen to pieces.' Ethan sighed.

'Poor lad. What about Saul and Max?' Philip said, asking about his youngest nephews.

'We are going to tell Saul tonight,' said Ethan 'but Max, only being two, we need to work out what best to tell him.'

'Can the hospital help with situations like this?' Asked Philip.

'Liam, who is my clinical nurse specialist, he seems a decent bloke, so I am going to ask him when he next comes around if he has any ideas.'

'That sounds like a good plan,' said Philip. 'I'll come by the hospital on Monday and do whatever I need to do.'

Philip was aware that his brother was finding it awfully hard not to cry on the other end of the phone. Their father had died when Philip was eighteen and Ethan twenty-four and that just left the two of them now.

'Thanks for being tested Philip, this means you could actually save a life.'

'Not a problem Ethan and let us just hope that I can be of help in any way you need me to,' replied Philip.

4:

7th October 2017

Rebecca

Rebecca Firth, at forty-four was showing her age, she had grey streaks running throughout her tired and drab hair and deep-set wrinkles around her eyes and mouth. These she found the most distressing. She used to dye her hair, but lately had lost interest. As a younger woman she had been attractive, but nowadays, much less so.

Somehow, she managed to maintain a slim figure, despite the amount of alcohol she consumed. Her nutritional intake however was the bare minimum, so Rebecca assumed this was probably what kept her slim. Being a heavy smoker for twenty-five years had taken its toll on her skin and to some degree her teeth. Most mornings she woke with that heavy feeling in her head, a feeling that reminded her that she had drank too much the night before.

'I'm never touching alcohol again,' was a phrase she often used.

Each new day started the same, with a hot shower, strong coffee, two paracetamol and an Alka-Seltzer. This process enabled her to get to her job as a pharmacy assistant in the local hospital. Her shifts were Monday to Friday 8:30am-1:00pm, which meant she was usually in the pub called The Lemon Tree by 1:30pm and her drink was finished by 2:00pm. However, this wasn't usually her first drink of the day!

On this Saturday morning, once she had been able to get out of her bed and have the briefest of showers, as standing was making her feel dizzy, she went downstairs and into her cluttered kitchen. Pushing the dirty cups and plates into the sink, she put the kettle on and sat at the breakfast bar, that her since divorced husband Terry had insisted that they had.

'It'll make us appear more upmarket than our friends,' he'd say.

'Elevate ourselves and be admired.'

Rebecca clearly remembered thinking,

'It's a bloody table Terry, not a swimming pool.'

Terry stayed around for two months after it was installed, then ran off with a woman he met at work. Rebecca was then left with a breakfast bar she had never wanted and two small daughters. If she was honest with herself, she didn't want them either. She hadn't been the maternal type, or at least she didn't think she had. When she was discarded by Terry and this is how Rebecca had felt, Amelia was nine and Alice was eight. Her relationship with both girls wasn't good then and wasn't good now either. Thinking back, she recalled the time that Amelia, looking at her as she stood in the kitchen and saying, in front of Alice,

'Has daddy left because you drink so much Mum?'

Head beginning to ease, Rebecca picked up her phone and decided to text three people. The first text was the easiest:

'Hey Amelia, do you fancy coming over tonight for something to eat? I can cook, or we can get a take-out. What do you think? Mum x.'

Over the years, Amelia had slowly warmed to her mother. She hated the drinking and the lifestyle her mum led, but equally had learnt that it was her mum's life. She preferred to meet up with her the day after she knew that her mother had had a heavy night drinking. Rebecca rarely drank the next day after such a session, so was usually sober when seeing her daughter that evening.

Text two she knew wouldn't get a response:

'Hey Alice, how is university going? Do you need anything? I would love to hear from you. Mum x.'

Alice was the opposite to her sister. She blamed Rebecca for the fact her dad had left. Watching her mother either drunk or less than sober, for want of a better phrase, had taken its toll. Rebecca turning up to a parent/teacher night excessively drunk was the last straw for Alice. She may have only been thirteen at the time, but on that night, she made a conscious decision that as soon as she could, she would leave home and never return. Alice was now at university in Scotland and Rebecca only knew what was happening in her youngest daughter's life due to Amelia.

Text three was potentially the most awkward. They had shagged the previous Saturday. It had not been the most romantic encounter that they had had, as it was downstairs in the cellar of The Lemon Tree. Knickers around her ankles, smell of damp, a head that was spinning and a screwing that lasted no more than five minutes. After he had finished with her and left her to adjust herself, she remembered walking back up the cellar steps slowly and into the bar. She noticed Arjun, the bartender, staring at her in disgust, or was it jealousy? Head held high, she remembered that she went over to the seats in the corner and joined the young lad, Lewis. Now, however, still sitting at the breakfast bar, she started to type her third text:

'Hi Philip, I'm still thinking of last Saturday, are you? Maybe next time we can go back to using your bed lol. Anyhow, I'll be back tomorrow for the quiz if you fancy a chat. Hugs Rebecca x.'

She looked at the text she had written several times and then pressed the send button. She just couldn't get to grips with Philip. At times he was all fun and laughter with her, then he would be indifferent and act as if he didn't even like her. They had slept together four times now, well, if you count a quickie in the cellar as sleeping together. Why was he treating her like this? Hadn't she been through enough with the way Terry had treated her?

'For Christ's sake Mum, dad left you eleven years ago, it's time to move on and do something to sort your life out.'

This was a frequent conversation she had with Amelia. So often in fact, that she heard her daughter reciting it in her head over and over again.

As frustrating as she found Philip's behaviour towards her, she was becoming obsessed with him. To be honest, he wasn't even that attractive. He was tall, which she liked, overweight with a developing beer belly and odd scars on his shoulders and the tops of his arms. He did however have ginger hair, which was a huge turn on, freckles which she liked, but also had the most beautiful rich blue eyes. This was a rarity for ginger haired people. Those eyes were bewitching and drew her in every single time.

She had only seen the ginger hair/blue eyes combination one other time and that was at work. She dispensed medication to an Ethan Oakes, who, as she found out recently at work, was Philip's older brother. A much better-looking man than Philip, but also tired looking, with signs of gauntness and worry in his face.

Rebecca poured herself her third coffee of the morning and took it upstairs to get back into bed. Her phone alerted her to a text and her heart raced with excitement. Once in bed, she studied the phone and the excitement faded. It was from her eldest daughter.

'Can't tonight, already going out for the evening.'

There was never a kiss at the end of Amelia's texts, but why would there be?

As she lay in her bed, on linen she hadn't changed in four months, Rebecca tried to picture Philip in her head. She was sure he must like her and she might even say love. She smiled and gave herself a hug. Yes, she was sure he must love her.

8th October 2017
09:30am

Rebecca woke and felt reasonably refreshed. She liked this feeling and every time she felt like this, she regretted that it didn't happen more frequently. Today was going to be a good day, she was feeling positive about things and was excited for the quiz night at the pub. Seeing Philip was what she hoped for most this evening.

She reached for her phone which was on the floor next to her bed. The bedside table she needed was still in the shop. She looked at the screen in excitement, but there were no new messages.

'Oh, for pity's sake, you're an arsehole,' she screamed out with utter frustration. The thought of love now very much at the back of her head.

She completely forgot Alice hadn't texted back either.

'Well Mr Oakes, I'll show you,' she thought to herself. 'I am going to spend the day pampering myself.' She studied herself in the mirror and mouthed, 'Long hot bath, face pack, dye my hair, nail treatments, shave my legs and dress to kill.' Laughing to herself, she walked into the bathroom and turned on the bath taps.

7:30pm

Walking into the bar that evening, Rebecca felt like a beautiful, desirable woman. She believed she was commanding the place in her green, strapless dress and believed that all eyes were on her as she walked over to the bar to order a drink. Sadly, if she had looked closer, very few, if any people noticed her. Stan, who was standing behind the bar, saw her approaching.

'Evening Rebecca,' he said with a sense of foreboding as he knew what Rebecca could get like. Why Philip hadn't barred her was a mystery to him.

'Usual?'

'No thanks Stanley,' she said, patronising the bartender. 'Can I have a soda water and lime please, I want a clear head for the quiz.'

She glared at Stan in a dismissive way. Stan's only redeeming quality was that he wasn't Arjun!

Quiz night was always good for business. The Lemon Tree relied on its weekend takings, as it could be slow during the week. Gazing around the bar, in the far corner, Rebecca saw a young man wearing green jeans, red Converses and a red t-shirt that was depicting the face of the latest Doctor Who and horn-rimmed glasses. His dyed black hair was expensively styled and was very impressive. Maybe this was Lewis, a young lad she got on well with when he was in the bar. She walked over and indeed it was him. As with Philip, she liked his eyes, she had a thing for eyes, she decided.

'Hey Becky,' he said with a smile and almost disrespectful tone, 'take a seat gorgeous lady,' he said with a wink.

Laughing, Rebecca sat and instantly started flirting with Lewis. However, all the time scanning the bar for Philip in the hope that flirting with a young man would fire up some jealousy within him.

'You look different tonight Lewis,' she said, 'have you coloured your hair, changed your glasses or something?' she asked with a quizzical expression on her face, 'I can't quite work it out.'

Lewis just smiled and said, 'I enjoy trying out all trends lovely lady.'

She laughed aloud as she threw her head back in an exaggerated way.

Arjun and Stan looked across from the bar at the pair laughing and almost at the same time said,

'What does he see in her?'

As the evening progressed, Rebecca and Lewis were only half-heartedly doing the quiz. He was asking her about her life and at the same time he was buying her the alcohol she was so determined not to drink this evening.

'What is the capital city of Estonia?' was the next question asked by the quiz master.

'Who cares,' said Lewis, 'go on, tell me about what you and the manager did last Saturday, sounds fun.'

Rebecca, after three large glasses of white wine, began to slur her words but managed to recount the whole story, with Lewis taking in her every word.

'You know that last Saturday was the fourth time we had done it!' she slurred. 'The other three times had been nicer, as it had been in his bed at his house and not in the pub cellar.'

'Where else would his bed be?' sniggered Lewis.

'Oh yeah,' she said, 'silly me.'

'Why do you like him Becky?' Lewis asked.

'He showed some interest in me I guess,' she said, with a sudden curious look on her face. 'I don't seem to attract men like I used to, not like when I was younger. Philip adores me and I'm hoping we can start living together soon.'

'Does he ever talk about himself to you?' Asked Lewis.

'Like what?' she said.

'Oh, I don't know, things about his past, present or future.'

'I know he has a brother who is sick with cancer.' She suddenly opened her eyes wide and an element of panic showed on her face, she stared directly at him,

'I shouldn't have said that, as I only know that due to work, Philip didn't tell me.' She was now worried.

'Hey, no worries Becky, I won't say anything to anyone I promise,' he smiled, raising his hand in a mock salute.

'Thanks.' She felt relieved.

'Has he always lived around this area?' Lewis continued with his questions.

'Yes, I believe so,' she said, 'his mum died when he was about four.'

'That's sad,' Lewis remarked. 'What did she die of?'

'He told me the first night we hooked up and if I am completely honest, I don't remember huge amounts of what he said.' Rebecca looked embarrassed. 'Although, I think it might have been a road traffic accident.'

'Blimey!' Lewis exclaimed, 'that's awful and especially if Philip was only four.'

'Why are you so interested in Philip?' Asked Rebecca breathing alcohol fumes over the young man.

'Oh, I'm not at all,' laughed Lewis, 'I don't really know him, I was just being nosey.'

Rebecca considered Lewis with an air of curiosity and he was regarding her at the same time. She seemed to him, to be mulling things over in her head, as she had stopped talking and this wasn't like her. She then smiled.

'I like him a lot,' she said, 'he's got a real charm about him.'

'He doesn't sound like a nice person Becky, he hasn't even turned up tonight and you made yourself so pretty too.'

She nodded and looked at Lewis with heartfelt gratitude in her eyes.

'My round, what are you going to have?'

Going up to the bar, she briefly thought she saw Philip walk past the kitchen entrance. She called his name, but he either ignored her or didn't hear her. She hoped it was the latter. Of course it was the latter. Wasn't it?

At the bar, Arjun was serving and sighed deeply when he saw her approaching.

'Was that Philip I just saw?' she demanded.

'Probably,' dismissing her question and asking, 'what can I get for you?'

In a crass voice overheard by many at the bar, she said, in a brazen way, 'If he thinks he can just shag me in the cellar and then ignore me, then he has another thing coming.'

Arjun, who was now outraged by her behaviour, walked away without serving her. She turned to the strangers at the bar and said with force,

'There is a shock coming Philip Oakes' way and then he won't be ignoring me.'

Unseen by Rebecca, Lewis pulled on his coat and had a menacing smile on his face as he looked at the pathetic drunk at the bar, talking to customers who just wanted her to go away. He slipped out into the night, laughing to himself.

5:

1985

Philip aged Four

Mr Oakes walked through his front door, drenched and wind swept from the storm that was raging outside. He did have an umbrella, however, it was useless in this type of weather. He stood in his wide Victorian hall, erect and stern and glanced at himself in the arch shaped mirror next to the portrait of his beloved wife and himself. The painting had been done before their two sons had been born. In the mirror, his face was showing signs of sorrow and heartache.

Mrs Temple who helped care for the boys, came forward to greet him. She was a pleasant woman, mid-fifties, pillow-like cheeks and always cheerful. As she stepped closer to the dazed looking man, she could see the pain in his eyes.

'Can you call the boys for me please, it is extremely important,' he asked in an off-hand manner.

'Oh, my goodness, is everything alright?' she replied. 'What on earth has happened?'

'Just please fetch the children and then leave us alone in the lounge,' he repeated loudly.

Mrs Temple went up the stairs and into each bedroom and told the two boys they were wanted by their father. The youngsters never argued when summoned by him. They both came downstairs and saw him pointing for them to go straight into the lounge. He followed them and Mrs Temple went back into the kitchen, although she was tempted to listen at the keyhole.

Mr Oakes paced up and down before addressing the two confused children sitting in front of him.

'Boys, I need to talk to you and I need both to remain quiet.'

They were both sitting on the floor, crossed legged, glaring up at their father with their eyes wide open.

'Ethan, take hold of Philip's hand will you please,' he spoke to his eldest son with little to no emotion in his voice.

Ethan looked strangely at his father, but did as he was told. As he reached out for his brother's hand and held it in a gentle manner, Philip turned and smiled at him. They both then turned back to their father.

In a loud booming voice and without any preparation, he viewed their small faces and spoke.

'Boys, I am sorry to say this but your mother was hit by a speeding car today and she died.'

Ethan dropped Philip's hand and instantly started to cry. Philip, aged four, looked at both his father and brother. He didn't know what he was meant to do and felt confused.

He started to cry and got up to go to his father for comfort. Mr Oakes stepped away from the approaching child and walked over to the fireplace.

'Philip, don't come over to me, please can you go to your brother and stay with him.' There was no feeling in his voice.

The young boy, who was bewildered and upset, stepped towards his brother, however, Ethan turned his back on Philip and Mr Oakes walked out of the room.

6:

15th October 2017

Jacob

7:30am

Sitting in their kitchen with its log burner throwing out heat and pictures of their two children covering one of the yellow painted walls, the married couple looked at each other and felt happy. For the past two weeks, each day had started the same in the Spencer household. Jacob had applied for a promotion at work, so each morning he was speaking aloud the answers he might give at his interview.

Tanvi, his beautiful South Indian wife, with silky, long black hair and rich brown eyes under her newly threaded eyebrows, stared adoringly at her husband.

'Can you please give me some ideas of what you would do in the first six months if you were successful in getting this job?' She asked Jacob, as she pretended to be the interviewer.

'Firstly, as I already know the staff I'd be managing, I would discuss with them my new role and how this would mean I was no longer able to be their friend.' That's absolute crap, he said, frustrated.

'Start again,' his wife said calmly.

'During my first six months I would discuss with my team, how my new role will be different from how they are used to seeing me, but it is an exciting time of change and I am looking forward to the new challenges ahead that we can face together.' He took a deep breath and looked at Tanvi with a puzzled expression.

'Better,' she said. 'Go on.'

'I would gain a better understanding of how the department runs from a Matron's point of view and how it impacts on targets and Trust policies.' He stopped and breathed, then smiled at Tanvi.

Currently, Jacob was a senior staff nurse working in the A&E department of his local hospital. He had applied for the Matron's role, which would mean bypassing the charge nurse grade, but he was sure he could make the jump, as he had worked hard in the department for the past seven years and had a lot of knowledge.

At thirty-six and a father of two young children, Rory aged two and Adrian at six months, he needed to be earning more money to help pay off some debts and start to secure his family's future. His concerns were that he lacked managerial experience and was terrible in interviews.

'We've been doing interview practice for two weeks Jacob, you need to start relaxing about this whole process and start having faith in yourself and your abilities,' Tanvi said beaming at her husband. 'You are a fantastic nurse and they would be lucky to have you as their Matron.'

Jacob was a tall, regal looking black man, with a rounded, handsome face and high cheekbones. He wore glasses for reading and these made him look very distinguished. He was proud of his firm body and knew he got lots of attention from the females at work. He was a real flirt, although he hoped his wife didn't know. His physique was probably inherited from good family genes, as he hadn't seen the inside of a gym for years. In their twenties, he and Philip, his best friend from school since they were three, did frequent the gym for a few years but that was a long time ago. Now they preferred drinking games and pub quizzes. Tanvi disliked Philip and always had.

'Sorry hun, I know I have been a pain with the constant interview questions.' Jacob kissed his wife with a slowness and passion she adored.

A sudden cry from upstairs alerted them to the fact that Rory had woken up. Jacob gave Tanvi one longer kiss and then raced upstairs to get his son. Adrian slept on. Jacob returned and put Rory into the highchair, so he was ready for breakfast. Tanvi was at the sink washing up. Jacob stood behind her, grabbed her around the waist, and nuzzled into her neck. She fell back into his enveloping arms and enjoyed the moment. She loved him so much.

'I'll feed the monster,' said Jacob. He reached for the Weetabix and mixed in the warm milk.

Rory was unimpressed!

'Are you seeing Philip tonight?' Tanvi asked.

'I am indeed,' he replied. 'Is that OK?'

'If I said no, would it make a difference?'

'Oh, come on, I have known him since I was three.' There was slight annoyance in his voice. 'He's my best friend and we have always been there for each other.'

'Has he mentioned the money you owe him again?' She asked with bitterness.

'Yes, but that was a while back and I am hoping he won't mention it tonight.'

'I hate you owing him money,' she said, 'let me ask my parents for the money, you know they have plenty.'

Jacob was feeding Rory his third spoonful and slowly turned to stare at his wife with a shocked expression on his face.

'Absolutely not!' he said with real force behind the words. 'I'd much rather owe Philip than that bitter old man you call dad!'

She rolled her eyes at him, but had to agree about her dad. At this moment, there were crying noises coming from upstairs. Adrian was awake.

8:00pm

Philip came out of the kitchen and viewed the bar area to see how many customers he had. Standing behind the bar was Stan, his senior bartender, who had worked at the pub for a few years now and loved his job. He was mid-thirties, slim, balding and had heavily tattooed arms. Everyone loved Stan and Philip was very protective of him.

'Hey, Stan,' he said to his friend, 'who is that lad in the corner wearing the black jeans full of holes and pink baseball cap?'

'Don't worry Philip, he's legal, I checked,' replied Stan.

'It's not just that,' said Philip, 'I thought he was staring at me earlier. Has he been in before?'

'Not sure, but maybe. Ask Arjun.'

Jacob came through the door. He spied Philip in the main section of the pub, nodded and then headed to the toilet.

'Stan, I'm going into the office, send Jacob through.'

'No worries,' said Stan.

'And bring through a large Sauvignon Blanc and half a pint of lager,' winked Philip.

Stan smiled. He really liked Philip.

In his office, which was a decent size with large square windows that let in lots of light and looked out onto the pub's car park, Philip was waiting for Jacob. He was going to ask him about the money he was owed and when he was going to either get it all back, or at least start receiving substantial payments each month. He had been happy to lend the money, as he had inherited a large amount after his dad had died, but that loan was now four years ago and Jacob had made no attempts to either discuss it or start repaying. Philip had asked a few months back, but not for a while now. Nonetheless it had started to irritate him and was becoming an issue. Jacob had been the one to ask to come along tonight, so maybe Philip thought, I won't need to be the one to mention it and he would bring the subject up.

The office door opened and in walked Stan with the drinks, closely followed by Jacob.

'That woman at the bar, bit drunk and loud,' said Jacob.

'What about her?'

'She works at the hospital in the pharmacy department,' was Jacob's reply.

'So, what of it?' snapped Philip.

'I was just saying, don't bite my head off.'

They both laughed and had a mouthful of their drinks.

The two then chatted about current events happening in their lives. Jacob talked of the pending interview; however, he was keen not to linger too long on the fact it was a promotion, in case this ignited the thought of money in Philip's head. Philip was genuinely pleased for his friend.

'When is the interview?'

'20th mate and I can tell you I am shitting myself.' Jacob said with real fear in his eyes.

'Why are you so nervous?' Asked Philip.

'Because there is a lot riding on this,' he answered. 'No more weekend or night work. I can do Monday to Friday 9:00am-5:00pm and have more time to spend with you.'

They both roared with laughter. They had a good friendship, although it was now beginning to get tested.

When Philip told Jacob that he was gay, but with a little element of fluidity in him, Jacob had been stunned. Philip had always been the more aggressive one and hadn't given off any vibes that he was anything but straight. It hadn't been a problem for Jacob. He had always been there for Philip, even when the self-harming had started when his friend was thirteen years old. Jacob remembered asking Philip why he had started to cut himself and all Philip would say was,

'Stuff Jacob, just stuff, please don't ask me again.'

The money was beginning to be a problem and it was coming between them. Jacob had borrowed £25,000 four years ago to pay off his gambling debts. He hadn't wanted Tanvi to know he had an addiction, so she believed his debt was from a poor investment. Paying off the debts was a huge relief and in secret, Jacob had attended support groups to stop him gambling again. However, all he had really done was move the debt. Owing this money to Philip was playing on his mind. He had promised to pay him back within two years. Four years later and not a penny had been paid back.

The idea of using some of his wages and start betting on the horses had started to be a thought in his head. Jacob started silently praying that he'd get this promotion, then at least he could maybe think about a Direct Debit into Philip's account.

'Did you hear me?' said Philip.

'No mate, sorry, miles away.' Jacob grinned and then asked, 'have you had your test results back yet?'

'Not yet, they are due on the 19th, so just got to wait four more days.'

'How is Ethan getting on?' Asked Jacob. As a senior nurse, he was keen to know.

'Well not great to be honest, the chemotherapy is going OK, but psychologically he isn't in a great place,' replied Philip, who had visited his brother at the hospital two days ago.

There was a knock at the door and Arjun, the junior bartender, came in with fresh drinks for the two men.

'Hey Arjun, you must have read my mind,' Philip leered at Arjun, an expression that lasted a little too long.

'Cool, just thought you could both do with another drink,' Arjun smiled back.

As Arjun left, Jacob observed Philip with a bemused look in his eyes,

'You fancy him,' smiled Jacob, 'you dirty old man.'

Philip just smiled and said nothing.

'I can't drink that, I'm driving,' said Jacob pointing to the half pint, 'so back to Ethan.'

'He has started to lose his hair and his blood counts are low.'

'That's normal with chemotherapy I believe,' said Jacob.

'Oh, is it? I didn't know, but was told his white blood cell count falls because of the treatment. They usually fight infections, so as they are low, he is vulnerable to germs.'

Philip was doing his best to remember what his nephew Adam had told him.

'Part of the white cells are something called neutrophils and they are the main part of the white cells that fight infections.'

'It is complicated,' surmised Jacob. 'Remind me what test you're waiting on?'

'Ethan has to have a transplant as the best chance of a cure, so they have tested my blood cells,' Philip continued, 'If I am a perfect match, meaning my blood cells match Ethan's, then they will use my cells as the transplant.'

'What if you don't match?'

'In that case they have to do searches using databases of people on the donor registers and that's happening already in case I don't match.'

The two men looked at each other for a few moments, both a little confused, but Jacob more so.

'Jacob,' Philip said, 'you asked to meet tonight, was there a reason?'

'Do I need a reason?' was the response.

'You know full well you don't, but you particularly asked to meet tonight, why?'

Philip was now hoping to start hearing about a Direct Debit or payment plan etc.

'OK, can I use your house on the 19th?'

Philip looked bemused at Jacob and asked, 'why?'

'Well, I know you're working and I could do with the peace and quiet to plan for the interview the next day.'

'Can't you use somewhere at work?'

'No, not really, as I don't want people seeing me as then I get distracted and start chatting.'

'OK, go on then,' said Philip. 'I assume you still have the spare key I gave you?'

'I do indeed,' was the happy reply.

10:35pm

As both men left the pub, they stood by Jacob's car and chatted some small talk for a few minutes. The two men embraced and Jacob got in his car and drove off in the opposite direction to that which Philip was heading. As Philip walked, he couldn't help thinking that Jacob asking to use his house on the 19th, was strange. Was Jacob up to something?

Philip lived about ten minutes from the pub, so the walk was good to clear his head. He was a lazy man and did on occasions still drive to and from work. Not tonight though, tonight was all about fresh air and exercise, well if the short walk counted as exercise.

Philip walked through the streets, not really taking notice of anything. It was a crisp October night and the moon was clear in the sky. As he walked into his road, which was a long street with mostly Victorian houses, Philip's attention was on his test results and whether he'd be a perfect match for Ethan. He honestly hoped he was going to be. He smiled to himself.

As he looked ahead, he thought he saw someone standing in the road.

They were quite far off, but just standing in the middle of the road. Philip stepped off the pavement and onto the road to have a better look. In the distance stood a figure, silhouetted by the moon, just standing. From what Philip could see, he, or she, was standing still with their hands on their hips and not moving at all. Their hair appeared curly and wild but it was difficult to tell from such a distance.

Thinking nothing more of it, Philip went over to his front door and went inside. He had noticed Mrs Ferres, his nosey neighbour, was at her curtains. Once in his house, he went upstairs and removed his clothes and came back down to the kitchen and poured himself a large glass of wine. He went through to his lounge, put on his TV and in the background put on the news as he played his turn of Scrabble on his phone.

Outside, the figure in the road, stood for a few moments longer, then smiled and walked away.

7:

19th October 2017

Philip

08:30am

It was the morning of Philip's test results and he was excited to know if he was a full match for Ethan. Lying in bed, he allowed himself a huge yawn, then got up and headed downstairs to make coffee and have some breakfast.

As he waited for the kettle to boil, he grabbed his phone, went into the bathroom and sat down for his morning call of nature. He knew instinctively there would be many text messages.

Ethan: *'Fingers crossed for good news today, Philip. I'm relying on you bro.'*

Adam: *'Please God you're a match for my dad. See you later.'*

Ethan: *'Sorry, didn't mean to put pressure on you, can't wait to see you later.'*

Jacob: *'Don't forget I'm coming to use your house today. Cheers mate.'*

Stan: *'Hey boss, I can do that shift for you tomorrow but Arjun's on at 2:00pm and I am sure he would stay on. Anyways, let me know what you think.'*

Philip had plans for Arjun so a quick text back to Stan asking him to come in from 6:00pm was instantly sent.

Ethan: *'I'm so nervous Philip. Love you.'*

'Love you!' when had Ethan ever said he loved me, thought Philip.

Then he saw an old message from Rebecca that he'd never replied to.

'Hi Philip, I'm still thinking of last Saturday, are you? Maybe next time we can go back to using your bed lol. Anyhow, I'll be back in tomorrow for the quiz if you fancy a chat. Hugs Rebecca x.'

Philip looked at the message and said to himself, 'silly bitch!'

He had to think hard to remember what had happened on that Saturday. When he remembered, he frowned in disgust at himself.

Stan: *'No worries, see you at 6:00pm tomorrow.'*

The kettle had boiled so he walked back into the kitchen and was slapping his buttocks in a rhythmic motion, like he was playing drums as he went.

After breakfast, he showered and went back upstairs to dry and get ready for the day. He sat on his bed opposite his mirror. Both shoulders and tops of his arms were covered in small, healed cuts. Philip looked for a long time at these marks. Self-harming had been a big part of his life from age thirteen to about eighteen. In his twenties, he had been very body conscious and wanted to look his absolute best. He enjoyed the gym, especially going with Jacob. As he now observed himself in the mirror, he just saw a scarred, overweight man, who at thirty-six, was still single and at times, very lonely.

A text message alert brought him out of his low mood and he picked up his phone, saw who the text was from and pulled an irritated face.

Ethan: *'What time are you getting to the hospital?'*

Philip looked at the text for a few moments before he texted back.

'I'm leaving the house in 5 minutes.'

'Screw that,' thought Philip, 'I'll have another coffee, Ethan can wait,' he told himself.

When Philip was nearly ready to leave the house, he did his usual tidying up routine. He hated coming home to an untidy house. Breakfast things were in the dishwasher and worktops were cleaned. He put bleach in the toilet and ensured the toilet roll was in the correct position. Philip then headed upstairs to do the most important thing for him, which was to make his bed to a luxury hotel standard.

8:

19th October 2017

Ethan

11:30am

Philip pulled into the hospital car park in his red BMW. He hated car parks as he was nervous his car would get scratched or dented. There was no point in trying to park away from other cars, as this car park was always full. Philip paid for his ticket and put it on his dashboard and then headed to the main entrance. Apparently, he was searching for Silver Birch haematology ward. He found the hospital directory on the wall and saw that he needed to go to the 11th floor and head to the East Wing.

'Please let me be a perfect match,' Philip said as he entered the lift.

When the lift doors opened, he walked to the ward and pressed the intercom.

'Philip Oakes, I am here to see Dr Kelleher.' The door buzzed to allow him to enter.

'Uncle Philip.'

Philip looked along the ward and saw Adam coming towards him, calling his name.

'Hi Adam, how are you?'

'I am so nervous Uncle Philip, please be a match.'

'Firstly, stop with the uncle stuff, just call me Philip, you're eighteen for Christ's sake.'

'Sorry,' Adam said in an embarrassed tone.

'Everybody's putting so much pressure on me and it isn't fair,' declared Philip.

'Oh, I'm so sorry Unc... I mean Philip, please don't be mad.'

'It's fine Adam, how's your dad?'

'He's a bit stressed as he thought you'd have been here ages ago.'

The two then walked along the ward and into the room. Ethan's face wasn't happy.

'Where have you been?' he said in a raised voice. 'I thought you said you were leaving in five minutes, which meant you should have been here ages ago.'

'I know you're stressed Ethan, but don't have a go at me.'

'I wasn't having a go at you Philip but this is a big day for me and I am petrified that if you aren't a perfect match, then I might die.'

Adam's eyes opened wide and tears started to appear. Ethan reached over and rubbed his son's shoulder. Before the conversation escalated into a family argument, Liam arrived with a cheerful bounce in his step.

'Hey everyone.'

'Morning Liam,' Emma answered for everyone.

Liam surveyed the family and could sense there was anxiety amongst them. He took a deep breath,

'As these are Philip's results, he has the right to be given them by himself.'

Ethan was stunned and looked around at his brother and his eyes enlarged.

'Are you kidding me Liam?' Ethan said with anger and slight aggression.

'No Ethan, but...'

Philip interrupted.

'It's fine, I am happy to hear the results along with everyone else.' Philip nodded at Ethan.

Liam agreed and took them to the quiet room on the ward to see the consultant. He walked with Emma and Adam, followed by Ethan and Philip, who were in silence.

Dr Kelleher was waiting for them as they all arrived. She smiled as they took their seats.

She could tell there was a huge amount of tension in the room and Adam was already shaking in his seat.

'I know this is a very tense moment, so I am not going to delay things any longer,' she said with compassion as she looked at both Ethan and Philip. 'You're a 100% match Philip.'

Emma held her husband's hand as he started to shake, just before the tears started to flow and she took a deep breath and closed her eyes. In the room, sobbing could be heard. Liam went over to Adam and put his arm around the teenager as he cried. Through tears in his eyes, Ethan glanced over at Philip and beamed. Adam then came over and hugged his dad. Philip sat on his own with a huge smile on his face.

'What happens now?' Asked Emma, who was the pragmatic member of the group.

'As we have already done all our tests and investigations on Philip to ensure he is well enough to be the donor, we need to harvest, meaning collect his stem cells,' Dr Kelleher said, still radiating a huge grin. 'We need to ensure that Ethan is in remission from the intensive chemotherapy regimen he has had and start the transplant as soon as we can.'

Ethan was now grinning and his tears had gone. Adam was still holding on to his dad.

'Ethan, do you have any questions?' Asked Liam.

'I think over the past few weeks waiting for these results, we have talked lots and I think I'm OK and understand what happens next,' Ethan was cheerful as he held Emma's hand tight and kissed his son's head.

'Does this mean my dad will be cured?' Asked Adam, with hope in his voice.

'As we have discussed Adam, having Philip's stem cells is very important and they are your dad's best chance of a cure, but even with the transplant we can't be sure.' The consultant addressed the entire room.

Everybody was smiling and the tension in the room had now turned to excitement and relief. Ethan was kissing his wife and then nodding over at Liam. Adam was texting his friends at the paint company, as he was so relieved by the news and knew they all wanted to know what the outcome was. Philip had stood up unnoticed by anyone, even though the room was small and positioned himself over by the window.

'I'm very pleased about this result Ethan,' Dr Kelleher said, 'I was reluctant to tell you all, but the donor searches we did in case Philip wasn't a match, came back with no definite matches.'

She continued, 'There were a couple of potential donors that were a 7/10 match, but for your type of Leukaemia, you really needed a full match and especially a sibling match.'

Everyone in the room, apart from one person was celebrating and crying, Philip looked on.

'What if I don't want to donate my cells?' Philip said in a loud and authoritative voice that filled the room.

The room went silent. Everybody turned to stare at him with dazed expressions on their faces. Nobody said anything for about fifteen seconds.

'Why are you asking this?' Asked the doctor with surprise on her face.

'If I don't donate my cells, what will happen?'

'Philip, are you seriously asking this question?' Asked Emma.

Ethan was silent.

'Ethan's best chance of a cure is to have your cells Philip. There are no other fully matched donors available,' said Dr Kelleher. 'There are treatments existing and trials that Ethan could be placed on if necessary but, without the transplant, his chance of survival is extremely low.'

'Philip, you're alarming me,' said Ethan, 'are you just asking this question to make sure everything is out in the open and to make absolutely sure it's necessary?'

'Uncle Philip,' said Adam, with a sense of despair in his voice.

'Philip!' Emma said, with assertion, 'why are you saying this?'

Philip surveyed the room and smiled at each person. Liam looked back with a questioning stare.

'Are you simply scared? Do you need more time to ask questions?' He asked of the man who was standing by the window and commanding the room.

Everyone turned back to look at Philip. Dr Kelleher just glared at him with an astonished expression. In all her time as a transplant consultant, she had never been in this situation before. She couldn't work out if he were just seeing what alternatives there were or scared about the harvesting process, which meant collecting his cells. She prayed he hadn't really meant what he was implying. That would be disastrous for Ethan and would be signing his death warrant.

'No, I understand everything thank you Liam.' Philip nodded calmly.

'Philip, please can we be clear here, what exactly are you saying?' Asked Dr Kelleher.

The tension was now back in the room. Ethan was showing signs of extreme anger. He was shaking and biting down on his lip and there was blood.

'WHAT are you saying?' shouted Ethan.

'I don't want to donate my cells.' Philip said assertively.

'Are you worried about the effects that it could have on you?' Asked Dr Kelleher.

'No!' was the clear response.

'Then what is your concern?' She asked.

'I don't have any concerns,' he smiled at the doctor.

'Philip, please,' begged Ethan, 'don't do this to me.'

'Do you want time alone with Dr Kelleher and Liam without us?' Emma asked.

'Nope,' was his answer.

'Uncle Philip, please don't do this to us,' Adam said, choking back his tears.

'Please don't put me through this.' Ethan stared longingly at his brother.

Philip moved towards the door and as he opened it, he turned to look at Ethan.

'I won't be giving you my cells.'

Philip turned and walked out of the room. He had a huge smile on his face as he headed to the car park.

9:

19th October 2017

Philip

12:15pm

Philip walked out of the hospital and over to his car. He could hear footsteps running behind him.

'WHAT ARE YOU PLAYING AT?' Emma screamed at him.

Philip ignored the screams, got into his car, closed his eyes and smirked. He was aware that his breathing was rapid and pulse rate was fast. The shaking first started in his legs and soon was evident in his hands and arms. Suddenly there was a loud thud on his window. Philip took a deep breath and slowly opened his eyes. Standing looking at him with a face like thunder was Emma. Philip could tell she wanted to rip him into pieces. Taking a moment, Philip opened the door, got out and faced the hysterical woman.

'What do you want Emma?'

'What do you bloody well think I want?' she hissed at him.

'They are my cells and I have decided that I don't want to go through with the harvesting.'

'Please,' she begged, 'he will die if you don't go through with the procedure.'

'I'm not doing it Emma.' Philip was now getting irritated.

'Think of the kids then,' she was frantic. 'Adam is distraught and Saul and Max just won't understand.'

'Can I go now please?' he said, smirking at her.

'Do you hate Ethan that much?'

'I don't hate Ethan.'

'Then why won't you let him have your cells?' she was confused, 'I don't understand.'

Philip stared directly at her for one more moment. Smiling, he opened the car door and got inside.

'YOU'RE PURE EVIL!' she bellowed at him and thumped the car. 'You're so evil Philip.'

Emma walked away from the car and Philip could tell she was crying. He did genuinely feel desperately sorry for her and the kids. He watched as she bumped into a young man due to not watching where she was going.

Sitting in the car, he picked up his mobile phone and rang The Lemon Tree. After a few rings, it was answered.

'Good afternoon, The Lemon Tree, Arjun speaking.'

'Arj, it's me. How are things at the pub?'

'Hi Philip, it's OK at the moment, a few people in,' was Arjun's reply.

'I'm going to take the day off, is that OK?'

'You're the boss mate, you can do what you want.'

'What's the staffing like?' Asked Philip.

'It's me and Hannah at the moment and Stan comes on at 6:00pm to work with you but I'm happy to stay through to closing, if that helps you?' Arjun was always keen to please his boss.

'Great, thanks Arj, you're a star.' Philip ended the call.

He didn't want to be bothered by anyone for the rest of the day, so he turned off his phone.

As Philip drove out of the car park, he was unaware that a young man was watching him, the same one that Emma bumped into. He was wearing dark green trousers and a black jacket, he had dyed grey hair, sunglasses on and was smoking a cigarette. He had followed Philip to the hospital and had just watched the spat with Emma. The youngster whistled as he went over to his car and climbed in.

Philip drove around for a couple of hours to try and clear his head. He'd been to a drive-through KFC and then parked outside the pub, but didn't go in. He ate in the car. Feeling slightly awash with emotions, he drove back to his house and as he pulled up outside, he saw Jacob's car.

'Bugger, I forgot he was here,' he said to himself.

Not wanting to see anyone, or more importantly talk to anyone, Philip parked up and took himself off to the nearest tube station. He decided he'd go into London's West End and eat in Chinatown and then see a musical. He'd come to a decision about which one after he'd eaten.

Sitting on the tube, Philip questioned if he was being too harsh with Ethan, but soon concluded that he had every right to act the way that he had. He knew no one would agree with him on this matter but that didn't bother him at all.

The tube train was making so much noise as it rattled along that it disrupted his thoughts. Metal scraping against metal was a dreadful sound. It was crowded but he had a seat, so what did he care. The couple next to him were discussing how excited they were to have seen Big Ben and Buckingham Palace. He got bored of them very quickly.

'Excuse me, I'm sorry to disturb your day.' The homeless man was standing in the carriage and telling everyone that he needed £18 for a place in a hostel. The whole carriage of people looked in any direction but his. Philip called him over. As he neared, Philip could see the state of his matted hair, the bruise above his right cheek bone and the general filthiness of the young man. Philip thought that he had soft, gentle eyes and the poor soul just seemed exhausted.

'What's your name mate and how old are you?' Asked Philip.

'Paul and I'm nineteen,' came the answer.

'How did you end up in this situation Paul?'

'Long story,' he said as his eyes dropped to the floor of the tube train.

'It's still a few stops until I get off so I am happy to listen, if you're happy to tell me.'

Paul looked at Philip. He wasn't used to anyone showing any interest in him. He was used to being beaten on the streets, hence the bruise and spat at and usually totally ignored.

'My dad died when I was eleven,' the young man started to say. 'Mum quickly hooked up with a bloke who turned out not to be too nice to me.'

'Did your mum know? What did she do about it if she did?'

'Told me I was making things up and refused to listen.'

The people who had refused to even look at this young man now seemed to be gaining interest in him, as they glanced in his direction.

'Let's get off at the next stop Paul and I'll buy you a late lunch.'

Paul smiled broadly and showed his teeth. Philip realised he'd need to buy Paul some toiletries too, like toothpaste and a brush.

They went via Superdrug for the few things to help freshen Paul up and then headed to McDonald's. At the table with a Big Mac, large fries, milkshake and dessert, which Paul treated like a full Christmas dinner, Philip asked a few more questions.

'Can I ask what your mother's boyfriend did to you?'

'Step-dad actually, they got married.' Paul said. 'He was a bully and would run me down and tell me I was worthless. Then, when I turned sixteen, he started to hit me, usually where a bruise would be covered up with clothes.'

'That's dreadful Paul, I am sorry you went through something like that.'

'I think mum knew that he was treating me badly but turned a blind eye, as she was more scared of being on her own than standing up to him.'

'So, what got you on the streets?' Philip asked, genuinely concerned.

'The beatings got more frequent and then when I turned seventeen, he raped me.'

Philip couldn't help himself and reached out and touched Paul's arm. Paul looked at Philip and swallowed hard to fight back his emotions.

'Is it bad on the streets Paul?'

'It's not great, especially as the weather is now so cold,' the teenager said. 'There is a lot of violence but you learn how to dodge it, well, if you're lucky enough.'

'Is there no other family you can stay with?' Asked Philip.

'I am an only child of parents who were only children too.'

Paul had now finished his food and was already slightly brighter in his face. However, underneath the dirty, grubby beard, Philip could see Paul's crystal blue eyes but they appeared tired and frightened.

'Thank you for showing an interest in me and my life and thank you for the food. I didn't eat yesterday so this was very welcome.' There was a very wide grin on his face.

'Come with me,' said Philip.

They went to a Lloyds Bank cashpoint and Philip took out £300. Paul was confused.

'Paul, this is for you. Don't flash it around, just get yourself a hostel for a week or so and use the rest for food, etc.'

Paul was again stunned.

'I really don't know what to say,' he said, clearly choking on his words and having tears in those blue eyes.

'Stay safe and it was lovely to meet you. Here is my email address on this card and you contact me if you need help.'

Philip handed Paul the Superdrug bag and gave the young man a hug. He then turned and walked away.

Philip walked into Chinatown. He loved the buzz of this part of town. The smells coming from all the restaurants and the multicultural people going about their business, looking like they loved life. This was London at its best. He took himself to one of the restaurants and asked for a table for one. When eating out, Philip always liked to sit looking out over the restaurant. He refused to eat with his back to everyone.

The menu was already on the table, so he picked it up. This was just a motion to go through, as he already knew what he was going to have.

'Are you ready to order?' Asked the waitress, in a discourteous and slightly aggressive way.

'Yes, I will have the hot and sour soup, then sweet and sour chicken with fried rice and a large glass of the house white wine.' He smiled at her in a smirky way. 'Oh, I would also like some prawn crackers too.'

The waitress took his order and walked away without saying another word.

'Kinky Boots,' Philip unexpectedly said aloud and was then aware people had started glaring at him.

The Adelphi Theatre was only about a 10-minute walk from Chinatown, so he'd see Kinky Boots. He'd seen it twice before but it was a very funny show to watch and right now, Philip felt he needed to laugh. It was also a relatively short show and the music was also great.

9:30pm

Philip came out of the theatre having enjoyed what he had just seen. He breathed in the night air and considering this was London and the amount of traffic, the air smelt good. He looked around to decide if he would walk to a tube station or order an Uber. It had been a very strange day and because of this, Philip's phone was still switched off, however, he knew as soon as he turned it on, it wouldn't stop buzzing.

From across the street, Philip saw a McDonald's, thought of Paul, and hoped he was now safe in a hostel bed somewhere. For a brief second, he did contemplate getting himself a burger to eat on the way home, but decided a KFC and a Chinese meal had been enough calories for today, well, at least until he got home.

As he wasn't yet ready to turn his phone back on to order an Uber, Philip hailed a taxi, as a treat to himself as the thought of a tube was not tempting him. He got in ready to sit and relax but his driver had other plans.

'Alright mate?'

'Yes, thanks,' Philip replied in a disinterested voice.

'You been to see that show tonight?' indicating Kinky Boots.

'Yes,' said Philip, again answering as little as possible.

'My wife wants to see it, but it has drag queens in it, hasn't it?'

'Is that a problem?' Philip asked with a touch of aggression.

'Not at all mate,' the driver said. 'Sorry, I was just asking and didn't mean anything by it.'

'It's been a very tough day; do you mind if I just sit and not talk?' asked Philip.

'Yeah, no worries mate.'

The conversation ended and the peace was welcome.

Once the car pulled into his street, Philip noticed that Jacob's car had gone and this pleased him significantly.

'I'm sorry if I was a little moody,' he said as he paid the driver.

'Not a problem mate,' was the chirpy reply.

As Philip headed into his house and straight through into the kitchen, he could tell that Jacob had been there, as the kitchen was untidy. This really angered him. He had no issue with his friend helping himself to any food or drink but what really irritated him was the mess that had been left. Two tops-off lager bottles were left on the side and he had obviously had toast as not only had he left the buttered knife on the worktop but also all the crumbs that had been created. Philip could not stand mess, especially of other people's doing.

'This is disgusting,' Philip said aloud.

Quickly, he cleaned up the mess and contemplated whether he wanted anything to eat. He decided that he did, so opened up the fridge, took out some cheese, and cut off a few slab-like slices. He also thought about not having wine but this decision was short-lived and he poured himself a large glass and headed into the lounge. Rather than putting on the TV, he played music via Spotify.

As he sat on the sofa, he concluded it was time to turn on his phone. This was a moment he had been dreading! After it had re-booted and within a minute of turning it on, the text messages, WhatsApp messages, emails and voicemails started coming up on the front screen. This was all too much for him, so he left the phone on the sofa and headed upstairs. He'd deal with the messages tomorrow, or maybe not.

As he walked into his bedroom, Philip knew something wasn't right. His bed wasn't how he had left it. It was poorly made and was trying to mimic the perfectly made bed he had created before he left this morning. Straight away, Philip assumed that Jacob had got tired doing his interview practice and slept instead, as he may have been up during the night with the kids. This was a step too much as far as he was concerned. No one got into his bed, unless invited.

Philip was now truly angry, but not as angry as he was about to get. As he walked around to the other side of the bedroom he noticed on the floor, an empty red box of condoms. Philip swiftly felt like his blood pressure was rising high and about to cause a stroke. He violently pulled back the duvet and immediately felt sick. There were obvious signs on his sheets that Jacob hadn't just slept in the bed. At first, he didn't know how to react as he couldn't quite believe someone would do something like this in another person's bed.

'You dirty bastard,' Philip said to himself as he continued to look at his sheets.

The sight of them was still making him feel nauseated and the anger he felt was causing pains in his chest and head. Everything had to be washed and it all had to be washed now.

'You are going to pay for this Jacob!'

Philip started to angrily pull off the bed linen, swearing with each movement.

10:

20th October 2017

Arjun

07:00am

As she walked through her sunny hallway, looking at the wallpaper that was beginning to look shabby and in desperate need of re-doing, Mrs Singh got to the bottom of the stairs.

'Who's in for dinner tonight?' she called up to her three sons, two of them getting ready for the day ahead.

Rohit, her youngest at sixteen and still very boyish in appearance but with the beginnings of facial hair and alluring good looks called down to her.

'I am, as have no choice, seeing that I am kept a prisoner in this house.'

Mrs Singh was fifty but looked older with worry lines evident on her face. She had a rounded figure that her husband adored and always called her his gorgeous lady.

'When you are eighteen you can do as you please,' she called back and then added, 'like your brothers do.'

Rajan, the eldest at twenty-six, leisurely walked down the stairs stating that he would also be home. He always appeared to carry the weight of the world on his shoulders, with looks and a personality less captivating than his brothers. A lonely person in some respects. Sitting in the newly furbished kitchen having breakfast together was an enjoyable time for the Singh family.

'It was the best time of day,' were always Mr Singh's thoughts.

The only time that he knew all of his beloved family would be together, catching up on the events of the day before. Only Rajan tended to be quiet but he did still engage, just from a distance.

Mr Singh passed away eight months ago after battling pancreatic cancer for eighteen months. It was the usual story of being too advanced once symptoms started showing. During those last few months of his life, the family found their love for each other incredibly supportive. The time since he had passed had been very tough, each member worrying about another. Mrs Singh concerned about Rohit as the youngest, Rohit more anxious about Rajan as the more isolated brother. The truth being that each person missed the father figure of the household but each had learned to adjust as is necessary to continue with life.

Arjun, the last into the kitchen as usual, was dressed in just his boxer shorts. He had a body that Rajan, who had his mum's roundness, envied. He was a twenty-two-year-old Indian man with an athletic build, a swimmer's body many had said. Thick black hair and gorgeous brown eyes. He was often described by his female and even his male friends as an incredibly 'fit' guy. Arjun was aware of his attractiveness and enjoyed the attention that he received because of it. He worried about Rajan and the unhealthy road to food he seemed to be taking.

'Are you in for dinner tonight Arjun?' enquired his mum.

'Maybe, don't know, depends if Philip needs me to stay on at the bar like he did yesterday,' he said.

She frowned.

'He needs to give you regular hours, so you know what you are doing,' she frowned and continued, 'why do you like working there? He seems a smutty, dislikeable man.'

Arjun raised his thick, groomed eyebrows and carried on with his cereal without answering. Instead, he gazed at Rohit.

'Hey, how are you Rohit?' He asked his brother.

'I'm ok thanks,' he replied. 'I am glad it is half-term next week.'

'Why is that? I thought you loved school,' Rajan said.

'Oh, I do,' said Rohit, who was starting to look increasingly like Arjun, 'but I need a rest from the ladies, as they are totally into me.'

Arjun beheld his younger brother and beamed the biggest smile. He adored him.

He then turned his attention to his older. more serious brother.

'Rajan, you OK?' He asked.

'Fine thanks,' came the quick response which ended the conversation.

'Rohit, do you want to see a movie with me soon? We haven't been out together in a while.' Arjun asked.

'Yeah, that would be really nice, thanks Arjun.'

'What about you Rajan?' Asked Arjun.

'I'll pass,' he replied.

This was the exact answer he knew he would get from his brother. He truly wished Rajan would engage more.

'Maybe we could plan a family dinner, go out sometime soon?' Arjun said. 'Try out a new restaurant in town?'

There were murmurs around the table of this being a good idea.

'Why you up so early Arjun?' Asked Rajan.

'Bed is for lazy people.' Arjun said as he raised his right eyebrow. He then looked at Rohit and pulled a face that said 'I'm talking to you little bro.'

Rohit laughed and said, 'ah, but I love my bed.'

They all laughed, even Rajan.

The DJ on the radio station, Kiss FM, announced that it was 7:30am. Both Rajan and Rohit put their breakfast things onto the side near the sink, kissed their mother and gathered up their things needed for the day from the hall. Rohit came back into the kitchen and gave Arjun a hug. This was something he had started doing to his brothers if he was going out and one of them was staying behind. A result of his dad's death, the rest of the family surmised. Arjun enjoyed his brother's hugs; he relished being around Rohit.

As the two lads left, slamming the front door behind them, Mrs Singh looked at Arjun.

'What are your plans today young man, if I can know without being scowled at?' She asked.

Arjun put his breakfast things on the side and kissed his mum.

'Shower, shit and shave Mother dear, then working from 2:00pm,' he said with annoyance.

As he left the kitchen and headed up the stairs, his mother started huffing as she cried out,

'Try the shit before the shower Arjun my love, it works better that way.'

Before his shower, Arjun stood observing himself in his bedroom mirror and he was satisfied with what he saw. His hard work at the gym had really paid off and he felt attractive. Life since leaving university was difficult. He had studied Business and Management studies at University College London, but since graduating he felt that he had lost direction.

He had been able to live at home during the three years, but this was not what he had hoped for, despite the fact it saved him a lot of money. It is true that he didn't incur the debt his mates had, but he felt he'd missed the proper university experience. Now one year since his course had finished, he felt deflated and to some extent depressed. Not like Rajan who always seemed low in mood, but he knew that he lacked motivation and drive to start something new. Staring again in the mirror, just for a moment, he thought maybe he could go into modelling. He liked the idea of this but what would his family think? He certainly had the body to do it.

Working in the bar was good, he liked Philip, despite what his mother said about him but the actual job with Philip wasn't exactly stretching his capabilities. He'd need to think about finding a job soon. If not modelling, then one that recognised what he learnt at university.

Arjun took off his boxer shorts and grabbed his towel off his radiator and headed into the bathroom which, like the hallway downstairs, needed redecorating as the paintwork was flaking off and it was a drab green colour.

He liked his shower to be as hot as he could bear it, however, this meant edging his way in slowly and allowing his body to get used to the temperature. The water felt good against his skin and it was helping to relax his cluttered mind. He knew his head was full of thoughts and feelings that, at present, he didn't know how to process. Philip featured within these thoughts. His mother would not be happy if she knew this.

After his shower, as he was drying himself in his bedroom, Arjun was excited at the thought of going to work. He liked most of the customers and the banter that happened between them and his co-workers Stan and Hannah. A customer called Lewis, young lad, was a strange character. Each time he came in, he had changed his style. He never had the same colour of hair, nor was it styled the same way. Different dress sense and accessories. When he had time to talk, Arjun was fascinated by his company. However, it was Philip's company he relished the most.

The Lemon Tree was a friendly pub/restaurant that had a large bar area with exposed beams and wooden floors for easy cleaning. The furniture all matched throughout the pub and on the walls were pictures of London throughout the ages.

Walking into the pub ten minutes before his four-hour shift was due to start, Arjun scanned around the bar. No sign of Lewis but Rebecca was in her usual and frequent place, a stool up at the bar. He disliked her intensely which, wasn't usually in his nature to take against someone so severely. As he turned to go and hang his coat up, he saw Philip talking to the chef, he felt himself take a deep breath.

'Afternoon Arj,' bawled Philip with enthusiasm.

Arjun hated being called Arj and if anyone else had done it, he would have corrected them straight away. But not Philip. Why not Philip? His head was driving him mad.

'Afternoon boss man,' joked Arjun.

He savoured the way Philip looked at him.

'You doing anything after work today?' Philip asked.

'No, so I am happy to stay longer if you need me to?' was Arjun's quick response.

He suspected he'd said this too eagerly and looked down to avoid Philip's gaze. Philip reached out and touched Arjun's arm.

'No, I don't need you to work, but wondered if you fancied coming back to mine for a couple of drinks and a catch-up?'

Philip tried to read Arjun's face, once Arjun had raised his head again. Not wanting to seem too pleased, Arjun smirked.

'Sounds like a plan boss, looking forward to it.' He turned, feeling flustered and headed into the bar.

Philip watched the slim, athletic man walk away and he felt pleased with himself. He enjoyed the way Arjun moved and didn't want to stop studying his shape.

A million things were going around Arjun's young head. Those thoughts that he had earlier in the shower, some of them were now very much at the front of his mind. His breathing was fast and he knew this was a mixture of panic, excitement and sheer amazement.

As he arrived at the bar area, he quickly saw the look he was getting from Rebecca and he knew exactly why.

'So, Rebecca, are you ready for another drink?' Arjun gave her his best fake smile.

'What was that about?' She asked almost too directly. She pointed to the space by the kitchen where Philip and Arjun had just occupied.

'What?' said Arjun with an air of flippancy. 'He is my boss and from time to time he needs to talk to me as I arrive for my shift.' He then glared hard at her and said, 'so what does it have to do with you?' Annoyed, he forcefully asked, 'do you want another drink as your glass is empty?'

Rebecca nodded to him. He didn't need to ask what she wanted as he already knew, in fact every staff member knew what her poison was.

At about 4:30pm a couple of lads came in. They were in their early twenties. Arjun hoped one of them was Lewis, as the shift was going slowly and he wanted something to think about apart from feeling nervous about seeing Philip later. Sadly, neither was Lewis. He could never tell in what guise Lewis would arrive in, so never really knew if someone was him or not. Checking their ID proved they weren't who he was hoping for. He gave them their Rekorderlig, both having strawberry and lime flavour and continued to clean around the bar and put the dirty glasses in the dishwasher. Rebecca thankfully had gone home.

Philip was now in the bar area over in the corner. He was talking on his mobile and not looking very happy. In fact, Arjun had never seen him appear so angry. Every so often, he raised his voice enough for those few people in the bar to hear the things he was saying.

'Because they are mine,' and, 'I don't care, I really don't care,' were two of the strange things he said. Maybe the strangest thing Arjun heard him shout was, 'his neutrophils really don't concern me.'

With this, Philip got up and as he left the bar he winked in Arjun's direction. This was now freaking Arjun out. Was Philip gay? He knew he'd slept with Rebecca at least once, but other than that knew very little about him. He only knew about Rebecca because she was very drunk one evening (most evenings) and told Arjun and a couple of other customers who were at the bar.

Arjun was gay, a fact his family were not yet aware of. He had stayed closeted, but hated this fact. He was troubled by what his brothers would say and how they would react. Especially Rohit. He had had a fair amount of sex during his university years but usually far away from where he lived. In these times he usually told his family he was staying on campus with his mates. The truth was that he was usually in Brighton visiting the gay scene there. He used the apps on his phone, Surge, Tinder, Chappy and occasionally Grindr, but this one only when he was in Brighton. As soon as he left, he 'paused' his profile. This meant it was hidden until he next visited. But did Philip know he was gay? Is that why Philip asked to meet tonight? Arjun's head had gone into overdrive and his mind was all over the place.

'I said three lagers mate,' a loud voice said.

The voice shocked Arjun out of his thoughts.

'I'm erm, sorry, I was miles away.' Arjun slightly stuttered.

As he finished with the customer, he noted the time was 5:45pm. He took out his mobile and sent a text to the group 'Family Singh' on his WhatsApp.

'Not home for dinner, mate from uni has been in touch and a few from my year are meeting up tonight and we are heading out for a few beers and a pizza. Don't wait up, Arjun x.'

Replies wouldn't happen for at least thirty minutes; experience told him that.

6:00pm arrived and Stan came into the bar to start his shift. Arjun talked briefly and then said goodnight. He got his coat and looked around for Philip but he wasn't anywhere to be seen. Feeling slightly frustrated, he just stood there scanning around him. At 6:05pm he saw Philip in the bar area and Philip indicated with his eyes for Arjun to look in his coat pocket. Inside was a piece of crumpled paper and written on it was Philip's address, his mobile phone number and a message 'Go to my home, it's a ten-minute walk from here, use Google Maps. I went back earlier and left the back door unlocked. Grab a wine from the fridge and I'll be there by 7:30pm. Sorry, but need to sort out a bit of business with a friend of mine. Don't worry, it will be worth the wait.' Arjun nodded slightly to Philip to acknowledge what he had read. He then turned to the entrance of the bar and stepped out into the October night. It was cold but that didn't worry him. He was excited. He took out his phone and opened Google Maps and entered the postcode.

11:

1986

Philip aged Five

Philip and Ethan were sitting in the lounge watching television. Philip had wanted a cartoon on but Ethan snatched the remote control and had put on a dull programme about science.

Ethan glared at Philip.

'When mum died, it was probably your fault and that's why dad never stays in with us and just leaves Mrs Temple to care for us.'

Philip stared at his brother in confusion, but didn't say anything.

'He leaves me to look after you when she isn't here,' indicating Mrs Temple by pointing in the direction of the kitchen.

Philip wasn't sure why Ethan was saying these things. Sometimes his brother was horrible to him and then at other times he was fine. Mrs Temple then entered the room with a plate of sandwiches and milk.

'Share nicely,' she said as she glared at Ethan.

Once she had left, Ethan grabbed all but one small square of a sandwich.

'Mrs Temple said you have to let me have the same as you Ethan.'

'I don't care and if you tell her or dad that I had more food than you, he'll send you away.'

Philip slowly ate the only bit of sandwich he had and seemed to be thinking about something, as his face kept screwing up. Pondering on what Ethan had said a few moments ago, Philip looked at his brother.

'Why was it my fault mummy died?'

Ethan glared at his brother with disdain.

'They never wanted you Philip, you were a mistake, I heard them talking about it one night.'

Philip's lip started to tremble.

'She couldn't cope with two of us so she jumped in front of the car, so it's your fault.' Ethan snarled at his brother.

12:

20th October 2017

Jacob

6:30pm

Philip went through into his office to wait for Jacob. When in there, he stared out of the window onto the car park. Very few cars were there and that wasn't good for business. At times and more so recently, he thought about possible changes in his life. The money Jacob owed would be needed, as he had spent most of his inheritance, mainly on his house, but now had little usable funds.

Philip had thought long and hard about his friend and he was still extremely angry with him for using his bed for an affair. He had hoped to meet up with him earlier, as he was keen to walk home with Arjun. However, Jacob's interview had been moved to 4:00pm so it wasn't possible. When he had texted him earlier asking to meet, Jacob had been very reluctant.

'Can't meet tonight mate, need to get home ASAP and tell Tanvi about the interview.'

'Does Tanvi also want to know about the red box of condoms?' was Philip's reply.

'6:30pm OK?' was Jacob's.

There was a knock at the door, quite a firm knock which caused Philip to jump a little.

'Yes,' he called out.

Stan put his head around the door.

'Drink?'

'No thanks, I am only going to be about half an hour and then I am shooting off home.'

Stan nodded and left to go back to the bar.

'Did you find the house OK?' Philip texted Arjun.

The office door banged open and Jacob stood there looking tremendously anxious.

'Before you say anything, let me explain,' said Jacob with an air of urgency.

Philip received a text message, so held his hand up to stop his friend from saying anything else for the time being.

Arjun: *Yes thanks and I've done what you said and poured a drink out for myself.'*

Once Philip had read the text, he turned his focus to the fretful man standing in front of him.

'This had better be good because I am exceptionally angry and disappointed with you.'

There was very obvious friction between the two men that Jacob had never felt before. He could tell Philip was on the verge of exploding and it wasn't a good feeling.

'I am waiting for your explanation as to why you not only shagged in my bed, but why you thought it was OK to leave your DNA all over my sheets!' Philip was furious and Jacob knew this. 'I have to leave here by 7:15pm at the latest, so start telling me, NOW!' he slammed his fist down onto his desk.

'OK, OK, don't yell,' Jacob was very sheepish. 'Since Adrian was born, Tanvi and I haven't had sex.' He looked at Philip for signs of compassion but there weren't any.

'Go on,' was all he said.

'I work with a nurse called Maria and she has designs on me, you know, she fancies me,' Jacob exhaled. 'About a month ago, we were finishing a night shift together and she asked me around to hers for breakfast and I thought it would be nice.'

Philip could see where this was heading, but let the explanation continue, as he was relishing seeing Jacob squirm as he told his story.

'As we were having a bacon sandwich and a coffee, she said that her husband was away for a few days with his work and asked if I wanted sex.

She was as blunt as that.' Jacob was feeling uncomfortable with the situation. 'I was shocked that she had said this, well maybe shocked isn't the right word.'

'How does my bed get involved?' interrupted Philip.

Jacob was seething as he looked at his so-called friend. He had no idea what was happening and why Philip was acting the way that he was.

'We've seen each other a few times and this is usually at her place but she sent me a text yesterday and asked if I wanted to meet up, as she was on a day off.' Jacob took a deep breath. 'I said I was studying at yours for my interview and she asked if she could come around and I said yes.'

'Keep going, I sense we are getting to the sordid part,' Philip smirked.

'Don't be a prick, you know exactly what happened and why are you acting like a total arsehole?'

The atmosphere between the two, was getting worse. Philip took a deep breath and for a moment gazed at Jacob with shame and disgust.

'You left my kitchen in a filthy mess. You used my bed to have sex in and left your DNA all over my bedding. I had to wash it all, at gone midnight.'

'I know it was wrong of me and I am truly very sorry, however, you're making a mountain out of a molehill mate.'

'Really?' Philip said with anger in his voice, 'and would Tanvi think it was a molehill?'

Jacob eyeballed directly at Philip and seriously contemplated his next sentence before saying it aloud.

'Keep Tanvi out of this as this this is my business and no-one else's, do you HEAR ME?'

'You thick idiot, you've made it my business,' Philip yelled back.

The two men spent the next minute looking at each other, but neither saying a word. This was the first crack in their friendship.

'What about my £25,000?' Asked Philip.

'Where the hell did that come from?' was the tormented response.

'It has been four years and I want it all back.'

'Philip, what has got into you lately?' Jacob was perplexed.

'What about my £25,000?' repeated Philip.

Jacob scrutinised Philip's face for any sign that would help him understand why he was behaving like this, but all he saw was an irate expression. He got up from his chair and went over to the door. Without turning around, with disappointment in his voice and his head hung low, he said.

'I think my interview went well today, so I should be on a much higher wage from next month. They have two more people to interview on the 27th so I will know later that day. I will then set up a payment plan.'

Jacob walked out of the office and left the door open. Philip sighed and then looked at his watch.

7:15pm

As Philip left the pub he was feeling frustrated that his friend hadn't really understood why he had been so upset and revolted. Jacob really should have known.

'What has got into you lately?'

These words his friend had said were going around in his head. Philip was aware that since his decision to deny his stem cells to Ethan, he had been feeling different inside but also more positive, assertive and in control. These were new qualities for him and he felt determined to do as he pleased and not care about anyone else.

As he walked home, a distant memory stirred inside Philip and he remembered a time when he knew he had been a nicer person and cared about other people. However, things happen and those things, can and do, change a person. Those things changed him. Philip tried to put those thoughts to the back of his head, as he was now looking forward to seeing where this evening with Arjun was going to go. Nevertheless, he was also aware of the expression; *'don't crap on your own doorstep!'*

Yet there was something special about Arjun and Philip couldn't wait to get home and start getting to know him better.

When he turned into his road, softly singing to himself, his eyes saw a figure in the distance. It reminded him of the figure he had seen standing in the road a few days previously. This time, however, it was standing on the pavement. He frowned and wondered who it was.

As he got further along the road and nearer to his home, he saw that the figure hadn't moved. It had the same pose as the other night, with their hands on their hips, but it was nearer Philip's house this time. As he approached his gate, he looked at the figure just standing there in the distance. He squinted his eyes to try to focus on what he was seeing. The hair was still wild and all over the place and the face appeared strange but it was too far away to really tell.

'Why is it just standing there?' Philip thought to himself.

Fascinated by what he was staring at, Philip took one last look and really tried to focus his eyes. Then he suddenly realised what he was seeing and started to shake all over.

'Jesus Christ!' he screamed out as he held onto his gate to stop himself from falling over, 'it's a fucking clown!'

13:

20th October 2017

Arjun

7:30pm

Arjun was sitting in the kitchen holding a glass of wine when he heard Philip's key turn in the lock. He was nervous and excited all at the same time. What did he think was going to happen tonight? He had no idea but he hoped it would be thrilling. Exciting things didn't really happen in Arjun's life, well, not at the moment. He half stood, then sat again and then fully stood. Nerves were getting the better of him. Should he wait in the kitchen or go towards the front door? He had no idea what he was doing. The front door closed and Philip walked into the kitchen. He saw Arjun but said nothing. Arjun wondered why he hadn't spoken to him.

'Arjun,' Philip finally said and saying Arjun's name in full for the first time, 'did you see a figure just standing in the street when you arrived?'

Arjun just looked bemused and shook his head. Philip was behaving oddly, like he was mulling things over in his mind.

'Philip, are you OK? What's happened?' Arjun was concerned.

Philip looked at him for a few moments and then back at the front door.

'Hang on a minute,' he said and went back out into the street.

Philip, as terrified as he was of clowns, had to know if it was still there. He looked in the direction of where it had been standing, but now the pavement was empty. He stared at the window of his neighbour, Mrs Ferres, but for once even she wasn't peering out. He looked once more up and down the street but nothing strange was going on, so he headed back into his house and through to the kitchen, where he found a confused young man just standing there.

'Sorry Arj,' Philip said. 'Actually, can I call you Arj?'

'Well, as you've asked and if you don't mind, can you call me Arjun please?'

'Yeah, sure, sorry.' He was still a little unnerved, hence saying these three words as if they were each a sentence in their own right.

Philip went over to the fridge and took out the wine. He topped up Arjun's and poured himself a large glass.

'Cheers,' he clinked glasses with a still confused man.

'Can I ask why you had to go back outside and why you were so worried?'

'I saw a clown!'

Arjun was even more confused now and it showed on his face. Philip then continued.

'About five nights ago, when I came home, I saw a figure just standing in the road. It was far in the distance but with the moonlight and streetlights I could see it was standing with its hands on its hips and it also had wild hair, or from what I could see I thought it did.'

Arjun just stared at Philip and was totally mystified as to where this conversation was heading.

'Tonight, the same figure was standing on the pavement instead of on the road, but it was nearer to me. It held the same pose but this time I made out that it was dressed as a clown.'

'Well, it is approaching Halloween time, so maybe it's just an idiot messing around,' volunteered Arjun.

'Yes, you're probably right,' agreed Philip, 'but I have a real issue with clowns, they petrify me.'

Arjun looked directly at Philip. He appeared to be trembling.

'Philip, are you alright? Would you rather forget about tonight and I can head off home?'

Philip appeared like he was contemplating the idea but then seemed to snap out of his trance.

'Don't be silly, I am OK, just being stupid.'

'Why do you hate clowns so much?' Arjun asked.

'Oh, it was a stupid prank when I was younger.'

Going back to the fridge, Philip topped up his glass with wine. He looked at Arjun's but it was still full.

'I can heat up a chilli if you want?'

'I'm a vegetarian, so don't worry about me.'

'I didn't know that about you,' Philip said. 'We are learning new things about each other already.'

Arjun nodded and agreed.

'I'll call out for a take-away, what do you fancy?' Philip asked, 'you choose, as I like everything.'

Forty minutes later, the two were sitting in Philip's lounge with its open fireplace burning a newly placed log and enjoying a Thai meal whilst laughing about the customers that came into the pub.

'There's a young lad I see in the bar sometimes who stares at me in a very odd way,' Philip was saying, 'I think it's the same lad but he doesn't always look the same, different hair, clothes, glasses etc. Do you know him?'

'I think you must mean Lewis. He's a top bloke, slightly strange, but I like him,' was Arjun's reply.

'How old is he?'

'Eighteen, nearly nineteen.' Arjun had checked his ID.

'OK, I just get the feeling he glares at me and follows me with his eyes as I move around.' Philip said.

'He is a strange lad so I wouldn't worry about it. He looks at everyone.' Arjun said.

The two were getting along well and there had been no lulls in the conversation, just giggles and at times loud laughter.

'So, is Stan a friend of yours?' Arjun asked Philip.

'I am very fond of Stan. I am not breaking a confidence here as Stan is open and honest about it, but he has mental health issues.'

Arjun's eyes widened.

'He has quite bad depression from time to time. He doesn't like to use medication, so every so often it can really take over and cause him to be very low.'

'Gosh, I had no idea.' Arjun said.

'He has had quite a long run of wellness lately, which is great. When he feels a bad period is approaching, he comes to talk to me and we sort his shifts out to help him cope with it in the best way.'

'That's really nice of you.' Arjun was genuinely pleased at what he was hearing, as he also had a soft spot for his co-worker.

'I'm very fond of Stan and will always find a way to help him through bad times.'

They were now sitting close on the sofa and there was a relaxed and happy feeling between them.

'More wine?' Philip asked.

'Yeah, go on then, but can I also have a glass of water?'

'Yes, of course you can.'

Philip went to stand but then leaned over and kissed Arjun on his lips. It was a spontaneous, quick and soft kiss. Philip walked into the kitchen, Arjun blushed and then grinned.

As Philip poured the wine into the two glasses, he looked at his phone, which he had purposely left in the kitchen. He had six messages.

Ethan: '*I hate you, you are the fucking scum of the earth.*'

Rebecca: '*Hey gorgeous, do you fancy meeting up soon for some fun? xx.*'

Jacob: '*Don't tell Tanvi, PLEASE!*'

Ethan: '*Please Philip, please do the transplant, I am begging you.*'

Hester: '*I'll be slightly late on Monday, got to take Molly and Kevin to school, as their no-good shitting father says he won't do it. Sorry luv x.*'

Hester was Philip's cleaner, who he'd known for a few years now and really liked her down-to-earthiness.

Ethan: '*I'm going mad here. Please come and see me in the hospital tomorrow so we can talk.*'

Philip deleted all the messages and turned his phone off.

In the lounge, Arjun took his phone out of his pocket, he only had three messages. All were from the Family Singh WhatsApp group, in reply to the message he sent just before leaving the pub earlier saying he was going out for the evening.

Rajan: '*OK.*'

Mum: 'OK *my dear.*'

Rohit: 'OK, *have a great night and stay safe x.'*

Arjun smiled when he read Rohit's message.

Philip came back into the lounge and handed Arjun his drink. He sat down on the sofa but this time ensured he was close enough to Arjun so that their legs were slightly touching.

'How did you know I was gay?' Arjun asked.

'Grindr app,' was the reply. 'If you're wanting quick sex then Grindr is the way forward,' laughed Philip.

'I only use it in Brighton as I don't want people in London knowing I use that app; in case it gets back to my family, as they don't know I am gay. Grindr has a sleazy reputation.'

Philip nodded in agreement.

'So, we must have been in Brighton at the same time because I saw you on the app and saw your profile picture and message, wanting sex, staying at 'The Old Ship hotel.'

Arjun was mortified and knew that he had blushed. He had started to feel uncomfortable.

'I don't remember seeing you on the app,' he said to Philip.

'I don't use my face, just a picture of my chest.'

They both laughed but Arjun's was more from embarrassment than anything else.

'So, are you gay?' Arjun asked his boss.

'Yes, I am,' Philip said.

'But Rebecca from the bar told a few of us that you'd had sex with her in the cellar.'

'I have had sex with her a few times, four I think, but I am gay. I do very occasionally have sex with women but still consider myself to be gay.'

Arjun wasn't fully sure that he understood this but it had nothing to do with him, so he let it pass.

The two men looked at each other and no words were spoken. Philip leaned over to Arjun and they kissed. It felt nice.

'Do you want to take this upstairs?' Philip asked with a soft voice.

Arjun nodded. They both stood up, picked up their wine glasses and headed upstairs after Philip had placed a fireguard in front of the fire, which was now just glowing embers.

Arjun entered Philip's bedroom and looked around. He thought he had entered a top luxury hotel in London. The room was stylish and immaculate with a matching colour scheme and accessories. It made his room at home seem like a train wreck.

'Wow!' he said.

Philip smiled. He was proud of his house and the way he kept it, but was especially happy with his bedroom. This was the main reason he had been so angry when Jacob had abused it.

Philip turned down the bed and then approached the nervous man standing in his bedroom. He took Arjun's face in his hands and kissed him. The kiss was long and intense. The two men smiled at each other and both indicated that it was time to start removing their clothes. Philip was quicker than Arjun, but still made sure he folded each item as it was removed. He then lay on the bed and watched the young man as he slowly took off each item of clothing and folded them neatly and put them onto the chair in the corner. Philip loved this similarity about Arjun.

He stared adoringly at the athletic build of this young man. His legs were long and solid, they also had the right amount of dark hair. Arjun's buttocks were tight and peach-like, only slightly darker in colour than his legs. Philip was beginning to feel like a complete obese whale lying on the bed awaiting a god. Arjun turned around and saw Philip on the bed, naked and smiling. He liked what he saw a lot. He had never really been attracted to men of a similar build to himself and had always preferred men who carried a few extra pounds.

Arjun continued looking at Philip and then his face screwed up a little as he noticed the scars all over Philip's shoulders and tops of his arms.

'Self-harm marks,' Philip volunteered.

'I'm so sorry, I didn't mean to stare,' Arjun said as he started to blush.

'It's not a problem Arjun, I didn't have a great childhood and when I started to self-harm it somehow eased my frustrations and helped me cope with life,' Philip happily told Arjun.

'I'm so sorry to hear you had a troubled past,' the young man said with real compassion in his voice.

He moved over to the bed and sat next to Philip. They kissed enthusiastically and allowed their hands to explore each other.

'We need to remember this moment,' Philip suddenly said, making Arjun jump a little.

'What do you mean?' Arjun asked.

'Let me go downstairs and get my phone, then we can take a selfie.'

Arjun felt uneasy.

'I don't know that I am happy with that idea, sorry.'

Philip thought for a few moments, then looked at Arjun with a puzzled expression.

'Take the photo with your mobile, that way you are in control and the photo is safe in your phone.'

Arjun thought for a second or two and then grinned,

'Oh, OK, let me get my phone,' Arjun replied as he jumped out of the bed.

This brought a smile to Philip's face as he got to see Arjun's backside again and it was certainly worth a second look. Arjun got his phone and then got back into bed.

'OK, let's do a selfie,' he said and put in his passcode.

1-2-4-5-7-8. Philip observed closely.

As Arjun positioned his phone at arm's length, the two men put their heads together and giggled. Arjun took the photo.

'Let's have a photo of a kiss,' Philip said.

Arjun positioned the phone one more time. This photo showed the tops of their bare chests too. The two looked at each other and kissed. Arjun took the picture.

They both acknowledged they were good pictures and a nice memory of their first night together. Arjun turned slightly and put his phone on the bedside table. He then turned back to face Philip. The two, edged closer to each other and started to kiss.

Outside, standing on the pavement and gazing up at the window where he thought Philip and Arjun were, a young man stood, a cigarette in one hand and mobile phone in the other. He put the cigarette between his lips and used his now free hand to move his dyed grey hair away from his eyes. He went over to his car and got into the driver's seat and drove off laughing to himself. Next door to Philip's house, the curtains twitched.

14:

27th October 2017

Rebecca

6:30pm

Rebecca had been excited for this evening all week. She loved a girl's night out and this evening she was meeting up with her three best friends and couldn't wait. She hadn't seen them for what felt like ages. It had actually been a year and a half. She knew they had met up a few times without her, as she'd seen their pictures on Facebook and Instagram but she didn't like to think too much about that. She was at least going tonight.

After work today, she had been tempted to go into the Lemon Tree and grab a quick drink and see if Philip was around. She had sent him a text message a week ago now and he still hadn't replied. She was missing him and she was sure he must also be missing her.

'I bet he didn't see it,' she thought to herself. 'He probably isn't a phone person, better face-to-face,' she tried to convince herself.

She sat at the breakfast bar in her cluttered kitchen and had her make-up laid out all over the place. She wanted to make herself appear stunning tonight, just in case they went into the pub and saw Philip. She knew he liked her looking pretty, although he seemed to have gone cold lately.

'Bloody Arjun,' she said aloud.

She'd seen the way that the two of them kept smiling at each other during the past week and it made her stomach turn. Rebecca wasn't homophobic, it was just Arjun she hated and the fact Philip seemed so keen on him irritated her.

She was aware that Philip had had sex with men and that didn't worry her. She'd been known to experiment with the same sex herself, especially in the few months after Terry had left her but she longed for Philip to take more notice of her.

Staring at the packet of cigarettes sitting next to her make-up, she reached over and took one out, lit it and took a long drag. Rebecca then crossed over to the fridge with the cigarette still in her hand and took out a gin and tonic ready-mixed can. She didn't bother with a glass as they were all dirty in the sink, so she just swigged out of the can.

Tonight was going to be great fun, her with Charlotte, Liz and Jessica, who had formerly been James. She had known Liz and Jessica for years, probably going on fourteen. They had all worked together at the hospital pharmacy.

Liz was tall and pretty and had mousey coloured hair. She walked with a slight limp due to a childhood accident, so never wore high heels. It was lucky that she was tall so didn't really need to.

Jessica had been a large, overweight male, named James. He'd been extremely unhappy and had no support from family to help with the transition from male to female. However, since her surgery she had worked hard at the gym and was slimming down nicely, well from what Rebecca could see from the photos online.

Charlotte was the raucous one of the group and she was also a heavy drinker like Rebecca. She was the shortest of them all, but always the one noticed in the crowd due to her hyena-like laugh. All three of them were younger than Rebecca as they were in their late thirties and when they had last met, all three were single, however, Jessica had started seeing a guy from the gym. Rebecca reflected on where those eighteen months had gone. It made her feel sad and lonely.

She picked up her phone as she dragged on her cigarette and blew the smoke into the air. She knew she shouldn't text Philip as he'd be busy at work, but equally knew she couldn't stop herself.

'Hey hun, out with the girls tonight. Hope you're OK. Did you get my text last Friday? Fancy meeting up soon? Missing you, are you missing me?'

She put the phone back onto the hated breakfast bar and went over to the fridge. No gin left, so she grabbed a vodka and coke can.

'I must remember to re-stock the fridge this week, they don't seem to last long,' she thought to herself.

Rebecca continued applying her make-up and thinking about Philip. Her daughters hadn't crossed her mind. Her phone started making a noise, it made her jump. She grabbed it quickly.

'Oh my God, it's him, he's replied,' she shouted out in surprise.

'Fine thanks, have fun tonight and don't forget we sell booze at The Lemon Tree!'

Rebecca was now smiling as wide as she could. Her mood had lifted ten-fold, she couldn't believe he'd replied and so quickly.

'He does care about me,' she thought to herself. 'He wants me in his pub tonight.'

It never occurred to Rebecca for one second that Philip was just thinking about the money she and her friends would spend and that was the only reason he texted back so quickly.

8:30pm

Rebecca walked into the dark wine bar and scanned around for the girls. She had texted them all to ask if they fancied Philip's pub but she got three very quick responses back, all saying 'no!.'

The music was already quite loud, so chatting was going to be difficult. She preferred places like The Lemon Tree, where the music was a background thing and talking to whoever you were with was a comfortable and effortless process. Rebecca started to walk around the dingy venue, looking out for her friends.

'Rebecca, over here,' shouted Liz.

'REBECCA!' screamed Charlotte with no effect as Rebecca carried on scanning for them.

As she obviously hadn't heard them, Jessica went over and tapped Rebecca on the shoulder. She jumped.

'We're over here,' Jessica said in her deep East London accent.

She nodded and followed her friend.

When they got to the table, Rebecca noticed that they had already had a round of drinks without her.

'Thought we were meeting at 8:30pm,' she expressed to her friends as she pointed to the empty glasses.

The three looked at each other and pulled awkward faces.

'Oh, blimey Becks, we thought we said 7:30pm and you were running late,' was a quick response from Liz.

'Oh, OK, shall I get a round in then?' Rebecca asked, not convinced.

'No, we have a whip going, so chuck in £30 and we can pay that way but seeing as you're up, you can go to the bar and get them in,' Liz winked and passed the whip money over to her.

Rebecca took herself over to the bar and after waiting for about ten minutes to be served, she ordered the drinks. She looked over at the table where they were sitting and realised that the reason she hadn't seen the girls for eighteen months or so was because she didn't really fit in with them anymore. A sadness passed over her as she watched them all laughing and she had a heavy feeling in her heart. Then she remembered the lovely text she had received from Philip this evening and started to smile again. She picked up the tray of drinks and as she walked over to her so-called friends, she was determined she was going to enjoy herself, no matter what.

'What's everyone laughing at?' She asked as she giggled, trying to fit in.

The evening was turning out better than Rebecca thought it would be after seeing how close the three were when she first arrived. They had been somewhat inclusive and at least the laughter hadn't stopped. Rebecca hadn't felt this happy for as long as she could remember. Looking at her friends having fun brought Philip into her mind. She wondered if they also had men in their lives.

'Girls, we haven't talked MEN yet,' Rebecca shouted out and started sniggering.

The three women glared at her and then at each other and pulled faces and then burst out laughing.

'I'll go first,' said Jessica. 'I was seeing a cute guy from the gym for a few months at the beginning of last year, sex was good but he was dull. His conversation was limited to repetitions and weights.'

The others stared at Jessica as if they thought there was more to come.

'That's it girlfriends,' Jessica said, snapping her fingers, 'It's been a dry spell ever since.'

'Bloody hell, that's over a year,' said Liz, 'have you dried up and scabbed over?'

The whole table now screamed with fits of laughter.

'Me next,' jumped in Charlotte. 'A few days ago, I finally met up with a guy I have been chatting to via Tinder for ages. There was always an excuse why he couldn't meet up.'

'Wife and kids,' the other three screamed out at the same time and then started laughing and snorting.

'Maybe,' Charlotte said, 'but I don't care. Anyway, he is tall, broad, stunning and black.'

'Lucky bitch!' Jessica said.

Again, everyone started laughing.

'He took me to his house and we shagged in his lounge and girls let me tell you, it is true what they say.'

'Jammy cow,' Jessica said as she pulled a comical face.

'Why did you shag in the lounge and not his bedroom?' Asked Liz with a baffled expression.

'Let's just hope it's because he likes the idea of doing it in every room in his house but probably he's married, with kids and a dog and he doesn't want to use his bed.' Rebecca raised her eyebrows and blew Charlotte a jokey kiss.

'Oh well, if he is married then that's her issue and not mine. We had to do it in the lounge as his bedroom is being painted,' remarked Charlotte.

'Does Mr Hung have a name?' Asked Jessica.

'Jacob,' replied Charlotte.

'My go,' volunteered Liz. 'I was seeing a lovely man over the summer, he was my age, slim, swimmer's body, Chinese guy called Frank and worked in the city as an investment banker.'

'Nice,' said the others in unison.

'Frank? Not very Chinese,' said Rebecca.

'He had a proper Chinese name but I didn't know it but he was a perfect, generous lover and made me feel very special,' Liz said as she acknowledged each person around the table.

'What went wrong?' Asked Rebecca, as she was sure the others probably already knew.

'I turned out to be one of about four people that he was stringing along and not all were female.'

'Typical!' laughed Jessica.

The attention was now on Rebecca. She scanned the girls and took in a deep breath.

'I've been seeing a great guy called Philip.'

'The overweight bloke from the pub you go to?' questioned Liz.

'Yes, that's right,' beamed Rebecca.

'I know him, he's gay,' shouted Charlotte, slurring her words.

'Not at all,' Rebecca said in a curt manner. 'He has had sex with men in the past but I've had sex with females so that isn't an issue. However, since August we have been exclusive and it's been amazing, he takes me to all sorts of lovely places.'

The three other women just looked at each other and then back at Rebecca. Rebecca hadn't noticed.

'He texts me all the time, our sex life is wonderful and he is so caring. The last time we made love, it was so romantic.' Rebecca hoped they couldn't see in her eyes that she was thinking of the cellar experience.

'Got a pic?' Asked Jessica.

'Oh, I don't, as he hates having his picture taken.' Rebecca was now worried. 'Oh, hang on, I think I have his Tinder profile pic on my phone as I did a screenshot of it cos I know how shy he can be and it's adorable.'

'Not that shy if he's on Tinder,' Liz said to Charlotte under her breath.

'Yes, here it is,' said Rebecca.

They all took it in turns to look at the picture and then at each other.

'Nice,' Liz said unconvincingly.

'Not bad, I love the ginger hair and blue eyes,' Charlotte responded.

Jessica read out the profile information.

'Exploring and trying to figure life out. Don't really know what I am on here for, but if we match, make sure you start the convo because I won't. Oh and PS, I am petrified of clowns.'

'Well that's dull, he can't get many matches and likes,' Liz said.

‘Oh, he wasn’t on it for long and well, we’ve been together since about August, so he has deleted the app.’ Rebecca was grinning. Even she was beginning to believe everything she had said to her friends.

‘OK, well nice one Becks, I hope it all goes well,’ Charlotte smirked.

‘Yeah, sounds amazing,’ Liz said, looking at Jessica and pulling a face.

‘Good luck with him,’ was Jessica’s sarcastic response.

‘It’s only going to get better,’ Rebecca said with excitement, ‘I’m about four weeks pregnant.’

15:

30th October 2017

Ethan

8:30am

Ethan was sitting in his large kitchen, in his favourite armchair over by the glass doors that led into the extensive family garden. He had tried to eat a bacon sandwich but due to the chemotherapy, his mouth was feeling sore and the medication had given everything a metallic taste.

Emma came into the kitchen.

'You haven't eaten very much,' she said to her husband and observing the almost full plate in front of him.

'My mouth isn't feeling great Em and I feel a bit sick.'

His hair was almost completely gone now due to the treatment. Just a few wispy bits left. Emma had offered to shave it all off but Ethan had declined. He thought that the image of the last strands of hair, bitterly holding on, might make his brother feel guilty and offer up his cells. The truth, however, was that Philip hadn't visited since the time he walked out of the hospital on the day of his results.

'Let me take your temperature.' Emma said.

'It'll be high, I know it will,' her husband said in a defeated manner.

She placed the thermometer under his tongue and walked over to look at the garden. It was a bright autumnal morning. Adam had left for work soon after his breakfast at 7:30am and Suzanne, Emma's mum, had come at 8:00am to take Saul to school. That just left Max who was currently still asleep. He hadn't been sleeping well lately, probably due to the disruption in the household. Emma watched a squirrel running about her garden and tears started to well up in her eyes. She wiped them away and turned back to Ethan.

'OK, let's see what this shows.' She took the thermometer out of his mouth and read the result. 'Oh, honey it says 39°C.' She knew and so did he what that meant.

'I'll go and wake up Max and then take you to A&E.'

'No, don't wake him, poor mite needs to sleep.'

'You have to go to the hospital with a temperature like that and you know you do. Your neutrophils are low and your immune system is compromised and that means you're vulnerable to all sorts of infections.'

These words that were so alien at the beginning of all this, were now second nature.

'I know I do,' he said back to Emma. 'Let me text Philip and just see if he will take me. If he won't, Neil from next door said he would always help when he could.'

Emma just stood and looked at him. He was so gaunt and unwell. There was no colour in his face, so he probably needed a blood transfusion as well.

'OK,' she said, mostly thinking of Max, but equally knowing there would be no response from Philip.

Ethan picked up his phone and smiled at Emma. She smiled back. She loved him so much.

'*Hi Philip, I have a high temperature which means I may have an infection; therefore, I need to go to A&E for blood tests and antibiotics. Max is asleep so Emma needs to stay with him. Please will you take me*?'

Ethan now stood up and placed his phone on the kitchen table and went upstairs to get dressed. If Philip hadn't responded by the time he came back downstairs, then he would go and ask Neil.

09:30am

Sitting in the car on the way to A&E, Ethan was beginning to shiver. This wasn't a good sign.

'Are you OK?' Neil asked.

'Not really, these are rigours which means a rapid feeling of cold with shivering along with a rise in temperature, sweating, especially at the commencement of a fever.' Ethan was aware that lately he was sounding like a textbook.

'Oh, sounds awful,' was Neil's baffled answer. 'Nearly there mate.'

As they pulled into the hospital car park, Ethan thanked Neil for bringing him but told him not to stay, as this was going to be a long day and probably even an admission to the Haematology ward. He watched Neil leave and then walked into A&E and headed over to reception. He was feeling weak and hot and cold at the same time.

The receptionist was a hard-looking woman, shaved head and a tattoo of a bird on the left side of her neck. Her name badge stated that she was called Sandra. He sat in the chair in front of her.

'Name?' was the very curtly asked question.

'Ethan Oakes.'

'Age?'

'42'

'Date of birth?'

'4th July 1975.'

'Why have you come to A&E?' Sandra wasn't getting any friendlier.

'I'm having rigours and feeling hot and cold at the same time,' Ethan responded.

'Take a seat and you'll get called in as soon as possible but there is a three-hour waiting time.' At no time during the conversation did Sandra look at him.

'No!' said Ethan trying his best to stay calm, 'I'm on chemotherapy and have no neutrophils, therefore I need to be seen as soon as possible as if not, it can be life-threatening. Now do me a favour and get me some help and in future try to be nice!'

Sandra finally glanced up at him, smirked, got up and went out the back.

Ethan took himself over to the chairs and sat down. He took out his phone and texted his wife.

'Just got here, stupid bitch on reception. I'll keep you posted. Love you x'

Ethan felt dreadful, he had been sweating profusely and was now feeling really cold.

'Ethan,' the nurse called.

Ethan looked up as he recognised the voice and standing in front of him was Jacob.

'Oh, hi Jacob, how are you?' He asked with little enthusiasm.

'You look dreadful mate, come around to curtain three and I'll take some bloods from you.'

Ethan, feeling like an old man, slowly got up from the chair and followed Jacob into the cubicle and got himself onto the bed.

'What's been happening?' Asked Jacob.

'I've had chemotherapy for the Leukaemia. They have only discharged me recently whilst I wait for the next stage of the treatment but I felt bad this morning and had a temperature of 39°C.'

Jacob nodded.

'Did Philip tell you I was sick?'

'Yes, he did and I'm so sorry to hear about it all. Is the transplant the next stage?' Asked Jacob.

Ethan just looked at Jacob with a bemused expression on his face.

'I'm not having the transplant,' he said with an air of anger.

'Oh, I'm sorry, wasn't Philip a match?'

'Jacob, are you taking the piss? Or has Philip really not told you?' Ethan asked in a confused manner.

'He said he had tests to see if he matched but to be honest, I had been so wrapped up in the job interview here for the Matron's post, I forgot to ask. Also, Philip and I have had a bit of a falling out recently.'

'He was the perfect match, 100% and he has decided not to donate and has therefore sentenced me to death!' Ethan said in a sarcastic and cynical way.

Jacob looked at Ethan and his jaw dropped a little as he realised that he didn't know what to say. He took Ethan's blood samples and sent them off, then came back and did a full set of observations including blood pressure, pulse, respirations and temperature. His blood pressure was low, his pulse was rapid and temperature still high. Possible sepsis was happening so Ethan was commenced straight away on antibiotics and fluids.

'I didn't know, Ethan,' Jacob finally said to the frightened man on the bed, 'I'm so sorry.'

Jacob knew that Ethan and Philip had had a troubled upbringing, but couldn't understand why Philip wouldn't give his brother the cells he so desperately needed. It did, however, make Jacob understand a little about Philip's recent behaviour towards him.

'I'll be back soon with the blood results,' Jacob said in a quiet voice.

'Did you get the job?' Asked Ethan.

'No,' said Jacob.

Ethan must have dozed off because when he woke up, he had a new bag of fluids running via the drip line in his arm and he could hear Liam's voice on the other side of the curtain. He picked up his phone and had just one message which was from Emma who was replying to his earlier text. Nothing from Philip. He re-positioned himself on the bed and reached for a glass of water that had obviously arrived when he had been sleeping. He suddenly found himself hoping that Max had slept too.

'Hey Ethan,' Liam called out as he entered the cubicle. 'Jacob asked me to come and let you know what is happening as he has now gone off duty.'

'So, what is the verdict?' Asked Ethan.

'We need to admit you to Silver Birch ward for blood and platelet transfusions and also a week of intravenous antibiotics,' was the unwelcome answer.

'Liam, what is a platelet transfusion? I have had a blood transfusion before but this one is new.'

'The chemotherapy affects all aspects of your blood, red cells which are your haemoglobin, white cells that fight infections which include your neutrophils and platelets that help stop bleeding. For example, when you cut yourself, the reason it stops bleeding is due to your platelets. Do you understand?' Liam looked at Ethan for signs of recognition.

Ethan nodded.

'Your platelet count is low, which means you are at risk of having a bleed, so we need to top you up to stop that from potentially happening. It is a usual thing to happen on your type of chemotherapy, so don't worry, nothing is going wrong.'

'I can't believe this is happening to me Liam, I'm a good person, I love my wife and kids, steady job and would help anyone.' Ethan sounded very frustrated.

'Sadly, it isn't based on how you are as a person, it is just bad luck,' was the sympathetic reply.

Liam exited the cubicle and left Ethan feeling sorry for himself. He inspected his surroundings and couldn't help but think about his brother. His heart felt very heavy and his mind was working overtime thinking of his relationship with Philip.

Knowing that he was going to be admitted and what that would entail, Ethan sent Emma a text.

'Keeping me in for a week as I have sepsis, need blood and platelets etc (I'll explain when I see you). I'll text Adam to bring me my things so you can concentrate on Saul and Max. Don't come up tonight, but come and see me tomorrow. Love you to the moon and back x'

Ethan next texted his son, who would still be at work.

'Hey Adam, I am in A&E as have sepsis and need to be admitted for antibiotics and other things, will work let you off for a few hours so you can go home and bring me things I'm going to need? Dad x'

Ethan now sent one more text.

'Philip, I'm unwell and need admitting. A visit from you would be nice, I am your brother after all.'

He put his phone down and drank some more water whilst he listened to the everyday sounds of an A&E department and praying that he would be fine.

Ethan must have dozed off again as he woke with a start and could hear some commotion in the department and assumed it must be a drunk causing issues with the staff. Then, just as he was going to use the nurse call button to ask for a bottle to pee in, due to the amount of intravenous fluids he had been given, he heard a familiar voice.

'Dad!' Adam was shouting, 'Dad, which cubicle are you in?'

'Your dad's in there,' he heard a nurse tell his son.

Adam pulled back the curtain with much force and just stood there looking at his dad in total shock.

'I couldn't find you and no one was on reception, I thought something bad had happened and I was worried and couldn't find you,' Adam was talking without taking a breath, repeating himself and staring at his dad with panic in his eyes.

'Calm down Adam!' Ethan said assertively.

Ethan then looked at his son standing in front of him. He was in his work uniform of white overalls and huge boots, still with paint splotches all over them. Under his right arm was a jacket and in his left hand he was holding a small holdall which hopefully had Ethan's belongings in it. Ethan started to chuckle and then this turned into laughter and before he knew what was happening, Ethan was laughing so hard he had the beginnings of tears trickling down his cheeks. Adam just stood and looked confused at his dad. However, the laughter was infectious and soon Adam started to laugh too. Ethan then opened his arms and called Adam over for a hug. Adam put down the jacket and holdall and went over to his dad, who was still laughing.

'Oh, Adam, you are the best thing that has happened to me in months. Seeing you standing there in your uniform, holding my stuff with an expression of panic on your face, was so funny.' Ethan hugged his son tightly.

'Well, I didn't think it was funny,' he replied, but was still laughing along with his dad.

The two men held each other for a while and Ethan kissed his son on the top of his head. Liam then arrived and saw the two of them and smiled.

'Bed is now available on the ward Ethan, so you'll be going up in a few moments.'

Ethan just nodded.

16:

8th December 2017

Philip: The afternoon of his death

12:00pm

Philip lay in the bath until the water temperature had dropped and the foam from his lavender bath gel had depleted. His head felt better and he believed that he'd now be able to face the day. Looking down at his body underneath the tepid water, he could see that his fingers had wrinkled and he suddenly felt very cold and his nipples had stiffened. He lifted his left buttock cheek and passed a huge burst of wind, which in turn caused a flurry of bubbles on top of the water. Philip sniggered aloud as this always amused him. His inner child was always ready to smile at childish games.

He stood up and then shook each leg as he stepped out onto the cold stone floor and started to dry his bulky frame. As he bent down to dry his shins, he passed wind again without even trying and started laughing. He was feeling so much brighter than when he first woke this morning.

'Today is going to be a good day,' he thought to himself.

Once he was semi-dried, he put both his towels onto the heated radiator and walked from the bathroom into the kitchen, switched the kettle back on as he prepared his cup for another coffee. As the water was heating up, he walked upstairs and into his bedroom and threw himself onto his bed.

As he lay there he felt around the bed feeling for his phone, however nothing came to hand, so he got up and lifted the duvet up. There at the bottom of the bed he saw it. He looked at the screen, five missed calls from Ethan, three from Jacob and sixteen from Arjun!

'What the crap do they want?' Philip asked himself.

There were also six voicemails, but Philip had no intention of listening to them just yet, especially as he had no memories of the night before and dreaded what might have happened. He plugged the phone into the socket next to his bed to recharge and then sat on the bed and contemplated for a moment. Today had to be kept quiet, a do not disturb type of day.

Sighing, he stood up and looked out of his bedroom window and into his garden. Suddenly and for the briefest of moments he had a strange feeling that he'd done this same thing last night when he came into his bedroom drunk and something didn't feel right. The feeling unsettled him for a moment but then he dismissed the thought and went back downstairs to make his coffee and then sat on his sofa and listened to his light opera.

Philip found this type of music not only up-lifting, but at the same time, peaceful and relaxing. He was able to lose himself within the music and find himself floating through space or lying on a secluded beach. He wasn't a full opera fan, as the likes of Tosca or Madam Butterfly were too deep and heavy, but he found certain songs or arias absolutely stunning and they lifted his soul. As he sat with his eyes closed, he could hear his phone upstairs making ringing, text and email noises. Taking a deep breath, he got up and walked slowly up the stairs.

He picked up the phone and saw a mixture of alerts. There was an email from Jacob and Philip was very tempted to read it. He hadn't heard properly from his friend since their massive argument a week ago and wondered if the email was an apology, as that would be too long to write in a text message or on WhatsApp. He looked at his phone for what felt like ages and reluctantly decided to see what Jacob had written in the email. However, as soon as he saw the subject heading, his eyes widened and he went cold all over.

'*Why did you send it to her? Watch your back!*'

Philip stared at these few words and felt sick. These were serious words from Jacob and Philip wondered what he had done to have caused his friend to write such a thing.

'What the hell did you do last night Philip?' He asked himself. 'Oh, dear God! Please say you didn't send Tanvi the video!'

Closing the app down and therefore not reading the main body of the email, Philip sighed and felt upset, as he already had the strange feeling that he'd upset Arjun and now he'd obviously done something to fire up Jacob. He couldn't bring himself to look at his messages to see if he had sent something to Tanvi, as that would be unforgivable. He'd only taken the video to help blackmail Jacob into giving him his money back, but had no intention of ever sending it.

'Why would I have her number in my phone? She hates me!' He thought to himself.

Pacing around his room trying hard to remember things from last night, he suddenly remembered Tanvi calling him once to tell him that Jacob had been admitted to the hospital with a suspected appendicitis and he had stored her number in case he needed it.

'Damn!' he screamed out.

Philip was now realising that a lot had happened yesterday and he was probably to blame for most of it. Shrugging his shoulders and opening up his wardrobe, he started to get dressed, as he had decided he needed to go for a walk to try to clear his head. Any messages, voicemails and emails could be dealt with and answered tomorrow.

1:30pm

As he stepped out of his house and into his front garden, he saw Mrs Ferres peering out of her window. Philip gave her a false smile and then pretended to take notice of his plants in the hope she would go away. She didn't! The weather was bracing with a sharp, icy wind, so Philip did his coat up using the belt and started off down the street in the direction of the park. A few houses away from Philip's, stood a young man. He was wearing a brown leather jacket with dark purple jeans and aviator type sunglasses, despite the fact there was no sun. His hair was black and spiked up and he had a cigarette between his lips. As Philip walked, the young man started to follow, but not without being seen by the nosey neighbour.

Entering the park, Philip was aware how empty it was. No screaming children or parents playing ball with their kids. There were a few people walking dogs but that was about all. It was a true winter's day and Philip was relishing the peace and quiet as he began laps of the park. Whilst he walked, he thought over the last few weeks and all the arguments with so many people.

'Should I have given Ethan my stem cells?' he contemplated to himself. 'Not for him, but for Emma and the kids.'

So many thoughts were swirling around his head. Had he gone too far in what he had done to Rebecca two weeks ago? Had he sent that video to Tanvi? What had he done to Arjun last night to warrant so many missed calls?'

'Bloody hell!' Philip yelled aloud as a Jack Russell dog ran past him, yapping and frightening him out of his thinking.

Taking a few moments to come back to his senses, he surveyed the park and noticed that there were still very few people around. In the distance coming towards him, he saw a young man and the only other person was an old man who obviously owned the yapping dog, but that was about all. He continued walking and put his hands in his pockets as the cold was getting to his fingers.

The wind was rising and although it was only 2:00pm the sky was beginning to get dark. The young man was now almost level with him and as they passed each other and even though he had a cigarette in his mouth, he smiled and nodded in Philip's direction. Philip felt oddly attracted to him, despite the fact he was wearing sunglasses in this weather and also felt that he'd seen him before.

'I need peace and to sit by an open fire and have a pizza,' Philip thought as he headed home, but not before checking out the young man's backside as he walked in the opposite direction.

4:00pm

After he had arrived home from his walk, Philip went upstairs to check his phone. To his utter amazement, there were no new messages or calls.

'Thank Christ for that!'

Pulling out the charging cable he placed the phone in his pocket and went downstairs to make coffee. As he got to the bottom of the stairs, the doorbell rang.

He froze on the spot and tried not to make any movement. He had no idea who was at the door, but he didn't want to know.

'I can see you standing there Philip, don't try to hide,' Ethan said in a firm and solid voice.

'Shit!' Philip whispered under his breath.

'Please open up, I haven't seen you properly since mid-October and I just want to talk.'

At first, Philip thought about running into the kitchen and out the back door. He really didn't want to face Ethan and have to listen to the begging that was bound to happen. He wanted this day to be quiet and relaxing, if he let his brother in then it would be far from that.

'We talked, or should I say argued on the phone yesterday Ethan, so I don't have anything more to say on the matter.' Philip said sharply.

'Please Philip,' Ethan said with truly little strength.

Philip's phone buzzed, so he took it out of his pocket. It was an email alert and it was from Rebecca.

'What the hell did she want?' contemplated Philip.

'Philip! Let us in!'

'Us?' cringed Philip, 'Jesus Christ, don't tell me he has brought the whole bloody family.'

'PHILIP!'

'OK,' Philip yelled.

He opened the door and on his doorstep was Adam and a very thin, gaunt and exhausted Ethan. Philip almost cried out. His brother looked like a completely different person and he hardly recognised him.

'Have I done this to my brother?' Philip asked himself.

Ethan's cheeks were sunken, he had nothing more than a few wisps of hair stuck to his head and his eyes were dark and swollen. Philip looked at his brother's once athletic build and now saw someone who could have been from a concentration camp.

'Stay strong,' Philip's inner voice said. 'Remember why you made your decision.'

'Can we come in?' Ethan asked.

Without speaking, Philip stepped aside and the two men walked in and stood in the hallway.

'You can go into the lounge,' Philip said as he gestured with his hands.

The lounge was warm, despite the fact that the log fire had not yet been lit. Ethan scanned around the room and noticed straight away that there were no Christmas decorations.

'No Christmas decorations?' he said to his brother.

'Well, you of all people should know that Christmas time for the Oakes brothers wasn't really a time for celebrations,' Philip said with an air of anger in his voice.

'I guess not,' was the reply.

'What do you want Ethan?'

'To see you.'

'Why?'

'You're my brother and I love you.'

'LOVE!' Philip shouted in shock. 'Ethan, when did you ever love me?'

'Philip, pleas...'

'You never loved me, in fact you hated me.' Interrupted Philip.

'I didn't Philip, but you know how tough it was for us growing up.'

The tension in the room was uncomfortable and having the word 'love' bandied about was even more so. As far as Philip was concerned, there had never been any love in the Oakes' household once their mother was dead. Their father had been worse than useless and the only time Philip ever felt liked in the house was when Mrs Temple was there and even that went sour.

'Ethan, why are you really here?'

Ethan took a deep breath, looked at Adam, then back at Philip.

'Why wouldn't you donate your stem cells?' Ethan said with a fatigued voice. 'They may not have helped, in fact they probably wouldn't have as my Leukaemia is so aggressive, but you kept saying how much you hoped you'd be a match and then when you were you walked out of the hospital after saying you wouldn't donate and we haven't seen you since, apart from that stupid five minutes when you came around and asked us about a clown and then left as quickly as you arrived.'

Ethan could see the pain in his brother's face, there were tears starting to roll down Philip's cheeks.

'I wanted to build your hopes up so I could finally cut you down to size,' Philip replied as honestly as he could.

'Oh my God Philip, why would you want to do that?'

'You know why,' said Philip, sniffing heavily but without looking at his brother.

'I don't Philip, please tell me.'

Philip glanced over at Adam and then back at Ethan.

'YOU KNOW WHY!' Philip said, looking straight into his brother's eyes.

'Oh Philip, I apologised for that, you know I did.'

'You think saying sorry is enough?' Philip said through broken tears.

Adam now gazed between the two brothers, but didn't understand what was going on.

'Philip, it was wrong of me and we both know that. I told you I was sorry! Please can we not go there?' Ethan looked drained as he spoke these words.

'What happened?' Asked Adam, his first words since arriving.

Ethan quickly looked at Philip.

'Your father wasn't exactly a model brother when I was growing up Adam.'

Adam was confused, but said nothing else. Ethan looked at Philip and bowed his head.

'Philip, I need to ask now that I am finally in the same room as you. I appear to be failing all treatments that they are trying to give me. The Leukaemia just keeps coming back and I am desperate.'

Ethan hoped for a response from Philip. There wasn't one.

'I don't even know if it is still a possibility, but will you please donate your stem cells? I am so deeply sorry about what happened when we were growing up, but please help me now.'

Philip went silent as he looked from Ethan to Adam. His heart was pounding and he was on the verge of bursting into tears. Adam stepped forward and looked at his uncle, tears were already staining his face and he was obviously struggling to find his voice, but he stared directly at Philip and mouthed, with all the emotion he could muster, a single word.

'Please.'

Philip looked at his nephew's swollen and exhausted eyes. He took on board the pleading he had heard from the young man. He then turned to Ethan.

'No,' he said, looking coldly at Ethan, 'please leave now.'

'YOU FUCKING BASTARD!' yelled Ethan. 'You are going to burn in hell you little shit!'

'Get out of my house, both of you,' Philip said through clenched teeth. 'I made my decision the day you asked me to get tested, so I am not going to change my mind now.'

Ethan just stood glaring at his brother in sheer disbelief.

Adam looked at his uncle with eyes full of sadness and pain and again he mouthed,

'Please.'

Philip started to usher the two men out of his house. He had had enough and wanted them gone.

'I HATE YOU!' screeched Ethan, 'you are going to pay for this Philip, I will get you back!'

'You'd better be quick in doing that,' Philip sneered, 'from what I can see, you haven't got long!'

Philip opened the door to let them leave and standing on his doorstep, with a face that wasn't at all happy, was Arjun.

17:

1987

Philip aged Six

Philip sat on his bedroom floor and looked at his new Star Wars jigsaw puzzle that Mrs Temple had brought around for him. She had two sons, Leon and David, who were teenagers, so now and then she brought along a puzzle after she had done some clearing out of her cupboards. In the past she had given Philip books, games and some toys, but jigsaw puzzles were his much-loved things to do. He especially loved anything to do with Star Wars.

This was a puzzle of his favourites, C3-PO and R2-D2. He also liked Chewbacca and Yoda, but the robots really were his preferred. Philip was scared of Darth Vader because he had strange breathing. In his young and impressionable mind, the robots were his friends and he often thought up things they did together.

Philip was proud of himself as he could now do one-hundred-piece jigsaws, but his friends at school, Daniel, Tom, Lauren, Josie, Maddie and Fiona, could only manage fifty-piece. This brought a smile to his face. As he looked down on all the jumbled pieces, he could tell he was excited, as he had that funny feeling in his tummy and his heart was making boom boom noises.

Philip took puzzles very seriously and planned every move. He started by finding all four corner pieces and putting them on his large piece of board that he did them on. Next, he found all the straight edged pieces and put those aside, making a large pile.

'This is going to be such a great, happy and exciting day,' Philip found himself talking aloud.

With the four corner bits in place, he started to work out where the straight edged pieces went.

'I really wish Jacob were here to watch me do this and complete this

puzzle,' thought Philip.

Jacob was his best friend at school, although he never came to the house for tea as that was not allowed. Philip's dad didn't like other children coming to the house and this made Philip feel sad.

As the excited lad concentrated hard on his puzzle, he was suddenly aware of a breathing sound behind him. He hated this feeling as he knew who was making this noise. Philip slowly turned around and saw Ethan standing in his bedroom doorway. Ethan glared at his brother without saying any words. This made Philip feel nervous, so he slightly moved his little body to hide the fact he was doing a jigsaw puzzle. The tension built up and Philip felt frightened. After about two minutes of no talking, Ethan turned and went into his own bedroom. Philip relaxed and continued with his puzzle.

An hour later, Philip was about two-thirds done. He realised he was going too fast and it would be over far too soon if he didn't slow down. He therefore decided to go downstairs and see Mrs Temple who was in the kitchen getting dinner ready.

Philip walked out of his room and saw that Ethan's door was closed, this pleased him a lot. He now descended the staircase and walked into the kitchen.

'Hello, can I get a large glass of milk and two chocolate biscuits please?' He asked.

'Well,' Mrs Temple grinned at the young boy, 'dinner is going to be at least two hours, so, Ok, go on then.'

Philip helped himself to the two items as he was now big enough to be allowed. This made him feel happy about himself.

Carefully walking back upstairs, as he didn't want to spill his milk and get into trouble, he went into his bedroom. He placed the drink and biscuits on the table in the corner and turned back to his puzzle.

There on the floor was now a jumbled mess. The whole puzzle had been broken up and several pieces had been cut up with scissors. Philip felt like his heart was breaking and tears started to fall down his cheeks. He stepped over the mess and climbed into his bed. He curled himself into a tight ball and cried as he heard, through the bedroom wall, his brother laughing.

In the corner, on the table, the milk and chocolate biscuits went untouched.

18:

1st November 2017

Jacob

11:00am

The mood in the Spencer household wasn't a happy one. Tanvi sat over by the doors that led into the large garden and was feeding Rory his lunch. Jacob was at the other end of the kitchen sitting in a large rocking chair and was giving Adrian his bottle.

Both of the children seemed content, but this wasn't something you could say about their parents. It was a good job that they were too young to pick up on dark atmospheres. This feeling in this house had been going on since Jacob found out that he hadn't got the matron's job. He had been so sure that the role was his. Bragging to his colleagues had now proved to be a very foolish thing to do.

The job had gone to Maria, the woman who had invited him back to her place when her husband had been away with work. Jacob had no idea that she was also applying and now felt disgusted with himself that she was going to be his boss. They had even had the interview on the same day as each other, the day after they had had sex in Philip's lounge and she had said nothing.

As angry as he was with himself for shagging his future boss, he was pleased that he'd found a place to have sex with random women. Hotels would cost a fortune and Tanvi would ask where the money was going. Jacob could go back to the women's homes if available, but he didn't like not being in control.

As well as Maria, he'd been with a woman called Charlotte, who he'd been chatting to on Tinder for a while. That had been a terrible date and he wouldn't be seeing her again. There had also been a few others. His tinder app was very well hidden on his phone, as he had placed it within another folder and then within another folder. Notifications had also been turned off. Tanvi therefore had no idea.

Later this afternoon, he was meeting someone called Kate at Philip's place. He had already checked that his friend was working, so knew he had the place until at least 7:00pm. Jacob told his conquests that upstairs was being redecorated, hence the need to only have sex in the lounge. He wasn't going to get on the wrong side of Philip again about using his bed.

'Remind me why we aren't talking to each other!' Jacob said in a loud voice.

'Not in front of the children,' was the snappy reply.

Jacob put Adrian over his shoulder and started to wind him. As he patted and did circular movements over the baby's back, he glared hard at his wife. She hadn't been happy that he didn't get the job.

'I'm sorry I didn't get the matron's role, but why are you punishing me?'

Rory was now fed up being in his highchair and was already trying to climb out. Tanvi lifted him and put him down on the ground. He staggered off to his toys and was happy.

'I am not punishing you Jacob, but we owe Philip £25,000 with no way of paying him back, unless you let me ask my parents.'

'NO!'

Rory jumped and quickly looked at his parents for reassurance. Adrian let out a huge burp.

'When I borrowed the money, I assumed our friendship was enough of a bond for the debt to never be a concern,' Jacob said, trying to explain. 'Something is not right with Philip at the moment, but I think I'm getting a pretty good picture of why.'

'Tell me,' Tanvi said with assertiveness.

'Ethan, Philip's brother...'

'I know who Ethan is,' interrupted Tanvi.

Jacob looked at his wife and was feeling very frustrated, which was now heading towards anger.

'Philip has decided not to give Ethan his stem cells for the transplant, which I told you about in September.'

Tanvi remembered the conversation, but couldn't now believe that a brother would do that to a member of his family.

'I have always said that he was a bad man,' she said to her husband.

'I don't know the ins and outs and I was as shocked as you when I found out two days ago, but Ethan and Philip have a bad history together.'

'Nothing would stop me helping my family,' Tanvi said with sadness in her voice.

'You don't know their history and something made Philip start self-harming at thirteen and that's something even I don't know about.'

'I didn't know that, what did he do?' She asked.

'One day after PE at school we were getting changed quickly to get to our next class, we never took showers, so no one really saw us without clothes on,' Jacob said. 'I noticed as Philip was changing from his sports t-shirt quickly into his school shirt, tiny cuts over both his shoulders.'

'Oh, that's awful,' Tanvi said.

'I asked him when it started and he told me he'd been self-harming for about two months. I asked why and he just said, 'stuff Jacob, just stuff'.'

'He wouldn't let me ask him any further questions and I respected that, so we never talked of it again.' Jacob looked at Tanvi and shrugged his shoulders.

'That's sad,' she said with heart, 'I wonder what made him start something like that?'

Rory was playing on his playmat and Adrian was just rolling his eyes and making baby noises. Tanvi got up and went over to the kettle to make them both a drink.

'What about the money?' she said without turning around. 'He wants it back Jacob and we don't have it and since you didn't get the matron's job, we can't even start a payment plan as every single penny is used by the end of the month.'

Jacob could see the tears welling up in his wife's eyes. He put Adrian in his crib and walked over to his wife and gave her a cuddle.

'What are we going to do Jacob? It's making me feel ill knowing how much we owe him.'

Jacob was moved by the way Tanvi had said we and not you.

'I'll sort it my darling, I promise.'

As they embraced and Tanvi cuddled tightly into Jacob's chest, he secretly glanced at his watch behind his wife's back. It was OK, he had four hours before he was meeting Kate at Philip's house.

2:30pm

Tanvi watched as her husband descended the stairs with a sleepy two-year-old in his arms. Rory's hair was all over the place and he still had his thumb in his mouth. As they reached the bottom, Rory put his arms out to his mum. Jacob passed him over and kissed his wife's cheek as he did.

'Do you have to go?' She asked

'Yes, I'm sorry, but I need to get these policies written and being in work is the best place to do it so I can refer to other documents etc,' he leaned in and kissed her again.

Tanvi watched her man put on his coat and check himself out in the mirror. She even noticed him wink to himself.

'I'm off love, I shouldn't be longer than about three hours at the very most.'

Jacob left without kissing the children and this upset Tanvi. She watched him get into his car and drive off.

'Why did he go in that direction? That's not the way to the hospital,' she thought to herself.

2:45pm

Jacob parked his car outside the local pharmacy shop and walked in. Skirting around the shop appearing like he was up to no good, he wanted condoms. He was feeling guilty as he picked them up, not only because of the cost of them, but because they wouldn't be used with his wife. He headed to the front of the shop to pay.

'£14.99 please,' the young lad said to Jacob. 'Would you like a bag for 10p?'

Jacob eyeballed the young lad's badge.

'No thank you, Ben, I'll put them in my pocket.'

'Cash or card?' was Ben's next cheery question.

'Cash!' Jacob said a little too quickly and loudly.

He wanted no record of him being in this shop and certainly not buying the condoms. He and Tanvi had a joint account and she would certainly question him on a purchase of £14.99 from a pharmacy, especially as they had to account for every penny that was spent at the moment.

Jacob thanked Ben and turned to leave. Just at that moment a woman entered the shop and Jacob was convinced he recognised her. Looking at her for a moment too long, he suddenly heard her say,

'Want a picture?'

'Oh, sorry love, just thought I recognised you.'

She stared at him as hard as he had looked at her.

'The Lemon Tree,' she blurted out and made Jacob jump a little.

It then became noticeably clear to Jacob who this was. The drunk and he suddenly remembered that she also worked at the hospital. This was beneficial that they had bumped into each other.

'Oh, yes, you drink there don't you. I've seen you in there a few times when I visit my mate Philip. Do you know him?'

Rebecca slightly blushed as her thoughts turned to Philip.

'I do indeed, he's very special to me,' she beamed.

'Is he?' Jacob asked with an air of confusion. He'd always thought he hated the woman.

'Yes, we are very fond of each other.'

'Have you just come from the pub?' He asked as he could smell the alcohol on her breath.

'I have yes, I only had the one drink,' she replied, as she patted her tummy.

Jacob really didn't care how much she had drunk and wasn't sure why she rubbed herself, but Philip had told him she was odd.

'Erm, was Philip working?' This would be good to confirm.

'Yes,' Rebecca replied, 'but he was very busy so wasn't able to spend any time with me, but I know he really wanted to.'

'OK' Jacob said, looking at her with a bemused expression on his face. 'Bye then.'

As he left the shop he looked back at Rebecca and shook his head. The fact she had told him that Philip was at work was good to hear, however as he drove to the house, he would quickly go via the pub to see if Philip's car was in the car park.

3:00pm

Not wanting to chance anything, Jacob parked his car in the road around the corner and walked to the house. Feeling more secure that Philip was at work, he let himself into the house with the key Philip had given him a few years ago.

As it was now November, the house was warm, he knew Philip hated coming home to a cold house. This was probably due to the fact he liked to get undressed as soon as he got in. Jacob now sat on the sofa and took out his phone to text Tanvi.

'*Hey darling, just wanted to let you know that I'm missing you already x.*'

Before he had time to put his phone back into his trousers, he got a text back.

'*Why did you go in the wrong direction in the car when you left?*'

'Shit!' he thought to himself.

'*I wanted to get some sweets and a drink, as they are more expensive in the hospital shop. You know me, always thinking of the pennies. Home by 5:30-6:00pm x.*'

He now put his phone into his pocket and got up to look out of the window. Knowing what the neighbour was like, Jacob carefully glanced to see if she was staring out of her window. Fantastic, she wasn't. As he stood there a red Vauxhall Adam pulled up outside. Getting out of the car was Kate. She had short brown hair that was in a bob style and she was slightly overweight, but Jacob liked the fuller figured woman. He especially liked Kate's big breasts and was looking forward to seeing them in the flesh. She had sent him pictures via his WhatsApp, but sadly he had to delete them so that Tanvi couldn't see them by accident, despite the fact his phone had a passcode.

As she was walking up the garden path, Jacob had a surge of guilt pass through him. He genuinely loved his wife, but the sex freeze since Adrian's birth had gone on far too long.

'I have needs,' he told himself, to try to dispel the guilt he felt.

The doorbell chimed and he studied himself in the mirror above the fireplace and liked what he saw. He grinned to show off his extremely white teeth and then went to the front door and opened it wide.

'Welcome to my home Kate.'

She stepped over the threshold and into the hall. As she took off her coat, Jacob could see the outline of those breasts he was eager to meet.

'I need a pee,' were the first words out of her mouth.

Jacob was pleased that the bathroom was downstairs, as he'd told her that the bedroom was out-of-bounds due to redecorating.

'Through the kitchen and the bathroom is there.'

As she went off in the direction of the toilet Jacob looked at his watch. It was now 3:15pm and Philip was probably due back about 7:00pm so he had plenty of time, although he wanted to be out by 5:30pm at the very latest. Why was he feeling so nervous? Music would help, so he put his music on via Philip's wireless speakers. It was a little loud, but he was happy with that.

A few minutes later, Kate came back and met him in the lounge.

'Nice place you got here,' she said.

'Cheers,' he said as he approached her to kiss. He didn't want to stand about having small talk.

Jacob liked to be in control at all times and enjoyed undressing his women and taking things slowly. He loved that moment when they were completely naked and he was still fully dressed. It added to the excitement of the situation and he viewed it very much as a part of foreplay. He placed a hand behind Kate's neck and pulled her closer to him. She felt the beginnings of his erection. Their kissing was deep and sensual. Jacob gently started to massage her breasts through her top. They felt amazing. The kissing stopped and he started to slowly undress Kate. He liked to do this unhurriedly and savour the moment. She smiled at him, but also checked out his wedding finger. No ring was being worn.

5:00pm

Philip sat in his car outside his house and put his head into his hands. His headache had progressively got worse as the afternoon had gone on, so he had left early. Seeing Rebecca hadn't helped either. He'd heard her boring a young man who was wearing aviator sunglasses indoors, with stories of her new boyfriend. Philip couldn't help but think whoever her boyfriend was, he'd probably be a strange bloke. He'd need to be to be able to cope with her, but at least it would mean she wouldn't be bothering him again.

As he sat in his car, he could hear music playing, which meant it was too loud, wherever it was coming from. The street was already dark and quiet and all he wanted to do was to get home and do nothing. As he took his head out of his hands, he looked up and saw lights on in his house. He then realised that the music was coming from his own home.

'JACOB!' he squealed out. He felt his anger levels rising and got out of the car.

As he approached his house, he peered through the tiny cracks in the closed blinds. He was able to just make out what Jacob was doing.

'I'll have you for this,' Philip said under his breath.

He put his key in the lock and turned it as quietly as he could. The loud music would cover up any noise he'd make. As soon as the door opened, he could hear the woman making very loud noises and calling out to a deity. The lounge door was open and Philip stood and saw the couple having sex. Jacob had his back to Philip and she was on all fours towards the fireplace. Despite his anger, Philip had to admire the arse on Jacob, it was pure heaven of pertness and muscle. Taking out his phone from his pocket, Philip opened up the camera app and placed it in video mode. This was going to help him get his money back. The couple had no idea that they were now being filmed and Philip would also have some blackmail material. After about one minute of filming, the video was stopped and Philip put his phone back into his pocket.

'JACOB!' he shrieked.

Kate's head hit the side of the fireplace and her forehead started to bleed. The shock of hearing his name screamed out and the terror he felt at that moment, Jacob, as he was thrusting inside Kate, propelled her forward. He stood up and turned to see Philip standing in the lounge doorway. As with his backside, Philip couldn't help but look at Jacob's huge erection. He had often seen it flaccid over the years and it was huge when soft, so he knew it would be massive when hard. Making himself look away from Jacob, Philip now noticed the woman sitting crossed legged with her hand up to her head. The blood was seeping a little from under her fingers. Philip turned and walked into the kitchen. There he tore off a few sheets of kitchen towel and ran them under the cold tap. He walked back into the lounge and handed them to Kate.

'Thank you,' she said, without eye contact.

Philip looked at Jacob who was now standing there wearing his Calvin Klein white jockey shorts. The contrast of the white against Jacob's black skin was amazing.

'Who wants to start?' Philip said to the dazed pair.

Kate looked at Jacob and indicated with her eyes towards the chair he was standing next to. He looked down and saw her clothes and instantly realised she was still naked, so he threw her the clothes. He then glared at Philip.

'Can we turn around and at least let her get dressed without an audience.'

Philip reluctantly turned around and heard Kate getting herself dressed. After a few moments, he turned back. Jacob now had a t-shirt on too.

'I'm really sorry Philip, please don't be mad,' Jacob said, staring at his feet.

'You fuck in my house, you're cheating on your wife and you say don't be mad.'

'Wife?' Kate said, glaring hard at Jacob. 'This isn't your house?'

'No dear,' Philip said to her, 'it is my house and I want to know what the hell you both think you are doing here.'

Kate looked directly at the quiet man standing with his head hung down in shame.

'I bring my Tinder matches here and have sex with them in your lounge, that way I don't use your bed.' There was an air of anger, frustration and guilt in Jacob's tone.

'What!' said Kate.

Jacob looked at her as if he now hated her.

'Yes, you silly cow, did you think you were the first? You are just one of many, so I suggest you leave.'

Kate stood up and glared at Jacob. There were tears in her eyes and blood trickling down her cheek. She grabbed her coat and stormed past the two men without observing either of them.

After she had left and they heard the door slam, Philip noticed she had left her handbag behind, so he ran out after her. He found her sitting in her car sobbing and he knocked on the window and caused her to jump. He indicated the bag he was holding in his hand and she opened the door and got out.

'Thank you and I am so sorry, I thought he owned the house as that's what he told me,' she said through her sobs.

Philip placed a gentle hand on her shoulder.

'It is not your fault and I'm so sorry you got hurt, that wasn't my intention.'

'It doesn't matter,' she said as she got back into her car and drove off.

Philip watched her go until she went around the corner. He turned around to go back into the house to confront Jacob and screamed. On the pavement, about four houses along was a clown, standing with its hands on its hips and staring at Philip with an evil grin. Philip started to shake and feel unstable on his feet. He felt his legs go from beneath him, so had to steady himself against his wall. The clown continued to stare at him without moving any closer, however it did use a finger to start beckoning. Philip looked at Mrs Ferres' window but she wasn't there. Philip then looked back at the pavement, but the clown was gone. He leaned over his wall and vomited and started to gasp for air. He felt that he was going to faint. After about five minutes, he stood and walked slowly to his front door. He walked into the hallway and saw a fully dressed Jacob looking at him.

'What's the matter? You look dreadful,' Jacob said.

'A clown!' was all Philip could say.

'What? You're terrified of clowns,' Jacob said.

'Three times now I've seen it. Each time it gets closer.'

Jacob just stared at his friend, but had no idea what he was going on about. The only good thing was that Philip seemed to have forgotten about the incident just now.

Philip looked at Jacob and Jacob saw the fear in his eyes.

'Go home Jacob, I want to call the police and I can't deal with you right now.'

'I'm happy to stay with you until the police come if you want me to?'

'Go home,' Philip said in a deflated and depressed manner, 'and give me back my key.'

19:

1st November 2017

Philip

9:00pm

Philip sat on his sofa with a glass of wine in his hand. He had called the police at 6:00pm and had been waiting ever since for them to turn up. The time had gone very slowly and he wasn't feeling any better. The shakes had gone, but the sick feeling he had in the pit of his stomach was still there.

Three times he had seen the clown now. Many thoughts were passing through his confused head. Was the clown coming for him, or just a person randomly dressing up? Who was the clown? Did whoever it was, know that he was petrified of them? His thought processes were now all over the place and he wasn't going to settle until he'd spoken to the police.

Philip picked his phone up and was surprised to see no messages. He had hoped to have got one from Arjun. The night they had spent together had been remarkably successful and so far, no issues at work because of it. Sadly though, the opportunity hadn't presented itself again, so Philip knew he'd have to plan something as Arjun was probably a little too shy. This made him smile as he thought of the young man.

Outside a vehicle pulled up, so Philip jumped up and stared out of the window, but it wasn't the police. It was the young lad who delivers Pizzas. He had delivered to Philip a few times now and Philip liked him. As he watched the lad go across to the house opposite, it occurred to him that he hadn't eaten. He walked into the kitchen, opened the fridge, and took out some eggs, peppers and an onion and planned to make an omelette. Topping up his wine, he looked again at his phone. He went into his photos app and saw the video there of Jacob. He pressed play and watched the minute of footage. Jacob really did have a fantastic body, but he was going to pay for using his home like a brothel and this video was going to help him get his money back too.

Just as the onion was sliced into, the doorbell chimed and caused Philip to jump a little. Knowing that the police were coming, he had kept his clothes on, so he went straight to the door and opened it. There were two police officers standing at his door, a female and a male.

'Mr Oakes?' said a tall female officer.

'Yes, please come in,' Philip stepped aside and let the two officers walk past him and into the lounge.

Philip joined them in the room and asked them to sit.

'Would you like a tea or coffee?'

'No thank you Mr Oakes, we're fine,' this time the shorter male officer spoke.

'My name is Police Constable Chaplin and this is my colleague, PC Bates.' The tall, attractive female then smiled at a nervous Philip. 'Do you want to start and tell us what the issue is?'

'Mid-October and I know this is going to sound strange, I first saw the clown.'

'Clown?' Interrupted PC Bates. His more experienced colleague glared at him.

'Yes, a clown! First time it was standing in the road in the distance, so I didn't know at that point what it was, but I could make out how it was standing and the fact it had wild hair.' Philip knew how this was sounding but he carried on regardless. 'The next time on the 20th October, I came home from work about 7:30pm, it was standing nearer this time and on the pavement and not on the road, but still standing in the same position and with its wild hair still all over the place, I was able to make out that it was a clown.'

Again, Philip could tell he was rambling and maybe not making much sense, but he could see both officers nodding slightly, so they seemed to be taking in everything that he was saying.

'You're doing great Mr Oakes, please can you continue,' said PC Chaplin. Philip liked her face.

'Well this evening about 5:30pm, my friend Jacob was in my house and I was seeing someone off in a car and when I turned around the clown was there again, but this time much closer, only about four houses away. The posture was the same, both hands on the hips and again the wild hair, but this time it beckoned me with its finger.'

PC Chaplin could see how shaken up Philip was.

'Do you have a phobia Mr Oakes of clowns?' She asked in a soft, gentle tone.

'Coulrophobia,' Philip said.

'What does that mean sir?' Asked PC Bates.

'Fear of evil clowns.'

Philip looked at the female officer and could tell she was processing things in her head.

'Mr Oakes, yesterday was October 31st and therefore Halloween, do you think it's possible someone is just messing about and you've been caught up in the prank?'

'It is possible yes, but I don't think so. The way it looked at me today and that finger calling me made me physically sick.'

'Do you remember last year in Canada and the United States of America, they had issues with people dressing up as clowns and terrifying people, could it be something like that?'

Philip just shrugged his shoulders and didn't really know what else to say.

'Can you describe the clown to me please, in as much detail as you can?' she spoke softly to try to make Philip feel at ease.

'Erm, it had a white face, a painted red, chilling smile. The eyes were dark and had what appeared like painted crosses over them, but it was too dark for me to tell you the colour.'

'Go on Mr Oakes, you are doing really well,' this time it was PC Bates doing the gentle voice.

'It was a painted face and not a mask, but it did have a red nose and wild hair.'

'Could you make out the colour of the hair?' Asked PC Chaplin.

'Orange,' was the quick response. 'It had on a clown suit, white with red pom poms and it had large red shoes and white gloves.' Philip felt sick again as he remembered all the details. 'Oh and a flower on the white suit.'

'That is excellent, well done. Now Mr Oakes, who knows you are terrified of clowns?' Asked PC Chaplin.

'Everyone I guess, I don't keep it a secret.'

'Is there a reason you are so scared of them?' she continued.

The police could see that Philip was struggling with this question, as they both saw his breathing becoming more rapid and sweat appearing on his brow.

'Yes, when I was younger, a silly incident, you know, kid's stuff.'

'Do you know of anyone who would want to frighten you?'

Philip instantly thought of Ethan, but he assumed that he was too ill to be hanging about in the streets dressed as a freak.

'No, I can't think of anyone at the moment, I'm sorry.'

'Thank you for reporting this, as I can tell how this has made you feel. We will start asking along the street if anyone has seen anything strange, but at the moment there isn't much more we can do.'

Philip understood this and nodded in both their directions, but he was pleased he had reported it.

'If you have more sightings, get back in touch, OK?'

Philip nodded again and then showed them both out after thanking them for coming. He watched as he saw them going across the road and knocking on a door. He closed his front door and headed back to the kitchen. Looking now at the food he had taken out of the fridge, he put away the ingredients as he no longer felt hungry, however he did top up his wine and then went into the lounge.

As he sat on the sofa, he could see the blood on the fireplace that Kate had left when she banged her head. Philip sighed and went back into the kitchen to get cleaning things to wash the blood away.

20:

4th November 2017

Arjun

11:00am

Arjun was running five minutes late for his shift at The Lemon Tree, so he was now hurrying through the streets as fast as he could. He was working until 5:30pm when he was then going home, picking up Rohit and taking his brother out Ten Pin Bowling and then for something to eat. It would be up to Rohit where they went, but Arjun was sure it would be Nando's or pizza. It had been a while since the two brothers had spent some quality time together, so Arjun was really looking forward to it. Rajan had also been invited, but predictably he had declined the invitation. Arjun wished he knew what his older sibling was all about. He loved him but didn't really know him and this had got worse since their dad had died. Rajan was becoming like a semi-hermit that went to work, but then hid in his bedroom until either food was ready, or it was time for work again. Rohit on the other hand was fun to be around, he said funny things and was kind and thoughtful.

'You're late,' Philip said, joking with his junior bartender as Arjun entered the pub panting.

'Sorry Philip, I got caught up at home.'

Philip then turned and went into his office and as he got to the door he turned back and called after Arjun.

'Aren't you coming?'

Arjun looked at Philip and then scanned back into the bar area. Hannah was busy serving coffee to an elderly couple and hadn't noticed Arjun arriving. Looking back in Philip's direction he went into the office. As Philip closed the door, he grabbed Arjun and kissed his mouth with passion and urgency.

'What's up?' Philip asked as he felt Arjun go rigid.

'I'm not comfortable doing this here. It doesn't feel right.'

'Have you gone off me? I haven't seen you properly since our first night together,' Philip asked with a questioning expression.

'It isn't that at all, I promise, but I'm not used to doing things like this and it bothers me doing it here, especially as you had sex with Rebecca in the cellar.'

'Oh, for God's sake, she means nothing to me, you know that!' Philip said with force.

'I do, but it is odd just the same.' Arjun looked brooding. 'I can come to yours soon if that's what you want too?'

'How about tonight then?' was Philip's quick response.

Arjun looked at his boss, or lover and grimaced.

'I'm sorry I can't tonight, I am taking my younger brother out for the evening and he is looking forward to it. I can't let him down, sorry.'

Philip's disappointment showed all over his face and for a few moments Arjun felt guilty.

'I saw the clown again!'

Arjun was shocked at what he had just heard, but also surprised as to where the statement had come from, out of the blue.

'Oh, where?' He asked.

'Four doors from my house on Wednesday about 5:30ish. It frightened the life out of me and so I called the police and gave a statement to them.'

'What did they have to say? Are they going to help?' Arjun was genuinely concerned.

'They were nice, listened, took down notes and said they would ask around the neighbourhood etc.'

'Do you have any idea who is doing this? It is three times you've seen it now. Is it not just a Halloween thing?'

Philip sat in his large leather chair that swung to the sides a little as he moved. He looked at the Adonis in front of him and thought how beautiful he was.

'I thought it was probably my brother, Ethan, but he isn't well enough to be doing it, or so I assume.'

'Why would your brother do it? Does he know you hate clowns?' Arjun was looking at Philip in a very confused manner. The whole thing seemed incredibly odd.

'Yes, he knows I hate clowns, as he is the reason that I do. I don't really get on with him, never have and at the moment he is angry with me for something that I don't want to discuss at the present time.'

This appeared to bring the strange conversation to an abrupt end. Philip nodded to Arjun that he could leave, but did call him over for a final kiss. Reluctantly Arjun obliged and then left to go into the bar, grinning as he went, as he did like Philip and hoped they could spend some time together soon.

'Hey Hannah,' he said, greeting his co-worker.

'Hi Arjun, good to see you,' she said as she went past him to clean some tables.

Arjun took his phone out of his pocket.

'Hey Rohit, looking forward to seeing you later, if you ever get out of your bed. Lane is booked for bowling for 6:30pm. Be ready for 6! x'

In the pub there was only the couple having the coffee that Hannah had given them, so Arjun picked up a cloth and started to clean the bar area. As he did this, he thought about Philip's clown and the relationship he had with his brother.

'Arjun,' Hannah called out breaking his trance.

'Sorry, lost in thought. How was your shift last night Hannah?' He asked after a while.

'Interesting,' she laughed. 'Rebecca was in and drunk as usual, though she kept patting her stomach and winking at Stan and myself.'

'Why would she be doing that? She is so weird.'

'Lewis was also in, looking all different again. His hair is going to fall out soon if he doesn't stop colouring it.' Hannah then pulled a face. 'He was a bit strange too last night. He kept asking me and Stan questions about Philip.'

'That's odd, why would he do that? What was he asking?' Arjun asked.

'How long had we known him? What did we know about his past? Did he have kids? What was he like as a person?'

'Blimey,' Arjun said with a screwed-up face. 'Why all the interest?'

'No idea,' Hannah replied. 'He had been drinking and Rebecca had been all over him.'

The two friends then got on with their work, unaware that Philip was watching Arjun with a leering expression. Arjun carried on clearing up the bar when his phone buzzed in his pocket. He took it out and read his message.

Rohit: '*Looking 4ward 2 it 2 Bro x*'

Arjun laughed.

6:30pm

The two brothers walked into the bowling establishment and headed up to the reception area. The place was huge with loud music playing, strobe lights doing their thing and the smell of greasy food being cooked. As they waited to be served, Arjun leaned on his brother's shoulders.

'Hey, I'm Peter,' the lad behind the counter said with a beaming smile, with teeth covered in braces. 'Have you booked for this evening?'

'Yep, two games for two people,' Rohit said with a happy tone to his voice.

'Shoe sizes?' Asked Peter.

'Eleven and eight please,' the brothers said in unison.

When they arrived at their lane, they changed their shoes and both picked the bowling ball that was right for them. Arjun chose a 12lb ball and Rohit chose the 9lb ball.

'This is great, thank you Arjun.' Rohit hugged his brother.

As he knew they were going out for something to eat later, Arjun just got them both a coke to drink as they played. Rohit was extremely competitive when it came to games, so he was out to score big. He had a particularly good technique and usually scored high. Arjun on the other hand tended to favour the gutter.

'It is a shame that Rajan is the way he is,' Rohit blurted out from nowhere.

'I know, but he has always been a loner, even before dad died,' was Arjun's response.

'Doesn't he like us?' Asked the younger brother.

'I think he does,' replied Arjun, 'but he is just not like us Rohit. He prefers to be by himself and we have to respect that fact. However, he worries me that he is putting on so much weight and quite quickly, but again, if he doesn't want help what can we do?'

The bowling alley was getting busy and there was a lot of noise, as people were laughing and enjoying themselves and not to mention the loud music that was playing. There was a great vibe in this place and Arjun could tell how happy Rohit was to be here, especially as he was winning. Making his younger brother happy was a wonderful feeling. There was so much love in the youngest member of the Singh family.

'Your turn bro,' beamed Rohit, 'but you won't catch me now.'

Arjun picked up his bowling ball and did all the right things to aim for a strike. He winked at his brother and gave himself enough of a run up to finally release the ball down the alley. He stood with his hands on his hips, as Rohit came forward and stood next to his brother.

'Come on, get a strike!' laughed Arjun.

The two of them watched as the ball travelled towards the pins. A strike might just put Arjun in the lead. Rohit's face screwed up as he willed the ball to enter the gutter. The two just stood there, as if frozen to the spot. Just as the ball was nearing its destination, it started to curve away and at the last minute took out just two pins.

'You are so lame,' shrieked Rohit, as the two laughed and gave each other a hug.

After finishing their two games, with a victory to Rohit on both accounts, they headed back to reception. Arjun handed the shoes back to Peter and Rohit went into the toilet. As Arjun stood there looking around, he thought he recognised the guy coming towards him.

'Lewis?' he said, with an element of doubt.

'Arjun, good to see you.' Lewis said, 'you here on your own?'

'No, I am with my brother and we have just finished and now off for some food.'

'Hey that's cool, nice to have some family time I guess.' There was an air of sadness in his tone.

'Do you have much family Lewis?'

'Erm, no, only child, mum dead and I don't know my dad, doesn't give much room for family time.'

Arjun was now feeling uncomfortable but hoped it wasn't showing on his face.

'I heard you were in last night, how was your evening?' He asked Lewis.

'I drank too much, I know that,' he laughed. 'Plus, I got lumbered with that awful Rebecca. Every time she sees me, she sits with me. I am just too nice.'

'Hannah said you were asking lots of questions about Philip.'

'Oh, was I?' Lewis said.

'Do you know him?' Asked Arjun, wanting to find out why all the questions, but without appearing too nosey.

'I don't know Arjun, maybe,' was all Lewis was prepared to say.

Rohit now joined the two by reception.

'Lewis, this is my brother Rohit,' Arjun smiled as he introduced his brother. He was so proud of him.

'Good to meet you,' nodded Lewis.

'You too,' replied Rohit.

At that moment, a young lady approached and linked arms with Lewis, as if she were claiming him as hers.

'This is Rachel,' Lewis said.

Everyone nodded at each other.

Once goodbyes had been said, the brothers left the bowling alley and headed to Rohit's choice of restaurant, which was Nando's, as Arjun had predicted. As they walked along the high street, sniggering and enjoying themselves, Rohit looked at Arjun.

'Who was he?'

'Lewis?' Arjun said, 'that my dear brother is an incredibly good question. He started coming into the pub a few months ago and is actually genuinely fun to chat to.'

'Go on,' Rohit said eagerly. He loved it when he and Arjun chatted, it didn't matter what it was about.

'Each time we see him, he appears slightly different. Hair colour changes, hairstyle changes, difference in clothing styles too,' Arjun was enjoying the expression on Rohit's face. 'Obviously when you start chatting you know it's him, but from a distance, you don't. Very odd behaviour don't you think?'

Rohit was nodding with wide eyes and a big silly grin.

'Go on,' he said again.

'Well last night, Hannah, who I work with, told me he was asking lots of questions about Philip, who I also work with.'

'I know who Philip is,' Rohit said quickly, 'mum doesn't like him.'

'Anyway,' Arjun said, ignoring the bit about his mother, 'Why would he be asking questions?'

The two lads shrugged their shoulders at each other as they arrived at the restaurant.

8:00pm

As this was a Saturday evening, the restaurant was packed with mainly student types. Big tables of friends, all laughing and happy. The smell of chicken was filling the place and it smelt good.

'Have you booked?' Asked the slightly geeky lad.

'Yes, table for two at 8:00pm in the name of Singh.' Arjun answered.

'This way please.'

The table they were given was great. It was towards the back of the restaurant and away from the larger tables, which were noisy. This table would mean the brothers could chat without too much commotion around them. They sat down and started to read the menu. Arjun was vegetarian, but Rohit wasn't. The two of them threw ideas at each other and giggled as they did so.

'Right, what are you going to have?' Arjun asked his brother.

'So much to choose from,' he said, pulling a nerdy face that made Arjun laugh aloud. 'I'll have chicken butterfly, with peri-salted chips, spicy rice and a coke.' Rohit's face was happy right now.

'Good choice. I think I'll have a roasted portobello mushroom and grilled halloumi burger, with normal chips and a mixed leaf salad, oh and I'm having a beer. By the way, who's paying?'

Rohit just glared at his brother, as if to say, get real!

As Arjun went off to place the order, Rohit took out his phone and checked in on Facebook.

'*Great night with my bro, bowling and now Nando's and he's paying ☺.*'

With the order placed, the brothers started to chat again as they sipped their drinks.

'Tell me about school Rohit, how are you getting on? Tell me about your friends.'

'All is good, GCSEs are going well and I'm excited to be starting A-levels next year. I want to get into film studies and be the next big film director to win big at the Oscars.'

Arjun loved that about his brother, he had always been so definite in his plans and where he saw himself in the years ahead. He was so proud of him for this trait alone.

'That's amazing Rohit, to be so sure, I love that.' Arjun couldn't help but feel delighted. 'So, tell me about your friends now.'

'What's to say? I hang about with Nabil and Jack mainly. They love films too and we play on the PS4 and that's about it.'

The food arrived and it was a feast. Arjun hadn't realised how hungry he was until he saw the food in front of him.

'Arjun, can I ask, I mean tell you something?'

Arjun looked at his brother with a slightly puzzled expression on his face.

'Rohit, you can always talk to me about everything and anything, that is what older brothers are for, well unless you're Rajan,' they both laughed at this.

'Promise you won't get mad at me?'

'Rohit, talk to me and I won't get mad.'

'Arjun, I know you're gay.'

Arjun had his halloumi burger half up to his mouth when he just froze. His legs started to tremble under the table and he suddenly felt like he wanted to be sick. There was a silence that lasted for a few moments, but it felt like years. Arjun just looked at his brother and didn't know what to say.

'It's OK Arjun,' Rohit said as he reached out to touch his brother's arm. He could feel Arjun shaking.

'I don't know what to say Rohit, you've stunned me into silence.'

'I love you so much Arjun, you make me happy and feel included. I really don't care who you fancy, as I know that whoever receives your love, is a lucky person. You're kind, generous, loving, smart and wonderful and the best brother I could ask for.' Rohit was still touching Arjun's arm. 'In fact, you're also my best friend.'

Arjun knew that tears were beginning to trickle down his face, but he was still frozen and not able to wipe them away. He just glared directly at Rohit, but was seeing straight through him. His legs were now becoming steadier and he placed his food back on his plate. Taking a deep breath and finally being able to wipe away the tears, he looked at Rohit.

'When did you get so grown up?' He asked as he touched his brother's hand, which was still on his arm. 'How did you know? Do mum and Rajan know?' Panic ran through him again.

'No, well, at least I don't think they do.' was his quick answer. 'I use social media and they don't and it's amazing what you can find out. Over the past two years I have followed you on Instagram and Snapchat and you've posted pics of you and your friends in various nightclubs.'

Arjun was just staring at Rohit, not at all sure where this was heading.

'Mainly men in the pictures, some and including you at times, with bare chests showing and kissing each other.'

Arjun was feeling mortified and sick, but as he looked across the table, he saw a young man laughing and smiling back at him with nothing but love in his eyes.

'Hey, hang on a minute, I didn't know you followed me on those apps!' Arjun blurted out.

'Ah, well, you wouldn't, as I don't have my profile pic of my face and

I go by the name of '*filmbuff_83.*'

'Rohit, you're a spy and bloody crafty and devious, that's what you are.'

'Also, Arjun, I see the way you are when Philip is mentioned. You sort of go a bit mushy.'

'I do not,' protested Arjun.

'Yeah you do,' said Rohit as he burst out laughing. 'Is he your boyfriend?'

Arjun knew that he was blushing at this point and couldn't believe he was having this discussion with his sixteen-year-old brother.

'Well as we are being so honest with each other, the truthful answer is, I don't know, but maybe.'

Rohit took this as an OK answer for the time being.

'Let's finish our food now, oh and by the way, in case you're wondering, I'm all about the ladies.'

The two now burst out laughing and it felt so good.

'Come here,' Arjun said as he opened and stretched out his arms.

Rohit stood up and went over to his brother and they hugged tightly.

'I love you so much Rohit,' Arjun whispered into his brother's ear.

'Likewise bro,' was the reply.

21:

5th November 2017

Lewis

5:00pm

The late afternoon air had an icy chill to it and grey foreboding clouds rolled over the darkening sky. The traffic was noisy as impatient drivers were leaving disgruntled fingers on their car horns in the hope of making others move over, so they could get to their destinations sooner. People hurried along the streets holding their coats tightly against themselves to keep out the cold. The rain started to fall and fall hard, so the pavements and roads became more frantic.

Despite the weather and commotion going on around him, Lewis just kept a steady pace as he walked towards The Lemon Tree, wearing his Duffle coat with an imitation fur lined hood that covered his face. His head was low as he looked down at the wet concrete and watched the rain splashing against his shoes and trousers.

Lewis' mood was as usual low and all encompassing. The medication he had taken for the past four years, since she had gone, had plateaued and therefore feeling depressed was now part of his everyday life and he didn't see a way around this. However, he knew he had one task to do and maybe once that had happened, maybe, just maybe his mood would lift and the world would be a better place again. He took one final drag on his cigarette and then flicked the end into the wet gutter. Stepping into the road, he heard a car horn blast in his direction. He turned to see the face of the driver in the car that had narrowly missed hitting him. Lewis held his hand up to say sorry, but this was met with the middle finger from the annoyed woman in the car. Crossing over and ignoring the woman, he entered the pub.

On this occasion Lewis had made himself more geek-like, well this is what he liked to call it. His hair was a silky, black colour and combed forward giving him an exaggerated fringe, he wore black rimmed large glasses and a rolled neck black jumper, black jeans with trendy ripped holes and his black converses. His clothing today was a good interpretation of his usual mood.

As he stepped into the bar area, he surveyed what was before him. His favourite seat over the far side of the bar, but centrally placed, was free. This gave him an unobstructed view of the comings and goings of the place, but more importantly, of him. He approached the bar still wearing his coat, but now with the hood down.

'Yes sir, can I help you?' Asked Stan.

Lewis was glad it was Stan, as he just did his job and didn't ask too many questions or do the niceties that often happened.

'A pint of the cider please,' he asked coyly.

'Can I see some ID please.'

Lewis handed over his driving licence and then waited for the now inevitable.

'Ah Lewis, sorry, didn't recognise you,' chirped Stan.

'Hey Stan, no worries my friend. How's you?' Lewis was now laughing and smiling and being the 'other' person, he knew he wasn't. 'Any news etc?'

'Nothing that I know of mate, enjoy your drink.'

Lewis took his pint and walked over to his chair and took off his coat and sat down, ensuring he could maximise his view of the surroundings. He could see that Arjun was on duty, as he just came out of the kitchen with three plates of food. Two plates went to the couple on the other side of the bar and the final plate was placed in front of the young man sitting four tables away from Lewis. This man was new as far as he could tell, as he hadn't seen him before, well, at least for the few months he had been coming to the pub.

The pub was beginning to fill up as workers were coming in for drinks before heading home. This was a good thing as it meant Lewis would be absorbed into the crowd and therefore less noticeable, but not hidden. He continued with his drink, played candy crush on his phone and constantly looked around. Then he saw him leaving the kitchen and going into the bar. Philip was untidy with his shirt hanging over the back of his trousers and his tie crooked. He stood at the bar talking to Arjun and then they both left and headed into what Lewis assumed was Philip's office. There was definitely something going on between the two of them, Lewis had noticed certain looks over the past week. However, Rebecca would say differently. Philip was certainly a complex man and Lewis knew he had to watch him for a bit longer.

'Hey Lewis, how are you doing?'

Lewis noticeably jumped, as he looked up and saw Arjun standing there appearing a little flushed.

'You scared me man, I didn't see you come back into the bar area,' said Lewis.

'Sorry, but didn't know you watched me leave the bar area,' was Arjun's response.

'Yeah, saw you leave with Philip, is that his name?' Lewis said, not wanting to appear too knowledgeable about his prey.

'Erm, yes, he is called Philip,' Arjun was blushing and a little concerned. 'Your glass is empty, so do you want me to get you another one?'

'Yes please, Arjun.'

As he picked up the empty cider glass and handed it over, Lewis looked at the bartender and pulled an odd expression.

'Is he a good manager?' Lewis asked.

'He's OK, why are you asking that?'

'Oh, no reason, just being nosey I guess.' Lewis was getting nervous. 'Is he nice, funny?'

'Lewis, what's going on, why are you asking these questions? I heard you were asking Hannah and Stan about him the other day too?'

'Oh, it's nothing mate, just thought I recognised him, that's all, I promise. Now where's my drink?' Lewis started to laugh loudly and gained the attention of the other customers. At that point, Philip came out of the kitchen and looked around the place. As he saw Arjun heading back to the bar with empty glasses in his hand, he also locked eyes with the young man towards the back of the pub. The two men looked at each other and held their stares for about ten seconds. Lewis then broke the moment and went back to his candy crush. Philip stood for a few more seconds and then joined Arjun and Stan at the bar.

Lewis knew he was shaking a little and hoped he hadn't been too obvious with Arjun. At that moment Rebecca walked into the pub and Lewis knew he could now join up with her. He despised the woman, but she was handy to know, well she was at first. Now Lewis used her to get what information she had and when she was drunk, as a distraction.

From his position, Lewis could see the scene at the bar. As soon as Rebecca had arrived and been seen, the faces of the three men behind the counter changed. Philip smiled and then tried to leave but she stood in front of him. Raising her hand, she tried to stroke his face, but Philip jerked his head back and she laughed. Without removing her gaze from Philip, Lewis heard her give either bartender her order, as her voice boomed out.

'Double gin and tonic please, not too much ice and lime not lemon and it's on Philip, isn't it my love.'

All three men just looked at each other and Lewis saw that Philip nodded his head at Stan and then gently shrugged his shoulders at Arjun. Rebecca then went to take hold of Philip's hands, but again he jerked them away from her.

'I have things to do in my office Rebecca I can't stay and chat,' then glancing at Arjun, 'can I see you in my office please.' This appeared to be an order rather than a question.

As he stepped around Rebecca and headed off, she called after him.

'I need to talk to you Philip! There is something important I need to tell you.' She rubbed her tummy as she said these words.

Arjun walked past her and she glared hard at him. He then took Lewis his drink and went to find Philip.

Stan handed Rebecca her drink and now with a glass in her hand she started to scan around the pub, looking to see who she could join and probably end up annoying.

'Hello, my darling,' she called out.

Lewis squirmed.

She moved in his direction and he found himself becoming that 'other' cheerful person again. However, she stopped at the table four tables away and joined the man who Lewis had seen earlier eating on his own. They obviously knew each other as they kissed on the cheeks as she sat down.

Lewis wasn't sure if he was annoyed that she sat elsewhere or pleased. He did however want to talk to her about what just happened with Philip. Damn the new man! Lewis could feel the anger building inside him, anger towards someone he didn't even know. Just then, breaking his concentration, he heard a shriek.

'Lewis!' Rebecca was looking directly at him from her seat.

Practically everyone was now recognising him on first sight, despite how he was dressed or arranged. He knew the time had probably come to stop trying to disguise his appearance, but did Philip recognise him yet?

'Hey gorgeous lady,' the 'other' Lewis called out.

Lewis knew how to hide his depression, but it was tough.

Rebecca got up and was heading over and also bringing the stranger with her.

'Lewis, this is Liam, we work in the same hospital.'

The two men shook hands and said hello.

'Can I get you both a drink?' Liam asked.

'I'm OK thanks,' Lewis said with a nearly full glass.

'Large Merlot please,' Rebecca said, as she guzzled down the gin and tonic, 'though I shouldn't really under the circumstances, but what the hell, go on it is Sunday.' She appeared to be rambling with a slight slur, suggesting the gin hadn't been the first drink of the day.

'What circumstances?' Asked Lewis.

'Tell you another time sweet lad,' she replied smiling and showing her smoked, stained teeth.

Liam arrived back with his pint and the wine for Rebecca and settled himself into his seat.

'Nice to meet you Lewis,' he said, 'how do you two know each other?'

Indicating Rebecca.

'Just from the pub really, I started coming here a few months ago and you know Rebecca, life and soul,' Lewis let out a small laugh as he grinned at her.

'Are you new to the area then, or I'm guessing and don't take offence, now able to buy alcohol?'

'Well both really and no offence taken. I'm from Looe in Cornwall, recently turned eighteen and decided to see what London had to offer.'

'Good for you, although I bet it's more difficult than you thought, yes?' Liam asked.

'Not as difficult as being in Looe for the past four years. However, I was left quite a bit of money recently due to a death so I'm doing OK really.'

'Ah man, sorry, I didn't mean to pry.' Liam was embarrassed.

As the evening went on, the alcohol flowed and the three appeared to be getting on well, each telling stories of work life, or travel they'd done and sexual experiences had. Alcohol was good for these types of conversations.

Rebecca was slurring her words as she re-told the cellar experience with Philip at the end of September and Liam was listening carefully.

'Not the best I've had, but it got the job done,' she now shrieked aloud and the three of them laughed hard, well two did and Lewis went through the motions.

Liam now looked discretely around him and then beckoned for the other two to come closer. His eyes were rolling and he knew he'd now have to phone in sick for tomorrow, as there was no way he could face going into the hospital.

'I can tell you something about Philip if you want me to?'

Lewis and Rebecca both smiled at each other and eagerly started nodding in Liam's direction.

'He's an arsehole.' Liam said as he belched.

'Yes, but he's my arsehole,' bawled Rebecca.

Both Liam and Lewis looked at each other at this point and then at Rebecca, but they both let the statement pass.

'Go on,' said Lewis, encouraging Liam to talk more.

'Well he has a brother who has Leukaemia and needs a stem cell transplant and Philip could have been the donor but wouldn't be, so now Ethan will probably die.'

Rebecca and Lewis weren't entirely sure they completely understood what they had just been told, but got the gist. Lewis knew that Philip's brother had cancer as Rebecca had let that slip out about a month ago, but he hadn't realised the seriousness of it.

'Philip won't help his brother live?' He asked Liam.

'Nope, no reason given, just won't.' Liam responded with a slurred voice that mirrored Rebecca's.

'Aren't you breaking some sort confidentiality type of thing by telling us that?' Asked Lewis.

'Oh, shit, yeah. Oh well. I don't care really, how could another human being do that to a member of his own family?' Liam was very drunk and his eyes were rolling.

The three sat there in silence for a few minutes without talking, but two of the three were so drunk that they didn't realise. Lewis looked at Rebecca and thought he'd try his luck.

'What circumstances Rebecca? Why shouldn't you drink?'

Rebecca smiled at Lewis, her head swaying. She lifted her finger to her mouth as if she were saying shush and starting to giggle.

'I'm pregnant and Philip's the daddy.'

Lewis could feel anger spreading through his body, he felt a tightness in his chest and a pounding in his head. He looked at the two drunks and felt nothing but hatred for both of them. The room started to spin and Lewis knew he needed to get out of here and get home as soon as he could. He grabbed his coat and pushed past Liam, causing him to nearly fall off his chair. Lewis felt a sickness rise up inside him as he ran from the bar. Stan and Arjun watched as he ran past them. Once in the street, Lewis crouched by the gutter and threw up the contents of his stomach.

9:00pm

The icy air of the afternoon was now Baltic and Lewis was aware his hands were like ice. He stood up and wiped his mouth with the back of his hand and then put his coat on. Looking up, he saw the sky was like a velvet sheet of nothing, no stars and no planes. A sadness swept through his body that he couldn't and didn't understand. Why was Rebecca being pregnant such an awful thing? Why had Liam upset him so much? No answers were coming and this frustrated him to a point of utter madness.

Lewis started to shake his head and then started to smack it with the palm of his right hand repeatedly. His main purpose of going to the pub tonight was to continue getting to know more about Philip, he just wasn't prepared for the amount and the type of information that he got. As he was now feeling so overwhelmed by everything that had happened, he called for an Uber, as he just wanted to get home as fast as he could.

9:20pm

Lewis had never felt so pleased to get home. He had left the heating on and the place felt exactly how he had wanted it to, warm and welcoming. It was only a one bedroomed rented flat above a shop, but right now it was his and he felt safe. The need to be jolly and excitable when in other people's company exhausted him and he knew he would now need to rest up for a few days to recuperate. His work was flexible so no worries there and he'd pre-planned needing to be alone, so the fridge was packed up with his favourite things that made him feel secure and protected. No one would be coming through his door for the next few days.

Lewis stood and looked around, trying to work out what he needed to do. His mouth still tasted of vomit and at the same time he felt hungry. Thinking about in what order to do things, he walked into the brightly lit kitchen and put the kettle on and then turned on the grilled sandwich maker to warm up and finally walked into his bedroom to remove his clothes. He liked his bedroom, he felt a connection to it. He now grabbed a towel off the radiator in the room and headed to the bathroom.

Standing in the shower felt amazing. The hot stream of water massaging his shoulders as it pulsated onto his skin was doing him some good and helped him to relax. His thoughts remained on the evening, but the anger and frustrations were ebbing away as he washed his hair and slim frame. He washed his right arm and saw his tattoo of a dolphin riding on a wave. She loved dolphins and it reminded him of her and that's why he had had it done.

Once dried and dressed in just his Lycra boxers, he went back into the kitchen and made himself a cup of tea and a ham, cheese and mayonnaise toasted sandwich. This was his perfect thing to eat and drink as it made him feel loved, wanted and needed.

'*Want a toasted special, Lewis?*' In his head he could still hear her calling this out from their kitchen in Looe and it gave him a warm feeling inside, but regrettably this was followed by a deep sadness that she had now gone.

'*Yes please mum, that would be champion,*' was always his answer and his mum loved it.

Just as he was lost in his thoughts and finally relaxing and beginning to feel calm, his phone buzzed.

Rachel: '*Are we still seeing each other? Haven't heard from you since bowling yesterday.*'

Lewis considered the message for ages, almost staring straight through it. He then focused on just two words, '*since yesterday.*' Jesus, he saw her yesterday and she's complaining. He texted back.

'*No*!' he then turned his phone off.

As he sat on his brown, lumpy sofa that had come with the flat, he turned on the television and went straight to Sky movies. The Green Mile was playing, this was his favourite film of all time. Lewis was enjoying his sandwich and knew he was now back in his happy place, he just wondered why Philip wouldn't help his brother and this worried him and would it therefore interfere with the task that he needed to do?

The next thing he was aware of was a different film playing on the television and a cup of cold tea in front of him.

'Time for bed Lewis,' he said to himself as he yawned and stretched out.

He cleared away the items he had used for his supper, as he hated waking up to a mess and he then went into the bathroom to brush his teeth and have the final pee of the night. Turning out the bathroom light, he went through into his bedroom and slipped off his boxers and then placed them on the wicker chair in his room. He'd only really just put them on after his shower so they would do for tomorrow. As he climbed into his king-sized bed, he studied the wall in front of him. It was covered with pictures of Philip and only small patches of the green paint showing from underneath.

'Night, Mr Oakes,' Lewis said as he reached over and turned off the bed-side lamp.

22:

10th November 2017

Rebecca

05:30am

The car was freezing and Rebecca's arms and legs were shaking with the cold, despite the thick checked blanket she had wrapped around herself and the hip flask of brandy by her side. She could see the early morning frost creeping up the car windscreen and forming patterns. As she breathed out, the breath she could see in front of her caused her to pull the blanket tighter around herself.

The street was still and silent and was almost haunting. Rebecca jumped as a fox ran in front of the car with something in its mouth. She glanced up at Philip's window and wondered if Arjun was in there too. She then remembered that the front bedroom was the spare room and that Philip's bedroom overlooked his garden, as this was the bigger room.

'Arjun is just a phase Rebecca; you don't need to worry about him. When Philip knows about the baby, he'll be thrilled and you can be together exactly how things should be.' She was aware she was talking aloud to herself, but that happened a lot these days.

Sitting in her car, her eyes rarely left his house. This was a place she had been in three times and was determined to get back inside, where she rightly belonged. This was a house where she and Philip had made love and had been a proper couple and now that bartender had come along and had started to ruin things. Her hands were making fists and her nails that were too long, were cutting into her palms and causing them to start bleeding, however she was oblivious to the pain.

'I like the name Molly if it's a girl and Edward if it is a boy.' Rebecca was talking aloud to herself again, but as if she were having a full-on discussion with someone else present. 'I don't like Molls, or Ted, Teddy, Ed, so I won't allow people to shorten the names, not unless Philip wants the names shortened.' Her rambling tongue just kept going on.

A light in the lounge went on and this shocked Rebecca out of her thoughts. Her heart started to pound and she felt a tingling sensation in her fingers and her breathing started to speed up a little. She looked at her watch and saw that it was 6:00am and wondered why Philip would be getting up so early. He didn't usually get to work before 10:00am so why was he already up? The front door then opened causing Rebecca to take a sharp in-take of breath that hurt her lungs. What she now saw turned her stomach and made her furious. Philip and that idiot bartender were standing on the front doorstep kissing and then hugging each other. Rebecca was feeling sick and had started to retch and feel faint.

'He's mine, he's mine, he's mine,' she started saying to herself over and over again. 'Get away from him, he's MINE!'

Her retching was getting worse and she was making far too much noise as she saw the two men had looked over in her direction. She lowered her head and hoped she hadn't been seen. She hadn't! When she righted herself, Arjun had gone and Philip was nowhere to be seen. The light was once again switched off. Rebecca started up her car, angry and with tears pouring down her face, she drove off in the direction of her home. She knew she'd need a gin to settle herself as soon as she got in, despite the fact it was a working day.

As she turned into the next road, she saw Arjun on the pavement and before she knew what she was doing, she had put her foot on the accelerator and had mounted the pavement. Arjun turned and saw the car and jumped into the nearest garden. Rebecca quickly got back onto the road and sped off as she started screaming.

'I HATE YOU! LEAVE US ALONE, HE IS MINE, NOT YOURS.'

7:00am

Rebecca lay in a hot bath with lemon sherbet bath foam that she had picked up in the pound shop a few weeks previously. In one hand she had a cigarette and in the other, a neat gin with ice. She was feeling more relaxed now and was again thinking of the future that she and Philip were sure to have and this made her happy.

'The baby will bring us back together and repair the damage that Arjun has done,' she thought to herself.

The hot water had helped to warm up her body after sitting in the car for three hours and the gin had helped too, but for a different reason.

She stepped out of the bath and stood in front of the mirror. As she observed her reflection, she saw nothing but sheer beauty and perfection. In reality, she was underweight, almost malnourished, her hair was lanky and drab and her breasts were becoming wrinkled folds of skin rather than pert like they used to be. Observing herself, Rebecca turned side-on and looked back into the mirror and cupped her belly in both hands and grinned, then started to gently rub where her hands had been.

From her bedroom, Rebecca heard her phone receive a text. She ran from the bathroom with her gin still in her hand and hastily started to search for her mobile. She put her glass on the floor and was frantically throwing clothes around the bedroom and getting angry with herself that she was so untidy.

'It's him, I just know it is,' she started calling out.

On the floor over by the linen basket, which she never used, she eventually found her phone under her Jeans that she had taken off when she got in. She desperately looked at it and her face dropped.

Amelia: '*Hi mum, can't make dinner tonight so see you next week instead. I have spoken with Alice and she is doing OK and just passed an assignment. Hope you're OK.*' As usual, there was no kiss.

Rebecca threw the phone back down where she had found it, then picked up the knickers she had taken off prior to her bath and put them back on. Sitting on the bed, she caught sight of herself in the wardrobe mirror. She wondered why it wasn't showing her the same image that the mirror in the bathroom had showed. Tears formed in her eyes and then started to glide down her cheeks.

She reached down to the floor and picked up the glass that still had a few mouthfuls of gin left in it. She swallowed what was remaining and then put her head onto the pillow that had no pillowcase on it. Arjun was to blame for her sadness and this thought caused the tears to turn into sobs and the sobs then turned into hysteria as Rebecca started to thump the bed and then got up and started to throw things around the room.

'Arjun you will pay for my unhappiness,' she said in a hushed whisper.

She then saw herself in the mirror again and stood there in just her knickers and looked hard at herself. Her hair was now wild and covered half her face, like some cave woman from the past. Deep breathing exercises that she remembered from when she was pregnant with her girls kicked in and her breathing began to slow. As she started to calm down, she searched around for her phone again and picked it up and sent a text.

'*Hi Philip, please can we meet up soon I have news for you and it is in your best interest to see me x.*'

11:00am

The pharmacy dispensary where she worked was extremely busy this morning, with people running around and being incredibly stressed due to staff sickness. Norovirus was doing the rounds and it appeared that half of the pharmacy staff had gone down with it. As she took two more paracetamol, Rebecca wished she'd been one of the many that had called in sick. The smell of the various tablets was more pronounced today, or so it seemed and the manager still hadn't addressed his body odour issues. The mixture of the two was causing Rebecca to want to throw up. With her head banging, she went over to the microphone to call the next patient forward to collect their medication.

'Number 103.'

As she stood there waiting for 103, she surveyed the waiting area and thought she saw Philip's brother. She had seen him once or twice collecting medications, so was sure it was him. He had been the only other ginger man with blue eyes that she had seen, apart from Philip. She looked at the board and saw the name 'Ethan Oakes 107'. She knew at that point she needed to speak with Ethan, try to find out what his brother was up to as he was clearly avoiding her.

'I'm 103,' said a meek voice.

Rebecca passed over the small packet of antibiotics without even talking to the person standing there. She then hurried up her pharmacist, who glared at her until it was time for 107 to be called.

'107.'

'Hi, I am 107,' Ethan said to Rebecca in a voice that no longer had much strength.

'Ethan Oakes is it?' She asked, already knowing the answer.

'Yes, it is.' He replied.

'I know your brother Philip,' she said with a smile that wasn't returned.

'Do you?' was the quick and uninterested response.

'Yes, very well in fact. Although I haven't been able to talk to him recently, as he always seems terribly busy.'

'What does this have to do with me?' Ethan asked in an annoyed manner.

'Oh, well, just asking if you had seen him lately?' She knew how unprofessional she was being, but needed answers.

'No, I haven't seen Philip for quite a while, now please just give me my medications and let me get out of here. I spend enough time in hospital without having to chat to someone about my heartless brother.'

Thanks to Liam's drunk discussions a few nights ago, Rebecca knew why Ethan said his brother was heartless.

'Oh, I am sorry to hear that, why heartless?' She asked hoping to get further information.

'Just give him his medications and shut the fuck up!' Emma said with a stern look on her face.

Ethan looked at his wife in shock, as she wasn't someone who usually swore, but he was so proud of her at this very moment.

'Number 108,' Rebecca called out as she shoved the medication packet at Ethan.

2:00pm

Arriving at the pub as soon as she had finished work, Rebecca headed into the car park and saw Philip's car. She then headed over to where she assumed his office was and looked into the window. There was no sign of

Philip, but she could see his mobile phone on the desk, so she knew he was working. She quickly ran around to the entrance and headed straight to the bar. Philip wasn't there either. Feeling very confused, she walked around and saw that Hannah was on duty.

'Hello Hannah, is Philip about as I need to speak to him?' She asked as sweetly as she could.

'Yes, he is about somewhere, so you'll just have to wait until he comes back from wherever he is.' Hannah disliked Rebecca as much as everyone else at The Lemon Tree. 'Do you want a drink whilst you wait?'

'Yes, I will have a glass of Merlot please.'

'Medium or large?' Asked Hannah.

Rebecca just smirked at the young woman as she knew all staff knew she only ever ordered large glasses.

With her drink in her hand, she strolled around the seating area and saw no one else.

'Quiet then?' she smirked at Hannah, who just ignored the question and walked away.

Nursing her drink, Rebecca remained in the bar area so she could pounce on Philip as soon as she saw him. There had been no answer to the text she sent this morning and she really needed to speak with him and let him know about the baby. More people knew now, her three friends and she had told Lewis the other evening.

She knew he'd be excited, so wanted to tell him herself before anyone else told him. A sense of warmth flowed through her and it wasn't just the red wine. She felt like her life was about to change and change for the better.

A noise from the left broke her concentration as she heard Philip's voice as he was leaving the kitchen.

'Absolutely, we can review the Christmas menu tomorrow.'

Philip left the kitchen and turned as if to walk into his office. Someone touched his arm and startled him.

'Jesus Christ, you made me jump!' he said with annoyance as he looked at Rebecca.

'Oh, I am sorry Philip my love, but you haven't been returning my text messages and I need to talk with you,' Rebecca responded with an open smile.

'I don't have time today, I am really busy as we are beginning to get ready for the Christmas period and to be honest I can't see why we need to talk!' Philip was almost shouting.

'I have important news and I want to tell you, but not here, over dinner at my place.' Rebecca was still smiling.

Philip just stood staring at her, he now hated the very sight of her and regretted ever having anything to do with her, especially the sex. She clung on to his arm as she looked into his eyes.

'Go away Rebecca and maybe find another pub to drink in, I think that would be best.' He turned to walk away to enter his office.

'I saw your brother today and he looks awful and I know what you are putting him through.' She was now glaring at Philip.

'Is that what you came here to tell me?' He asked with no real interest.

'No, but Liam his nurse, told me and another person that you wouldn't donate cells to save your brother's life.'

The door to the pub opened and Arjun walked in. He eyeballed the scene in front of him and went straight into the bar to find Hannah. Rebecca saw how Philip looked as the young man walked away and it made her feel nauseated.

'He hates you, do you know that? He hates you!' she snarled at Philip and bared her stained teeth.

'Who hates me?' Philip asked, for a moment thinking she meant Arjun.

'Ethan does, he told me today that you were heartless. We went for a coffee and he told me everything and how he hates you and is going to make you pay,' Rebecca hoped Philip wouldn't see through her lies. She often hoped that people didn't see through the untruths that she told.

'Arjun,' Philip called out, 'come into my office please.'

He turned his back on the physical wreck in front of him and waited by the office door for Arjun to arrive.

'I'M PREGNANT! AND YOU'RE THE FATHER!' Rebecca shrieked.

The four customers who arrived through the entrance just as Rebecca screamed out, hurriedly found themselves seats and read the menus. Hannah's eyes widened and Arjun was shocked and started to tremble. Philip just stood where he was and glared into the eyes of Rebecca. A pounding in his head was causing a pain at the back of his eyes. Inside, he started to feel sick and his thoughts were numb.

'Go away, you're a vile creature!' was all he said, as he turned and went into his office.

23:

13th November 2017

Ethan

07:45am

Ethan stood in the bathroom and observed himself in the mirror. The scars where he'd had medical lines put in, bruises due to low blood counts and the hair on his head that was barely hanging on, just re-enforced to him that his life was ebbing away.

He knew he hadn't been the best brother to Philip, but surely not bad enough that Philip would let him die. Ethan opened the bathroom cabinet and stood looking at the shelves filled with medications and all with his name on them. These were the things keeping him alive at the moment and yet he hated, no, despised taking each and every one of them. This disease was robbing him of his life, his family and his future.

Ethan reached for his toothbrush and special toothpaste to help fight bacterial infections in his mouth and looked back into the mirror and saw a frowning old face glaring back at himself.

Lost in his own world as he brushed his teeth, he didn't see that Adam had suddenly appeared from nowhere.

'Bloody hell son, you made me nearly crap myself and with the side effects of these meds that is relatively easy these days.' The two then half smiled and half laughed.

'Sorry Dad, I can't find my boots for work and was coming up to ask you and mum if she knew where they were?'

'In the garage as they were covered in more paint than usual,' Emma called from the bedroom down the hall.

'OK, thanks Mum,' Adam called back and then turned again to Ethan. 'You OK Dad? I know that's a stupid question, but I don't really know what else to say.' He looked down at his feet.

Ethan picked up the hand towel and wiped away the foam around his mouth from the toothpaste and beckoned for his son to come into the bathroom.

'You are amazing Adam and each and every day you show me how much you love and care for me and I really appreciate that. However, I don't want you feeling upset and guilty every time you are near me.' Ethan put his finger under Adam's chin and gently raised his son's face until it was level with his own. 'We don't know how much longer I have and if it is a short time then I want us as a family to be strong and happy and show the world how united we are.'

Adam put his arms around his dad, but instead of the firmness of a parent that was once so warm and comforting, that he remembered fondly as a child growing up, there were now ribs and bones. Panic was in his heart that he was going to somehow break his father.

'I know Dad and I am trying to be strong, I promise I am.' Adam pulled away and kissed his dad's cheek. 'I'll get my boots and head off to work and drop Saul off at school.

Ethan watched his eldest and most sensitive child walk away with drooping shoulders and his head hung low and inside his heart was breaking. Adam had always been his special boy. There was a sweetness and vulnerability about him that made him unique. Most lads of eighteen weren't as gentle and thoughtful as Adam. Ethan looked towards the bedroom and saw Emma looking at him watching Adam who was slowly descending the stairs and she smiled. She was aware that there was a special bond between this father and son that couldn't be broken. Ethan winked and turned back to the bathroom cabinet to start the daily drug routine. His first tablet was his antidepressant. It wasn't working!

As he walked back to the bedroom, he stepped into Saul's and Max's room and he saw his youngest still asleep in his cot.

'You're getting too big for that my little man, time for a small bed I think.'

Ethan then felt his wife's hands on his shoulders and he relished the feel of her touch.

'Isn't he so beautiful?' she said in a whisper.

'He's adorable,' was Ethan's response. 'Emma, I am worried about Saul, he doesn't say anything, or ask questions and he won't even come near me anymore.'

'I know I've been watching him. He's scared Ethan and I think he is trying to distance himself from you because he's afraid of losing you.'

'Does an eleven-year-old think like that?' Asked a perplexed Ethan.

'Let's sit with him when he comes in from school and ask him how he is feeling.' Emma kissed her husband.

'Em, once we have seen Dr Kelleher today, can we go to the shops and do something for me?'

'Yes, of course we can honey, what is it you want?'

'I want to get a few presents and cards for the boys, in case I don't get better. Do you know what I mean? Happy 10th, 13th, 18th, 21st, graduation,' at this moment Ethan started to cry but kept going, 'wedding, passing your driving exam.' He was now sobbing into Emma's neck and she held her husband tight.

'That is a precious idea my darling,' she whispered into his ear.

09:30am

The exhausted couple were sitting in a consulting room that was all too familiar now. The pictures on the wall advertising the 'flu jab' and the examination table with the blue paper that ripped as soon as you sat on it. Neither one was talking, but felt connected. Ethan's phone buzzed.

Philip: *I am coming around about 8:00pm tonight as I need to ask you something. Also, Liam is telling people about your condition when he visits the pub. Get him sacked!'*

Ethan stared at his phone and then at Emma and then back at his phone.

'What?' Emma asked.

Ethan showed her the text.

'Do you think he is coming around to tell me he will donate his cells?' Ethan's breathing was increasing. 'Why else would he say that about Liam? Does this mean he actually cares about me after all?'

'Ethan, slow down, it doesn't mean anything. You know what Philip has been like, please don't start getting your hopes up.' She sounded almost incensed.

There was now a very confused atmosphere in the room, where they were still sitting on their own. Ethan was optimistic, but Emma just knew that Philip's text wasn't the news that her husband was hoping for.

The door opened and in walked Liam.

'Hey guys, Dr Kelleher is just finishing seeing someone next door and will come straight in. How are you feeling? Your latest blood counts are holding, so that's good.' Liam then took a breath and saw the concerned faces of the two in front of him.

'Liam, look at this text please.' Ethan held out the message from Philip.

'Oh my God!' Liam was fully aware that his cheeks were turning red and his heart beats were becoming rapid, as was his breathing. 'I am so sorry Ethan, Emma, I was drunk and I know that isn't an excuse and he wants me fired? I was so stupid, I don't know what to say.'

'Liam calm down,' Ethan said, 'I actually think that by shaming him up to a few people in the pub has made him want to donate his cells. He is coming around tonight to talk to me.'

'Ethan!' Emma sharply said, but was stopped from saying anything further as the doctor came in.

'Hello, how are you getting on Ethan?' She asked in her usual positive manner.

'I'm OK I guess, hospital admissions for infections etc, but OK.'

'Good, good. Your latest blood results are reasonable at the moment, so the treatment is doing its best to hold back the Leukaemia. The best plan is to carry on the way we are going and try to keep you out of the hospital for longer periods of time.' She turned away from the computer and half-smiled at them both.

'Does this mean I'm doing well and that things are more positive now?' Ethan asked as he held onto Emma's hand.

'Ethan, we have known from the very beginning that this is a very difficult and complex Leukaemia to treat and therefore I cannot raise your hopes,' she said, taking a deep breath. 'The bloods are good at the present time. I will see you in a week and review where we are then. I am sorry that I can't be more positive.'

Once the consultation was over and the doctor had left the room, Liam approached Ethan.

'Do you want me to report myself? I did break your confidentiality and that is an unbelievably dreadful thing to do, I truly am sorry.'

'It's not a problem Liam, we know that overall you were angry with Philip and in a roundabout way, were just trying to help.' Ethan looked at Emma for her to also acknowledge she agreed with him. She nodded.

Both could see Liam exhaling as his breathing was beginning to slow down again as he wiped off the sweat on his forehead.

'Thank you, I am so sorry.'

4:00pm

Ethan sat in his favourite chair in the kitchen watching Max playing with his toys. Emma was at the oven preparing Saul's favourite dinner of Spaghetti Bolognese with mountains of grated cheese. There was a delicious Italian smell in the kitchen from the oregano and garlic. She was also enjoying a glass of her favourite red wine.

Saul was in the lounge watching his kid's television programmes. Ethan stood up and went over to the fridge and took out a carton of chocolate milk. Pouring some into a glass, he then headed off to talk to his middle son.

As he approached the lounge door, he could hear laughter and this made him feel happy. It had been ages since Saul had laughed, or that Ethan had heard him do so. He opened the door quietly and walked in. Saul looked up and saw the drink and took it from his dad without saying anything.

'Don't I get a thank you?' Ethan asked.

'Thank you,' was the curt reply.

'Hey Saul, what's up? You don't come near me anymore and I miss our chats and our cuddles.'

Saul took a huge gulp of his milk but said nothing.

'Do you know when your uncle Philip was younger, he also loved chocolate milk, just like you do.'

There was still no response from the young boy and he just kept staring at the television. Emma put her head around the door and looked at Ethan and gestured with her eyes for her husband to keep talking.

'Ask me anything you want to and I promise that I will answer with the truth.'

Saul picked up his glass and took another gulp of his drink. He then stood up and went to leave the room by pushing past his dad.

'SAUL!' Ethan regretted shouting as soon as he had done it.

He ran into the hallway and up the stairs where he had heard his son heading and approached the youngster's room. As he stood outside, he heard sobbing coming from the other side of the door. Upon entering the room, he saw his son lying on his bed and he was crying into his pillow. He walked over and sat on the bed next to his son and gently touched his back and started to stroke it. The young lad flinched, but Ethan continued. After a few minutes of no talking, Saul finally spoke through his tears.

'You don't look like you anymore, I want my dad back.'

Ethan started to well up, but knew he had to stay composed, especially at this vital moment.

'I know I don't and I am so sorry for that. The medications have made me lose my hair and the treatment has also made me lose lots of weight and I can't do anything about that Saul.' He took a deep breath. 'I love you Saulie and I hate the fact we haven't talked for ages.'

'Don't call me Saulie, I am not a kid anymore and you're always in the hospital, so it isn't my fault we haven't talked.' Saul's tears were beginning to dry up.

'Quite right Saul, but I can't help being in the hospital, but I know we don't usually let you visit because we were worried it would be too upsetting for you to see me there, but in the future, if I need to go in again, do you want us to let you visit?'

Saul didn't move his face away from the pillow, but he did move his head up and down.

'I'm sorry I haven't been around much for you, but I will try harder and I love you so very much,'

As Ethan got up to leave, he heard mumbled words coming from his son, but muffled by the pillow. He hoped they were 'I love you too Dad,' but he wasn't sure.

'Dinner at 5:00pm darling and it's your favourite.'

Ethan then closed the door and headed downstairs and back into the kitchen. He walked straight over to Max and picked him up and as he cuddled him tightly, he burst into tears. Emma looked on from where she was standing. She knew this was a moment that she shouldn't interfere with, but it broke her heart to watch the pain her beloved husband was going through, but she also worried more about what was to come in the future.

8:00pm

With Max asleep and Saul in his bed reading his Marvel comics, Ethan, Emma and Adam sat in the lounge with a huge log fire roaring away which added real atmosphere to the room. Ethan kept looking at his watch and then in the direction of the front door. He was hoping that Philip wouldn't be too much longer, as he had to know what that text message had meant. Emma could tell how anxious he was getting.

'Do you think he finally wants to help dad?' Asked Adam, almost as anxious as his father.

'I don't know Adam, I really don't know,' was the rushed response.

'What did the doctor or Liam say? Is it still OK to use uncle Philip's cells?'

'Adam, stop asking your dad questions. He didn't mention it to the doctor.' Emma responded for Ethan.

'Why didn't you?'

'Because I thought I should see what Philip had to say first, now can you please not ask any more questions, as I am stressed enough as it is.' Ethan looked at his watch again.

The three of them just sat in near silence for the next twenty minutes. Each of them with a book or magazine, but none of them taking in any words on the pages. Ethan looking at his watch every few seconds until the doorbell rang.

'I'll go,' said Adam.

Ethan sat on the sofa and took in a very deep breath. Emma noticed that Ethan had fingers crossed on both hands.

The lounge door burst open and caused both Ethan and Emma to jump.

'Are you the clown?' demanded Philip.

'What?' Asked Ethan with total shock on his face.

'Are you the fucking clown that has been terrifying me since 15th October?'

'Philip, I don't know what you mean, please calm down.' Ethan was trembling.

'Some bitch from the pub said you both went for coffee the other day and you told her I was heartless and that you hated me and you were going to make me pay. ARE YOU THE FUCKING CLOWN?'

Emma at this point stood up and approached Philip.

'Keep your voice down and don't swear in my house. We obviously don't know what you are talking about, so calm down and explain.'

'Are you the clown that has been frightening me? I have seen it three times now and each time it gets closer to me and always in my street, but closer each time I see it. Are you the clown? You of all people know how scared I am of them.' Philip glared at his brother.

'Philip, I am not the clown. The woman I assume you speak of, is the pharmacy assistant who gives me my tablets. She was asking questions about you and yes I said you were heartless, but we certainly did not go for a coffee.'

'I am scared shitless of clowns and you know why Ethan.' Philip was pointing directly at his brother and at the same time pacing around the room.

'I'm scared shitless too Philip, but I'm scared of dying, do you care about that?' Ethan stared at his brother until Philip turned his head away.

'Get out!' all eyes turned to Adam, who was standing in the corner of the room.

Philip just glared hard at Adam and then screwed up his face. It looked like he was about to say something in return, but instead he stormed out of the lounge and slammed the front door as he left. Ethan turned to Emma and his face said it all.

'I should have known,' he said with sorrow in his voice.

Adam stood by the lounge door and was shaking, as tears fell onto his cheeks.

11:00pm

Ethan and Emma sat in bed with cards and wrapped presents around them. Emma was drinking her wine and Ethan was having a cup of hot water with fresh lemon. Alcohol tasted metallic these days and therefore he no longer bothered.

As he sat there propped up against his pillows, he read the labels on the presents they had bought today.

Adam 21st

Saul 13th

Max 5th

Adam 25th

Saul 16th

Max 8th

Adam wedding

Saul 18th

He knew he still had more to do, but they would have to wait for another day as he wanted to do one more thing tonight before he went to bed. He picked up his phone and selected video and then started to film himself.

'*Hey Adam, happy 21st birthday my gorgeous son. To say I am sorry that I can't be with you today is the biggest understatement. You were my world, you and your brothers. I know that I am missing you grow into such a wonderful man and I hope life is being kind to you. How's work? Still wearing those huge boots? Have you got a girlfriend? Or boyfriend? You know I was always a very welcoming type of person, so I just hope you are working hard and happy. Hopefully, the boys are looking to you as a role model now that I am gone.'*

Ethan pressed pause as the tears started to pour down his face and his voice started to break up. He could taste the saltiness of his tears as they trickled into the corners of his mouth.

'You're doing great my darling,' Emma whispered across to him, 'keep going.'

'*As you can tell by my tears, this isn't an easy thing for me to do, but I wanted to be with you on your 21st. I hope this is a lovely surprise and isn't too shocking or upsetting. I know you will be in tears, as you were and I guess still are, such a sensitive soul and you should be proud of that. I was always immensely proud of you and knew how much you loved me. You were my first and I doted on you. I hadn't always been a great brother to Philip, so in some ways, I made sure I was the best father I could be. When I first saw your little toes and fingers, I knew then how much I loved you. Adam, I don't want to stop recording because I could tell you a million reasons why you are so special, but you also need to get on with celebrating your 21st. I hope you are having a huge party. I so wish I could be there with you. Bye for now Adam, love Dad.*'

Using the back of his hand to wipe the tears off his cheeks, he turned and smiled at his wife as she smiled back at him.

24:

1988

Philip aged Seven

Philip sat in his bedroom playing with his toy cars. This is where he spent most of his time when he wasn't at school. He still wasn't allowed to invite friends round and this made him sad. He knew his other friends went to each other's homes because he heard them talking about it. Philip's dad had made it noticeably clear to Mrs Temple, that no children were allowed in the house and Philip was to come straight back after school. Philip's best friend Jacob had stopped asking now and this also made him sad.

Today was Sunday, which meant the boy's dad was in the house. They had had breakfast together in the dining room and then at 9:30am Mr Oakes took himself off to his study and wouldn't be seen again until dinner time. Ethan and Philip used to sort lunch out for themselves.

As he was playing with his toys, Philip could hear Ethan on the phone downstairs arranging something. His brother was thirteen now so was allowed to go out and do things with his friends, but they weren't allowed to come to the house either, Ethan had to meet them at theirs. Philip hoped he could also be allowed when he was older, as he missed his friends at weekends, especially Jacob.

'Philip,' Ethan said, standing in the doorway of his brother's bedroom. 'Do you want to come out with me and my friends?'

Philip was shocked. Why was Ethan asking him this? Ethan was never nice! He turned and looked at his older brother.

'What did you say?' He asked, still confused.

'I am going to the park with my mates and they are also bringing their younger brothers and sisters and I wanted to know if you would like to join us?' Ethan was smiling at his brother, a grin that went from ear to ear.

Philip just looked at his brother and felt his eyebrows moving above his eyes.

'Philip, serious offer, we are meeting in the park and playing some cricket and football and then we are going over to Matthew's house and his mum Shirley is making us all pizza. Do you want to come?' Ethan was smirking.

'Really?'

'Really,' Ethan responded.

'I'd love to come Ethan, thank you.' Philip was so happy, for once Ethan was being friendly towards him.

'You don't want to? Why not?' Ethan asked with a grin that was transforming into a smirk.

'No Ethan, I said I would love to come. I love playing cricket.'

'I don't understand you Philip. You say I don't do nice things for you and here I am, asking you to come out with me and my friends and you don't want to come!'

'I do Ethan, please listen, I really want to come.' Philip was now almost pleading.

'OK, well if you don't want to come and have all the fun that we are all going to have, you may as well just play with your cars.'

Ethan walked away laughing as loud as he could.

Philip watched his brother as he walked down the stairs and put his jacket on. After a few moments he turned and walked into his bedroom and uttered just five words before he started to cry.

'I love cricket and pizza.'

As the devastated boy lay on his bed, he heard his brother laughing as he slammed the front door shut.

'I love cricket and pizza,' he whimpered again.

25:

17th November 2017

Philip

It had now been one week since Rebecca had blurted out her pregnancy news and four days since Philip had accused Ethan of being the clown. He sat in his bed feeling like his world was closing in on him.

Sitting there with a lukewarm cup of coffee and a now soggy piece of wholemeal toast with Marmite on it, all he could think about was Rebecca and this made him want to retch. He didn't like the woman and the idea of the baby was something that repulsed him.

'She can't be pregnant, she's too old!' he kept thinking to himself.

His mobile phone was by his side and since he had woken at 6:00am, ten text/WhatsApp messages had come through.

'She can't be pregnant, she just can't be! Please God, no, just no.'

He took a gulp of the coffee and this made him feel a little sick, he hated cold coffee but was not motivated enough to go and make a fresh one.

'She can't be pregnant.'

His head was spinning and he was now getting angry at himself for having sex with her, for not wearing protection and for talking to her in the first place.

Feeling a throbbing pain building up in his head, Philip took himself downstairs and into his bathroom and turned on the shower to warm up. He hated getting into a cold shower and always had done, even as a kid. He looked at himself in the mirror and saw he was getting heavier.

'You're stressed Philip, what with Ethan, Rebecca and that bloody clown, no wonder you're putting weight on.' His thoughts were all over the place.

The scars on his shoulders and the tops of his arms were more pronounced, even though he had stopped self-harming years ago. Everything he saw in the mirror stressed him out and it was all her fault.

'She can't be pregnant, she just can't be!'

After taking some painkillers for his headache, Philip stepped into the shower and stood there for a few minutes without moving. The hot water was pounding his body and it felt good. He hated showers that were directly above your head, as it felt like the water was in control. Water coming in from the side was nice and manageable.

He stayed in the shower for at least twenty minutes as he contemplated what his next moves were going to be. Ethan was sorted, as he wasn't the clown, but then who was? Although the clown was still a concern despite the fact that he hadn't seen it since 1st November, but then that was only just over two weeks ago, his priority right now was Rebecca and getting rid of that thing growing inside of her.

'Aaaaggghhh!' Philip shouted, 'I am going fucking demented!'

After his shower, he sat on the edge of his bed and picked up his mobile phone to see who the earlier messages were from. He had called in sick for the week as he couldn't face Arjun and the other people who were there when Rebecca screamed out what she did. In fact, he couldn't even remember who had been present, apart from Arjun.

Despite the fact it was November, he felt like he was going to explode with the heat he was feeling and the sweat dripping from his groin and moving down the back of his legs was not helping matters. Looking at his phone was now just adding to his anxiety, especially when he saw who some of the messages were from.

Ethan: *'Philip, I'm worried about you and this clown stuff, talk to me please. We don't need to talk about me at all, please let me help x.'*

Arjun: *'Can we talk about what happened please?'*

Arjun: *'Philip, we need to talk.'*

Hester: *'Hey Philip, just to let you know that I can't clean on Monday so will come Tuesday if that's OK? Molly has a parent/teacher thing going on.'*

Stan: *'You OK mate?'*

Stan's text brought a much-needed smile to Philip's face and this is why he liked his senior barman so much.

Number withheld: *'I'm watching you Philip Oakes!'*

Philip looked at this text and a shiver went through his spine. He felt nauseated and due to still feeling hot, a little faint.

The rest of the messages, apart from the one he dreaded, were from suppliers for the pub and his dry cleaners.

Rebecca: *'I am giving you until Friday 24th November. I expect you to be at my house for 7:00pm.'*

Reading all the messages, Philip wasn't sure which frightened him more, Rebecca's or number withheld.

As he stood to go downstairs and make himself a coffee, he thought about calling the police about the mystery text, but also sadly thought that he hadn't heard from Jacob in over two weeks. This was unheard of. Philip missed his best friend, but was equally torn over the money he was owed and the fact Jacob had been using his house as though it was a cheap brothel.

He picked up his phone and spent a few minutes looking at it. His heart was thumping and he was still breaking out in sweats. Text messages needed to be answered and Philip knew this, plus he needed to send one to Jacob and ask to meet up and discuss where their friendship was heading. He took a deep breath and as the water in the kettle was heating up, he started the replies.

Stan's: *'Hey Stan, doing OK*

I think, don't want to have a long text convo, so call in mate, be good to see you.'

Arjun's: *'Hey gorgeous, I am so sorry for being like this, but she has really put the shits up me. I'm dealing with it. Talk soon, I promise x.'*

Number withheld's: *'If you're the clown, you've been reported, so crap off!'*

Hester's: *'No worries hun, see you Tuesday x.'*

Philip ignored Ethan's.

The last two messages were the hardest to do, as he wasn't sure what he wanted, or needed to say, so he therefore made his coffee and took it back upstairs and got into bed. A million thoughts were circling in his mind.

Rebecca's: *'Fine, I'll be there.'*

Lastly and maybe the most difficult.

Jacob's: *'Hey, over two weeks mate, longest time ever. Can we meet? Soon? I don't know what's happening between us.'*

Philip took a deep breath and put his phone onto his bedside table. As soon as he had, he received a text.

Jacob: *'1st Dec, your house 7:00pm, it's the soonest I can do.'*

26:

24th November 2017

Rebecca

6:45pm

Rebecca stood in the doorway of her kitchen that led into her overgrown but small garden and smoked her cigarette. She didn't usually do this, but wanted her house to smell of the mulled wine spiced candle she had burning, rather than smoke from a cigarette. She was feeling excited, but at the same time full of trepidation. Taking one final and long drag of the cigarette, she flicked the butt into the garden and then shut the door.

Slowly pacing over to the fridge, she took out a gin and tonic can, although she had promised herself not to drink before Philip's arrival, she now felt she needed it. She pulled off the can ring and started to drink. The cold liquid felt good as it trickled over her dry, tobacco tainted tongue and down her throat.

Walking over to the kitchen table where she had left her phone, she looked to see if she had any messages and hoped he wouldn't have sent one to cancel. There was only one message.

Amelia: *'Mum, what the hell do you mean you're pregnant?'*

Rebecca hadn't remembered telling her daughter her news, but thought she must have sent her a drunk text. That was a frequent thing she did. Often in the mornings, she would scan through her messages and see who had been the recipient of one of these types of messages and then cringe.

Things would be different soon, as in a little while it would be Philip, her and their new baby.

'Oh Philip, we are going to be so happy together.' She took a huge gulp of her gin.

Looking at her watch she saw he was due to arrive in five minutes and her stomach turned over, as she felt a mixture of euphoria and unease. A chilli con carne was cooking on the stove because although she didn't know for sure, she was confident Philip would love it and it would set the tone of the evening beautifully. The table had been set for dinner for two, with candles and paper napkins, however the other part of the table still had a pile of newspapers on it and a huge pile of ironing that needed to be done.

Rebecca continued to pace up and down and was constantly talking to herself. She went to take another swig of the gin, but it was already gone. She glared strangely at the empty can, as if she couldn't believe that she had drunk its contents so quickly. Dithering about by the fridge, fighting with her conscience and debating with herself about having another drink or not, she opened the fridge door and stared into the void in front of her. There was practically no food and only two more cans of ready to drink alcohol. There was some semi-skimmed milk, but that was now two days out of date and some remnants of garlic and onion, left over from making the chilli. However, what was in the fridge was a bottle of New Zealand Sauvignon Blanc as she was sure this was Philip's favourite. She half-remembered that he had given her a large glass of it when she went to his house, the first time they made love. Looking at her watch she saw that Philip was now five minutes late. She shut the fridge door and sighed and then opened it again, this time taking out a can of whiskey and ginger ale. That just left the vodka and tonic and Philip's wine.

'Just going to help settle your nerves that's all, you're great and it'll be fine,' she tried to convince herself as she drained half of the can in one long mouthful.

As she wandered back to the stove to stir her chilli and put on a pan of salted water to boil, so she could cook the rice as soon as he arrived, she saw herself in the kitchen window.

'You're beautiful Rebecca, Philip is a very lucky man,' and then she smiled at her reflection.

The mobile phone on the counter suddenly made a loud noise that startled Rebecca and caused her to jump, but she still grabbed it as fast as she could.

Amelia: *'Mum! Answer my text messages! What do you mean you are pregnant? Who is the father? Are you just pissed still?'*

Rebecca put the phone back down and paced the kitchen again, but this time she was rubbing her stomach and singing softly to herself as she took small dance moves.

7:30pm

The doorbell sounding brought Rebecca back into the real world, she must have been singing and dancing to herself for about twenty minutes without realising. The whiskey can was still in her hand, so she quickly finished its contents and then hid the empty tin, along with the gin and tonic one. She then smoothed out her green, strapless dress and ran her fingers through her hair to try to give it some volume. Finally, she looked back into the kitchen window at her reflection.

'Stunning Rebecca!'

Gliding to the front door with as much feminine grace as she could muster and a huge grin on her face, she touched her belly again and then opened the door and saw Philip standing there, he was as fetching as it was possible to be.

'Come in handsome,' Rebecca said as she stepped to the side to let him enter. 'Go through to the kitchen.'

Philip entered without looking at her and went to where he had been directed. His first impressions of the kitchen were filth. The whole place looked like it hadn't been cleaned and de-cluttered in years. He could see the saucepan on the stove and could smell the food. To be honest he thought it actually smelt nice. On the draining board next to the sink was a large wine glass that appeared clean. Rebecca came into the kitchen rubbing her tummy. This really annoyed him, but he knew he'd need to stay calm and try to get her on his wavelength if he was to convince her to have the thing terminated.

'Would you like a drink?' She asked.

'Do you have any white wine?'

'Of course, I have got your favourite in my love.'

Philip had winched when she said, 'my love,' but continued to smile at her. He watched her walk over to the fridge and was fully aware that she was like a bag of bones in her ill-fitting dress. Her hair was also lanky and lifeless.

'I didn't know you were cooking,' Philip said, 'smells good.' Observing how grubby the kitchen was, he dreaded the fact he might have to eat some of it.

'Just a basic chilli con carne, but home-cooked and made just for you,' Rebecca said.

'Great,' Philip lied.

Rebecca handed over a large glass of wine and then got herself a glass of water.

'Aren't you having a glass of wine with me?' Philip asked.

She touched her tummy and said, 'I've practically cut out all alcohol these days as I don't want to harm our baby.'

Philip recoiled.

Rebecca started to take two dinner plates out of the cupboard and as she did so, shouted over her shoulder.

'I hope you're feeling hungry.'

Philip really didn't want to eat the food so thought of ways to delay.

'Hey, I can't eat off cold plates, why don't you put them in the oven on a very low temperature to warm them through?'

'OK, my love, good plan,' as she did what he had suggested and also turned the gas off under the boiling water for the rice, as she didn't need it just yet.

Philip started to pace the kitchen as he didn't know how best to start the questions he needed to ask and when to do it. He knew he didn't want to eat the food, at least not sober, so he took a large gulp of his wine and then asked for some more. Rebecca topped his glass up and beat him to the questions, although they weren't the sort of questions that he was going to be asking.

'What names do you like for a boy? I like Michael, but not Mike. I did like Edward, but I wouldn't want people to shorten it. I remember when we first met and you said your name was Philip and I said, 'nice to meet you Phil' and you said straight away, 'Philip, never Phil'. I have always remembered that. Do you have any thoughts? Or do you think it will be a girl?'

Philip could hear that she was talking and not taking a breath and could see her mouth moving quickly but was trying not to take in what she was saying.

'Have you done a pregnancy test? Is that how you know you are pregnant?' Philip spoke over Rebecca, who was still talking about names.

'I did, of course I did,' she lied, 'and it was positive. I was so pleased.'

Rebecca knew she was pregnant even without the test. After all, she had had two children, so knew what it felt like. Plus, she hadn't had a period for two months now. She didn't need an expensive test from a pharmacy to tell her what she already knew.

'Rebecca sweetheart,' he gave her a sickly smile, 'I don't want to be a father.'

She just stood there looking at him. Inside she died a little.

'Oh, my love, your glass needs refilling, let me do that for you.' She swiftly walked to the fridge.

'Rebecca, I will not be a father and therefore you need to have a termination,' he said as calmly as he could.

She stood by the fridge, gripped the handle, and then took ten deep breaths. She slowly turned around and started talking as if she hadn't heard a thing he had just said.

'I was extremely well when I carried Amelia and Alice, so no reason to expect different this time, although I am slightly older this time around.'

'I will not be a father and therefore you need to terminate this 'thing' and say no more about it.' Philip was getting steadily more irritated and he was now beginning to glare at her as his breathing became more rapid.

'It'll be a June baby, so we could think of names that have a summer vibe to them.'

'REBECCA,' Philip bawled as he slammed his fist down on the table.

Half of the ironing and newspapers fell to the floor and his wine glass toppled a little but stayed upright.

'We could be like the famous and call it something like Daffodil if it were a girl, but then that's more Easter than summer isn't it?' She was trying not to listen to him.

Philip moved slowly towards her. He wanted to try a different approach and get her on his wavelength.

'Hey, my love,' he thought using her words might get her on side. 'We are too set in our ways to have a kid, don't you agree?' He put his arm around her shoulders and felt her lean against him. This made him cringe as he touched her leathery, dry skin, but he continued.

'Why don't I make an appointment at a clinic and I'll come with you and pay for it too.'

'I want to keep our baby,' she said in a quiet, mouse-like manner.

He took in a deep breath.

'You can't keep it, you need to get rid of it as I will NOT be a father.'

She jumped as he raised his voice and was beginning to feel a little frightened.

'I think the chilli might be burning, I need to turn it off,' she pulled away from him.

Philip used his right hand and started to run it through his hair. He was getting angrier and could feel the tension rising up inside of him. Rebecca was serving up the chilli without rice on the warmed plates, but Philip could see she was visibly shaking.

'Will you sit down and have some dinner?' She asked with trepidation.

Walking over to the table Philip kept his eyes on her, he looked at her stomach and felt nothing but hatred. As he got to where she was, she held out a plate for him. He was still looking at her and before he knew what had happened, he had taken the chilli and thrown it against the wall. The plate shattered and the chilli went everywhere. Rebecca jumped and put her hands to her mouth in silence. Philip started to pace up and down again like a caged lion.

'You can't be pregnant, just look at the state of you,' his anger was building. 'How old are you? Fifty-five? Late fifties? You're too old to be pregnant!'

Rebecca had never felt pain like it. Terry had been awful to her, but this felt a thousand times worse. She turned to look into the kitchen window again, as she had done before Philip had arrived. That time she had seen herself as a stunning, vibrant woman, but now she was glaring at a tired, thin, corpse-like creature. She started to cry.

'I'm forty-four,' she said in barely a whisper.

'Jesus, I thought you were approaching sixty. Look at the state of you. You're ugly, your hair is disgusting, you live in an absolute pigsty and the very thought of you repulses me.' Philip was still pacing.

'Why are you being so cruel? I thought you loved me?' She stepped towards him.

'Love!' he glared at her as he stepped back to get away from her. 'You make me feel sick and the fact I even shagged you makes me feel dirty.'

Rebecca blanked these words from her thoughts and continued to look at him with adoration.

Philip took a deep breath.

'Can we please talk about terminating the baby? I'm sorry about throwing your lovely food, I didn't mean to get so angry.' Philip smiled to try to make the frightened woman in front of him feel more secure, as he lied about her food.

'I want the baby Philip, I'm sorry, but I want it.' Rebecca seemed almost childlike as she spoke.

Philip gritted his teeth and at the same time he was clenching his fists and trying to stay calm. It wasn't working.

'Being a father fills me with absolute dread. My own father was a complete waste of space, a spineless idiot, who abandoned his two children from a physical and psychological attachment. I had a brother who hated me growing up and therefore I really don't see the point of children. Rebecca, you WILL NOT have this child!'

'Don't say that, please!' she ran at him with her arms out wide.

Philip saw her coming and with the back of his hand he smacked her in the face. She screamed out as she fell against the wall, her face sliding in the chilli that was still stuck to the peeling wallpaper.

'Please,' she called out. 'Please don't hate me, I love you.' She stood and approached him again.

This time he kicked out and got her straight in her abdomen.

'I HATE YOU!' he screamed, but with sheer exhaustion in his voice.

She staggered for a third time towards him and he pushed her over. As she lay there on the filthy floor looking up at him, he kicked her once more in her stomach.

Rebecca lay there now curled up into a ball and screeching as she held her wounded and harmed belly. Philip just watched the pitiful wreck at his feet for what seemed like ages. Finally, he put his head into his hands and spoke softly.

'I'm sorry Rebecca, I shouldn't have done that.'

As soon as these words left his lips, a cold and sinister shiver ran through his body. He remembered these exact words being spoken to him.

'I'm sorry Philip, I shouldn't have done that!'

These words had haunted him for at least twenty-three years.

His concentration was broken when he heard a key in the front door. He jumped up and ran towards the door. As it opened, Amelia pushed her way in as Philip rushed past her. She turned to see who it was but didn't recognise him. Amelia then heard the sobs coming from the kitchen and rushed towards them. As she entered the kitchen, she screamed out.

'MUM!'

9:00pm

Philip walked into the Lemon Tree and went straight into his office. Hannah and Stan were on duty, but he knew he didn't want to see anyone. He wasn't even sure why he'd come to the pub and not gone home. After he'd left Rebecca's and was driving away, he had the feeling he was being followed. This had unnerved him and broke his concentration. This is probably how he ended up at the pub.

Now in his office, he thought he'd have calmed down, but he was still wound up and pacing. He hadn't gone there to hurt her, just to try to convince her to have an abortion. Did he see blood on Rebecca? He wasn't sure as it could just have been the chilli. However, if it were blood, does that mean he'd caused trauma?

'You bloody idiot!' he said as he banged his head with his fist.

This was the first time he had ever shown such aggression and violence to another person and it had scared him. He knew he was causing psychological pain to Ethan and in a way physical distress due to Ethan's deteriorating body, but such actual physical violence was something new to him and Philip didn't really understand where it had come from. He then unexpectedly remembered someone in his past, who had also been psychologically hurt by him.

Wandering up and down, Philip kept glancing out of the office window and into the car park as he was sure a police car would turn up soon.

'Who was that girl?' he said to himself.

The office door opened causing Philip to cry out. Stan also jumped.

'You OK Philip? I saw you rush past. My God! You look dreadful.'

'I'm fine Stan, thanks for asking, but I just need to be alone. You understand?'

'Sure thing mate.' Stan left.

Philip took his mobile out of his pocket but for once there were no messages or missed calls. He put it back and paced some more. He then went back over to the window. Nothing there.

'Oh my God!' he said to himself. 'You went too far, she will get you for this, she will send the police.'

Deciding that he needed a drink to try to settle his nerves, he went through to the bar. His heart was beating fast and his breathing was rapid. He touched his forehead and it was wet. Hannah was serving.

'Double brandy please.'

'Sure thing boss, are you OK?'

'I'm fine.' He finished the drink she handed to him in one swallow, he then indicated for her to repeat the order.

He now headed back to his office. Once inside, he knocked back the drink and headed over to the window to see if the police had arrived. There in the car park and parked directly in front of his office was a car, not a police car but a normal everyday car. Philip started to shake and then the sick feeling started to overtake. Sitting in the front seat and looking straight at him was the clown. Philip couldn't move his eyes away. The clown started doing pointing movements with its fingers, like it was dancing whilst sitting down. It next started to use its left hand to wave, not a full-on wave but just using its fingers. Next it started to point at Philip and laugh and it was then holding both hands next to its tummy and moving them around like it was doing a belly chuckle.

Philip felt the sweat pouring down his face. He went to grab the phone from his pocket. As scared as he was, he needed to take a photo to prove he wasn't lying. His hands were clammy and trying to get the phone out of his pocket was proving difficult. He finally managed and tried to open the camera app. He looked back at the clown who was now sitting still, but with its head slightly on one side. Philip raised the phone to take the picture, but it slipped from his hands and onto the floor.

The clown smiled and then raised just one finger and dragged it across its throat, then pointed at Philip and started to laugh again. Philip turned from the window and vomited over his desk. When he had finished, he wiped his mouth with the back of his hand and looked back at the car park. It was once again empty.

27:

December 2013

(4 Years before Philip's death)

Lewis

4:00pm

This was definitely one of her favourite times of the day. She felt like a curtain twitcher, but she really didn't care. Watching him get off the bright yellow school bus at the bottom of the road and walk up with his friends brought tears to her eyes. He was always dressed smart in his school uniform, even at the end of the day. His light brown hair caught the sun and this gave it a reddish tinge. His constant smile allowed his face to become more radiant and he was so handsome.

'Look at my boy laughing,' she said to herself as she smiled so deeply that she felt the sides of her mouth almost touch her ears.

Lewis knew his mum looked out for him and secretly he cherished the fact she did. Although being fourteen he didn't let her know he loved it.

'Come on Lewis, I haven't seen you all day, hurry up!' she was always eager to see him but did like the fact he had lovely friends to talk to and engage with.

That was it, she had to move away from the curtain, so he didn't know she'd been watching. He'd said goodbye to Manish who lived four doors away, so that was her cue to move. As she turned, she stubbed her toe on her oxygen cylinder and cried out.

'Ouch!'

Janice Mayhew was thirty-two and lived in Looe, Cornwall. She was unmarried, single and mother of Lewis. She was tall and once had a full figure that caused men to turn and desire. She had had Lewis after a romance that she considered life long, but he obviously didn't! Janice had worshipped him, even though they had only been together for about twelve months. She honestly believed she'd found her true love and best friend.

They had met at the local cinema where she was behind the counter selling tickets and popcorn and he'd been a film fanatic. She remembered those deep blue eyes used to penetrate her soul and bring her otherwise boring existence to life. They used to spend every spare moment together and tell each other everything, or, so she thought. When she looked at Lewis, she could see him and this made her happy in one way and terribly sad in another.

Lewis hadn't known or met his dad and this had always tormented Janice. When he was six, Lewis had started asking more and more questions.

'Why don't I have a dad? Who was he? Why doesn't he love me?'

Janice had done that awful thing that you read about in books and see in films. She told her son that he had had a dad who loved him more than life itself, but he'd died when Lewis was only a baby. Now that she was dying herself, she regretted with all her heart telling him this, as she now needed to tell him the truth and she was scared he'd hate her for it.

Two years ago, Janice had been diagnosed with a lung disease. She had never smoked. Treatment hadn't been successful, so she was now on oxygen for most of the day. Sadly, her prognosis was now only a few months. Lewis knew everything that was happening to his mum, but he chose not to talk about it. In his head, if he didn't talk, it wasn't happening. Arrangements were in place for Lewis to go and live with his aunt, her sister who couldn't have kids of her own and was ten years older, so Janice knew her son would be loved and cared for.

However, this evening she needed to tell Lewis the truth about his dad, the man she had once and probably still loved, the man with deep, rich blue eyes, ginger hair and little scars over his shoulders and the tops of his arms.

'Mum, I'm home,' Lewis called out from the hall as he kicked off his school shoes without undoing the laces.

Janice put her hand up to her mouth in a fit of emotion and wished she could hear those words for years to come, but she knew she wouldn't.

'Hey gorgeous, how was school? Anything exciting to tell me?'

'Nah, just the usual.' Teenage boys never revealed much.

Lewis came into the lounge and went straight over to his mum and kissed her cheek and then gave her a hug. He knew he was going to miss being able to do this, but he said nothing.

'What's for dinner? I'm starving.'

'Well,' she said, 'I can make you a toasted special for now and then I thought I'd order in your favourite at about 7:00pm for dinner. What do you think?'

'Chinese?' He asked with excitement.

'Yep, Chinese,' she responded, equally enthusiastic.

'Can I have spareribs in barbecue sauce and sweet and sour chicken? Not the balls but the one they call Hong Kong style I think.'

'You can have whatever you want my darling.'

Lewis then helped his mum up and together they went into the kitchen to make the toasted sandwich that they both loved so much.

7:30pm

The two of them were sitting on the large sofa in the lounge with foil cartons opened on the floor and Lewis' plate was full. Janice was only able to manage small amounts of food, but she so enjoyed watching her son tuck in and enjoy his favourite cuisine. As he was gnawing on a rib, he looked over at his mum, aware that he had the barbecue sauce dripping on his chin. He blew her a kiss and her heart broke a little.

'Lewis, I need to talk to you about something serious and if I am honest, I don't really know where to begin.'

'Is it about your health Mum? If it is, please don't, it scares me and makes my depression bad.'

Since Lewis had been told of his mum's diagnosis and the full impact it would have, he had suffered badly from depression. He had been through counselling and cognitive behavioural therapy, but as yet no medication had been started.

'No love, it's not about my health,' she took in as deep a breath as she could manage. 'It's about your dad.'

Lewis looked at her with a large piece of sweet and sour chicken half in and half out of his mouth. He bit down and half the chicken fell back onto his plate.

'What about him?'

'Lewis, I told you a very bad lie when you were six. I told you that your dad died, but in truth,' tears started to form in her eyes, 'he isn't dead, he just didn't want anything to do with us. When I told him that I was pregnant, he went into a rage and split up with me. That's when we moved to Looe, to be nearer your aunt, who was going to help me with you.' She now just stared at her son.

Lewis carried on eating without saying a word. Janice found this disconcerting and would have preferred that he had screamed at her.

After about ten minutes of silence, apart from the sounds of Lewis eating, he put his fork down, picked up his coke and drained the glass. He then turned to her for the first time since she last spoke.

'What was he like? No, what was his name?' Strangely, Lewis had never asked this question before.

'His name was, well is, Philip Oakes. We were both sixteen when we met. He had a brother called Ethan, but for some reason that Philip never told me about, they didn't really get on. Your dad was a quiet lad when we met, very introverted.'

Lewis didn't stop looking at his mother and was taking in every word she said.

'Go on,' he said.

'We met at a cinema. He used to come in with his best mate, who if I remember correctly was called Jason, no, Joseph, no, Jacob, yes, definitely Jacob.'

'Go on,' Lewis repeated.

'Lewis, I loved your dad and I thought he loved me. We were together for a year and I know we were only sixteen, but I loved him with all my heart.' Janice was starting to cry but Lewis didn't move. 'Just as I turned seventeen, I found out I was pregnant with you and I told Philip and he went crazy. He said some things that I won't tell you, but I never saw him again because of his words.'

'Is he why you have never had a boyfriend?'

'Maybe, probably. I know I was only a kid myself, but I adored him and he hurt me so much when he just left me after the vicious things that he said.' At this point, Janice was now trying to hold back the floodgates of tears and Lewis could see this. 'I didn't know a young lad would know such hateful, hurtful and terrifying words.'

'Why did you lie to me?'

'I was just trying to protect you. The things he said to me when I told him about you scared me, psychologically wounded me and I saw a side to him I'd never seen before and it really frightened me. I just assumed that if you knew about him and wanted to try to meet him, he'd be horrible to you too.'

'OK, so why now? Why are you telling me now?' Lewis was being harder on his mother than he had ever been.

'Because,' she took a breath, 'when I am not here, I want you to know who you are as a whole person. Maybe when you are eighteen you can see if you can find him and see if he wants to know you. Maybe he has changed.'

Lewis just sat there almost like he was in a frozen state.

'Lewis?' Janice said.

'I'm going to bed.' Lewis got up and left the room, but then came back and kissed his mum goodnight. 'Toasted specials tomorrow morning Mum and I'll ask more questions then.'

Janice watched her son leave the room and then silently cried into her hands.

10:00am

Lewis came down the stairs and found his mum asleep in her armchair. He often found her like this as she was no longer able to manage the stairs but hated the hospital bed that had been set up in the dining room. He walked over and gently kissed her on the cheek. She opened one eye.

'Toasted special?' she said.

'Yeah, go on then that would be champion.'

As they ate their breakfast, Lewis started with his questions.

'So, I know he was a strange person, really nice and then really horrible, but what did he look like?'

'He had a slim build and ginger hair, beautiful deep, rich blue eyes. If I am honest, not the most attractive guy, but not the ugliest. Luckily, you take after me in the looks department.'

Lewis could never stay mad at his mum, not even over something like this and especially not with her health like it was.

'What was his favourite food?'

'Ah, that's an easy one, Hawaiian pizza.'

'OK, tell me something more about him.' Lewis was like a child in a sweet shop displaying such excitement.

'Sadly, his mum, so your gran I suppose, died when he was only four, she was hit by a car in a road accident. He didn't have a good relationship with his dad, or his brother, but I never knew why. I mean his dad became isolated after his wife died, but I meant I don't know why he and Ethan didn't get on.'

'Does he know I'm a boy?' Lewis asked.

'No sweetheart, he doesn't know anything about you or where we moved to.' Janice couldn't bring herself to tell her son that she'd sent a message to Philip just before leaving for Looe, that she had lost the baby due to the stress he'd put her through and never wanted to see him again.

Lewis finished his breakfast and started to do the washing up. Janice slowly followed him, not to help, but just to be with him as every moment mattered.

'So tell me something weird about him,' Lewis asked as he cleaned plates.

'Well, that's a difficult one, let me think. Oh, got one, he was petrified of clowns. They made him feel physically sick and he would vomit, he was terrified of them.'

'Why was he so scared?'

'Something to do with Ethan, but I never found out what.'

The two laughed as Lewis cleaned up. As it was a Saturday, they always watched a film after breakfast, well Lewis did and Janice tried her best each week to try to stay awake for it. She never managed to.

As they settled down and chose a DVD, Janice smiled at Lewis.

'Only go searching for him if it's something you really feel you need to do, as I don't want you getting hurt by him, he isn't worth it.'

'OK Mum, I promise to only search if I really feel the need to.'

28:

1st December 2017

Jacob

3:00pm

Jacob stood in his bedroom looking out of the window at two kids kicking a football around the street. Part of him was smiling as he liked to see kids enjoying themselves away from today's technology, but the other part of him was ready to kill either one of them if that ball hit his car.

The sky was dark and stormy and small raindrops started to hit the bedroom window. Jacob could hear Tanvi in the shower in their en-suite and the boys were both staying at his parent's house for the night. Having a night without the kids was rare, but neither had suggested having a romantic night in, or out together. Maybe this was a sign of the direction in which their marriage was going.

Tanvi was meeting her friends for dinner and Jacob was meeting Philip. This was not a meeting he was looking forward to. It had now been a month since Jacob had met Kate at Philip's house and he had hit the roof and then flipped more when the clown appeared. Jacob had tried to be nice to his friend and had offered to stay with him, but this gesture was rebuked and it had hurt Jacob. He felt his friendship with his best friend was damaged and he wasn't sure how it was going to heal. He didn't have the money to even start paying some of the debt back and the fact he'd been using Philip's house as a love nest was just more ammunition against him. In his head Jacob knew Philip had every right to be angry, but in his heart, he couldn't understand why his friend was behaving the way he was.

'I was there when you started self-harming and never pushed you to tell me why!' Jacob was talking loudly to himself as he walked around his bedroom.

'Even when your dad died, I was there and when you had your troubles with Ethan, I WAS there!'

'What did you say? I couldn't hear you,' Tanvi was calling from the bathroom.

'Nothing, just talking to myself,' Jacob responded.

His wife emerged from her shower with the obligatory towel wrapped around her head and a towel around her breasts and body. Jacob looked at her and wished that things would get better between them. He loved her, but with all his issues with Philip he felt himself becoming more and more distant.

'You look thoughtful,' she said to her husband.

'I'm not looking forward to seeing Philip tonight as I know he is going to ask about the money.'

'Then let me ask m...'

'NO!' Jacob made Tanvi jump as he interrupted her and her towel around her body dropped to the ground. 'You will not ask your father!'

Jacob stormed out of the bedroom and went downstairs to pour himself a large brandy. Tanvi just sat on the edge of the bed and started to weep into her hands.

A few minutes later Jacob came back into the room looking sorrowful.

'I'm sorry love, I shouldn't have shouted, but this is my problem not yours.'

Tanvi glanced up and straight into her husband's eyes. She was sick and tired of feeling the way that she did.

'Then do something about it because I can't live like this, I'm scared to open my mouth around you these days. Over the past few months you've kept disappearing for a few hours at a time, never telling me where, no, my mistake, telling me you are off to work to do some paperwork. I have been too frightened to challenge you on that.' Now that she had started, she wasn't about to stop. 'So, what have you been doing? Or should I say who?'

Jacob got up and as he left the room he shouted back at his wife.

'I'm not going to answer that, either you trust me, or you don't!' He was glad she couldn't see his face as he spoke these words.

6:00pm

Jacob opened his eyes and saw that he had fallen asleep on the sofa. That large brandy was probably the reason. He looked at the lounge door just as Tanvi walked in.

'Wow, you're stunning.'

'It's been a long time since you've said anything like that to me,' Tanvi said, even though she was delighted at his words.

'I know and I am sorry, but you look amazing and I do love you so very much.' Jacob meant every word.

He got up from the sofa and walked over to his wife, he took her face into his large hands and just looked at her for a few moments. He then kissed her lips and she let out a huge sigh, a sigh that made her happy. She kissed him back.

'Tomorrow we can talk,' she said to him, 'tonight try to sort something out with Philip, otherwise you'll make yourself ill.'

Jacob slowly nodded. He now helped Tanvi into her coat and wished her a pleasant evening as she left to get into her taxi. He went into the kitchen and poured himself a glass of water and headed upstairs to get ready before leaving for Philip's.

7:00pm

Jacob stood outside Philip's house for what seemed like hours without ringing the bell. He was remarkably close to turning around and going home again. Not knowing how this evening was going to turn out was causing him amount of anxiety. If Philip didn't bring up the subject of the money, Jacob wondered whether he should and try to clear the air and put their friendship back on track, but how could he do that if Philip mentioned the loan?

A noise behind the door startled him and he nearly ran off, however he knew it was just his friend tidying up. Jacob hoped on this occasion Philip would be clothed. He was used to seeing him naked but today wasn't a time for that, it would make things more difficult and the evening was going to be hard enough.

A sudden glimmer of light from his left caused Jacob to turn and as usual Mrs Ferres had pulled back her curtains just enough to be nosey. Jacob hadn't made a sound so how did the old bat know he was standing there. He gave her a sarcastic smirk and as she closed the curtains, he stuck two fingers up and laughed, quietly.

'No more dithering, just push the doorbell,' he told himself, but that was easier said than done.

Jacob somehow knew or felt that this evening wasn't going to end well, so he may as well get it started. He pushed the bell and waited and almost immediately the door was opened.

'Hey Jacob.' Philip was fully clothed.

Philip stepped aside to let his friend enter and then went to hug him like normal. Jacob flinched and pulled back. He had no idea why he did this. Not a great start to the evening.

'Erm, sorry, yeah, erm sorry,' Jacob leant in to hug Philip.

They walked through to the lounge, where the last time they had seen each other Jacob had been the one to be naked and there was a woman bleeding and sitting on the floor. There was a log fire burning away and as usual the place was immaculate, not a thing out of place.

'Would you like a drink?' Asked Philip.

'Gin and tonic please if that's OK?'

'Of course it is,' was the answer.

They were both behaving like this was a first date and not like two people who had known each other for thirty-three years.

As Philip went into the kitchen to make the drinks Jacob checked his phone. He wished he'd asked Tanvi to call him at 8:00pm in case he needed a reason to leave. Why did he need to even think this?

'Here's your drink,' Philip said, coming back into the room and handing over the gin. 'I have a rhubarb and ginger gin in the kitchen if you want to try that one next.'

'Sounds nice,' said Jacob.

'Shall I put some music on in the background?' Said a nervous Philip.

'Sure, but none of your opera crap, or that 'gay' music.' Jacob smiled, probably for the first time since he arrived.

'Gay music! How very dare you!' They both laughed aloud.

Philip turned on his Spotify and selected a compilation playlist that they could both enjoy.

'So how have you been?' Asked Jacob.

'Not great if I'm honest. Had a massive row with Rebecca.'

'Who's Rebecca?' queried Jacob.

'Well you know her as the 'drunk' from the bar, or the woman from the hospital,' laughed Philip.

'Oh, she is so weird, I saw her the last time I saw you, she was in a pharmacy shop and she was talking really oddly. Said that you were special to her.'

'Jacob, she says she is pregnant with my child.'

'WHAT! You had sex with that? And without protection?' Jacob couldn't believe what he had just heard.

'Four times,' Philip was embarrassed as he said these two words. 'Last week I went around to hers to discuss her terminating it and things turned ugly. I don't want to say how, but it ended badly.'

'Bloody hell mate, you should have called me.' Jacob said with real compassion.

'I wanted to call but, well you know how it's been between us,' Philip looked at his friend and sighed. 'Also, after I left her place I went to the pub and sitting in a car outside my office window was that fucking clown making all sorts of gestures. It scared me so much that I vomited over my desk.'

'Shall I go and fix us more drinks? It sounds like you've had a very tough week,' Jacob got up to go into the kitchen and Philip stood too and put his arms out to hug this friend. This time the hug was returned.

'Make those gins extra strong,' Philip said, calling out as Jacob headed towards the kitchen.

9:00pm

After spending a couple of hours catching up, there was now much laughter between the two men. The log fire was still roaring away, the crackling sounds were adding to the atmosphere in the room. On the coffee table was the now empty gin bottle and two bottles of wine, one red and one white, both were half empty. Despite the alcohol consumed they weren't too drunk, just merry and both had let their guard down, which at the beginning of the evening had been fully in place.

'It's so good to be laughing again, isn't it?' Stated Jacob.

'Totally mate, but to be fair it was your fault that we stopped, I mean I'm just saying,' was Philip's clumsy reply.

'What!' Jacob said in an irritated manner.

'Well be honest, the fact that you were using my home like a brothel wasn't the best thing you could have done, was it?'

'Agreed, but you didn't need to be such a twat about it, we are supposed to be best mates.'

The warm atmosphere that had developed throughout the evening was now beginning to turn sour again and a frosty feeling was beginning.

'I come home and find you naked and shagging some female on my carpet and you think I'm the twat? You need to look nearer to home mate!' Philip was beginning to raise his voice.

'You didn't seem to mind at first, I saw the way you were perving at me, or should I say my knob!' A bitterness was coming through in Jacob's tone.

'And what is that supposed to mean?'

'I've always known you have fancied me over the years, but the way you looked at me in those few moments made my skin crawl. We are, or should I say were friends and you shouldn't have viewed me in that way!'

'I have never fancied you, but yeah, I looked, seen it soft enough over the years, so what's wrong with seeing it hard for once?' Philip knew this hadn't sounded great and not the best thing he could have said.

'I think it's time I left. This evening was obviously a mistake.' Jacob got up to leave,

'MONEY!' hollered Philip, 'I want my money.'

'Where the hell did that come from?'

'You owe me £25,000 and I want it back and I mean now. I don't mean in chunks or instalments, I mean all in one payment.' Philip sneered at Jacob.

'I don't have it and you know I don't. Why are you being like this? What has happened to you? To us?' Jacob was genuinely confused and sad.

'It's my money and I want it back!'

Jacob started to move haphazardly around the lounge and was scratching his head at the same time as glaring at the man still sitting on the sofa.

'Can you prove you gave me the money?' Jacob said through gritted teeth. He then ran at Philip and grabbed him by his clothes, yanked him up from the sofa and brought his face in line with his own. 'Prove that you gave me the money. Where is your proof?'

Philip was scared as he had never seen this side of his friend before and if it came to a fight, he knew full well that Jacob would come out on top. The difference in their bodies and strength was huge, Philip wouldn't stand a chance.

'I have a bank statement that proves that I paid £25,000 into your bank account.'

'Very good,' snarled Jacob. 'Now prove that you said I had to pay it back.'

'What do you mean?' Philip asked bewildered.

'There is no paperwork, documents, signed statements etc, saying that I have to pay you that money back. I will just say that you gave it to me as a gift because of our friendship over the years.' Jacob grinned at the man in front of him. It was a grin full of victory.

Standing there for a few minutes with no words being spoken, the two men just stood staring at each other.

'I have a video on my phone that tells me that you'll pay me back my money,' Philip was now smirking a winning smile.

'And what is that supposed to mean?' probed Jacob.

'I'll show you,' Philip said as he reached down to pick up his phone and opened the picture app where videos were also stored. He highlighted a certain film and pressed play.

Jacob just stood there open-mouthed as he watched the minute worth of footage. Footage of him having sex with Kate, in Philip's lounge. Jacob went to grab the phone from Philip.

'No point in you doing that Jacob as I have copies of this film on other devices. If I don't get my money back in, let us say a month, then I will send this piece of evidence of your behaviour to Tanvi.'

Jacob's veins in his neck were now very prominent and his clenched fists were shaking.

'You are an absolute piece of scum, you are the lowest of the low. Philip, I hate you and there is no coming back from this.' Jacob felt the nausea rush up inside of him.

'Get out of my house.' Philip said as he pointed towards the door.

'Please don't ever show Tanvi that video!' Jacob pleaded, but it appeared to fall on deaf ears.

Philip ushered Jacob out of the front door and was fully aware of the tears falling down the cheeks of the man standing in front of him.

'GET OUT of my garden and go home,' shrieked Philip.

'Don't you EVER show my wife that video or I swear to god that you will be sorry.'

Curtains twitched next door as Mrs Ferres spied on the argument.

'Pay me back my money and I won't have to.'

'I DON'T HAVE IT!' screamed Jacob.

Philip watched a few more moments at his childhood friend breaking down in front of him and he then closed the door. He felt an intense sadness and straight away wanted to open the front door again and make things right. However, he didn't and as he walked back into the lounge, he heard Jacob screaming outside, but couldn't make out the words.

Across the street, standing behind a lamp post, a young man had witnessed the scene that had just unfolded. He had stood in this spot many times before looking at Philip's house.

'Not the nicest of men, are you dad?' Lewis said as he turned and walked away.

29:

7th December 2017

Philip

7:30pm

Philip was really excited for tonight. With the past couple of weeks being so awful he was ready to have some fun and especially with Arjun who was coming around at 9:00pm. Philip was falling for him in a big way. Recent events had meant they hadn't spent huge amounts of time alone together, so after drinking in the town it would be back to Philip's for hopefully a passionate time.

Standing in his kitchen Philip went over to his fridge and took out a bottle of his favourite wine. He poured himself a large glass and took a mouthful. He loved the way it tasted and its coldness just added to the experience.

Philip noticed that he had put on his expensive Rolex watch, which he had bought with money left to him in his father's will. He very rarely wore it as it reminded him of his useless father. Remembering the dodgy places he might end up in tonight he thought it best to take it off and leave it on the kitchen worktop. This was not something he'd usually do, as everything has a home, but he was feeling a little reckless tonight. He looked at the watch, sniggered and went over to the fridge to top up his wine.

'Don't go mad Philip, you don't want to get too drunk tonight,' he thought to himself.

Just as he was feeling in a good place his mobile phone started ringing. Assuming it was Arjun, he picked it up quickly without noticing the name on the screen to see who it was. It wasn't Arjun.

'Hello gorgeous, I'm ready if you want to come around sooner than

9:00pm.'

'Philip? Is that you?

'Ethan! What do you want?' Philip was now regretting answering the phone.

'Please Philip, can we talk? Can we come around and talk to you?'

'No, I am going out tonight and don't want to talk about your health.'

'Philip, I am probably dying, don't be so selfish and let me come and try to talk to you. Please!' Ethan was sounding desperate.

'No, I just told you I am going out so I don't have time.' Philip was getting annoyed.

'How about tomorrow? It'll just be me and Adam as Emma has taken the kids to her mother's house for a few days. Or I can come on my own. What do you think?'

'Ethan, when are you going to learn that I am not interested in talking about your health.'

'Uncle Philip, it's Adam, would it help if I just came around to talk to you tomorrow? Is that an OK idea?' Please Uncle Philip!' Adam was pleading as hard as he could.

Philip could sense the anger building up inside him. He took the phone away from his ear and pulled a face. He then put it back to his ear.

'Adam, I don't want to talk to either of you now kindly fuck off!'

'Philip,' It was Ethan again. 'Please, whatever happened between us growing up, please be the bigger man here and try to help me.'

'No, so go away.'

'Philip, you selfish prig! HELP ME!'

Philip again took the phone away from his ear, but this time just ended the call. However, he was now feeling extremely angry and agitated. Downing the wine that was left in his glass, he stepped back over to the fridge and filled his glass back up to the top. The bottle was now practically empty, but that was fine, as there were still another two bottles to go.

9:00pm

Philip was still feeling furious following his phone conversation with his brother and nephew and the wine hadn't helped subdue feelings. He found himself pacing the kitchen with a hundred things going around his head. None of which were nice things. Hopefully, once Arjun arrived he'd calm down and start enjoying himself. His phone alerted him to a text.

Jacob: *'I am warning you Philip, if you ever send that video, then you will pay for it.'*

'Big words Jacob, big words,' Philip uttered to himself.

The doorbell chimed to let Philip know that Arjun had arrived. He rushed to the door to open it. Standing on his doorstep was his Indian Adonis. Arjun was stunning in his black designer jeans and shirt covered in small blue flowers. His hair, as always was beautifully presented and velvet in look. Philip stepped aside and let him enter. As they walked into the lounge Philip grabbed Arjun and started to kiss him.

'Hey! Hang on, don't be so rough.'

'Sorry,' Philip said.

'Woah Philip you reek of booze, how much have you had?' Arjun was genuinely concerned.

'I'm sorry, I had a phone call from Ethan and it got me all wound up and angry. I've had about three glasses but I'm great, don't worry.'

'Would you rather not go out? We can stay in if you'd prefer?'

'Not at all, I have been thrilled for this evening and my shitty brother isn't going to ruin things for us.'

'Why do you hate him so much? What did he do to you?' Arjun was genuinely confused.

'Doesn't matter Arjun, now let's get going please.' Philip was assertive with his answer.

'I really don't understand Philip, I'd die for my brothers, especially Rohit.'

Philip opened the front door and they waited for the Uber that he'd ordered. There was an uncomfortable silence as they stood in the cold. The first the two of them had had.

10:30pm

The evening seemed to be going from bad to terrible. They both sat in a crowded pub which was playing music so loud that they could hardly hear what the other was saying. From where they were sitting, the smell of toilet cleaner was wafting around every time someone used the loos. The place was poorly lit and the tension that had started off in the house had now escalated.

'We should head back to the Lemon Tree, at least we can talk properly there,' said Philip as he learned in towards Arjun.

'To be honest,' Arjun could see Philip's face was struggling to hear him so raised his voice. 'To be honest, I don't think the evening is going too well, so I might just head home.'

'Why would you do that?'

'Because if I am being truthful, I don't understand someone who wouldn't try to help a family member who is ill, regardless of what went on before and therefore I don't really want to be in that person's company. Plus, you're completely pissed and slurring your words. This is a dreadful evening.' Arjun was angry and didn't care that Philip knew.

'Arjun, you have no idea what Ethan put me through growing up and therefore have no right to dictate to me what I should and shouldn't do.' Philip could hardly focus on Arjun as his head was nodding from side to side and his eyes were half closed and fluttering from too much wine.

'This isn't working for me,' Arjun yelled.

'Fine, then let's move to a different pub then, a quieter one.' Philip stood to leave but drained his glass first.

'No, I don't mean this pub, I mean us. I don't like what I am finding out about you Philip and it makes me uneasy that you'd let someone die. It's been playing on my mind since I found out.'

Philip sat back down and just looked as best he could at Arjun, but his focus wasn't great.

'Screw you bar boy, what does it have to do with you?'

Two more drinks arrived that had been ordered via the pub's app.

'Great, just what you need, more alcohol. It's over Philip! I'll get a new job. I'm going to the toilet and then I'm going home.'

'Don't be silly you just don't understand my life, that's all.'

'I know I don't, but after tonight I really don't care to.'

As Arjun stood up, unbeknown to him his mobile phone had slipped out of his pocket and onto the seat. As soon as he had entered the toilet, Philip leaned over and picked up the phone. It was password protected, but Philip had remembered the number from watching Arjun entering it. 1-2-4-5-7-8. The phone opened up and Philip went straight to the photo app. Luckily there were only a few pictures held on the phone. A few of his family, especially the younger brother who did look an awful lot like Arjun and the two Philip wanted to see were still there. The pictures of their first night together, the selfies of them in bed together. Quickly Philip closed the app and opened WhatsApp. He opened the 'Family Singh' group and added the two pictures and pressed send.

'Let's see how you like being judged.'

Philip downed both drinks that had just been delivered, put Arjun's phone on the table and stepped out of the pub and then wandered down the street laughing to himself. People were standing out of his way as he went. Some were pointing at him, as he was laughing aloud to himself. At one-point Philip tripped but luckily fell into a pile of bin bags that were by the side of the road, so he didn't hurt himself. However, it did take him a while to get himself back up again and when he did, he tripped and fell down again. This caused him to start giggling and then he did his favourite thing and farted as loud as he could. Philip was now sitting on the pavement next to sacks of rubbish and was singing to himself.

'Screw the lot of you!' he shouted out and tried to stand up.

The next thing he was aware of was sitting in a car that was hopefully an Uber and more importantly taking him home.

'If you're going to puke mate then give me warning to pull over,' pleaded his driver.

Philip didn't respond as he was too busy looking at his phone, especially the last message which had been from Jacob.

'I am warning you Philip, if you ever send that video, then you will pay for it.'

'Well guess what Mr Spencer, you don't scare me, you don't scare me at all. In fact, I think Mrs Spencer needs to know what type of man she is married to.'

'Did you say something mate?' Asked the driver.

'No, sorry, just talking to myself,' the slurred words were barely audible.

As he had done with Arjun's phone, Philip opened up his WhatsApp and searched for Tanvi. When he had found her, he started to up-load the video of Jacob and Kate. Once it had finished up-loading he pressed send.

11:45pm

Philip staggered up his garden path after paying his driver, who was relieved Philip hadn't been sick. He struggled to get his key into the lock and therefore stood in the cold longer than necessary. Once he was in, he went straight upstairs and removed his clothes. Despite being drunk he put his clothes where they needed to be, either in the washing basket or put back on hangers and placed into the wardrobe.

He staggered downstairs, luckily not tripping and falling and went through into the kitchen. As he went to the fridge he had a strange feeling he was being watched. Reluctantly he went over to the window above the sink and looked into his garden. He hated doing this, but there was nothing to be seen, so relieved he went back over to the fridge and opened a fresh bottle of wine and poured himself a large glass and headed back upstairs to his bedroom.

As he sat in his bed he scrolled through his phone, but as soon as he saw the message that he had sent Tanvi, he shuddered and dropped the phone.

'I'm going to have such a bad head on me tomorrow,' Philip said as he picked up his wine glass and took a mouthful.

Sitting there, he tried to contemplate tonight's events, from talking to Ethan and Adam, to the text from Jacob and the disaster of an evening with Arjun. Philip thought he heard a noise in the garden. This type of thing terrified him and at moments like this he hated living by himself. He climbed slowly off his bed and headed over to the window.

'Why are you doing this? You know you're frightened!' Philip thought to himself trying to ease his nerves.

As he looked into his garden his worst fears were realised. Standing in his garden staring up at his window was the clown. Waving at him and laughing. Philip quickly turned from the window and felt on the bed for his phone. He wasn't able to focus too well, but eventually found it.

'Get a picture this time, don't fail,' he slurred to himself.

With his phone in his hand, he opened up the camera app, pointed the phone into the garden, and took two pictures before the clown disappeared. He then got back into bed and took a large mouthful of his wine until only about a third remained and then looked at the two pictures he had just taken. Sadly, they were both extremely blurred or was that just Philip's vision at this precise time, but he could just make out that it was a clown. Philip then put his phone under the duvet and passed out.

30:

8th December 2017

Arjun

01:30am

Arjun sat in the Uber that was taking him home and felt sick to his stomach. He had come out of the toilet to find Philip gone, but his phone which he hadn't realised was missing until he saw it, had been left on the table. He had picked it up and saw he'd received WhatsApp messages from his family. Arjun then saw why he had messages. The pictures of him and Philip in bed together and one of the pictures showed them kissing.

Rajan: *'You disgust me, why would you send us this filth'*

Mrs Singh: *'Arjun, what is going on? Why are you sending us pictures of you and this ghastly man?'*

Rohit: *'Arjun, your phone has been hacked or something, be careful coming home as Rajan is going mad'* This message had been sent just to Arjun and not via the family chat.

Arjun had been so shocked by what Philip had done, that his first Uber had taken him to Philip's house to have it out with him. The bedroom light was on, but after walking around the street for a while Arjun lost his nerve, nevertheless he wanted to hurt Philip.

The driver seemed to be taking his time and this suited Arjun, as he was in no rush to get home. His thoughts turned to Philip and why he would have done such a vindictive thing. What did he have to gain by doing it?

Rajan: *'You'd better be on your way home to explain yourself.'*

'What can I tell them?' thought Arjun. 'Maybe I could say that the photo had been altered,' he then realised the stupidity of this and that it was time to now acknowledge to them who he was.

At least he had Rohit on his side. He wasn't sure about his mother, but Rajan would hate him.

'Oh, damn, this is such a mess!' he reflected to himself.

After another ten minutes of having a million things going around in his head and the queasiness feeling only getting worse, Arjun heard the driver's voice in the distance.

'We are here buddy.'

Once the car had driven off, Arjun stood on the pavement outside his house. He was aware of the breath coming out of his mouth, but somehow wasn't feeling the intense cold, despite the temperature of this freezing December night. Shouting was coming from his house, but he couldn't make out what was being said but he knew it was because of him and this made him feel distressed. Everything inside him told him to leave, run and face this another day, but he knew Rohit was probably trying to defend him and he couldn't leave him to deal with this on his own.

As he walked slowly towards the front door he took his keys out of his pocket. This evening was meant to have been fun, with his so-called boyfriend, but it had turned into absolute chaos and he now didn't know how it was going to end.

'Philip Oakes, you'd better be suffering wherever you are,' Arjun said through gritted teeth.

As he got close to the front door the voices were now clearly heard and they weren't encouraging him to enter the house.

'It's disgusting and he needs to know. Our father would be revolted by his actions,' Rajan's voice was terribly angry.

Arjun slowly put the key into the lock and turned it, gradually pushing the door open. The first thing he saw was his older brother yelling in the face of his younger brother. Arjun flew into the house begging for Rajan to leave Rohit alone.

'Get off him I said!' wailed Arjun, as he pushed his heavier brother.

Without letting go of Rohit's collar, Rajan lashed out and hit Arjun across the face. Mrs Singh was crying as she watched.

'Stop it! Just stop it!' she was sobbing.

Arjun ran back at Rajan and pushed him off of Rohit. Rajan fell to the floor and his substantial weight was making it difficult for him to get himself back up again.

'You disgust me,' he yelled at his brother who was standing above him with clenched fists.

'I'm gay Rajan, get over it. We don't all live our lives like we were dead!'

Mrs Singh was now weeping as her three sons were all yelling and bawling.

'Please boys, stop this, please!'

None of the three seemed to take any notice of her.

Rajan was now back on his feet and shrieking straight into Arjun's face.

'There is nothing wrong with Arjun being gay,' yelled Rohit. 'He is our brother and that's all that should matter.'

Rajan looked at Rohit in absolute horror.

'You repulse me Rohit, for not seeing this as the abhorrence that it is.'

Arjun now grabbed his older brother by his T-Shirt and pulled his face into his. Rajan knew he didn't have the same level of strength as his brother.

'You leave Rohit out of this. He is the brother that I care most for and you have no right to talk to him like that. You are a sad, lonely and miserable excuse of a man. Don't you dare judge me for who I am. You are meant to be the head of the household since dad died and look at you, nothing but an overweight, slug of a human being. You disgust me as much as I revolt you! '

Rohit, like his mother, was sobbing as he viewed the scene in front of him. Mrs Singh was trying to break up the two brothers as they continued to bellow at each other, but in the heat of the moment she received a fist to the side of her cheek. Neither brother was sure who had hit her, but she fell back against the wall and continued to wail.

'STOP it!' cried Rohit, 'please, please, please, just stop this.'

Arjun pulled away from Rajan and bent down to help his mother.

'I'm so sorry Mum that you got hurt but I am gay and I am not sorry for that and it's something that you will have to get used to.'

These words seemed to spark off the anger in Rajan again as he flew at his brother and knocked him to the floor. He sat on top of Arjun and punched him in the face.

'Our mother never has to get used to the fact that you are evil.' Rajan then threw another punch as Arjun tried to push his brother off.

'GET OFF HIM!' screamed Rohit, who was now hysterical and sobbing as if his heart was breaking. 'He can be who he wants to be and I love him because of that! GET OFF HIM!'

Rohit was now inconsolable and was moving around in a haphazard way.

'He is EVIL!' screeched Rajan, as he went to punch Arjun again. His strength coming from sheer anger.

'STOP!' cried Rohit. The situation was so traumatising for the young man that he turned to run away from the devastating scene in front of him. Arjun had left the front door open when he'd arrived and Rohit ran out into the garden. There he stood and sobbed as loud as his shaking body would allow. Inside the house he could still see the violence happening.

'STOP!' he screamed as he turned and ran into the street and then into the road.

He only stood there for a matter of moments when a car came from nowhere and hit Rohit hard and it then drove off. In the wing mirrors the driver could see three people were running to the person who had been hit. One of these people started to cradle the young man in his arms.

The driver turned into the next road, pulled over to the side, and started laughing. The laughing soon turned into hysterics.

'So that's the end of you Arjun.'

She had parked up to watch the Singh's house and couldn't believe her luck when 'he' had stepped into the road. In a split second she made the decision to knock him down.

As the car started up again, Rebecca had no idea that she had just hit the wrong brother.

31:

8th December 2017

Jacob

9:00am

The smell of bacon wafting up the stairs from the kitchen is probably what gently awoke Jacob from a good night's sleep. He hadn't as yet opened his eyes but was welcoming the delicious aroma. Stretching his limbs felt like the correct thing to do and made the start to the morning feel good.

As he opened his eyes, he could see that it was one of those crisp winter mornings where the sky was blue and the sun was brightly shining. Downstairs he could hear Tanvi going about the kitchen, obviously making his favourite, a bacon sandwich and real coffee, not instant.

Jacob was however aware that he couldn't hear the children and this was unusual as both were normally up by 6:30am. Rory, when he was awake, was never quiet. Lying there in his comfy bed, he knew he needed to go to the toilet but was reluctant to move, though when nature calls she needs to be listened to.

When he got back to his bed he plumped up his pillows, got in and awaited the arrival of his breakfast. He was on a day off today and was looking forward to it. He reached over to the bedside cabinet and picked up his phone. There was nothing of much interest on the screen. Just two notifications, one telling him it was his turn on scrabble and the other was from the BBC news app.

He could hear Tanvi coming up the stairs, so he put his phone down and got himself ready for his food. Tanvi walked into the bedroom with a tray and placed it on the bed.

'Wow, this is a lovely surprise, thank you my darling,' Jacob said, smiling at his wife.

'You're welcome and I hope you enjoy it,' was her reply.

'I can't hear the kids, are they awake? I am assuming not as I can't hear them,' Jacob asked.

Before she answered, Tanvi went over to the wardrobe and took out a large suitcase.

'My mother collected them this morning at about 7:00am, they are staying with my parents for at least a few days.'

'Nice, just the two of us then. Why the case? Are we going away?' Jacob seemed confused.

'You are, I'm not!' was the curt response.

Jacob stopped eating the sandwich he had in his hand and glared strangely at his wife.

'What is that supposed to mean?'

'What it means, is that the bacon sandwich you are eating is the last meal you will ever eat in this house. What it means, is that you are the scum of the earth. What it means, is that you are a foul, disgusting, cheating piece of filth. Now finish your breakfast, pack your case and leave.' Teardrops were falling down her face as she said these words to the dumbstruck man sitting in the bed.

'I don't understand Tanvi, why are you behaving like this?'

'I awoke this morning to a WhatsApp message from your so-called friend, Philip.'

Jacob's eyes widened as he adjusted himself to be sitting more upright.

'Well, judging by the frightened expression on your face you seem to know what the message was!' Tanvi was now pacing around the room as she glared hard at her husband. 'But just in case you don't, Philip sent me a video of you having sex with a woman.'

Jacob now got out of the bed and for the first time ever he felt uncomfortable being naked in front of his wife. He rushed to the bathroom to get his bathrobe and came back to the bedroom.

'I can't believe he sent it to you, I am so sorry.' He went to touch his wife, but she flinched and dramatically pulled away from him.

'Don't you even consider touching me, just get dressed and get out of this house. Oh and the message sent with the video was, *'she isn't the only one, there have been many more.'*

Jacob looked at his wife, then lowered his face to face the ground, he was embarrassed and ashamed.

'I'm so sorry,' he said.

'Actually, there was no message, just the video, but thank you for confirming my suspicions. Now GET OUT!'

1:30pm

Jacob had spent most of the morning and early afternoon pleading with his wife to forgive him. He had tried to get hold of Philip and had called him three times but there had been no answer, which wasn't exactly surprising.

He had now been sitting in his car for about an hour and in between crying and pleading phone calls to Tanvi, he had sent Philip a damning email.

'Why? Philip, why?' was all he could muster to say as he sobbed into his hands.

Jacob knew the email was probably going to be deleted rather than read, but he felt he needed to do something. Tanvi was standing at the lounge window and could see her husband just sitting in the car, he glanced up and saw her staring at him. She turned and walked away from view.

With anger surging through him, Jacob started the car and headed to Philip's house. As he drove, he just couldn't believe that his best friend had done this to him, had basically destroyed his marriage and devastated his family life. With the extreme anger coursing through his body, Jacob kept banging the steering wheel with his hand to try to relieve just a small amount of the rage and frustration.

As he arrived at the house, he rang the doorbell continuously and banged with his fists on the front door.

'Answer the door you bastard!'

Mrs Ferres came to her window as soon as she heard the first fist thump on the door. As she looked out, she saw a screeching, almost tortured soul pacing in the front garden. Jacob was aware she was spying on him, but he really didn't care.

'PHILIP!' he shouted as he started to kick the door, 'GET OUT HERE, NOW!'

There was no answer, Jacob went around to the back of the house to look through the kitchen window, but he saw nothing so returned to the front.

'PHILIP!' he yelled.

When he got no answer, he finally assumed that Philip wasn't in and got back into his car.

'I will be back,' he said to himself through gritted teeth, 'and when I do, you are going to wish you'd never been born. I hate you Philip Oakes.'

Jacob drove away, tasting the salty tears that had passed over his lips.

32:

1989

Philip aged Eight

It was the usual type of evening with Mr Oakes and his two sons sitting around the dinner table all eating what Mrs Temple had made them for their dinner, in near silence. Once the food was finished, Philip had gone into the lounge to watch a Star Wars film on video. Mrs Temple cleared up and went home, Mr Oakes returned to his study and Ethan must have either gone out, or into his room. This meant that Philip was able to enjoy his film in peace.

It was Saturday tomorrow, so it meant he was allowed to stay up a little later than on a school night. As the film was coming to an end he had been surprised that his brother hadn't come in and disturbed him. Ethan liked annoying his brother, especially when he was watching films. Philip used films as a form of escapism from his lonely home life.

The credits for the film ended, Philip took himself into the kitchen and poured himself a glass of chocolate milk, he also grabbed a few biscuits and then headed to his bedroom. As he walked past the study he called out.

'Goodnight Dad.'

He waited for a moment or two, then got his response.

'Goodnight Philip.' His father's voice always sounded stern and vacant.

Walking into his bedroom he was aware he could hear no sounds coming from his brother's room, so decided that Ethan had probably gone out to a friend's house. He was fourteen now so was allowed. Philip loved it when Ethan went out.

Putting his milk and biscuits on his bedside table, he undressed and put on his pyjamas. Brushing his teeth could wait until he had finished his snacks. Before getting into bed he turned on his night light so he could read and then turned off the main light. Once in bed he opened up his Spider-

Man comic and took a mouthful of his milk. He was feeling happy and this wasn't a common occurrence.

As he turned the pages, Philip thought he heard a creaking noise and quickly looked up, but there was nothing to be seen. This was an old house and therefore strange noises often occurred. He went back to his comic. Doctor Octopus had just entered the story and it was getting exciting.

Philip picked up a biscuit and had some more of his milk. Another creaking noise and again Philip looked up, a little more concerned this time but again nothing to be seen. As he continued to read, from the corner of his eye he saw a slight movement opposite his bed, on the other side of the room. He lowered his comic. The door of his wardrobe began very slowly to open and a white gloved hand slowly started to emerge. Philip swallowed hard but couldn't take his eyes away from what was happening in front of him. He could feel his heart racing and was aware his hands were shaking. He went to get out of bed, ready to run, but the wardrobe door opened up more and a colourful arm was now visible. Philip stood up and was transfixed by the arm. His legs were now beginning to shake as his heart started to beat faster and felt like it was getting ready to burst out of his chest. The wardrobe door sprung open and a grotesque creature jumped out and bellowed.

'PHILIP!'

The clown ran at the terrified child baring its large, fanged teeth and its painted white face and red lips.

'PHILIP!' It screeched for a second time, as it again rushed forward.

Philip now started to squeal, as he jumped from foot to foot and was shaking all over. His screams turned to hysteria. He was aware that his left leg was very wet, as the urine trickled down his leg. The clown was now staring at him, laughing, waving and pointing to the wet patches on the pyjamas. Philip was shrieking and sobbing as he turned towards his bed and vomited.

'What the hell is going on?' Asked Mr Oakes as he stormed into the bedroom.

Ethan had now taken off his wig, fangs and red nose and was staring at his father. He knew he'd be punished but sitting in that wardrobe for a few hours after dinner had been worth it. It couldn't have gone any better.

Mr Oakes surveyed the scene he was presented with, looking hard at both of his sons.

'Ethan, you're grounded for a week, now go to your room.'

Chuckling as he went, Ethan grinned at Philip as he left and went off to his own room. Philip stood by his bed silently sobbing and still shaking. He was also feeling cold due to wetting himself.

'Philip, take your bed linen and put it in the bathroom. Take off your pyjamas and place them there too. Mrs Temple can deal with them tomorrow when she arrives, I will leave her a note.'

The frightened lad just stood and looked at his father. He wanted to be cuddled and told everything would be alright.

'When you have done that,' continued Mr Oakes, 'go and have a shower and then put some clean pyjamas on. I suggest you get the sleeping bag from the cupboard and sleep in that for tonight.'

With that, he turned and went back down the stairs to his study.

Philip started to weep louder as he tried to take off the soiled bed linen. Through his bedroom wall, he heard laughter.

33:

8th December 2017

Philip: The evening of his death

5:00pm

Philip looked over Arjun's shoulder and watched Ethan and Adam getting into their car. However, at the last minute a distraught Adam jumped out from the passenger side and ran off down the street. Ethan drove off in the opposite direction from where his home was. Philip then turned his attention back to the man in front of him, who appeared like he was going to punch him.

'What do you want?'

'You're an absolute bastard,' Arjun said with pure hatred in his voice.

'Why?' said a confused Philip. 'What have I done?'

'You know exactly what you did.'

'I don't have any idea what you are talking about,' Philip said with an edge of anger.

'You sent the pictures of you and me in bed together to my WhatsApp family group last night.'

'Did I?' Philip said, sounding very muddled.

'Why would you do such a horrible thing?' Arjun was close to tears.

'I didn't know I had.'

Philip was really trying hard to think back to last night, but nothing much was coming to him. He had refused to read his messages today, so had a limited idea of anything he may have done the previous night. Then he swiftly remembered the evening in question, when the pictures were taken.

'I didn't have the pictures on my phone, we took them on yours,' Philip said. 'Also, I don't have your family group on my phone, so what are you going on about?'

Arjun looked to the left and indicated to Philip that his neighbour, Mrs Ferres was gazing out of her window.

'I don't care Arjun, I am not in the mood to have a massive argument, so I am not inviting you in.'

Arjun tried to step forward into the house but was blocked.

'I went to the toilet last night and when I was gone you used my phone which had slipped out of my pocket and sent the pictures to my family.'

'Your phone is password protected, isn't it?' Asked Philip.

'Yes, but you must have seen me put the code in at some point.'

A faint memory started to form in Philip's head and then recognition started to show on his face.

'Oh, shit Arjun, I did.' Philip was ashamed. 'I was so drunk last night, we weren't getting on and somehow I thought it would be funny.'

'FUNNY!' screeched Arjun, straight into Philip's face. 'MY BROTHER IS FIGHTING FOR HIS LIFE AND YOU SAY IT WAS MEANT TO BE FUNNY!'

Arjun was exhausted with his shouting. He was also crying and quaking with emotion.

'What do you mean?' Philip asked with genuine concern.

'Rohit was standing up for me to Rajan about me being gay and the emotional situation got too much for him and in the heat of the argument he ran out of the house and into the road and was hit by a car.'

'Oh, Arjun, I am so sorry,' Philip said, 'but how is that my fault?'

Arjun just stood on the doorstep still aware that the neighbour was watching him. He looked directly at Philip and then with as much aggression as he could muster he screeched,

'I COULD KILL YOU!'

'Why, what has it got to do with me?' Asked Philip in a mystified way.

'If you hadn't sent the pictures, then there wouldn't have been an argument and Rohit wouldn't be lying in Intensive care after having surgery to have a clot removed from his brain.'

'Go home Arjun.'

'You're pure evil,' the young man said in a defeated voice.

Arjun just stood at the front door as it was shut in his face. He sobbed hard as he turned and walked away. As he reached the road he glanced back at the house and bawled.

'YOU'LL PAY FOR THIS PHILIP!'

7:30pm

Philip had promised himself that after last night and the way he felt this morning, that he would not be having any alcohol this evening. However, after the arguments with Ethan and then Arjun, he felt in need of a drink. His liver was probably in need of resuscitating, but to hell with it. He was sick to death of everything being his fault. Everybody blamed him for the issues in their own lives.

Philip was sorry to hear about Rohit and hoped the lad would come out of intensive care. Sending the pictures was a stupid thing to do and he accepted that, however, he didn't ask the kid to go running into the road without looking. Arjun had been so mad and Philip had never seen such hatred in someone's eyes before. He had seen anger and violence behind someone's eyes, but not such hatred.

Whilst he was having this melancholy moment about Rohit, his thoughts turned to Adam. As he left earlier, Philip could see the pleading in his eyes.

'What was it about eyes this afternoon?' Philip thought to himself.

He was now alone and was determined to relax and enjoy his evening. His clothes were off, the open log fire was happily burning away, he had poured himself a glass of Sauvignon Blanc and he had put on his favourite film, The Green Mile, with Tom Hanks.

'There is something about Tom's voice that was soothing in a crisis,' Philip reflected.

Using an app on his phone he had ordered a pizza, which was due to arrive within the next fifteen minutes, so all he needed to do was wait and enjoy his wine.

His phone chimed which let him know he had received a text message. It was from Ethan. He didn't bother to read it.

'They can all go screw themselves,' he softly spoke to himself.

As he sat there watching his film, Philip did think about recent events and fall outs. He was aware he'd already done this whilst walking around the park, but he couldn't stop himself. The one he was most upset about was Jacob. He didn't give a toss about Rebecca and Arjun was unfortunate as he was fond of him. Ethan however was a completely different thing altogether.

'Bugger the whole lot of them,' he snorted.

He grabbed at his wine glass and was shocked to see that there was only a mouthful left. He hadn't realised he had drunk it so quickly. He picked up the glass and headed into the kitchen to replenish it. He put his phone next to his wallet and watch (which was still on the worktop), as he didn't want to look at it anymore this evening. It was all too depressing each time he looked at it.

Philip turned and caught sight of himself in the window over the sink. It was dark outside, so his reflection was noticeably clear. He had put weight on, quite a bit of weight and the evidence was staring back at him. It did at first make him feel sad and frustrated and he knew extremely well that wine and a Hawaiian pizza weren't going to make him slimmer.

'Tomorrow is another day, think about a diet then,' he said as he laughed.

He grabbed at his growing belly and jiggled it around and sniggered to himself.

Knowing that his pizza would soon be here, he took out a plate. He hated eating straight out of the pizza box, it was somehow a dirty thing to do in his opinion. He also took out a sharp knife so he could re-cut it into triangles. The pizza place never did it enough and that meant tearing at the pizza and this was another thing he disliked doing. He knew he had his quirks, but he liked that about himself, even if no one else did. He opened the fridge and took out his bottle of wine and filled his glass up to the top. He then took a gulp and topped it up again before putting the bottle back. Standing in the kitchen he could hear Tom Hanks's voice coming from the lounge. Taking another look at himself in the window, Philip grinned and took his wine back into the lounge. He had just sat down when he heard the moped arrive outside. This meant his pizza was here. He jumped up and ran to the window. It was the young man who had delivered to him many times over the past three or so months. This would be fun.

He went into the hallway and put on his dressing gown but only very loosely tied it up. The doorbell rang and Philip waited for a few seconds before answering. As he opened the door, he was aware that his gown had started to gape in the middle. This excited him.

'Evening Mr Oakes,' the delivery lad said with an air of cheekiness.

'I've told you that you can call me Philip.'

As this was about the ninth time he had delivered to this address, he was used to the way Philip was presenting himself. The first few times had been uncomfortable, but now it didn't bother him. In fact, it made him sad to see how a grown overweight man got his kicks.

'Nice to see you again,' said Philip. 'How are you this evening?'

'All good mate, cheers.'

Philip looked closely at the lad and thought he recognised him. Not from delivering pizza but from somewhere else.

'Do you come into my pub? The Lemon Tree?' Philip asked.

'Might do,' the lad answered quickly. 'You do realise that your knob is on show?' he said changing the subject.

'Is it,' Philip said, leering at the lad. 'If you're not busy you're welcome to come in and have some of the pizza with me.'

The young lad just shook his head.

'Nah mate, I'll pass this time.'

He began to walk away, shaking his head.

'This time!' Philip called out, allowing the gown to become fully opened. 'Does that mean you like what you see and there might be a next time?'

'Listen pops,' the lad was suddenly assertive. 'I prefer my conquests to have a much slimmer body and a very different frontal arrangement.'

'Pops!' Philip said bemused, 'you are a cheeky git.'

'Have a good evening sir.'

'What's your name,' shouted Philip.

'Lewis,' was the quick response.

'Well Lewis, come and see 'Pops' again and maybe we can change your way of thinking.'

Lewis noticed as Philip said this that he was also touching himself. He turned and walked away. As he reached his moped, he glanced back and saw him still standing by his door.

'You are very soon going to regret talking to me like that!' Lewis said under his breath.

Philip shut the door tittering to himself and was aware that the lad was still outside on his moped. Finding his next delivery address Philip assumed. There was something about Lewis that reminded him of someone he used to know. Philip put the pizza down on the hall table and ran up to the front bedroom. He looked out of the window but there was now no sign of the lad. Coming back slowly downstairs, he picked up the pizza and headed into the kitchen. He had the beginnings of an erection.

'Damn you Lewis!'

He put the pizza on the worktop and opened the box, picked up the knife, and started cutting up the pizza. His tummy was making noises and he couldn't wait to start devouring the food. He loved pizza and especially with pineapple and ham.

As he was preparing his food he heard a noise in the garden and looked up. Staring at him through the kitchen window, with its head as close to the glass as it could get and eyes wide open was the clown grinning at him.

'Fuck!' screamed Philip and nearly lost his balance. 'Jesus fucking Christ!'

The clown looked straight at Philip and smirked with its large, exaggerated red lips and painted dark eerie eyes. It then used its right hand and waved, just using its fingers and appeared to start laughing at him.

Philip dropped the knife onto the pizza and glared at the face. The clown just looked at him. Philip's worst nightmare was now glaring at him with only a pane of glass between them. His body started to shake and he felt dizzy and queasy. He focused directly on the clown and couldn't stop himself, as much as he wanted to.

'Was it different this time? How could it be?' Philip thought to himself.

He was frozen to the spot and when the clown started to blow kisses at him, Philip felt frightened and panic-stricken. His head felt ready to burst and he didn't know what to do for the best. Then suddenly Philip darted towards the back door, still looking at the creature who was glaring at him. The clown saw his fast movement and it quickly ran off. Philip opened the backdoor as speedily as he could. He was shaking so much that he couldn't turn the key at first.

Once the door was open he dashed into the back garden and around the side of his house. Where this bravery was coming from he had no idea, but fear and stress had taken over his body and he had just gone into action mode. He found himself standing in the street, his dressing gown was fully open. He was shaking and shouting out.

'WHERE THE FUCK ARE YOU?'

He saw his neighbour's curtain open and witnessed Mrs Ferres looking directly at him. She indicated with her eyes that his gown was open. Philip didn't care but he pulled it around himself and held it in place.

'WHERE ARE YOU? YOU BASTARD?' yelled Philip.

He looked up and down the street but there was nothing to be seen. Where had the evil, vile thing gone to? He stood in the street for about 5 minutes hoping, or maybe hoping not, to see the clown. He wanted, no needed, to know who it was and why it had been terrorising him since October. 'Did they know he was petrified of clowns? They had to,' Philip thought to himself.

Still shaking and feeling sick, Philip walked back into his garden and towards his back door. There were a million thoughts running around in his head and he was terrified. He stepped into his house and turned to lock the back door as he needed to feel safe. His bravery had been short lived and he craved to feel protected. He wanted to phone the police and maybe this time they would do something more concrete to help him.

Philip looked up and into the glass of the back door and screamed. He turned dramatically around and gazed at the person standing in front of him.

'What the bloody hell are you doing in my house?'

The intruder just looked directly at him.

'GET THE FUCK OUT OF MY HOUSE!' thundered Philip. 'What are you doing here?'

Philip quickly scanned the situation in front of him and the realisation hit him. This was the unmasked clown. The wig was now on the counter by the pizza, but the white gloves were still on.

'You?' Philip said, shocked. 'It was you terrorising me since October?'

The intruder winked and then shrugged their shoulders and could tell that Philip was uncontrollably shaking and saw that rage was building up in his face.

Philip was so angry that he ran at the clown. The bravery had returned. He wanted to hurt the person standing in front of him and needed to cause pain, enough to reflect what he had been through for the past few months.

He didn't know quite what had happened, but he was aware that there was a sharp pain in his chest. He knew that he could hear Tom Hanks' voice coming from the lounge and was aware of the clown's painted face looking into his eyes and lastly he knew he could smell pizza. Philip stared back into the dark eyes of his attacker and fell face down onto the floor. Already there was blood seeping from his body and onto the kitchen floor where the now murderer was standing. Stepping back and viewing the scene, the clown placed the knife by Philip's head and picked up the wig, kicked the body and then stepped over it to leave via the back door. Before they left, they grabbed up a piece of the pizza out of the box and picked off some of the mozzarella from the pizza to eat on the way out.

34:

11th December 2017

Isaac

7:00am

Isaac Davidson was forty-one and shared a detached bungalow with his younger brother Alan, who was thirty-three. They had lived together since Alan's car accident eleven years ago. The driver who had caused the accident, had walked out of his car without a scratch. Alan had been left unable to walk again.

Following the accident, Alan was allowed home after fourteen weeks in the hospital. Isaac had been the main carer for a while thanks to his work allowing him some compassionate leave. A private nurse had also been hired to help. Alan had suffered with severe depression and lacked any motivation to try to help himself. The psychological recovery had taken so much longer than the physical.

Today the brothers lived a happy life together and shared the same interests of fishing, board games, seafood, especially oysters and white Rioja. They also had individual interests and in Isaac's case they were going to the theatre, tennis, cooking and currently learning Swedish. For Alan, it was wine, photography, city breaks (with Isaac when his work allowed) and practising mindfulness. In the evening, the two of them looked through recipe books and planned different cuisines for the coming month. Isaac would then cook them and Alan's part was to find the perfect wine to go with each recipe.

The two men worked well together, which was fortunate, as they only had each other. Relationships seemed to have passed them both by. Alan had had a girlfriend at the time of his accident and they had been together just over a year. However, he was concerned he would be a huge burden, had ended that relationship as soon as he could after the crash and had remained single ever since. Isaac on the other hand had never really grasped dating. In his late teens and early twenties there had been a few sexual encounters, but none of them had led to a long-term partner. He was a strikingly handsome man, very noble with defined features and he had alluring, crystal blue eyes. His brown hair was slightly thinning, but like the other male members of his family they had all lost their hair mid-twenties, including Alan, he had done well to keep as much as he had. Body wise he was also doing OK. He was not overweight, maybe the slight beginnings of a protruding belly, but equally not worried to take off his top on a beach and show off his once gym perfect body.

'I'm just getting into the shower,' called Alan from the hallway.

'Coolio fella, then get my breakfast!' was Isaac's quirky reply.

Isaac was a DCI; a Detective Chief Inspector and he loved his job. When he had been to his career's lesson at school, it had been pointed out to him that he was probably destined to work at a bank, or a similar type of institution. He had always excelled in exams and in tests he was usually the top scorer. When it came to making choices he knew crime fascinated him. Watching Agatha Christie's Death on the Nile as a child had enthralled him, especially the moment where the murderer was being revealed. It was almost a done deal that in his mind he would end up in the world of crime, especially murder.

As he lay in his bed he could hear Alan finishing up in their specially adapted wet room, so he knew he'd be cooking breakfast as soon as he had dried himself and dressed. In the Davidson household the younger brother did breakfast and the older brother did dinner. Lunches were usually made together the night before and placed in the fridge ready for the next day.

The detective stretched out his arms and legs and it felt amazing. He then recoiled himself and started to count. At one hundred he'd get up and have a shower, however the rain that was lashing down outside made him hide under his duvet and count to two hundred instead.

'Isaac, I'm going to start breakfast now, so you have twenty minutes to haul your arse out of your pit and get it into the shower. I'm doing

Cumberland sausages with homemade baked beans, grilled tomatoes and sourdough toast from the bread I made at the weekend.' Alan knew this would be all the incentive his brother needed.

As he lay in his bed, Isaac realised he enjoyed hearing his name said aloud. At work, he was only ever known as Guv, Davidson, or mostly just Sir. He flung back his duvet and headed straight into the shower. As he passed the kitchen he could already smell the coffee and it smelt good.

He stood under the hot water with it cascading over his body and he wondered what the day would bring. The thing he loved most about his job was never knowing what would happen from one day to the next. This meant there was always excitement but also constant learning. People always amazed him from case to case as to how they reacted to the devastation around them. As he turned his face towards the shower and took a full blast of water, he heard his brother calling through the door.

'Ten minutes and it'll be on the table.'

'OK, I'll be ready in time,' was his reply.

As he walked back into his bedroom he could smell the sausages and he then appreciated how hungry he was feeling. He dressed quickly and glanced at his phone that was still plugged into the charger. There were no messages yet, so today might be a quiet day. Funds didn't allow for a work phone, so his personal phone doubled up.

Isaac walked into the kitchen just as his brother was dishing up the food and it smelled great. The coffee was strong and smelt wonderful and that was a perfect way to start the day.

'What does your day have in store for you?' Isaac asked his brother.

Alan worked in the local college within the photography department and enjoyed every moment of it. He loved watching his student's faces as they worked on the given assignments each week.

'We are doing 'things with stripes' this week,' Alan replied.

'I see, hence the blue and white striped jumper you are wearing?'

Alan looked down at what he had on and rolled his eyes.

'I hadn't realised I had put this old jumper on, I'm so stupid,' both were laughing now.

After breakfast had been eaten and dishes loaded into the dishwasher, the two finalised getting ready to leave the house. Isaac was first to go and as he opened the front door to leave, he heard his brother's usual words.

'Keys, both house and car, phone and money?'

Isaac went through his pockets to check he had everything. His brother knew him so well, however on this occasion the checklist was complete.

'All present and correct. Have a good day and see you later,' shouted the detective as he shut the front door and headed to his car ready to see what delights the day ahead was going to bring.

10:00am

Isaac sat at his desk draining the last few drops of coffee from his 'Doctor Who' mug, which Alan had given him for Christmas. They were both huge fans of the programme but tended to keep that to themselves. No-one had ever questioned him about the mug.

'The amount of paperwork/admin this job requires is getting to ridiculous levels,' he thought to himself, shaking his head. 'More time is spent at a computer than on the streets solving crimes.'

Isaac looked around the room and saw that most people were hard at it with administration work. There were about twenty people who worked out of this space and ten of those were members of Isaac's team. The place was in real need of re-decorating as the paint was peeling off the walls in many areas and the small kitchen area was depressing to see. Isaac had once suggested that the team all came in one weekend and paint the place themselves, but this had been met with sour faces, hence he didn't raise this subject again. The carpet had seen better days too. The crime board which stood off to one side had been wiped clean and was ready for when the next misdemeanour occurred.

People-watching was of particular interest to the DCI, especially amongst his work force. Emily Morgans who was his Detective Sergeant was a tall woman of slim build, she had what was described as mousey hair that sat just above her shoulders. She was thirty and was a favourite with the others. She was also a hard grafter who excelled at her job. Isaac knew he couldn't keep her much longer as a promotion was bound to start calling soon.

A phone started to ring and this snapped him out of his thoughts about Emily. He looked around the room to see where it was coming from before realising it was coming from his jacket which was hung on the back of his chair.

'Davidson,' he said into the phone.

Emily looked over at her boss and saw the changing expression on his face. Over the past few years she had become familiar with what his face was saying even when she couldn't hear the conversation. This face was saying he was talking to someone about a murder. She recognised the raising up of his left eyebrow and his lips were constantly moving as if kissing the air. Emily enjoyed working in this team and especially with her DCI. He was a kind, fair and knowledgeable man.

Isaac ended his call and again scanned around the room.

'Hey team,' his voice boomed across the office.

Those who worked with him came over and Emily led the way.

'There has been a fatal incident involving a male. His cleaner arrived this morning and found her employer dead in the kitchen. Forensics have already arrived at the scene.'

There was a sea of nodding heads just glaring back at their boss.

'Emily with me, the rest of you start clearing some of your paperwork so you're ready to start assisting us once we have a better idea of what has happened.'

'Sir!' was the word used by all of the team as they hurried back to their desks.

Isaac grabbed his coat and winked at his DS.

'Ready Emily?'

'Ready sir!'

35:

11th December 2017

Crime scene

11:00am

The detectives pulled up outside Philip's house and saw the crime scene tape in place. There were already lots of people standing on the streets trying to get a good glimpse at the proceedings. At this point they both put on their rubber gloves and shoe coverings and then approached the house. The police officer guarding the entrance to the garden nodded and stepped aside. As they went past him, Isaac noticed the next-door neighbour peering out of her window. Emily noticed her too.

Walking into the house the pair could smell something rotten and heard crying coming from the room on the right. They entered and saw a woman in her mid-thirties sobbing into a soggy piece of tissue, with a police officer trying to console her.

'That's the cleaner who found the body,' said a uniformed officer. 'The body is in the kitchen.'

They stepped into the kitchen. The rancid smell caused them both to take a step backward and put their hands over their noses. A member of the fully dressed forensic team handed them both a mask to try to lessen the pungent smell. Isaac started to peruse the surroundings. The kitchen was immaculate in every detail. On the worktop there was a pizza in a box with one slice missing and a small green hair-like material by the box, an expensive watch and a wallet which was rather thick. This suggested substantial amounts of cash, or a lot of cards. On the floor was the body lying face down. He was wearing a dressing gown that was splayed open rather than being tied around his waist and had nothing on his feet. There was a large brown stain where his bottom was and this indicated he had opened his bowels as he died, which was obviously contributing to the awful smell in the room. Positioned by the victim's head was a long, bladed knife stained with blood.

'Morning Alex,' Isaac addressed the lead forensic scientist. 'What have we got here?'

'Morning both,' Alex nodded in the direction of both detectives. 'Adult male, mid-thirties, overweight and first impressions I'd say he has been dead for at least 2-3 days. I haven't turned him over yet but judging by the knife and no signs of trauma so far, I assume he was stabbed on his front.'

'What are your thoughts Emily?' Isaac asked his DS.

Emily took her time to scrutinise the crime scene, taking in everything she could see before she spoke.

'Well sir, the fact the watch and wallet are still here suggests this wasn't a break in.' She took a deep breath but soon regretted it due to the smell. 'He is only wearing a dressing gown and there are no signs of any disturbance, so that implies that he probably knew the person who did this. He was in for the night as he'd ordered food in.'

'I agree,' Isaac said as he looked at Alex who was also nodding.

'His feet are filthy and have bits of gravel stuck to them, they are also cut badly and stained with blood.' Emily was walking past the body and taking in everything she could see.

'What does that either tell you or suggest to you?' Asked her DCI.

Emily pondered the question for a few moments.

'It suggests that he was outside for some reason. The cuts and blood also tell me that he must have been running around out there to cause the damage to his feet. He was probably disturbed and ran out, otherwise I assume he'd have stopped to put on some kind of footwear and maybe even have got dressed.' Isaac nodded.

Alex was finishing off all that he could before turning the body over. Photos had been taken and dustings for fingerprints had been completed. He was very thorough at his job.

Philip's body was gently turned over and more photographs were being taken from all different angles. It was clear now that the dressing gown was all he was wearing. His face was mottled in appearance and his right eye was wide open, but his left was half closed. Philip's chest was covered in his blood that had seeped out of him.

'Look there,' said Alex. 'One entry site, straight through the ribs and into the heart. Death would have been very quick, practically instant.'

Isaac crouched down and examined the knife mark, he then visually examined Philip's face and as he always did in these circumstances, he wondered what had got the victim to this moment.

'I'll know more when we get him back to my domain.' Alex said.

From the lounge, sobs could still be heard. Isaac scanned around the kitchen once more and then let Alex know that he'd seen all he needed to. The scientist could finish off as necessary and he and Emily would go and talk to the cleaner. They both left the kitchen and entered the lounge.

A face streaked with tears looked up at the two of them and then started to cry again.

'My name is DCI Davidson and this is DS Morgans,' Isaac smiled at the woman in the hope of calming her down. 'I am sorry to do this now, but can you tell me your name and what happened when you arrived this morning?'

'I'm Hester,' she said through sniffs and sobs. 'Hester Greening and I am, was, Philip's cleaner.'

Remembering how clean the kitchen was and apart from a wine glass on the table in this room, Hester was obviously excellent at her job.

'Can you go on please?' said the DS.

'I arrived at about 9:15am, I was running fifteen minutes late, but Philip never minded as long as I got my work done. He was a really nice bloke.' Hester looked concerned but continued. 'As I opened the front door, I was aware of a very unpleasant smell, but I entered the hall and went to the cupboard under the stairs where the hoover is.'

'You're doing well and everything you tell us is very important.' Isaac gently nodded towards the distraught woman.

'The stink was so awful that I was really concerned. I called out his name to let him know I had arrived because he was a naturist at home and rarely wore clothes. It didn't bother me, but he kept a dressing gown by the front door for guests or deliveries, you know what I mean?'

Both detectives looked at each other and smiled back at Hester.

'The smell was now really bad and as I walked into the kitchen I saw him on the floor and all that blood.' The cleaner started to visibly shake but continued through her sobs. 'I then did that thing they do on TV when they see a body and started screaming. I rushed to the front door and into his garden where I continued to be distraught.'

Isaac was taking down all that was being said and at the same time he was formulating thoughts in his head.

'Hester, did you call the police?' Asked Emily.

'No, I was standing in the front garden crying and the street started to get busy with people having a stare. A woman came into the garden and asked what the matter was, so I told her and she ran into the house saying she'd call for help.'

'Did she give you her name?' Asked the DCI.

'No, but she reeked of alcohol even though it was only about 9:30am.' Hester looked exhausted but continued. 'That's everything I can tell you as I just stayed in the garden until the police arrived.'

'What happened to the woman who called the police?' enquired Emily.

'Oh, erm, she, erm, just left after she made the call, I think. Sorry.'

'Nothing to be sorry about Hester, but did you see what she looked like?' requested Isaac.

'Thin, very thin with lanky hair and brown stained teeth, but I don't know anything more than that.'

As the detectives left the house to head back to the police station, they again saw the woman from next door peering out of her window and knew they would be back soon to interview her. However, they didn't notice the young lad on the other side of the road staring at the house.

Getting into the car a thought went through Emily's mind.

'Sir, I didn't see the victim's mobile phone!'

'Good point Emily and who was that woman who rushed into the house to call the police?'

2:00pm

Isaac went over to the crime board and in the centre of it, placed a picture of Philip. He then called his team around and started the brief.

'This was Philip Oakes,' he said pointing to the picture. 'He was a thirty-six-year-old man who was found this morning by his cleaner dead on his kitchen floor. Initial thoughts and most probable cause of death was a knife into the heart. The victim's laptop and iPad have been taken away for fingerprinting and I want you Anne,' Isaac was pointing at the detective constable sitting at the back of the room eating a donut and slurping a Starbucks caramel latte, 'to start going through both devices as soon as forensics have finished with them.' The portly officer just nodded as she licked her fingers.

'Sir, what about his mobile phone?' Asked Jian, another DC on Isaac's team.

'Good question, but we didn't find one, yet! That doesn't stop us searching his phone records etc, so Jian can you find out his phone number and start seeing if you can find anything of importance.'

Isaac glanced at his near empty board and began pacing around it. His team just looked at him until he suddenly turned and spoke loudly.

'There was a woman who arrived at the scene, thin, lanky hair and apparently poor dental hygiene. She ran into the house on the pretence of calling the police which she obviously did, but did she do anything else in the house before she left. Let's see if anything comes up that might lead to her involvement.' There was a lot of respect for the DCI. 'Everyone else start doing background checks, googling and checking out social media etc, let's see what Philip Oakes was all about.'

The team went back to their desks and Isaac saw the enthusiasm in Jian's face, however Anne was still finishing her snacks. As he got back to his computer Emily appeared.

'I have spoken with his GP and there is an Ethan Oakes down as the victim's next of kin who is the brother. She also said that Ethan wasn't at all well so we should tread carefully.'

'Did she indicate what was wrong with him?'

'No, she just said he wasn't in the best of health so we should be mindful of that when we tell him that his brother has been murdered.'

Isaac sat pondering for a moment as Emily stood by his desk. She was eager to start the investigation and start filling up the crime board.

'Right! DS Morgans, let's go and talk to Mr Ethan Oakes.'

36:

11th December 2017

Ethan

3:30pm

Ethan stood perfectly still. His head was turned in such a way that he could see out into the street. There was no movement to be seen, no sounds to be heard. Tears were falling onto his cheeks. Opposite his house he could see into two homes, both had their Christmas tree up, one had colourful lights which were blinking and the other had white still lights. In the distance he could hear a voice talking to him, but for a brief moment he wasn't sure where it was coming from.

Without turning his head he took in a deep breath and spoke to the detectives who were sitting on his sofa.

'Philip has been murdered?'

Emma moved close to her husband and took his hand in hers. Ethan squeezed it tightly. The warmth from it made him feel secure.

'Yes Mr Oakes, the forensic team believe it happened on Friday evening.' Isaac spoke softly.

The front door burst open and Adam ran into the lounge with a shocked expression on his face. He had obviously just come from work as he was still in his uniform.

'For pity's sake Adam,' yelled Ethan, 'look at the state of you. Those bloody huge boots are covered in paint and you're a bloody mess! Don't you ever clean them?'

Adam just stared at his dad, as he wasn't used to being shouted at by him. Isaac sat and looked at the image of Adam, standing there in his white overalls and boots that looked too big for him. He had to bite down on the inside of his cheeks to stop himself from smirking. He turned around to his DS who was also trying to hold in a smile.

'Sorry Dad, but Brian from opposite texted me to say he saw some official looking people going into our house, so I asked if I could leave and get home.' Adam appeared embarrassed.

'It doesn't matter,' Ethan said to his son. 'Adam, uncle Philip is dead and they believe he was killed. Sorry detective Davidson, please continue.' Ethan was staring at the ground and Adam's eyes were as wide as they could be.

The two detectives looked at each other and Isaac nodded for Emily to continue.

'Mr Oakes, your brother was found in his kitchen and he had been stabbed.'

Ethan pulled an agonising face and reached for the nearest chair to fall into. Adam rushed to help his dad sit down.

DS Morgans continued. 'Do you know any reason why someone would want to hurt your brother?'

Both detectives were very aware of the glances made between the family members.

'Is there something you need to tell us Mr Oakes?' Asked the DCI.

Ethan looked at Emma and then Adam.

'You may as well hear it from me, Philip had the chance to potentially save my life. I have Leukaemia and need a stem cell transplant.' Ethan paused to see if what he was saying was being understood.

'I have a friend whose father needed a transplant, so I understand what you are saying,' said Isaac.

Ethan carried on.

'Philip was a match and therefore could have been my donor but he refused to donate his cells. They may not have worked but we will never know and I am now palliative. I probably have no more than six months left to live.'

Everyone in the room was aware that Adam had started to shake, so Emma went over to him and put her arms around his shoulders.

'I am very sorry to hear that Mr Oakes, but I have to ask, where were you on Friday evening from about 7:00pm onwards?'

Ethan looked towards both detectives and made a loud sigh.

'I was out driving around trying to clear my head from thoughts of dying. I am weak, but still able for now, to get myself about.'

'When did you last see your brother?' Asked DS Morgans.

'It was mid-November I think; he came around here accusing me of being a clown and after I told him it wasn't me, he stormed out again.'

'A clown?' Isaac asked, with an air of confusion in his voice.

Emma looked at her husband and could tell how distressed he was getting. She stood up and approached the officers.

'Philip was terrified of them and one night he burst into the house accusing Ethan of dressing up as one and periodically appearing in his street. Each time Philip saw it, he said it was getting closer. The clown wasn't Ethan!'

'Why was Philip so petrified of them?' Asked DS Morgans.

'Something happened when he was a kid I suppose,' volunteered Ethan, 'I don't remember what.'

'Were you close to your brother?'

Ethan looked at the female officer and again lowered his head.

'I wasn't the nicest of brothers to him growing up. Our mother died when he was four and I was ten. Our father was useless therefore we tended to sort ourselves out. We had help from a woman dad employed, but generally we fended for ourselves. I wasn't particularly kind to Philip, but maybe just the usual sibling issues.'

Isaac stood up and stretched out his legs and paced a little around the room. He observed the Oakes family and believed they were a close household, especially with their son.

'One more question for today, why do you think that your brother refused to give you the stem cells?'

Silence fell in the room and the atmosphere was decidedly cold.

'Because he was a shit!' bellowed Adam.

Ethan looked at his son and then spoke.

'I don't know DCI Davidson, but I guess he had his reasons. Philip was a complex person and had been since his early teenage years. You will soon discover that Philip used to self-harm. He cut into his shoulders and the tops of his arms. This went on for years and we never knew why.'

'Do we need to identify his body?' Asked Emma.

'No,' said Isaac, 'his cleaner has done that already, but once we have done everything we need to do, you will get a chance to view his body if you want to.'

The detectives made their way to the front door after thanking everyone for their time and headed back to their car.

'Just one more question,' Isaac called back to Ethan who was standing on the doorstep. 'Did Philip have a mobile phone?'

'Yes, of course he did,' was Ethan's reply.

'Thanks, we will be back in touch soon.'

37:

12th December 2017

Jacob

8:30am

Isaac sat in his cramped office with one too many grey filing cabinets. He watched through the internal windows and could see his team gathering around the crime board. He was still feeling slightly bloated from the breakfast Alan had made him that morning, but it had tasted so good.

As the team gathered he mentally appraised certain members, just quick thoughts but this helped him understand the directions he saw them going in. Emily was definitely moving towards promotion, as was Jian, who had shown real skill and had intelligent thought processes. Isaac liked Jian and hoped he'd take over from Emily once she was promoted. He was a stunningly handsome man, tall, slim and seemed to have unblemished skin. Although he spoke perfect English as he had been in the United Kingdom since he was seven, his voice still had a slight Chinese edge to it and this gave him a very influential sound. He was immensely popular with the team and the others enjoyed working alongside him.

Then there was Anne. She was slovenly and always appeared disinterested. She had already been through a disciplinary and was on a final written warning. Her desk was always covered in food wrappings and old coffee cups and when it came to her presence in the team, she was the complete opposite to Jian. There were also two other Detective constables, DC Potter and Asher who were very new to the team.

Isaac joined his squad by the crime board and 'good mornings' were exchanged.

'OK everyone, forensic report is in. The knife entered the body between the 3rd and 4th ribs and pierced the right ventricle of the heart.

Death would have been almost immediate. There were no signs of a struggle such as a bruise or cuts, apart from on the feet caused by the victim going out into the street and there was nothing under his fingernails.'

Isaac now pointed at the board. A picture of Ethan had now been placed on it, as well as a picture of a random clown. Isaac could see the baffled faces in front of him.

'So, this is Ethan Oakes, forty-two and was Philip Oakes' brother. He is terminally ill with Leukaemia and only a few, maybe six months left to live.' Isaac scanned the room. 'He does have a motive for killing his brother, which is revenge for want of a better word.' The DCI explained the stem cell issue and watched and listened to all the responses.

'Sir,' Jian said, pointing to the picture of the clown. 'What's that about?'

'That is a very good question DC Wong and something we need to act on and find out about.' Isaac enlightened everyone on the sightings. 'DC Michaels, I want you to see if Philip Oakes reported seeing a clown to our police colleagues and then take DC Potter to start door to door enquiries with the people in Philip's street.'

Anne Michaels slightly nodded in the direction of her boss, but she wasn't pleased. She hated going out and talking to people as she much preferred desk work. Another dislike of hers was taking out new team members with her, as was the case with Potter.

'OK team, now please feedback what you were able to find out since we last spoke yesterday.'

'Sir,' Jian was first, 'I checked phone records and it was extremely full. On the day of his death he had many missed calls, which I have traced and got details. Someone named Arjun Singh called sixteen times, a Jacob Spencer called three times and his brother called five times. Philip didn't answer any of these calls.'

'Sir,' Anne said as she placed a panini into her hand, took a bite and then swallowed what was in her mouth. 'Email records that I have seen so far, found one received from a Jacob Spencer and it wasn't nice.' Anne slowly plodded over to her desk and came back with a piece of paper that was now stuck to her fingers. She read from it to the rest of the team. 'The subject heading is this, '*Why did you send it to her? Watch your back!*' The rest of the email reads. *'I can't believe you sent Tanvi that video, you really are the scum of the earth and you'd better watch out Philip as I am coming for you! I may owe you £25,000, but that doesn't mean that you can destroy my life. Tanvi has left me and taken Rory and Adrian with her. Don't ever step out of the shadows because I'll see you and I will be waiting!'*

Isaac thanked Anne and turned to Jian.

'Anything on phone records re-sending a video?'

'Not yet sir, but I am working on it.'

'Right, thanks team. Anne, you go and see about the clown and Jian and DC Asher, I want you to go and interview a Mrs Ferres. She was Philip's next-door neighbour and from what I understand she was a curtain twitcher. DS Morgans and I will go and speak to Mr Jacob Spencer.'

10:00am

Jacob was sitting in a grotty room that hadn't been decorated in years. The smells wafting into his room were a combination of the odours coming from the shared toilet which was next to his room and the kitchen which was opposite. He sat on his bed wearing just a pair of white briefs and he hadn't shaved since Tanvi had kicked him out four days previously. He had phoned in sick for work. The tiny room he was now subjected to was hospital residences and he hated it. He spent most of the day looking at his phone in the hope of a *'come home'* message from his wife.

As he lay on the bed staring at the ceiling, he heard a knock at the door.

'Who is it?' he said, hoping whoever it was would just go away.

'Mr Spencer, this is DCI Davidson and DS Morgans, please open up.'

Jacob sprang to his feet to yank open the door in fear that something had happened to Tanvi or the kids.

'What's happened, are my family OK?'

Standing there in just his pants the detectives looked him up and down, reassured him that his family were safe and asked him to get dressed so they could speak to him about another issue.

When he was ready he opened the door and invited them in. There was only one chair to use after Jacob had pushed things onto the floor. Isaac used this and his DS stood by his side.

'Mr Spencer, do you know a Philip Oakes?' Asked Isaac.

'Call me Jacob and yes I know Philip, but right at this moment I wish I didn't.'

'Why do you say that?' Asked Emily.

Jacob now took in the scene of the two detectives in his small room and screwed up his face.

'What's this all about?' he directed the question to Emily.

'Jacob, Philip is dead, he was murdered on Friday evening.'

'Oh my God!' was all Jacob could say.

There was a strong smell of fish curry wafting into Jacob's room, despite the fact it was still only about 10:00am.

'The guy down the corridor does batch cooking, he told me yesterday that he cooks on Monday morning for the whole week. Philip's dead?' Jacob said with shock written all over his face.

'Yes, I am sorry to say but he was killed Friday evening.' Isaac continued. 'Jacob, we know you sent an email to him the day of his death and you stated, '*Don't ever step out of the shadows because I'll see you and I will be waiting!*' We know that Philip sent your wife a video via his phone. What was that video of?'

Jacob put his face into his large hands and took several deep breaths.

'I'm not proud of this, but it was of me having sex with someone who wasn't my wife.'

'What was your relationship with Philip?' Asked Emily.

'We were best friends since we were three-years-old. We were remarkably close, but recently he changed and became, for the want of a better word, an arsehole.'

Sitting on his single, uncomfortable bed, Jacob began to shake and tears began to trickle down his face. He turned away from the detectives, but they could hear him sniffing and could see him wiping away the tears.

The room was badly lit and the smell from the kitchen was getting stronger.

'Jacob,' Isaac said softly, 'We know from your email that you owed Philip a large amount of money, can you tell us about that?'

'A few years back he lent me £25,000. I promised to pay him back, but I never had the money to even start. Lately he started questioning me about it, this was upsetting my wife and he used the video as a bargaining tool. He told me if I didn't give him the money back he would send it to Tanvi. For some reason he sent it to her.'

'When did you last see Philip?'

Jacob looked at the DCI and shrugged his shoulders.

'I don't know, maybe a week or so ago. I was so angry with him, therefore I kept out of his way.'

'Where were you on Friday evening?'

Jacob stood up and paced up and down in the small space and pushed his hand through his hair.

'I was very distressed, Tanvi had kicked me out of our house without letting me see the children. She had sent them round to my in-laws before I had woken up. I spent ages pleading with her to let me stay and also kept thinking why Philip had done this to me. We had been through so much together over the years that I just couldn't fathom why he was acting so shitty towards me.' Jacob was getting visibly anxious as his pacing was getting more furious. 'When it was obvious that my wife wasn't going to let me back in, I drove off and ended up drowning my sorrows, but I don't remember where.'

Both detectives were nodding in appreciation of what Jacob was telling them but equally knew he wasn't telling them everything.

'Thank you, Jacob,' said Isaac, 'we can nearly end it there, but we have just two more questions for you. Did you know he hated clowns?'

'Yes I knew. Something happened when he was a kid. He didn't just hate them, he was petrified of them.'

'Last question. You made three calls to his phone on the morning of his death, you obviously wanted to speak to him, you also sent him an email. Knowing the devastation that he had caused you; didn't you at least attempt to go and see him and have it out with him?'

'No, I didn't,' was the curt reply.

'Thank you Mr Spencer, we will need to speak to you again.'

38:

1990

Philip aged Nine

Breakfast time in the Oakes' family home was always a quiet time for the three males as they sat around the large, polished walnut table. The dark wood was as depressing to look at as the dreary atmosphere in the room. Mrs Temple wasn't able to come to the house today, so it was just toast and cereal. Philip sat with one slice of toast and jam, Ethan had cereal and Mr Oakes was just having a black coffee.

'Dad,' Philip coyly said, 'It's my school sports day on Friday, will you come and watch me? I am running in the relay race.'

'No, I won't be there,' was the cruel reply.

The hurt lad just looked at his half-eaten piece of toast and sighed. He knew that that was going to be the answer he would get from his father, but he really wanted someone to be at the event to cheer him on. All his friends had parents who called out their name, egging them on to cross the finishing line.

The feeling around the table was even more miserable than before.

'I'll come and cheer you on Philip,' Ethan said with a smirk.

Mr Oakes lowered the paper he was reading and gazed at his eldest son, he then went back to reading without muttering a single word.

'Why would you do that?' Asked Philip.

'Because little bro, I think it would be a nice thing to do and my cheering might just be what helps you cross the winning line in first place.'

Philip looked at his brother with a worrying stare. He wasn't used to Ethan doing anything nice for him.

'Well?' said Ethan with a harsh tone, 'do you want me there or not?'

Philip gawked at Ethan and felt sad. He wanted to say yes but knew it wouldn't turn out in a good way.

'Will you be nice?'

'What's that meant to mean? I am always nice.' Ethan beamed at Philip.

There was no movement from their father.

'OK, you can come and root for me, thank you.'

'Think nothing of it.'

Sports Day 3:00pm

It was the perfect afternoon for the sports day. Philip was used to having no one cheering him on. This would be the first year he would have someone in the audience, standing on the side of the running track calling out his name. He was so excited. Year after year he had had to endure hearing the names of his friends being called out and seeing the excitement on the faces of those screaming their lungs out for their beloved child. This year however, Philip was going to finally hear his own name and see Ethan's face full of happiness as he watched his brother running down the track and at last winning a race.

The wind was blowing gently through the trees and making a soft whooshing noise. The sun was shining down on all the excited children. Philip looked around and saw at the end of the track his brother. This made him feel so happy, as he knew Ethan would be right there to call out his name and cheer him on.

Philip stood on the starting line, he was the fourth and final person to run in the relay, so it was up to him to make his yellow team win. Jacob was in the green team, which was a shame as Philip had wanted to be on the same side.

'Don't worry Philip,' he said to himself, 'Jacob's team can come second.'

The whistle sounded and the first four ran off as fast as they could. All around Philip could hear shouting and exhilaration and he couldn't wait to start running. He glanced over at Jacob and the two boys were both thrilled that they would be running the final leg together. They both turned and saw that it was about to be their turn to run. The green and yellow runners that were coming up fast to the two excited boys were beating both the blue and red teams. There were enthusiastic noises progressively getting louder around the sports field.

'Good luck Jacob,' said Philip.

'You too,' said his friend.

Philip got himself into position and put his arm out behind him ready to grab the baton. Jacob was in exactly the same pose. At the same time, they were passed the baton and shot off down their lanes as fast as their legs would permit. As he ran around the course, Philip was starting to make out what people were yelling.

'Come on Jacob, you've got this Jacob.'

He started to smile to himself, he could see Ethan jumping up and down and shouting. He knew he was about to hear his name for the first time at a sports day. Ethan's voice was booming.

'Come on Jacob! You can do this. Run Jacob, run!'

The track in front of Philip started to get hazy as he slowed down in disbelief at what his brother was yelling out. Philip started to find it difficult to breathe as he tripped over, fell to the floor and witnessed Jacob crossing the winning line. Then he spotted the blue and red teams as they ran past him. As he wiped the tears from his eyes, he could see Jacob running towards him, but Ethan was nowhere to be seen.

39:

12th December 2017

Mrs Ferres

10:30am

Molly Ferres was a lonely woman and looked and felt older than her sixty-three years. Her face was wrinkled and her eyes told the world that she had been through very hard times. She was widowed at thirty-six, had no children and very few friends. Standing at the window in her dreary dated lounge, she peered out onto the street and saw a car pull up outside her house, which she instinctively knew was the police. She had known they were going to call on her as soon as she had heard about the murder next door and she couldn't wait.

As the detectives walked along the garden path, they saw the woman dash from the lounge and opened the front door as fast as she could.

'I knew you'd be coming to see me, I just knew it I did. He died on Friday and was found on Monday. I saw him on Friday evening, probably just before he was killed. I always keep an eye on what's happening in this street.' Mrs Ferres wasn't stopping for breath. 'Naturist he was, didn't bother me, I have seen all things in my life-time. Mrs Latimer from across the road could see him through his window, she didn't like it, mind you, didn't stop her watching, shall I put the kettle on?'

The two men eyed each other, then back at the retreating woman and entered her house.

After they had introduced themselves and taken hold of the cup and saucer being presented to them, Jian started to ask his questions. DC Asher was there to observe and learn.

'Mrs Ferres.'

'Call me Molly my dear.'

'Erm, Molly, you said just now that you think you saw Mr Oakes just before he died, why do you think this?'

'Outside he was, just in his dressing gown, which was open, but like I said, it doesn't bother me. He was angry and shouting and searching up and down the street. He was clearly searching for someone. 'Where are you, you bastard?' he was yelling. 'Oh please forgive my bad language.'

'Did you see anyone?' Asked Jian, ignoring her apology.

'Not that time no, but plenty of other times. The things I could tell you about him next door, God rest his poor soul. Biscuit?'

In a bemused way, Jian took the plate of custard creams and handed them straight to his colleague.

'Mrs, erm, Molly, we need to focus, please tell me about what you've seen over the past few weeks in relation to Mr Oakes. Don't leave anything out, even if it doesn't seem that important to you.'

Mrs Ferres was in her element and couldn't wait to start answering this next set of questions. This was probably the most exciting thing to have ever happened to her and she was going to make the most of it.

'Well, firstly there was a woman, perhaps in her late fifties, drab lanky hair, thin or maybe emaciated would be a better word. She came around a few times a couple of months ago. I saw them go into his house once, he didn't seem keen, but she did. Then she just stopped. However, I am sure I saw her once or twice watching his house from her car.' Mrs Ferres looked at both men in the hope they were happy with what she was telling them.

'Did you see the make of the car?' Asked Jian

'White Ford Fiesta, I know that because my Meals on Wheels gets delivered in one, mind you that is a red one.'

In the corner of the room DC Asher was writing everything down in his notebook. He wanted to make a good impression. Jian smiled at Mrs Ferres and asked her to continue.

'Then there was the Indian lad, very handsome, very exotic. Am I allowed to say that?' She looked at the detectives. 'These days you never know what you're allowed to say or do. A woman I sat next to in the doctor's surgery last week said...'

'Sorry Molly, can we get back to the young lad you saw?'

'Oh yes dear, sorry, I do let my mind go off in all different directions. So, this young man, about mid-twenties started coming around towards the end of October. Mrs Latimer didn't approve, but as I told her, it takes all sorts to make a world.' She smiled at both men. 'I assumed they were together, as he would arrive in the evening and leave early the next morning. I heard the door opening and then closing as I am a light sleeper, plus I would glance out of the window. Oh, that was only to help keep the street safe you understand, always keep an eye out.'

Jian took a few moments to let his mind settle, as Mrs Ferres talked so fast it was at times very distracting.

'This is great Molly and it is so helpful. Is there anything more you'd like to tell us?'

'Oh, my dear, I have only just started. The day he died, well, was murdered, he had four visitors. The first was a black man, very beautiful and do you know if I was a few years younger,' she smiled to herself at this point. 'He was yelling for Mr Oakes, well Philip, to get out and see him. He was really angry. I knew there was no one at home because I'd seen him go out and a young man in purple jeans and wearing sunglasses even though it wasn't sunny started to follow him. I had seen that young man a few times, but the odd thing about him, was that he always appeared slightly different each time. Why do you think that was?' Mrs Ferres looked directly at the detective taking notes.

'I don't know,' was his simple reply.

Jian stood up and walked over to the window and peered out. This really was a good spot to see up and down the street. In the distance he could see his co-worker Anne and her side-kick DC Potter knocking on doors and asking, Jian assumed, about the clown.

'Did you ever see a clown in the street?' He asked without turning back.

'A clown?' she sounded surprised. 'Why would I see a clown?'

Jian continued to look out of the window and then turned again to face Mrs Ferres.

'So Molly, the black gentleman, what did he do?'

'He banged and hollered and eventually left. Philip arrived home about four o'clock, I think. Then, almost straight away, a man and a younger man turned up. The older man looked really ill. They were also bellowing to be let in and eventually he opened the door and they went in. There was lots of shouting coming through the walls, but I couldn't quite hear what was being said, but they were all incredibly angry.'

Mrs Ferres was enjoying herself, as she hadn't felt so needed in an exceedingly long time. She knew her inquisitive nature would come in handy one day.

'As they left, I saw them get into a car, but it stopped abruptly and the younger man got out and ran off and the car then turned around and went off in the opposite direction.' She glanced at both men and then continued. 'As the two men left, the Indian lad was on his doorstep and he was also yelling at Philip. No wonder he was done in with so many people angry at him.'

'Why was he angry? Did you hear what he was saying?' Asked Jian.

'Well, I don't like to pry or be nosey, but it was something to do with his brother being in hospital and he felt it was Philip's fault that he was there and then he said something like 'I will kill you'. Oh my, that's rather telling isn't it. After he left it all went quiet for a couple of hours. A pizza was delivered by a person on a motorbike type of thing about 7:45 and then shortly after that, Philip was in the street shouting.'

Mrs Ferres looked at the DC in front of her and could tell he was mulling over what she had told him. She liked the way his tongue rolled gently over his top lip.

'You said there was a young lad who followed him, but that you'd seen him a few times, is that correct?' Asked Jian.

'Yes, that's odd isn't it. He used to stand opposite my house. Go and look, there is a post box that you can see outside number forty-five. The lad stood there.'

Jian went over to the window again.

'How do you know it was the same lad?'

'Well you can tell can't you? He changed his hair colour and style, wore different clothes, but always wore the same type of sunglasses and you can't change your height and build, can you?' She smiled a smug grin. 'Saw him about six or seven times I think, do you think he did it? Oh, my lord!'

'No Molly, we have no evidence yet about anyone, we are just at the beginning of our investigations. You have been extremely helpful, but we must leave you be now.' Jian stood to go.

The detectives thanked Mrs Ferres and got back into the car. Jian was silent and DC Asher was finishing off his writing.

'I actually think my ears hurt,' Jian said aloud.

'Yes, I can understand why. What a nosey parker she was,' said the DC.

'Nosey yes, but what a good job she is.' Jian started the car and returned to the office to report the details of the interview to his DCI.

40:

13th December 2017

Arjun

9:00am

Isaac's team sat around the crime board waiting for their boss to come and do the usual round up of information already gathered and to be given their next jobs for the day. The board was beginning to fill up and become busier. Joining the Oakes brothers and the clown, there were now three new pictures. Jacob and two cartoon sketches of a teenage lad and a thin old woman. These had been placed there yesterday following Jian's feedback to the team the previous evening before heading home.

'Good morning,' Isaac called out as he entered the room. 'Let's get straight to business. We heard yesterday about the sightings of Mrs Ferres from DC Wong, so DC Michaels can you tell us what you found out about the clown.'

All eyes turned around to look at Anne, who was taken by surprise as she had just taken a bite of her apple Danish. Swallowing hard and quickly, she wiped the back of her hand across her mouth and started to speak, spraying a few crumbs from her mouth as she did so.

'I spoke with a PC Chaplin who had visited Mr Oakes on 1st November who had reported that a clown had been making several appearances, well three at the time. Each time the clown got closer and made finger gestures such as beckoning and taunting.' The DC now reached for her water and took a few sips before continuing. 'PC Chaplin then said she knocked on a few houses to ask if anyone had seen a clown in the street, but no-one had. However, when I did my investigation yesterday, one person,' she stopped to pick up her notebook, 'a Mr Teasdale did report seeing a clown in the street on 1st November, but assumed it was something still to do with Halloween and thought nothing more of it.' Anne stopped talking and took another bite of her Danish pastry.

Isaac now paced the floor and looked at his board. He ran his right hand through his hair and left it on his head and remained in deep thought.

'Right,' he shouted a little too loudly and made everyone jump. 'Jian, I want you to find out who this thin woman is with the lanky hair, as she is pivotal I am sure. She was at the crime scene and according to the woman next door, appeared to be stalking Philip Oakes. Check to see if Philip had reported her, check phone records again for messages of a flirty, or even nasty tone and see who sent them. We assume his phone is switched off but check GPS signals because as soon as that phone gets put back on, I want to know exactly where it is. Anne, can you start looking to see who this young lad is? Why are at least two people observing Philip?'

Emily started to gather up her belongings as she knew that she would be going to interview the next suspect with her boss. Isaac, after going back into his office to pick up his phone and keys joined her.

'Emily, we need to go and talk to Mr Arjun Singh. Why did he call Philip's phone so many times? I assume he's the Indian lad that Mrs Ferres spoke of?'

10:30am

The detectives pulled up outside Arjun's house and got out of the car. The front door to the house was open and angry voices could be heard.

'Please Rajan, come to the hospital with me and see your brother. He is broken-hearted and he is praying so hard for Rohit. Won't you come and be with him?'

'No, I have told you, I will not be in the same room as that demon!' Rajan looked deep into his mother's eyes.

'Do you care for Rohit? Do you not have a responsibility to be with him Rajan? He might still die. You stayed with him for the first forty-eight hours after he was hit and you didn't once leave his side. Why won't you stay anymore, just one hour a day is all you do.' Mrs Singh was pleading with her eldest child but with little success.

'If he dies, then it will be the fault of Arjun and that man he worked for. I will not say his name. One hour is enough for Rohit to know I am there.' Rajan said in a cold and clinical manner.

Isaac and Emily now knocked on the door and called through. They had heard all that had been said.

'Hello, I am DCI Davidson and this is DS Morgans, we are here to see a Mr Arjun Singh.'

Mrs Singh came to the door and was very flustered. She was aware of the tears staining her cheeks and was even shaking a little. Rajan skulked upstairs but not without being seen.

'Arjun is at the hospital with my other son, I am his mother, what is this about please?'

'Mrs Singh, we need to speak to your son urgently, where can we find him in the hospital?' Emily smiled at the concerned parent.

'Bad things have happened lately, please tell me why you need to talk to my son.'

Isaac looked at the frightened woman and spoke gently.

'Mrs Singh, we are investigating the murder of Philip Oakes and just need, as routine, to talk with your son.'

'See what I told you. They are both evil and have caused this. Have nothing to do with him again,' called Rajan from upstairs, who, despite leaving, was clearly listening intently.

'Rajan shut up!' Mrs Singh hollered at her son as he ran down the stairs shrieking.

'Arjun is a good boy, don't listen to my eldest. He is at the hospital with my youngest in the ITU department.' Mrs Singh closed the front door and the detectives heard her burst into tears as she slumped against the door.

11:00am

Arjun sat by his brother's bed and held his hand. Rohit was ventilated following surgery to remove a blood clot from his brain. He had also broken his left leg and both arms in the accident.

'I'm so sorry, I'm so sorry,' Arjun kept repeating the same words in a softly spoken voice.

'Mr Singh?'

Arjun looked up and saw two people in front of him. He had been so deep in thought he hadn't seen them approaching.

The detectives introduced themselves and asked if he would come with them to the relative's room to talk. Arjun was at first reluctant to leave his brother, but soon realised that he didn't have a choice.

'Mr Singh, we are investigating the murder of Philip Oakes and we believe you knew him.'

For a moment Arjun appeared shocked at what he had just been told, but then a smile crept across his face momentarily.

'Yes I knew him, unfortunately.' Arjun hissed at the pair. 'Why do you need to speak to me? I want to go back to my brother.' He made a movement to the door, but Emily stood firm.

'What was your relationship with the victim?' Isaac said.

'He was my boss at the pub he managed or owned, I never knew which,' was Arjun's aggressive reply.

The atmosphere in the small and dingy room was very cold. The young man was hardly maintaining any form of eye contact with the detectives. He was fidgeting in his chair and entwining his fingers over and over again.

'Is that the extent of your relationship?' Emily said.

'Look,' Arjun shouted as he stood up, 'I was in a sort of relationship with him, which I totally regret now. That man is the reason my brother is fighting for his life. I hate him and quite frankly I am glad that he's dead. He was pure evil. Death is too good for him.'

Both investigators eyeballed each other and the DCI indicated for his DS to continue.

'Mr Singh, where were you around 7:00pm-9:00pm on Friday the 8th December?'

Arjun dropped back into the chair and bent forward with his head in his hands.

'Do you think I killed him?'

'Just answer the question please.'

'Where do you think I was? I was here with my brother, in ITU following his brain surgery.'

'When did you last see Philip? Why are you so angry with him?' Asked Emily.

'I was with him the evening before, the 7th, he was drunk and disgusting, so I got an Uber about midnight and left. I later found out that he had sent my family a picture of us in bed together. This caused my eldest brother to go mad and he got violent. Rohit ran out into the road because, I guess he was scared of what was happening and a car hit him. That's why I hate him, or should I say hated him. He was a terrible person.' Arjun took a breath and looked about him.

'Did you see the make of car that hit your brother?' Asked Emily.

'What has that got to do with anything? I think it was a white Fiesta, but it was so quick. Do you know he was letting his brother die? I want to go back to my brother now.'

Sitting in his chair, Arjun looked like a defeated man. It was obvious that he hadn't slept or eaten since the accident and blamed himself for what his brother was going through. He felt like the experience had aged him ten years. Arjun curled into the chair like a scolded child trying to protect itself.

'Mr Singh, I will ask you once more, when did you last see Philip Oakes?' Emily had an air of irritation to her voice. 'Before you speak, we have an eyewitness that states that she saw an angry Indian man yelling at the victim just hours before his death. Now I'm not saying it is you, but it's in your best interest to speak now if it was.'

A slow eerie, cat-like noise started to escape from Arjun as he straightened himself out, tears were evident on his face and he got up and started to pace the room like a caged tiger.

'Yes it was me, I needed to see him to tell him what his actions had done. I needed him to know that I hated him.'

'Did you threaten him?' Asked the DCI.

'No, well, I don't remember doing so. Why?'

'When one of my detectives interviewed Philip's neighbour, she said that you said, "I will kill you".'

Arjun's breathing was becoming more rapid as his pacing quickened in the small area that he had to walk about in.

'If I said that, it was the heat of the moment type of thing. He is the reason my brother might die, therefore I had reason to be angry, but that doesn't mean I killed him! Does it?'

'No Mr Singh, it doesn't,' said Isaac. 'Where did you go once you left Philip's house?'

'We, I mean my mum and older brother stayed in the hospital from the moment Rohit was taken in. I was the first to leave, but only to confront 'him.' I then went home and showered, changed my clothes and headed straight back to be with Rohit. My mother and brother were both still there.'

'What time did you get back to the hospital?' Asked Isaac.

'I don't know, maybe 9:00pm or slightly later, but definitely by 9:20pm. When I got back, Rajan got up and left as he didn't want to be with me any longer.'

'One more question for now, did you know Philip had a clown phobia?' Isaac watched the young man's face very carefully.

'Yes.' Arjun now pushed pass the detectives and headed back to sit with his brother.

5:00pm

Arjun's picture had now been added to the crime board and Isaac was pleased to see that a photograph of a thin, tired looking woman had been added and the drawing of her removed. Social media was a great way of getting these pictures. Jian had obviously made progress.

'OK team, before we go home this evening I need just a little more of your time. You've heard Emily's account of Arjun Singh, so now it's time to hear about the others. Anne, any news re the young man?' Isaac called out.

'Nothing so far sir, but I'll keep at it tomorrow.'

Jian now stood up and he was rightfully pleased with himself. He walked over to the board and pointed at the newly placed picture.

'This is Rebecca Firth and is known to our victim. She was also not liked by him. I firstly, with the help of DC Asher, thought a good place to start was the Lemon Tree pub.' Jian was always good at making sure he included the other DCs he was working with. 'We spoke to a bartender called Stan, who was devastated to hear about Mr Oakes. He said that Rebecca was a regular in the pub but somewhat of an alcoholic. She was a nuisance and occasionally caused trouble, but the interesting part is that she was obsessed with Philip. One evening she screamed out that she was pregnant with his child.'

Lots of murmurs started around the room and Isaac needed to hush everyone up to allow Jian to continue.

'I read through police records to see if Philip had reported anything re stalking etc and although he hadn't, I found this report.' Jian handed out a few printed copies. 'Rebecca's daughter took her mother to A&E on 24th November and called the police at the same time to report that someone had violently attacked her mother. Rebecca however didn't want to take things any further, so the police took pictures of the injuries and contacted the domestic unit for follow up. I spoke with the domestic team and they have never been able to get hold of Rebecca to discuss the attack.'

The department was now awash with murmurs and noises as people were trying to get things sorted out in their heads.

'This is great work Jian, thanks,' Isaac nodded over to his DC, soon to be a DS he hoped.

As everyone stood to go back to their desks to log off computers and go home for the evening, Isaac called them all back.

'Sorry everyone, just two more minutes to summarise. So far we have five main suspects. Ethan Oakes a wronged brother, Jacob Spencer an angry and vengeful friend, Rebecca Firth a scorned woman and possible victim of Philip's violence? Arjun Singh a man potentially seeking revenge and a clown!' Everyone was staring at the crime board. 'Tomorrow I will go and interview Rebecca Firth with Jian, Emily, I want you and Anne to carry on searching for the young lad. Start at the pub like Jian did today as he may have gone there. Everyone else, I want you to trawl through all his emails and bank transactions. That is going to help us continue putting together a picture of Philip Oakes.

41:

14th December 2017

Rebecca

06:30am

Somewhere in the room a clock was ticking but was going unheard. There was a mountain of laundry that needed to be cleaned and a stack of glassware that had started to grow mould. On the worktops and on the floor were empty cans of anything alcoholic that Rebecca could find. She had been like this since Amelia had brought her home from the hospital after Philip had attacked her.

Rebecca started her day the same way every day. She no longer went to work having been signed off sick for at least three months following the attack. In her heart she knew Philip hadn't meant to hurt her and that was why she still loved him. That is why she needed to run her car into Arjun, so Philip would be hers again.

She sat at the breakfast bar she hated so much because the table was full of clutter and there was no free space. Rebecca lifted to her mouth the can of whiskey and ginger ale and looked at Philip's mobile phone that she held in the other. She softly wept as she put down the can and picked up her cigarette.

Three weeks ago she was as happy as she could be. Philip was nearly hers again and she was having their child. They would have been so happy together. She couldn't help these thoughts running through her mind. Now, she had nothing. Philip was dead and the hospital had told her there was no baby, she wasn't pregnant but starting her menopause.

'What do they know?' she screeched and flung her arms about knocking more clutter to the floor.

Taking a long drag on her cigarette caused Rebecca to have a coughing frenzy and she felt dizzy. She picked up the can and between coughs took large gulps and then headed to the fridge for whatever drink she could find. Everywhere she went, Philip's phone went with her.

When Rebecca had taken the phone from his house on that dreadful morning, it had no battery life left. As soon as she got home she started charging it, but instinctively knew she mustn't turn it on, or they would know she had it and it was hers now. However, she was desperate to see what messages he had on it and to see all the pictures of her that he was bound to have taken and stored.

'We would have been so happy together,' she said as she wandered out of the kitchen and back upstairs to her bedroom. Rebecca thought it was probably password protected but it was certainly a code relevant to her.

'I bet it's my date of birth, or the first date we made love,' she thought to herself as she climbed onto her bed with no bed linen on it.

As she lay there, she rubbed her tummy and smiled and spoke softly to herself.

'I'm going to call you Philip or Philippa because that hospital knows nothing, I've been pregnant twice before and I know the signs and they don't.' Rebecca took a deep breath and reached for her can of drink. 'I'm sorry it had to end this way Philip, but you did do wrong by me and so did that bloody Arjun, but I took care of that, he won't be bothering us again my love, I can promise you that.'

11:00am

As discussed the previous evening, Isaac was working with Jian today and Mrs Rebecca Firth was first on their list. Jian had stayed late at work and had looked at social media to try to find more out about her. He was keen to show his boss what he had discovered.

'She works at the local hospital as a pharmacy assistant, according to the bartender at the pub which Philip managed. She frequented it and was nearly always drunk before she left to go home. She has two daughters, divorced and as I said before sir, she said she was pregnant, but the hospital report said this wasn't the case.'

'Thanks Jian, that's some good work done.'

Their car arrived at the address required and both got out. Rebecca's white car was on the driveway.

'Now let's see what Mrs Firth has to say for herself,' said the DCI.

After five minutes of knocking on the door, ringing the bell and calling her name through the letterbox, the two men finally heard some movement from inside the house. The front door opened and the sight that met them caused them both to grimace a little.

Rebecca stood and looked at the two men. Her hair was dirty and tangled, she had a cigarette drooping from the left side of her mouth and the smell of body odour was overpowering.

'Mrs Firth?' Isaac enquired.

'Who's asking,' was the curt reply.

Introductions were made and the reason for their visit, so reluctantly Rebecca opened the door wide and let the men in and led them into the kitchen. The detectives couldn't help but look at the state of the place. The over spilling bins of rubbish mainly cans and bottles. The whole place was filthy, with a smell like rotting vegetables.

'Mrs Firth, please...' Jian was interrupted.

'Just call me Rebecca, as I can't be doing with that Mrs crap.'

'Rebecca, can you please tell me what relationship you had with Mr Oakes.'

'I can't believe he is dead, why is he dead?'

'He was murdered last Friday.' Isaac said.

'I know that you bloody fool,' she said, slurring her words. 'Why would someone want to kill him? Philip was my love and we were going to be parents. I loved him.'

'Rebecca, can I ask where you were on 8th December in the evening about 7:00pm-9:00pm?' The DC asked.

'Mmm, let me think, I don't remember, I have these blackouts from time to time.'

'Mrs Firth, can you please tell me about the evening of 24th November, did Mr Oakes assault you?' Isaac asked.

'Is that relevant? Why is that important? I don't want to talk about that evening, he wasn't himself as he'd had a long hard day at work. Stop asking me questions, my head is hurting and I just want to go back to my bed. Can't you see I am grieving and I just want to be left alone.'

Isaac could tell that they weren't going to get much information from Rebecca today, but he had three questions he needed to at least ask and plant the seed if nothing else.

'Rebecca, was it you who used to sit outside Philip's house, watching?'

'No.'

'Was it you who went into Philip's house the morning his cleaner found him dead, called the police and if it was you, did you take his mobile phone?'

'No.'

'Did you know he was terrified of clowns?'

'Yes.'

Rebecca, we will be back and if necessary take you into the police station for questioning. Do you understand me?' Asked Isaac.

Rebecca shrugged her shoulders and watched as the two men left and got back into their car.

As she watched the car turn the corner and disappear, Rebecca smiled to herself and spoke in a whisper.

'It's OK Philip my love, they've gone.'

42:

18th December 2017

Isaac

05:30am

Isaac lay in his bed on his right side studying a Van Gogh print on his wall. There was something so peaceful about the picture he'd picked up in a museum gift shop that helped ease his mind. He had already turned on his bedside light as he was unable to sleep. He could tell that Alan was asleep as no movement or noise could be heard through their adjoining wall.

The two men had enjoyed the weekend together, as they always did. They started with some Christmas shopping and then onto the cinema to watch Star Wars: The Last Jedi. They were both fans of the previous films, so it was an afternoon spent well. Sunday was about reading the newspapers, cooking a new recipe and catching up on TV.

Knowing that any chance of sleep was gone, Isaac propped himself up on his pillows, yawned until the sides of his mouth ached and then threw back the duvet and headed to the kitchen to put on a pot of coffee. Within five minutes Alan joined him.

'Ah mate, I'm sorry, I didn't mean to wake you so early.'

'No matter,' Alan said through a huge yawn and stretch. 'What's up?'

'Got the case going around in my head. Emily and that bloody awful Anne drew blanks when it came to the young lad who had been seen watching our victim. They talked to staff in the pub, but although they verified a young lad kept coming in, changing his appearance and asking about Philip, no one knew anything more about him, apart from the fact he was called Lewis, but no one knew his surname.'

'You'll find him, you're great at your job and the case has only been going a week. Stop worrying. Do you want me to start breakfast?' Alan asked.

'I think I'll drink some coffee, have a shower and then have some food. Is that OK?'

'Absolutely,' his brother replied. 'Do you want to run anything by me? Would that help?'

Isaac poured them both a mug of coffee and paced the kitchen mulling things over in his head.

'OK, so far I have four suspects who all need to be interviewed again. I believe they are all hiding something, or not telling me the whole truth, but that's fine I will go back to them. Then we have the young lad, but as you say, I will hunt him down. There are bound to be further suspects as he didn't sound like a nice person.' Isaac swallowed a mouthful of his coffee and then looked at his attentive brother and frowned before he next spoke. 'It's the clown I don't get.'

Alan's expression went from understanding to disbelief in moments.

'A clown? Are you serious?.'

'Oh yes. Philip reported seeing a clown three times to our uniformed friends. On each sighting the clown got a little closer and scared him to the point of vomiting. We don't know if he saw it again before his death but if he did, he didn't report it.'

'Is the clown important? I mean do you think it is involved in the murder?' Asked Alan.

'That my dear brother is something we don't know yet.'

Isaac drained his coffee cup and poured himself another and offered Alan one too. Once they both had their drinks they headed back to their bedrooms. As Isaac got back into his bed and pulled the duvet over himself he heard his brother shouting through the wall.

'DCI Davidson, you can do this!'

'You're a bloody marvel,' came the response.

09:00am

Everyone was sitting around the crime board which now featured an array of pictures and drawings. Isaac scanned his colleagues as he thought through questions silently to himself. The investigation had now been going for one week. The DCI was pleased with the suspects collected so far as he reviewed the board.

'OK, time to test them and see what they think so far.' Isaac thought to himself. 'DC Michaels, what questions should we be asking ourselves at this point?'

Anne jumped when her name was called out and spilt some coffee down her front. She grabbed her notes and started to flick through them in a haphazard way.

'Sir, what part does the clown play in all of this?'

'Jian,' Isaac called next.

'Sir, where is the victim's phone?'

'Faisal,' indicating DC Asher.

'Erm, what was the green piece of material doing next to a pizza box?' said a shaking DC.

Isaac stopped what he was doing as he gazed directly at the novice detective and was extremely pleased.

'Very good question. The fibre analysis showed the material was a synthetic fibre used for making all sorts of things. DC Hamish Potter you're next.'

'From everything that has been fed back to us, I'm wondering why the victim, Philip, wouldn't help out his brother and why he self-harmed?'

The DCI again was pleased and nodded in the DC's direction.

'Emily?'

'Well, we have liars. Jacob we have to assume was the black guy Mrs Ferres saw, yet he told us he didn't try to see Philip. Also, I heard this morning that Jacob has gone missing since we interviewed him four days ago. We are obviously looking for him. Mrs Ferres also saw a man and a younger man. Do we assume this was Ethan and Adam?'

'Back to Anne,' cried out the DCI. 'Anne! Put down that bloody food and concentrate!'

'Sorry sir, erm, who is Lewis?'

Without being asked, Jian stood up and gazed closely at the board and around the room.

'Sir, please can I have a look at the crime scene pictures again?'

Isaac walked into his office and took out the pictures from his drawer.

'What interests you about them Jian?'

'The murder happened between 7:00pm and 9:00pm. I want to see the name of the pizza company on the box, so I can check what time the order was placed, how it was placed and what time it was delivered and by whom. The delivery person would have therefore been in the area and may have seen something.' Jian was pleased with himself. 'The post-mortem revealed that there was just wine in Philip's stomach and no pizza, so did the killer come for dinner or just take a slice? Oh and what is Rebecca hiding?'

'DC Asher?'

'Philip was scared of clowns, but why?'

'His brother said something in his childhood but volunteered nothing more,' Emily answered.

'However, we do need to know who knew Philip was scared of them, I mean apart from his brother. DC Potter, what are you questioning?' Isaac then asked.

'So far we get the impression that Philip was not a nice person,' the team all nodded. 'Yesterday as I was going through his emails I found one from a Paul Tovey. It makes our victim sound like a really decent bloke. I'll read it out.'

'*Dear Philip, I hope you don't mind me emailing you, but you said I could. Don't worry I am not asking for help, but to say thank you. No one had ever been that kind to me before since I ended up on the streets and scared. The McDonald's meal was really needed as were the toiletries. No one had ever asked my story before and that's why I think I told you about my Stepdad and the rape and why I needed to get away. The £300 you gave me went to clever use. I booked myself into a hostel and had a shower. The next day I bought some new clothes, got a haircut and then a train ticket to Leicester (no idea why Leicester). I walked the streets and saw a sign in a small cafe window asking for someone to do the washing up and odd jobs. The woman who owns the shop is really lovely and gave me the job. Philip, it gets better, the café had a small one-bedroom flat that needed doing up as it was in a bad way, so she said I could stay for free if I did some DIY on it. I get some wages (not much due to living in the flat) and I get breakfast and lunch every day. I'm doing OK thanks to you. I'm off the streets and working for someone who is as kind and lovely as you. I will never be able to thank you enough Philip. I really hope you are well and if you are in Leicester, the place is called 'Lucy's One Stop Cafe.' Thank you Philip, with hugs Paul x'*

The team now looked at each other and Emily was first to speak.

'Well that doesn't sound like the person we have been finding out about. Why so nice and kind to a homeless person? What did Paul say that resonated with our victim?'

Isaac paced around the room and then assigned jobs.

'DC Michaels and DC Potter, I want you to see if you can track down Lewis, whoever he is. DC Wong and DC Asher, I want you to follow on from your thoughts Jian, re pizza company. Emily, you and I will visit Ethan Oakes again as I am sure he is hiding something from us.'

'Sir,' said DC Asher. 'What question do you think needs an answer?'

The DCI acknowledged the question with a perplexed expression on his face.

'I think you all came up with some good and relevant questions, but there are three words going around in my head and I don't know why and I don't know if they have any part to play but they are beginning to annoy me.'

'What are the words sir?' Asked Jian.

'White Ford Fiesta,' was the DCI's reply.

43:

18th December 2017

Ethan

11:00am

The drive from the police station to the Oakes' house was done in silence. Both detectives thinking through the details of the case. The weather outside was stormy and the strong wind caused the car to swerve slightly from time to time. An unexpected crack of thunder jolted them both back into reality, just as the heavens opened and a torrential rainstorm started.

Five minutes later their car pulled up outside Ethan's house, but they decided to wait until the rain had died down a little.

'Right Detective Morgans, by the end of today I want to know why Ethan lied about going to see his brother the day he was murdered, if indeed it was him and his son. We need to find out more about their relationship because denying your sibling the chance of survival must have come from a very dark place and does it have any bearing on why Philip started to self-harm?'

The weather was not calming down and interviews needed to be done. The pair got out of the car and headed quickly to the front porch. Despite their speed they still got very wet and looked like drowned rats. From inside they heard someone approaching. Emma answered the door.

'Oh dear, you'd better come in and I'll get you both a towel to dry yourselves off. Would you like a cup of tea?'

Once they were both as dry as they were going to get and seated with their hot drink, Emma spoke.

'I assume you're here to speak to Ethan? Unfortunately, he's back in hospital with a fever, so he is once again back on antibiotics and fluids.'

'We will need to go and see him after we leave here then. Mrs Oakes, I need to ask, where were you on the evening of your brother-in-law's murder?'

'Ah, I wondered when it would be my turn to be asked that pivotal question. I was at my mother's house. I had gone to stay with her for a few days.'

'Was there a reason you had gone away?' Asked the DS.

'My mother only lives a few minutes from us, so I was near enough to get back if Ethan needed me, but the reason I went away was because of Saul.'

Emma picked up her cup to take some of her tea but grimaced indicating to the pair staring at her that it had already gone cold.

Getting up and strolling over to the kettle to turn it back on, Emma continued to speak, although her audience could both tell how difficult this was for her.

'Saul, as you both know, is our middle child. He finds it exceedingly difficult to see the physical changes that have happened to his dad. We do explain what is going on, but Saul can't cope with the situation. Ethan and I agreed that I would take Saul and Max and stay with my mum, just for a few days. On the Saturday, my mother and myself took the boys out for the day. We went to London Zoo. By the evening everyone was exhausted. I came back home on the Sunday, the day before we heard about Philip.'

'Mrs Oakes, do you have any idea why Philip wouldn't donate his cells?' The DCI asked.

'Firstly call me Emma,' she said in her rich, silky tone, 'and secondly I don't really know. Ethan very rarely talks about his childhood. I obviously asked many times after Philip refused, but my husband would say very little. He said he wasn't the nicest of brothers but loved Philip. He also said they had a rough up-bringing but said nothing to indicate why Philip was so cruel and vindictive.'

Emma finished making the tea and gave the detectives a fresh cup each. Isaac could see the pain in her face and behind her eyes. This was the image of a person that had had to stay strong for so long. It was clear to Isaac that this woman was the backbone of the Oakes' family.

'Ethan is very close to Adam,' Emma continued. 'The two of them have an extraordinarily strong bond that even I don't understand sometimes. Maybe it's Ethan's way of making up for not being such a good brother, but that's just a thought. Lately it worries me that they are so close to each other.'

Emily sat looking at Emma and as she took a sip of her drink she screwed up her face a little as Emma had forgotten the sugar. Another crack of very loud thunder caused all three to jump and again the rain fell hard.

'Why does it worry you?' Asked Emily.

'Ethan isn't going to survive this. He told you at your last visit that he probably only has six months to live. Truth is, I spoke with his haematologist and it's more likely two to three.'

Tears were now freely flowing down her cheeks. Emily went over and sat next to her and gently put her hand on the weeping woman's arm. Emma patted it and smiled through her tears.

'Are you able to continue? We can wait or come back later?' Emily's words were soft and gentle.

'No it's no problem, I can go on. I always thought that saying goodbye to my wonderful, loving, kind, generous and devoted husband was going to be the hardest thing I would ever have to do,' Emma took a deep breath. 'I now believe dealing with Adam once his dad has died is going to be.'

These last words proved to be the breaking point for Emma. Her gentle weeping had now turned into loud sobbing. Her breathing became rapid and she started to shake all over. Emma fell against Emily's shoulder and continued to cry hard. No one said anything for five minutes.

As her tears settled and her breathing regulated, Emma apologised.

'There really is no need to be sorry Mrs Oakes, they looked like tears that you had held onto for too long,' Isaac could see how traumatised she was. 'I hate to ask, but is there anything else you think we might find useful?'

'I don't think so but will call if I do. When you see Ethan, please be gentle with him.'

The three walked from the kitchen and back into the hallway. The rain had stopped, but the weather outside was still dark and gloomy and so the hallway was poorly lit. As he turned to face the front door, Isaac tripped and nearly went over.

'Oh I'm sorry, you've fallen over Adam's stupid work boots. Truth of the matter, he won't go to work since you told us about Philip last week, so those bloody boots just sit there getting in the way. His work are being understanding but, I don't know for how much longer. I am trying to get him to do normal things such as work, seeing his friends, going for a pint. He won't leave his dad's side though. It's like he is just waiting for him to die.'

As they walked back to the car, Isaac threw his keys to his DS.

'I think I have sprained my bloody ankle, so you'd better drive to the hospital.'

12:30pm

The black, looming cloud seemed to be following them as they drove to the hospital. The car park was nearly full, with the only available spaces at the far end. No doubt this was due to the lousy weather. The rain was once again torrential and drenched people were either running towards the hospital or back to their cars. Different coloured raincoats with soaked bodies darting all over the place was actually amusing the detectives, at least until it was their time to get out of the car.

Isaac opened the passenger door and went to step out, but as soon as he put his left foot on the ground, pain shot through him and caused him to shout out.

'Bugger me that hurt!'

Emily jumped out and ran to her boss' side to offer some aid. He took her arm as she helped him stand and then once standing up he leant on her shoulder for added support. To add insult to injury as he slammed his door shut in anger the trees above dropped a fair amount of water onto his head. Emily bit the inside of her cheek to stop herself laughing.

After hobbling through the car park and into the main hospital, Isaac made the decision to first call in to minor injuries. Once he had flashed his badge he was seen straight away and strapping of his ankle and painkillers were administered. They were now on their way to Silver Birch haematology ward to find Ethan.

As they walked (or limped in Isaac's case) on to the ward they headed for the nursing station and asked to see Mr Oakes.

'Can I help?' said a male voice behind them.

They both turned and saw a very good-looking man with sparkling white teeth smiling at them.

'And you are?' Asked Emily.

'My name is Liam and I'm the clinical nurse specialist for Mr Oakes, what do you need from him as he isn't feeling great at the moment.'

'We are investigating the murder of his brother and need to ask him further questions. However, could we ask you a couple of things first?'

Ten minutes later the detectives were in Liam's office with hot drinks and Isaac had his foot up on a stool to help relieve the pain.

'This is very kind of you,' the DCI said. 'Grim question first, but what is the prognosis for Mr Oakes and would the stem cells from Philip Oakes have saved his brother's life?'

Liam took a deep breath and as he did, Emily noticed his muscles stretching his scrubs.

'Prognosis is unbelievably bad, Ethan is now palliative, meaning there is nothing more we can do for him, apart from keep him comfortable, give him blood products when needed and painkillers if he wants them. It is never easy to say exactly how long he has but I think no more than about three months, although his strength and determination are both still good.' Liam took a sip of his coffee and scratched the top of his lip. 'The second part is harder to answer as we will never know. Ethan has a very complex type of Leukaemia and it is difficult to treat. Philip's cells may have cured his brother, but they might not have.'

Isaac raised his leg and placed it back down on the chair, the painkillers were beginning to work slightly. He looked over to Emily, suggesting to her that he wanted her to ask any questions that she thought relevant.

'Liam, how did Ethan take the news that his brother wasn't going to give his stem cells?'

'That's an easier one to answer, the whole room was dumbfounded, including myself and Dr Kelleher. We had never come across a situation like it. It seemed to us that Philip was milking the time to his own satisfaction.'

'What do you mean?' Asked Emily.

'All the way along, from the beginning of the process, Philip kept saying how much he hoped he was a match and when he was, on the day we told them all, he let them all rejoice and then he dropped his bombshell.' Liam could tell he was getting angry again. 'The whole family was devastated and I don't blame them. I found myself getting really incensed by what was happening in front of me. After his announcement he just walked out like nothing mattered to him.'

Emily thanked Liam for his honesty and then pondered a few moments before asking her final question.

'Philip was murdered on 8th December between 7:00pm-9:00pm. I'm sure you have read in the papers that he was killed with a knife penetrating his heart. In your opinion Liam, was Ethan capable of murdering his brother? Was he physically able to carry out the crime?'

Liam took several moments to think over the question before answering.

'Ethan is weak and getting weaker, but I'd say he probably would have had enough strength, yes, just about.'

They both thanked Liam for his time and the much-needed hot drinks.

1:30pm

Ethan was in a side room towards the end of the ward. Outside his door were big notices that told the pair that they needed to wash their hands and put on gloves and aprons before they entered. Once they were ready, Isaac knocked on the door and entered. Lying in bed curled up on his left side Ethan was asleep. In the chair next to the bed was Adam, who awoke as the door opened. Straight away he put his finger to his lips indicating the detectives should not make any sounds. Adam then made gestures with his hands telling the pair to leave the room and he would follow.

Once outside, they found themselves ushered into a quiet room where they were joined by the angry teenager.

'What do you want? You can't speak to him now as he is sleeping, and I won't let you wake him up. He is unwell and needs to be left alone!'

Isaac let Adam calm down and then spoke in a gentle voice.

'I totally understand, but we are investigating your uncle's murder and therefore there are questions we need to ask.'

'Ask me then, I'll answer what I can for you,' was the stubborn reply.

'Your father lied to us when he said he last saw his brother in November as we have an eyewitness who saw you both at Philip's house the day he was murdered at about 4:00pm. Can you explain this?'

'That's a mistake! That wasn't us.'

'That's OK Adam, I'll go and ask your dad then.'

'OK, dad just wanted answers as to why uncle Philip did what he did, that's why we went around to his house.'

Isaac looked closely at the young man in front of him. He was still a teenager at eighteen and had already had so much to deal with and he genuinely felt sorry for him.

'What did Philip say?'

Adam was clearly trying to think back to that time as his face was making all kinds of expressions.

'He said that he wanted to get my dad's hopes up so he could drop them again, or something like that. Dad then asked why, but I don't remember the exact words.'

'Adam you're doing great, but this is really important, what did your uncle say?'

'He said something like, you know why and when my dad said he didn't, my uncle said the same words again but this time he shouted them. Dad then said he had already apologised.'

'What did your dad need to say sorry for?' Asked Emily.

'I don't know, nothing was said.'

The room they were in was designed as a quiet room for the ward, a place where private conversations were had, or people came to get away from the horrors that were happening inside rooms. It was a drab looking space that evoked depression and claustrophobia.

'Adam, you and your father left Philip's house and you initially both got into his car and started to drive off, however you stopped the car, jumped out and ran off. Why did you do that and where did you go?' Asked Isaac.

Adam raised both hands to his forehead and gently tapped the sides of his head with the lower part of his palms.

'It is all too much for me DCI Davidson! My dad is dying, people are yelling at each other. My entire world is changing. Don't you think it is reasonable for me not to be coping well and I just needed to get away?'

'I do Adam, I really do, but I need to know where you went and for how long?'

'I ran off down the road, went through the park, found a bench, and sat there for a while. I then got cold and went to the cinema to see a couple of films.'

'What films?' volunteered the DS.

'The new Jumanji film and, erm, the new Kingsman film.'

Realising that Adam was trying his best but clearly getting upset, Isaac changed the line of questions.

'Your uncle was scared of clowns and your dad said it was due to a childhood issue. Someone was clearly trying to scare Philip, make him feel vulnerable and intimidated. Do you know anything about this? Could it be your dad trying to scare his brother for not giving him his cells?' Isaac looked at his notepad for dates and then continued. 'Philip first saw it on 15th October, your dad had finished his first lot of treatment by then and wasn't in hospital. I know he is your dad, but you can't hold information back Adam, you have to tell the truth.'

Adam didn't appear to be listening to the question he had been asked and was rolling his eyes and screwing up his face. Both Isaac and Emily were unsure what he was doing, when suddenly he spoke.

'15th October?'

'Yes,' said the DCI.

'You said uncle Philip had been seeing the clown since 15th October.

Right?'

'Yes,' repeated Isaac.

'It wasn't until the 19th October that he said he wouldn't help dad, so why would my father be the clown in his road on the 15th?'

'That is a very good point young man.'

Adam got up, smirked at the detectives and left the room.

44:

21st December 2017

Lewis

09:00am

The team were once again sitting around the crime board contemplating what evidence they had accumulated so far. Christmas was just around the corner meaning days would be lost investigating and the staff Christmas party was tomorrow night. The cheerless police room was anything but Christmassy. Isaac wanted to know what information had been gathered over the last few days and after he had informed everybody of his interviews with the Oakes family, he went round the room starting with DC Anne Michaels.

'Well sir, myself and Hamish (turning to DC Potter) drew a blank as far as Lewis is concerned as there is no information out there about him, or so we thought. When we got back here last night after a few days of searching, Jian had unexpectedly found out a little about our mystery man.'

Isaac was pleasantly surprised to see that Anne spoke without eating, drinking or wiping things off herself.

'OK Jian, let's hear what you and Faisal found out about Lewis.'

'Sir, myself and DC Asher studied the crime scene picture and saw the pizza was in a box from 'Tony's Authentic Pizzas.' We googled it and found that there is only one. It's a family run business and only six minutes from our victim's home.' Jian looked over at his partner and indicted for him to continue. DC Asher smiled back at Jian and nodded.

'We went to the restaurant and discussed the night of the murder and asked how the order was placed and who delivered it. We stressed no one was in trouble but we wanted to ask the delivery person if they may have seen something etc?'

Tension was building in the room as it felt like a big reveal was about to happen. The team weren't disappointed. Faisal continued.

'The order was placed via their app and the pizza was delivered by a lad called Lewis Mayhew.'

The moment felt like there needed to be thunderous applause and fireworks being set off. They could now link Lewis with Philip. Each and every one looked at each other as if the case were solved. Isaac raised his voice and got the attention back into the room.

'Excellent work, both of you, but please continue.'

Jian took the lead again.

'Lewis Mayhew is eighteen years old and lived in Looe in Cornwall. Mother, Janice Mayhew died four years ago and Lewis moved in with Janice's sister. We called her and she said that she hasn't seen or heard from him since he left in the summer. However, before he went he told her that he was heading to London to make things right for his mother's sake. She wouldn't say any more than this. I checked his birth certificate and it states father unknown. Tony's Pizzas only know his name and previous address as it's a cash in hand job, but they do have his 'pay-as-you-go' mobile number, which is now permanently switched off.'

Isaac acknowledged the work his team had done before asking a couple more questions.

'Emily, any news on Jacob?'

'No sir, still nowhere to be found and his family haven't heard anything either.'

Isaac scrunched up his face.

'Why has he gone into hiding? Where is Philip's mobile phone? And where is Lewis?' The DCI scanned around the room at his DCs. 'Jian, Anne and Hamish, I want you to spend today and tomorrow looking into these questions and see what you can find out.' Isaac then faced DC Asher. 'Faisal, when I was asking you all to float questions the other day, you asked me what I was questioning. Do you remember my answer?'

'Absolutely sir, you said "white Ford Fiesta." Why?'

'I was having dinner with my brother the other evening and at one point I slammed my hand down on the table and made him jump out of his skin. I had linked together why the car was important.' Isaac looked at the faces all staring in his direction. 'Jian stated that Mrs Ferres said she saw a woman in a white Fiesta lurking outside Philip's house. Arjun Singh thought a white Fiesta had knocked down his brother and when I went to Rebecca Firth's house to interview her with Jian, there was a what in the driveway?' Isaac pointed at Jian.

'A white Ford Fiesta sir.'

'Emily and Faisal, I want us to go and speak to Mrs Firth again as she really has some explaining to do.'

4:00pm

Lewis sat on his bed and listened to the cars outside his bedroom window. He could tell that the school holidays had started as the noise level from the street was much lower. From his bed he could see flashing lights from the corner of his eyes. The Christmas lights had been switched on a few days ago and already Lewis was sick to death of hearing festive songs coming from the shop downstairs.

Christmas had always been a happy time when his mum was alive. There was always a mountain of presents under the tree and usually a few more hidden around the house. It didn't matter if they turned out to be a colouring book, socks or something big like a PlayStation console, Lewis just loved opening them and as he did, watching his mum's face beaming back at him.

'I miss you Mum,' Lewis said quietly to himself as he leaned over to his bedside table and took a bite of his toasted special.

Life hadn't worked out how he had expected with his move to London. His sole aim was to find Philip and then gather as much information about him as he could. Once armed with all he needed, Lewis was then going to reveal who he was. However, that had all gone wrong.

Looking out of the window, Lewis reflected on Rebecca and how she had got in the way and had misled him with her obsessive stories about Philip. Hearing that she was pregnant with his dad's child had made him feel physically sick.

'How could you have had another baby when you rejected my lovely mum when she told you about me?'

These thoughts were continuously going around his mind. Anger was building up inside Lewis and staring at the walls that were still covered in pictures of his dad weren't helping matters. He jumped off the bed and went over to them and slowly started to rip some of them off the wall.

'Why did you have to flirt with me?' Lewis started repeating to himself. 'I'm your son. You made me so angry when I delivered your pizza the night you died. I knew you'd regret it once you found out who I was, but why did you flirt and open your dressing gown? I was nearly ready to tell you who I was. I wanted answers as to why you treated my mum so badly. Why didn't you want me?'

Lewis was now sitting crossed legged on the floor holding a picture of Philip that he had ripped from the wall. It showed just half of the face. Silence fell over the room as he sat there quietly gazing at the picture.

After about an hour Lewis stood up, gathered any washing-up lying around his room and headed off to the kitchen to tidy up. As he stood at the sink he had an urge to go to Philip's house. He wasn't sure why he felt the need to do this, but he knew he was going to.

Once the washing up had been done and the kitchen was again spotless, Lewis went to get himself ready. As he stepped back into his bedroom he heard a siren and he rushed to the window, it was an ambulance. The noise had unnerved him. So far he had avoided the police. He knew they'd be looking for him as he'd been the one to deliver the pizza and they must have found that out by now. Lewis was also concerned that they suspected him of greater involvement. However, now was not the time to be worrying about them, he knew he'd have to talk to them at some point, but that wasn't now.

Thirty minutes later and Lewis was parked up outside Philip's house. He sat silently staring at the deserted building and had flashbacks to the times he had been standing on the front door delivering food, or when he had been standing opposite and simply observing the comings and goings. That last time had been the most awkward. Philip had gone too far that time. The anger began to rise again and Lewis started to bang on the steering wheel. To help calm himself, he opened the car door and got out to stretch his legs. He then walked to the house and stood and began wondering what might have been. His thought process was interrupted by a sudden glare of light. He quickly twisted to his left and saw an old woman looking at him from next door. Lewis turned and ran to his car as fast as he could and drove off towards his home.

Once he was back inside his flat Lewis found himself beginning to calm down, although still annoyed with himself.

'Idiot, why did you go over there and let that nosey old bag see you?'

Continuously cursing himself as he made himself a cup of tea, Lewis couldn't stop thinking of Philip and the awkwardness that had occurred between them. When he had delivered the pizzas, there had always been an element of flirtatious behaviour from Philip, but this had got more blatant each time. Lewis thought he was fine with this as he knew all the facts and the truth would put a stop to the actions of his father. Once these were known, a new beginning would start and they could have become a proper family.

To help ease his agitation, once the tea was made, he sat on his brown lumpy sofa and held his cup in both hands to let the warmth help soothe his mood.

Unfortunately after a few minutes his thoughts again turned to his mum and the situation he was in and therefore the tea and heat hadn't worked.

'Why did you treat my mum so badly?' He asked aloud.

Lewis remembered his mum's words to him, *'Only go searching for him if it's something you really feel you need to do, as I don't want you getting hurt by him, he isn't worth it.'*

Lewis got up and started to pace around the flat.

'I had to come and find him Mum, he needed to be taught a lesson and I had to be the one to do it.' His agitation had returned and he started to use his right fist to punch his left palm.

Lewis started to cry and through his tears his words started to get shaky.

'I went too far Mum,' he was now looking out of the window and up to the sky. 'I went too far Mum, I shouldn't have done it, but he needed to be taught a lesson. Help me Mum.' Lewis sobbed.

45:

1991

Philip aged Ten

Ethan walked through the dark and wet streets to pick up his brother from a school concert that no-one had bothered to go and watch. He had been ordered by his father to collect Philip and with each damp step forward he was resenting them both, but more so his brother for being only ten and not able to get home by himself.

As he neared the school, the heavens opened and a heavy downpour soon started to flood the roads. Ethan's feet were drenched as he only had canvas shoes on. The anger was building up inside him and someone or something needed to pay! As he walked on, a ginger cat slinked passed, but it soon regretted this when Ethan's foot shot out and kicked it. The cat hissed loudly and then scurried off into some nearby bushes. Ethan laughed aloud.

The school was quite close to the local graveyard and Ethan chose to walk the long way round rather than go through it. Philip hated the cemetery as it scared him and therefore Ethan had already decided to go that way home.

As he approached the school, Ethan could see the kids coming out with their parents who had obviously attended the concert, watching their children perform. Philip was standing on his own looking out for anyone he knew, as he had no idea who would be picking him up. Ethan hid himself behind a car as he watched everyone else leave the building, get into their cars, and drive home. Philip stood alone and Ethan could see the worry in his brother's face and it highly amused him.

This game went on for another fifteen minutes as the older brother was enjoying watching the growing panic in Philip's face. The fun had to end soon as the teachers would start coming out.

'Five more minutes brother of mine.' Ethan chuckled to himself.

Philip descended the school stairs and searched up and down the street, he began pacing back and forth and started to get very frightened. At this point the young boy knew it would be his brother collecting him.

'Ethan,' Philip shouted out. 'ETHAN!'

Behind a car, Philip heard giggling and knew who it was coming from and headed in that direction. Ethan saw his brother approaching and just at the right moment, jumped up and screamed.

'PHILIP!'

The youngster screamed and dropped his school bag into a large puddle. Ethan saw the distress in his brother's face and smiled to himself.

'Come on, I want to get home. Did you know I had plans for tonight? I was going out with a girl from my class and she was going to have sex with me. You have ruined that and I'm not happy you little git.'

Philip didn't like Ethan talking about girls in this way. He didn't really understand why, but it felt wrong.

'I didn't know you were going out, I didn't ask you to pick me up. Why didn't Mrs Temple come?'

Ethan just scowled at his brother and grabbed him by the shoulder and pushed him forward.

At the entrance of the graveyard, Philip went to take the path Ethan had taken earlier but was pulled back by his brother and forced through the cast iron gates and into the dark and creepy church grounds.

'No Ethan, this place scares me and I am not going to walk through it.' Philip stood still and refused to move.

Ethan kept walking through the grounds, knowing that his brother would have to eventually follow him. In true horror style, an owl hooted from the trees and a near full moon shone on the gravestones. Ethan was now getting a little afraid too but continued to wait for his brother.

'Phillllipp,' Ethan said in a low menacing voice and dragging out the name for a scary effect.

There was no reply.

After another ten minutes went by and still no sign of Philip, Ethan became concerned that he had gone too far and something had happened to his brother. He retraced his steps and arrived at the place where he had last seen Philip, but there was no sign of him. On the floor and soaked, was the pamphlet from the concert with Philip's name in the top right-hand corner.

'PHILIP!' Ethan screamed and looked around him in a mad haphazard way. 'Philip, I'm sorry, where are you? PHILIP!'

Ethan paced up and down and then walked back to the school to see if his brother and returned there. The place was now in complete darkness. Ethan's breath quickened and he was aware he had palpitations and a dry mouth. Sweat was dripping from his forehead and he felt he wanted to vomit.

After searching around the school grounds, Ethan walked back towards his home, this time bypassing the graveyard. There were plenty of cars on the road and at times Ethan's vision was impaired by the blinding lights from the vehicles. The rain continued to fall and each step Ethan made was with a heavy heart. He was now really anxious that he had gone too far and something had happened to his brother. How would he explain this to his father?

'PHILIP!' Ethan called in desperation.

'Yes, what do you want?' The calm voice came from behind Ethan and caused him to scream out.

'Bloody hell Philip, where were you? You scared me to death.'

Ethan was secretly pleased to see his brother standing there in front of him but wasn't about to let Philip know this.

'You don't always get to win Ethan. I may only be ten, but I can out-fox you sometimes. I knew what you would do if I walked into the church grounds. You would hide and then jump out and scare me. I decided to keep you in sight but hide myself and then follow you quietly as I watched you get scared, which is exactly how I knew you wanted me to feel.'

Philip smirked at his brother and turned and walked in the direction of home.

46:

21st December 2017

Rebecca

05:00am

There was an early frost on the windows in the kitchen. It was a light dusting that would melt as soon as the sun started to rise. Rebecca sat and looked at the tiny frost crystals that had formed and thought she could see certain patterns. The room was as cold inside as it was outside, but Rebecca sat in her ill-fitting bra and knickers at the breakfast bar and dragged on a cigarette, unaware that her skin had a light blue tinge. Her hair hadn't been washed for many days and was beginning to have a slight odour. In her hands she held Philip's mobile phone, it was still switched off but fully charged.

Rebecca started to slightly rock back and forth as she hummed to herself. She looked at her reflection in the front of the phone and grinned. She then put the phone next to her heart and rocked herself with more motion.

'I had to do it my love, didn't I?' She whispered softly. 'You betrayed me my love and therefore as much as I loved you, you needed to be punished. You understand that, don't you? Please tell me that you do.'

After an hour of sitting thinking thoughts of Philip and unaware of the passing time, Rebecca walked over to the fridge and opened it ready to take out a can of drink, but the fridge was completely empty. There wasn't even a drop of milk for a cup of tea. She slammed the door closed, which in turn caused a pile of papers and clothes to fall onto the dirt-ridden floor. Her next move was to phone Amelia and ask her to drop off the things that she wanted before her daughter went to work. She went back over to the breakfast bar and picked up her phone, which was next to

Philip's and made the call.

Since the night of the beating, Amelia had stopped talking to her mother because her mum was covering up for her attacker and not letting the police or the hospital staff know who it was. Her last message sent was constantly going around Rebecca's head.

'I'm done with you mum, you're a total mess and I can't help you if you don't help yourself. You need to get to your GP and get some serious help. No wonder Alice has disowned you. You're a wreck.'

Amelia's phone went to voicemail, just as Rebecca knew it would. She left her a furious and bitter message.

'I don't need you, you stupid bitch, I can take care of myself, you never cared about me. I hate you, you and your bloody sister. I wish I'd never had either of you. Stay out of my life and I never want to see either of you again.'

Rebecca ended the call, fell onto the floor, and curled up into a tight ball and howled herself to sleep.

10:30am

In the distance Rebecca could hear a slight noise, it sounded like a ringing tone or a bell. The noise wasn't stopping. She then heard a voice shouting and it startled her as it was coming from her garden.

'I can see her sir,' said DC Asher. 'She is lying on the kitchen floor, but she's moving and getting herself up.'

Rebecca stood for a few seconds and then staggered, steadying herself on the walls towards the front door to open it. Standing there in her bra and knickers shocked the trio of detectives, especially her dishevelled look. Emily was quick to step forward and steered the emaciated female into the lounge and then went to find some clothes for Rebecca. Emily needed to help her.

Whilst the ladies were in the lounge, the men wandered slowly around the rest of the ground floor. The place was a mess, which alerted them both to the mental state of Rebecca, as she obviously wasn't taking care of herself or her home. They walked into the kitchen and the sights were even worse in there. The bins were overflowing, mainly with empty cans and bottles of drink, but there were a few microwavable containers as well. Isaac scrutinised the hovel and his eyes came to rest on the two phones on the breakfast bar. He put on a rubber glove and picked up the first one and as it lit up he was faced with a picture of his victim. Isaac then picked up the other phone and soon saw that it was switched off. He looked over at DC Asher and called him over.

'Let's see what happens when I turn this on.'

The button was pressed and the phone slowly rebooted back to life. The two detectives viewed the screen and eventually it was on. The home screen photo was of Arjun, naked and asleep. The young man obviously had no idea his photo had been taken. Isaac turned to his DC and frowned. He took out an evidence bag and placed the phone inside.

'Faisal, I want you to go out to the front of the house and examine the white Fiesta. Search for any signs of damage, blood stains and clothing fragments. If you see anything, anything at all, get forensics down here ASAP.'

DC Asher left immediately and passed Rebecca and Emily as they came into the kitchen.

'Mrs Firth, is this Philip Oakes' mobile phone?' He was pointing to the evidence bag.

Rebecca made no sign that she had heard him. 'Mrs Firth, Rebecca, we are examining your car for signs of a recent accident. Is there anything you want to say?'

'Sir, she isn't well. She isn't talking at all. I think we need to call for an ambulance. She is skeletal, her breath stinks of alcohol and I'm really worried about her.'

An ambulance was called and Rebecca just sat there and looked out of the kitchen window. A few moments later the door opened and DC Asher walked in.

'Sir, it's as you thought. The front of the car is dented and there are signs of blood. Forensics are on their way.'

'Thanks Faisal, we can finish up here once the ambulance arrives.'

Isaac's phone started to ring. It was Jian, so he put on the loudspeaker for the others to hear.

'Sir, Philip's phone has been turned on and we have a GPS report on its whereabouts.'

'Thanks Jian, we have the phone and will be sending it off to be analysed as soon as we get back.'

The three detectives stood contemplating each other and then at Rebecca, who had started to rock herself back and forth again and was also rubbing her tummy as she talked to herself.

'It's OK Philip my love, they will understand why I did what I needed to do. You needed to be punished and I needed to be the one to do it. They will see why I did it my love.'

The team looked at each other with their eyes wide open and then back at the woman who was now quietly singing to herself.

47:

27th December 2017

Arjun

08:30am

As far as Isaac was concerned, Christmas was now over and done with. He had spent a quiet few days with his brother and had had a very nice time. They had both cooked and chosen wines, read books and seen a few films. On Christmas day they had had some friends around in the evening, but they were both pleased to relax by themselves on Boxing day. However, he now stood in front of his team and was ready to summarise the case so far.

'Where's Anne?' Isaac asked in an exasperated fashion.

'I'm here, I'm here, sorry.' Anne came bursting through the door just as her DCI had asked about her whereabouts.

The reason for her lateness was obvious when everyone could see the coffee and a package of food in her hands.

'Right! Is everybody ready?' Isaac asked as he glared at his slovenly DC. 'We have all had a couple of days off and I know that at the end of last week lots of good things happened re this case. I will now talk through what we know so far.'

He turned to the crime board and it was now more succinct, or maybe tidy would be a better word. There were six pictures on the board.

'Ethan Oakes, brother of Philip, father to Adam, Saul and Max and husband to Emma. He is angry he has been allowed to die without his brother even trying to save him with his stem cells. Jacob Spencer, supposed best friend since aged 3, father to Rory and Adrian and husband to Tanvi. He may have sought revenge due to Philip sending a video of him with another woman to his wife. He also owed our victim £25,000. Philip's death has wiped that debt.'

Isaac walked around, then stepped over to Anne, took her coffee and started to drink it. She was annoyed.

'Lewis Mayhew, unknown link to Philip. Thanks to Mrs Ferres calling in and saying she saw a young man/lad standing outside Philip's house, we now have his number plate and today we will contact the DVLA and see where the car is registered to. Rebecca Firth, mother to Amelia and Alice and divorced from Terry Firth. She is a scorned woman who believes she is pregnant by Philip. She isn't. Blood samples from the front of her car match those of Rohit Singh. If she didn't murder Philip, then she can be charged with attempted murder, or second-degree murder, if we can prove she was driving. That brings me to Arjun Singh, brother to Rajan and Rohit. His father is dead but mother is still alive. Arjun worked for Philip and was his partner at the time of the murder.'

The whole team sat glaring at their boss and were taking in everything he was saying, except for Anne. She was busy trying to eat her croissant without anybody noticing her.

'Lastly, we have the clown. We know it had been stalking Philip since 15th October, but we don't know who it is, or why they are doing it. We have been able to take the picture from Philip's phone that shows the clown in his garden. The time the picture was taken would make us suppose that he took the picture when he got in very drunk after his evening with Arjun. Unfortunately, the photo is very blurred and not easy to make out, even though it has been blown up in size. What is important and please all pay attention,' Isaac glared at Anne, 'I believe this is the image of our murderer. Why do I think this? A green piece of material was found in Philip's kitchen next to the pizza. Forensics said it was possible it came from a fancy-dress wig. Now we have this photo, we can just about see that the clown is wearing a green hairpiece. So, which of our suspects is the clown? We know from questioning everyone, apart from Lewis, that they all knew he was scared of them.'

The room was full of everyone talking at the same time. Isaac allowed this for a few moments as he was glad of their enthusiasm.

'Anne,' Isaac's voice caused the DC to jump a little. 'You asked PC Chaplin about the clown sightings, what were the dates Philip saw the clown?'

Anne went over to her desk and started to work through the mess. She was aware that everybody was looking at her and this was causing her to stumble more. After frantically searching her pile of mess, she eventually found her notebook. She grabbed it and rushed back to the others.

'15th and 20th October and 1st November,' she said in short, out of breath bursts.

'15th October,' Isaac repeated. 'Adam Oakes said that Philip didn't refuse cells until after 15th, so that would therefore count out Ethan as our killer.'

The whole team started to write in their notebooks and then looked at their DCI for further instructions. Isaac drank the rest of Anne's coffee and scrunched up the cup and threw it in the bin.

'What questions do we need answering? Bear with me as I wander and speak, but please jot down what I say. Where is Jacob? Why has he gone into hiding and why did he lie about going around to see Philip the day he was killed? Where is Lewis? Let's see what the DVLA can tell us. Where was everyone, apart from Ethan on the dates the clown was seen? Why wouldn't Philip give Ethan his cells? I can't help thinking this is important. Why did Philip attack Rebecca? Why did she mumble that he had to be punished? Why do I not have any questions about Arjun?'

Once Isaac had stopped talking, everyone was scribbling away. Finding Philip's phone had really helped to open up the investigation. They had all seen the video sent to Tanvi, as well as pictures stored. The majority of texts and emails had already been checked but added nothing new to the investigation.

'Sir, what next?' Questioned Jian.

'Emily, I want you and Hamish to go to the hospital and see if you can get any more out of Rebecca. I know she's extremely unwell but try your best. Anne, I want you and Faisal to chase things up with the DVLA and then visit Tanvi Spencer and see if there is any news from her husband. Check his bank to see if he has used any of his cards since we last checked. Also check his phone records etc and see if he can now be tracked via his phone. Jian, you and I will visit Mr Singh and find out more about his last evening with Philip and where he was on the clown dates.'

As the whole team got up and went back to their desks to start organising their day, Isaac stayed by the crime board. He stared hard at the blurred picture of the clown and couldn't help but think he was missing something.

11:00am

The noises coming from the various machines were supposed to be a comfort. It meant Rohit was still alive. However, the noises just reminded Arjun how sick his brother was and that he had caused this. The pain was deep inside Arjun as he stared at Rohit with the breathing tube in his throat and tubes and needles everywhere. Mrs Singh was asleep in the chair by the door, but Arjun was sitting right next to his brother, holding his hand like he had done nearly every moment. Rajan visited daily and only stayed for an hour or so, but never uttered a word to his grieving brother.

Arjun looked over at his mother, her head was dropped forward and to one side. He knew that as soon as she was awake she would start to complain of a stiff neck and that the painkillers she got from the GP for her aches and pains were no good. He had given up telling her that sleeping in a chair was not good for her, but he also knew she didn't want to leave the hospital.

Arjun turned back to his brother and started to talk in nothing more than a whisper.

'Hey Rohit, mother sleeping in that awkward position, you know she's going to start moaning as soon as she is awake. I haven't been up to much, I just sit here and pray very hard that you're going to open your eyes. I'm so sorry little bro, I never meant anything like this to happen to you. Thank you so much for sticking up for me against Rajan, that was very brave of you and I don't deserve your loyalty.' Arjun lifted his brother's hand and held it so it was touching his cheek. 'When you're better, let's go bowling again. That was a great evening and I'll pay again. Oh, please get better little man, I miss you so much, just open your eyes and look at me.'

'Mr Singh,' a softly spoken voice came from behind.

Arjun at first thought he was hearing things, but after another calling of his name, he turned around and saw DCI Davidson and another person he had not seen before.

'Mr Singh do you remember who...' Isaac was interrupted.

'I remember who you are, it was only a few days ago, who's he?' Arjun pointed at Jian.

Introductions were made and a request for them to go into the ward's quiet room. Arjun went, leaving his mother still asleep in the chair.

'Mr Singh, it has actually been two weeks since we first saw you. We knew where you'd be if we needed you again.' Isaac addressed the man sitting on a low sofa whose head was angled at the floor. 'We do need to ask you a few questions, so will need you to concentrate and please take your time in answering. Did you know Philip Oakes was scared of clowns?'

'You've asked me that before and I said yes.'

'Where were you on 15th, 20th October and 1st November?'

'Why? What has this to do with Phi...' Arjun found he couldn't say the name in full as it caused him such pain. 'And what does it have to do with a clown? I want to get back to my brother.'

Jian stepped forward and explained the significance of the dates and why the question was being asked.

'I've no idea about 15th, I was probably at the pub, but I was with Phi... him on the 20th. I only found out about his phobia that evening because when he arrived home he was in shock as he had just seen it in the street. You're very welcome to check my messages for texts, times, and dates they were sent.'

Arjun handed his phone over to Isaac.

'I send all messages from WhatsApp, so look there, you'll also see, if you go into the group 'family Singh' the pictures that arsehole sent to my family which caused the fight and why Rohit is where he is now.'

Isaac spent a few minutes reading through the phone and was happy that Arjun was telling the truth. He then went on with his questions.

'Do you know a Rebecca Firth?'

'Yes, she is the drunk witch from the pub. She was in love with 'him' and said she was pregnant by him. When she entered the pub, you knew evil had arrived.' Arjun's face was all screwed up.

'That is a strong thing to say Mr Singh, why do you say it?'

Arjun finally looked up from the floor and stood up, he raised his hand to his head as if he were suffering from a headache.

'She was vile, which, if you are interested, is an anagram of evil! She's had a sort of thing going with 'him' before we got together. She resented me and made that clear. She was a gossip and her words caused damage.'

'Mr Singh,' Jian said, 'we have reason to believe that Mrs Firth was driving the car that hit your brother. From what you have just said, it may have been that she thought it was you that she'd hit. I'm very sorry.'

Arjun collapsed onto the floor in a kneeling position and started to howl. Both detectives glanced at each other. Jian moved closer to put a reassuring hand on the grieving man's shoulder, but it was flicked away by Arjun. Isaac glared at his DC, as that was information that he wasn't authorised to give. This would be a learning curve for Detective Wong. Isaac wasn't happy.

Minutes went by with the only sound coming from the man kneeling on the ground. The howl was now more of a low moan.

'He might die and it really is all my fault. I blamed myself because the reason he ran into the road was due to the argument between myself and Rajan, but he was hit because of her jealousy.' Arjun suddenly stood fully erect and fear spread rapidly over his face. 'Oh my God, she tried to kill me before. It makes sense now, but at the time, I just thought it was a drunk driver or someone being stupid, but it was her.' Arjun was now visibly shaking.

'What are you saying Mr Singh?' Asked Isaac.

'Beginning of November, it was early in the morning. I had just left 'his' house and was walking home. A car mounted the pavement and came straight for me, I jumped into a garden and the car sped off. It was a white Fiesta. Oh my God, she tried to kill me.'

Isaac and Jian stood there in silence trying to take in the information that they had just heard and Arjun began pacing. The room was very tense. Isaac was realising that the mental state of Rebecca was probably far more disturbed than they had first thought. When they could, she would need questioning about Arjun's statement.

'Oh my goodness, it's Rohit, Arjun, it's Rohit.' Mrs Singh had burst through the door and caused all three men to jump out of their skins. She now lay on the floor sobbing and was thumping the ground with her fists.

Arjun ran from the room as fast as he could. He jumped over his mother and headed for the ITU ward.

Isaac looked at Mrs Singh and bent down to help her up, however, she was still sobbing and showed no signs that she wanted any help.

'Sir,' Jian addressed his boss. 'If Mr Singh only knew Mr Oakes was scared of clowns after the second sighting, does this mean he didn't commit the murder?'

'Yes Jian, it is certainly seeming that way.'

48:

28th December 2017

Jacob

08:30am

‘And then there were three!’

The team looked at their DCI as he wandered around the crime board. Isaac had a pen in his mouth, with which he was tapping his teeth.

‘And then there were three,’ he repeated.

There was a silence in the room as ‘sir’ hadn’t given any instructions and each team member didn’t want to break the concentration that was showing on Isaac’s face. The room was dimly lit as two bulbs had blown and they were awaiting maintenance to come and replace them. Hamish went over to the kitchen to make a coffee and the rest were studying their notebooks.

Emily approached Isaac.

‘Sir, can we help with anything?’

‘OK, here we go, let’s look at the board.’

Hamish quickly walked back with his coffee and sat down. Isaac continued.

‘Six photos and two have a red cross over them. Ethan and Arjun. Both these men have been ruled out as our killer due to the timings and sightings of the bloody clown. Do we even know that the ‘clown’ did the murder? We have one piece of green fake hair, found by the pizza box that we are pinning our hopes on and that’s only because of this awful, badly blurred photo that links the picture with the crime scene. I hope we are going in the right direction with this theory.’ Isaac was clearly getting agitated. ‘That leaves us three suspects, Jacob, Rebecca and Lewis. Two of these we haven’t been able to get hold off, well, Jacob just once.’

'Well I have good news to report,' Anne had stood up. 'Our Mr Lewis Mayhew is a very organised young man. When we checked with DVLA, he had updated his details and we now have his London address. Faisal and I went around yesterday but there was no answer, we waited in the car for a few hours.' Anne handed her boss a piece of paper with Lewis' information.

'Well done both, Emily and I will try again today. Did you have any luck with finding Jacob?'

Anne looked over to Emily who had her phone to her ear. She ended the call and spoke.

'Sir, myself and Hamish went to the hospital, but Rebecca was sedated so no luck there. I called Anne to explain we were now free and said we'd head over to see Mrs Spencer and see if she had heard from her husband, she hadn't. However, I have just taken a call from downstairs and guess what?'

Everyone stared at her and were eager to know what she was about to say.

'Jacob is downstairs, he has just arrived asking to see you sir.'

Isaac was really pleased with what he heard from his team. He felt that they were getting closer to closing this case, despite his earlier agitation.

'Right, I will go with Emily to interview Mr Spencer and then head over to see if we can catch Mr Mayhew. The rest of you go over emails, texts, voicemails and statements again. See if there is anything that we may have missed. Check again with forensics. Hamish, I want you to check with the hospital to see how Rebecca Firth and Ethan Oakes are getting on. Ethan might be at home now. Oh, by the way, I meant to tell you all, Rohit Singh woke up yesterday, it appears like he will make a full recovery.'

09:00am

Jacob sat in a small room with no windows and he was starting to feel claustrophobic. He had been given a glass of water and told to wait. He was feeling incredibly nervous and found sitting at a table and waiting extremely difficult. Outside the door, he heard voices and muffled sounds.

The door opened slowly and in walked the two detectives who had spoken to him before. They did not look happy. They both walked over and joined Jacob at the table.

'Mr Spencer, so nice of you to come and see us,' Isaac couldn't help the sarcasm.

'In my defence, I didn't know you were looking for me.'

'I told you at our last interview that I would need to speak to you again Mr Spencer.'

'I know and I'm here. I went away for a while. Tanvi, my wife, had told me I wasn't to come anywhere near her or the children at Christmas. That was inevitably awfully hard for me. I needed to get away to try to think straight. I miss my beautiful family. I truly am sorry, I actually didn't give the issue of Philip a second thought. What I mean, is that I thought about Philip a lot, but not the actual murder. He was my best friend and I loved him. I really don't know what happened to him in the past few months. He had changed and it wasn't a nice change. I missed the Philip who was my mate.'

Isaac studied Jacob's face for a few moments and watched his body language at the same time. The DCI liked Jacob, there was something very genuine about him.

'What had changed about Philip?' Asked Emily.

'He got mixed up with a drunk woman from the pub. Philip started out as bisexual, but I thought he was now gay and had been for years. I have no idea why he went with this woman. I saw her a few times and I don't like to be rude about people, but she was rank. Old looking but not old, drank like a fish, decayed teeth and hair I wouldn't touch. I couldn't see why he went with her. Then he hooked up with the bartender, Indian lad. He was nice. Then Philip started asking me about the money I owed him. I know it was really bad of me to not start a payback scheme, but I genuinely don't have any spare cash. I'm a gambler, well was and I got into £25,000 worth of debt and Philip bailed me out. I had every intention to pay back every penny, but I'm embarrassed to say it never happened, never even started. I told you this the last time we spoke.'

Jacob picked up his water and took a long drink. When he put the glass back on the table it was empty.

'£25,000 in debt to a person rather than a bank, that's a real motive for killing someone Jacob. Add into that equation a video that broke up your marriage. That's a lot of reasons to kill.' Emily stared at the man in front of her.

'I do hear what you're saying, but I didn't kill Philip!'

'Mr Spencer, do you always tell the truth?' Asked Isaac.

'I do indeed, I have no reason to lie.'

Isaac pulled out his notebook.

'When we last spoke, you said that even though Philip had made you incredibly angry, you didn't attempt to see him. His neighbour, a Mrs Ferres says she saw an angry black man banging on his door and demanding he came out. Was that you Jacob?'

The atmosphere in the room was cold as was the tension. Isaac knew Jacob was hiding something.

'OK, yes it was me, but he didn't answer, so what does that prove?'

'It proves that you were in the area the night Philip Oakes was murdered.'

Jacob hunched up his shoulders as if in defeat.

'Mr Spencer, we know from our last interview that you knew Philip was petrified of clowns, so where were you on 15th, 20th October and 1st November?' Asked the DS.

'I can stop you right there. If you are trying to find out if I were the clown scaring him, I guess your thinking is that I was trying to scare him, so he'd confide in me and forget to ask me about the money I owed him. Well you're wrong. I was with Philip on the 1st November. He phoned the police straight after he had seen it. I was in his house, following my liaison with the other person in the video he sent my wife, so I am not the clown. Check the statement he gave the police.'

'And then there were two,' Isaac muttered under his breath.

49:

28th December 2017

Lewis

12:30pm

Once their interview was over Jacob was informed that he was subject to a RUI, released under investigation, meaning if new evidence came up he would be called for interview again. He was also told not to go missing again.

Isaac checked in with the rest of his team before leaving to find Lewis Mayhew. As he could have predicted, everyone was working hard except for Anne who had gone out for refreshments. The DCI knew the time was coming to have strong words with her. She was the weakest link in the team. Hamish and Faisal worked harder and in more detail and they were new to the team.

Isaac walked over to the crime board and looked hard at the blurred picture of the clown. Was he right in thinking this was his killer? Am I putting all my eggs into one basket? These thoughts were constantly in his head. There was something he knew was blatantly staring him in the face but wasn't revealing itself.

'If only it wasn't so distorted,' Isaac spoke softly to himself.

The atmosphere in the room was vibrant. Phone calls were happening and the tapping of fingers on keyboards was loud. Isaac studied his team for a few moments. Emily was still documenting their interview with Jacob and once she had done this, they were going to find Mr Mayhew.

'OK, listen up and come over here,' Isaac's voice was strong and commanding. 'I want your thoughts and your ideas, I want anything that is going to solve this case. If we are right about this murder and the direction of our interviews, questions and thoughts, then we are left with just two suspects as we have ruled out the others for the moment.' Isaac looked over to the door as Emily joined them. 'We have Lewis and Rebecca. Mr Mayhew is yet to be interviewed, which then might either solve this case or at least give us some more direction. Mrs Firth however is not in a great place mentally or physically at the moment. This is not terrific for us as I'm sure she hasn't told us yet what we need to know. She did however say that Philip needed to be punished. So, what thoughts and ideas do you have?'

Isaac scanned the room. There was total silence. Tension in the room was building as each person glared at another, all hoping someone else would speak.

'Sir,' Hamish stood up. 'What if it isn't one of the five suspects we think it is?'

Murmurs drifted amongst the team. Jian was next to speak.

'I have been reading through all the notes. It may not be anything, but I guess it may also be important.' All eyes were now firmly focused on the DC. 'Adam Oakes said he saw two films the evening of the death. Jumanji and Kingsman. I checked and Kingsman was out in September and not December. I can check with the cinema to see if it was still showing, but if it wasn't, where was Adam at the time he said he was watching the film?'

'That is brilliant Jian, great thinking so check that out now,' Isaac said with pride. Anne rolled her eyes.

Jian ran over to his desk as the others sat still. There was now a lot of face twitching and odd facial expressions as people were trying to think of anything they could say that would not only help the case but also score brownie points with the boss.

'Sir,' this time it was Faisal who spoke. 'I understand that we haven't interviewed Lewis yet, but based on what we do know, especially about his birth certificate saying father unknown, do we assume that Philip was his father?'

Isaac was now beaming at his DC.

'I have been thinking the same Faisal, but we just haven't said it aloud for some reason. I am hoping that today we will get the answers we need.' The DCI now turned to Anne. 'DC Michaels, do you have any thoughts?'

Anne looked at the crime board and then at the others. Nothing was coming to her and she felt like a naughty school child.

'I'm sorry sir, but I don't have any new thoughts at the moment.'

'Sir,' Jian came rushing back to the group. 'Kingsman wasn't playing, so Adam was lying.'

2:00pm

The detectives sat in the warm car. The heaters were blasting out hot air and making Isaac even more reluctant to turn off the engine, but he did. The weather outside wasn't as cold as it could be for December, but it was too cold to sit in a car for too long watching a flat for signs of movement, so they headed straight over to see if Lewis were at home.

They knew from the details collected from the DVLA that he lived in flat 1A, which was above a shop. Emily pushed the bell and they waited for a voice asking who was there or for the door latch to be released, but nothing happened. Emily rang the bell again and as she did this the door was opened by another resident going out. The man was at first unsure about letting them in, however once their badges had been shown he left them to it.

The building was relatively clean and tidy and in good decorative order. There was a post rack to the side of the main door with a different section for each of the three flats. Lewis' just had pizza and curry house leaflets in it. The pair climbed the stairs to the first floor and found flat 1A. They stood outside and listened carefully before knocking. There was silence. Isaac knocked again, only this time calling out for Lewis to answer.

'Mr Mayhew please answer the door. My name is Detective Chief Inspector Davidson and I would like to ask you some questions. Your car is outside therefore I am assuming you are in. Mr Mayhew!'

They waited a couple more minutes and then knocked again, only this time with real determination.

'Mr Mayhew please open up, we are not going away, so I suggest you unlock the door and let us in!'

This time they heard movement and the lock slowly turned as Lewis opened the door a tiny crack.

'Thank you Mr Mayhew, I am DCI Davidson and this is DS Morgans, can we please come in and ask you some questions?'

'Why do you need to speak to me? What's it about?' Lewis asked but knowing full well.

'Can we please come in and talk, it would be better than standing in your shared passageway.'

Lewis hesitantly opened the door wide and stood to one side to let the detectives in.

'Straight on is the lounge, we can talk in there,' he pointed down the hallway.

Emily noticed that the three rooms before the lounge had the doors closed. The three moved through to where Lewis had instructed them to go and sat down on the sofa. Lewis stood in front of them with his back to the hallway.

'You can sit down Mr Mayhew,' stated Emily.

'I'm happier standing, just ask your questions.'

Isaac decided that he would start off softly and see if Lewis would begin to relax.

'Do you know a Philip Oakes?'

'Yes,' came a sulky reply. 'I delivered pizzas to a guy with that name. Why?'

'Lewis, can I call you by your first name?' Isaac asked and Lewis nodded. 'Philip Oakes is dead, he was murdered on Friday 8th December and you delivered him a pizza, probably just before he was killed. So, I am very keen to know if you saw anyone hanging around, acting furtive or anything that seemed out of the ordinary?'

'No!'

'That's a very quick response, can you think about what I said again and let me know if you have a different answer.'

Isaac looked over at Emily and quickly back to Lewis.

'Nothing,' said Lewis, 'Is that it? Can you go now please?'

'You seem very keen for us to go. Is there a reason for that?' Asked

Emily.

'I have nothing I can tell you. I only delivered him pizza.'

The atmosphere in the room was very tense. Lewis was clearly uncomfortable as he kept moving from one foot to the other, the whole time keeping his back to the hallway. Isaac knew he needed to be more direct and start informing the young man more of what they knew and gauge his reaction as questions were asked.

'Lewis, we know that you did more than just deliver pizza to Philip as we have eyewitness accounts of you doing much more. Asking staff in the pub about him and standing opposite his house watching him. Would you care to explain?'

Lewis was aware that he had started to sweat on his brow, his movements were becoming more erratic and he was feeling really nervous.

'Erm... I don't know what you're talking about, I didn't know Philip.'

'Lewis,' Isaac said as calmly as he could, 'We know you stood outside his house. A neighbour saw you and your car's registration number. You were seen on a number of occasions. Please tell us what your connection is with Mr Oakes.'

'I don't have a connection, please leave now.' Lewis looked behind him down the hallway and started to breathe more rapidly. 'Can you go please?'

Both detectives were fully aware of Lewis' growing levels of anxiety and the fact he kept turning away from them. Emily spoke next.

'Can I use your toilet before I go please?'

'No!'

'Are you hiding something Lewis? Is there something you don't want us to see?' Asked Isaac.

'Just leave, don't use my toilet and just go!'

Lewis was now visibly shaking and constantly looking from the detectives to the hallway. Isaac stood up quickly and this caused Lewis to panic and run down the hallway to his bedroom. Emily was quick off the sofa and swiftly followed. She got to the door just as Lewis tried to close it from the inside. Emily gave a hard shove and the door flew open. Inside she saw a sobbing lad grabbing at the pictures on the wall. Pictures of

Philip.

'SIR,' she called out.

Isaac arrived on the scene. Lewis had stopped ripping the pictures off the wall and was slumped in the corner of the room snivelling as he held on to a picture of Philip.

Isaac walked gently over to Lewis and carefully put a hand on his shoulder.

'It's OK Lewis, we won't hurt you.'

Lewis continued to cry.

'Sir,' Emily said from behind her DCI.

Isaac hadn't heard her as he was focusing on Lewis.

'Sir!' she said with more force.

Isaac swung round and looked at his DS. She indicated with her head and eyes for him to look into the far corner of the room. Isaac turned and saw hanging on the back of the wardrobe door a full clown's costume. His heart sank as he turned back to see the weeping childlike person in front of him.

'Lewis Mayhew, I am arresting you on the suspicion of the murder of Philip Oakes. You do not have to say anything, but it may harm your defence if you do not mention when questioned something which you later rely on in court. Anything you do say may be given in evidence.'

6:00pm

Isaac sat at his desk with his head in his hands. He had asked his team to stay late tonight as he wanted a debrief with them once he and Emily had questioned Lewis with a lawyer present. Forensics had been at the house since 3:00pm and Isaac was also waiting for any news from them. Lewis had looked so fragile as he had his rights read to him and the only word he said that could be heard, was 'mum.'

Isaac had helped him stand up and as soon as he had, he fell into the DCIs arms as if he had no strength in his legs. Lewis had continued to weep all the way back to the interview room.

'Sir,' Emily said with a gentle tone. 'They are ready for us to go and speak to Lewis.'

DCI Davidson walked into the room where Lewis was and straight away knew he'd have to go calmly as he didn't want the lad to clam up. The recording started and Isaac introduced everyone who was in the room. Lewis was very distressed.

'This afternoon myself and DS Morgans found you in your bedroom with a wall half full of pictures of Philip Oakes. We also found a clown costume in your room. Mr Mayhew, will you please tell me why your room was like it was?'

Lewis looked up and the detectives could see how red and sore his eyes looked.

'I don't know what to say, I don't think you'll believe me.' Lewis' words were nothing more than a whisper.

There was not a sound to be heard in the room. The tense atmosphere was almost suffocating.

'Lewis, let's start by asking why you had so many pictures on your wall of Philip? Can you tell me?' Asked Isaac.

'I needed to…' silence returned for a few moments. 'I needed to try to get to know him.'

'Why?' Asked the DCI.

'Mum said he was my father, but he didn't want me.' Lewis was still talking as softly as he could. 'She told me not to search for him, but I needed to know things.'

'Lewis, did you kill your father? Even if it was an accident, did you do it?' Asked Isaac.

'I wanted to get to know him and let him get to know me. I thought he might end up liking me.' Lewis was either ignoring Isaac's question, or he hadn't heard it. 'I found out where he worked, that was the easy part thanks to social media. I'd go into the pub quite often. I dressed differently each time so I wouldn't be suspected of anything, stupid idea really as the bar staff started to know me, but I don't think he did.'

Lewis was talking freely and the detectives weren't about to stop him.

'I would stand outside his house quite often, just to get a glimpse of him. I once followed him to a park and to a hospital. I don't think he ever saw me. I just wanted to try to get to know him and things about him before I revealed who I was. I soon saw he was gay which I wasn't expecting but that was fine. My mum brought me up to be open to everyone. She used to make me these toasted sandwiches and we'd call them "toasted specials" it was our little thing. I loved Saturdays as that was our film day, not that she was able to stay awake for the whole film towards the end.'

Lewis looked at Isaac and a small smile crept onto his face.

'In my stupid head, I thought I might get some of those things back with him. Then he started to get funny with me, he started flirting with me every time I delivered his pizza. I only got the job because once, when I was watching his house, I saw one being delivered. I thought it would be another way of seeing him and getting to know him, but he went and ruined that.' At this point Lewis stopped talking and the room went silent again.

Emily looked at her boss and then back at Lewis, who had put his head into his hands.

'Can I have a cup of tea? Milk with two sugars. I promise to talk more but I'm thirsty.'

Isaac nodded to Emily who got up.

'Would you like some biscuits Lewis?' She asked and he moved his head up and down.

'Emily,' Isaac called out, 'I've changed my mind, tell everyone to go home.'

Thirty minutes later the interview continued. It seemed to Isaac that Lewis needed to tell his story. They were no longer asking questions but just listening.

'Philip was starting to flirt with me each time I delivered at his. That last evening was the worst. He was being very over friendly. His dressing gown was open and he had nothing on underneath. I thought to myself as I walked away that he'd regret doing this once he knew who I was. That was the last time I saw him. Sad really, I was getting mixed messages about him, but I wanted to get to know him. A woman called Rebecca, she was a drunk at the pub,' Isaac and Emily exchanged glances, 'she was obsessed with him and told me he used to shag her, but he was gay so I couldn't work that one out. She then blurted out that she was having his baby. That did my head in. Made me vomit at the thought.' Lewis stopped again and this time Isaac did ask a question.

'Can you tell us why you had a clown's costume in your room?'

'I went too far didn't I, I knew I'd gone too far. I shouldn't have done it. I went too far, but he needed to be punished so I had to do it. I sent him horrible texts from a withheld number. He hurt my mum and left her. She told him she lost the baby, me, so he'd be a thing of her past, but he needed to be disciplined for what he did to her. I needed to be the one to do this, but I went too far.' Silence fell again.

Both detectives were now unsure what Lewis was talking about. What had he done to Philip? What had he taken too far? Was this a confession to the murder?

'Lewis,' Isaac said, 'what did you do to Philip?'

He looked at both Isaac and Emily for a few moments and then lowered his head again, so he was facing the ground.

'Mum told me bits about him and one thing she told me was that he was petrified of clowns. The idea festered inside me for four years. I thought that as I got to know him, by watching and asking questions about him, I could also seek revenge for how he treated my mum. I only wanted to do it for a few months, until I was ready to tell him who I really was. I needed him to be punished first. So, I think it was on October 15th I made my first appearance of four. I stood in the distance and each time I made sure I was nearer to him. I'd make beckoning gestures to him. On the third occasion he vomited into his garden. My final appearance was in my car in the pub's car park directly outside his office window. I was a bit more sinister that time and pointed to him and then pretended to cut my throat as if I were going to do that to him. The expression on his face was absolute terror. That was my last time. I just really wanted to scare him so badly, that he'd have even the smallest idea how scared my mum was after how he treated her.' Lewis looked exhausted. 'However, I went too far. His last few months alive he was worrying about the clown; he even called the police to report it. He died and I never got to know him. I wasn't going to reveal I was the clown but once it stopped appearing things would be good.'

Isaac was feeling perplexed and Emily was also feeling very confused that Lewis' story stopped where it did. They both looked at each other and then back at the young lad.

'Didn't you also go to Philip's house dressed as a clown the night before he was killed and stood in his garden staring up at his bedroom window? Can you tell us about that?' Asked Isaac.

Lewis looked puzzled.

'No,' he said. 'I just played the clown four times. I never went into his garden.'

'OK, let's get things straight here,' Isaac was staring straight at Lewis. 'We found a full clown's costume in your flat. Orange wig, white overalls with red pom poms. We also found large red shoes, a flower and white gloves.'

'Yes that's the costume I bought,' said Lewis.

'But don't you have a less detailed costume with black boots and a green wig?'

'No I don't, why do you ask?'

'Bloody hell, there are two clowns!' Isaac muttered under his breath.

50:

Philip aged Eleven

It was a glorious summer's day. The sun was beating down on the playground and the usual hustle and bustle of the children laughing, screaming and having fun was not happening today. There were pockets of kids all around the place but near some shade. Running and playing had been swapped for sitting and talking. Over by the large tree near the sports field sat Philip and Jacob. Despite the fact that the tree was providing the much-needed shade, they sat alone.

Philip enjoyed times like these with his best friend. No one to disturb them or mess around. He rarely got to talk to anyone just on a one-to-one basis and he enjoyed that. Mrs Temple always tried when he came in from school, but she had dinner to make before Mr Oakes came home so preferred to crack on with the cooking.

Jacob was lying on his back with his hands under his head and was looking at the sun rays coming through the trees.

'Are you OK Philip?' He asked.

'What's brought that on? Why are you asking me that?' was Philip's reply.

Jacob sat up and brushed the dirt and leaves from his hair.

'You've been very quiet lately, more quiet than usual.'

'Ah Jacob, you know my life, it's hardly full of joy and happiness is it?' Philip half smiled at his friend.

'I get that,' Jacob said, 'but it's been going on longer than usual this time. I don't like seeing you so sad for so long. Is Ethan messing around with you again?'

'He never stops, last week I got to school on Monday and he had taken out all the books I needed and also my homework and put in the things I needed for later in the week. I got into trouble for not handing in my stuff for marking. It's never-ending Jacob.'

Philip lent over and grabbed his bag for his lunch box. Mrs Temple always made sure he had nice things to eat. He offered his friend half his sandwich and Jacob did the same thing back. The two boys grinned at each other as they ate.

'Do you know what it's like to never feel loved?' Asked Philip.

'No, you know I don't.' Jacob knew that Philip was aware of his loving family.

'I asked Mrs Temple the other day how long she would stay with us. She put down her rolling pin and came over to me. She put both her floury hands on my cheeks and said, "as long as you need me Philip, as long as that." I honestly think that was her way of telling me that she loved me, what do you think?'

Jacob had been listening intently to his friend and said straight away,

'Yes Philip, absolutely.'

'I'm scared she is going to leave.'

'What makes you say that?' Asked his concerned friend.

'I heard her talking to my dad in the kitchen and there were raised voices. She was saying, "he's only eleven Mr Oakes, please, you need to..." She stopped there and dad told her she was an employee and to not interfere with his children and him. I'm frightened that she will leave, or dad will sack her.'

'I hate your dad,' volunteered Jacob.

'I don't feel anything for him, neither love nor hate.'

The friends talked for the majority of the lunchtime, sharing each other's food and laughing where possible. Ten minutes before the end of the break, Philip looked at his friend and spoke of his mother for the first time.

'I don't really have any memories of my mum. She died when I was four. I sometimes wonder how different things would have been if she hadn't been knocked down. Would dad be different towards us? Would Ethan have been nicer to me? Last week a letter arrived for me by post. Unless it's my birthday that never happens. I took it up to my room to read. Guess who it was from?'

Jacob looked awkwardly at his friend and shrugged his shoulders.

'It was from my mother.'

Jacob's eyes widened and his mouth dropped.

'The letter said that she wasn't dead but living in another part of England. She faked her death to get away from me as she never wanted a second child.'

Jacob was puzzled.

'Ethan had obviously got a friend of his to write it. I knew straight away it was of his doing, but it did upset me. Not the content, but that he could be so nasty. He wasn't that clever either, he got his friend to write the letter, but he wrote the envelope. I recognised his handwriting.'

Jacob was lost for words and felt so sorry for his best friend. He lived in a house full of love and kindness which was a whole world apart from Philip's. As the two boys sat in silence, the school bell rang to indicate the end of lunchtime. They stood up and Jacob found his voice.

'I love you Philip. I don't mean in a boyfriend way, but as my best friend. Is it OK to say that?'

'I think it's a perfect thing to say.'

Jacob smiled and went to move off, but Philip gently took his arm and gazed into his friend's eyes, with tears in his own.

'Thank you Jacob.'

'Come on, double maths now.' The two boys walked off in the direction of their classroom feeling closer than ever.

51:

29th December 2017

Ethan

08:00am

There was only one light shining in the detective's room and it was coming from DCI Davidson's office in the corner. Two people were having a very heated discussion.

'I am really angry, fed up and disappointed in you Anne. You're slovenly in both appearance and in your work. Your desk is a total mess and you usually have half your breakfast stuck on the clothes you wear. You are often late and currently when you are here you don't perform as I think you should for your level!' Isaac was irate. He had a thumping headache after being awake half the night thinking about this meeting 'Do you think that is a fair thing to say?'

Anne just sat there like a child being told off at school. She hunched her shoulders and nodded slightly.

'I don't mean to be messy, it's just my way sir.'

'I can cope with your sloppy day to day personal habits, but it's your work Anne, it just isn't good enough. Do you have any idea why I called you and asked you to come in and see me before the others came into work?'

Anne shook her head and said no words.

Isaac looked up to heaven with tired eyes and then rubbed his temples on the side of his head to help ease the tension he was feeling. He was slightly distracted by a light being turned on in the main room and noticed Faisal had come in early. Isaac turned back to DC Michaels.

'We, as in myself and DS Morgans, interviewed Lewis Mayhew yesterday.' The DCI took a sharp in-take of breath. 'We found out that

Mr Mayhew was the clown who was terrifying Philip Oakes.'

Anne smiled and seemed pleased.

'That's great isn't it sir? Is that the case over with then? Is Lewis our killer?' Anne seemed to have forgotten she was in the middle of an off the record disciplinary. She was also already on a final written warning.

'NO! It is not great Anne,' Isaac noticed from the corner of his eye that Faisal had glanced in his direction when he had shouted.

Anne shuffled in her seat. She felt like she needed to cry but was keeping it inside. She also knew she was hungry and thirsty and was wondering how long this telling off was going to take.

'Mr Mayhew was the clown freaking our victim, but he WASN'T the clown who killed him.' Isaac was getting very pent-up.

Anne jumped in her seat and was now genuinely concerned where this conversation was heading.

'He very clearly gave us the dates and times that he dressed up as the clown and the reasons for doing so. Lewis Mayhew did not kill Mr Oakes. He is a messed up teenage lad who is still grieving for his mother and searching for the father he never knew. He wanted to scare his dad as a form of punishment for the way he had treated his mother and then when he had done that, he wanted to get to know him and hopefully have another parent to be cared by.'

Anne was still not understanding where this was heading. She didn't need to wait much longer to find out.

'You spoke to PC Chaplin about Philip's meeting with them to discuss the sightings of the clown, didn't you?' Isaac had a stern and irritated appearance on his face.

'Yes sir, I did and I told everyone in a briefing one morning,' Anne said in her defence.

'Yes, you told us all that there had been a clown sighting, getting closer each time, but can you now go and get your notebook, come back in here and read out to me what you wrote.'

The DC looked confused but left to go to her desk. The room was now full of her colleagues who were all just staring at her. Anne kept her head low and got her book and headed back into her boss's office. The rest of them got on with logging on to their computers, making coffee and starting their days.

Anne had her book open at the relevant date and time and handed it to her DCI.

Isaac read the notebook, took in a deep breath, and spoke.

'Large red clown shoes, white overall with red pom poms and an orange wig. It also wore a flower and white gloves.'

Anne grimaced slightly as she wasn't sure what was going to happen next.

'I've just read out a description of the clown that you were told about and wrote in your notepad to disseminate to me and your fellow detectives. You had a RONALD, FUCKING MCDONALD clown on your paper and all you said to us, was that he had seen a clown!' As soon as he had shouted and sworn he was disappointed in himself. 'We have been studying a blurred picture of a person dressed as a clown, that we believe, if we are going down the right road, is our killer. Not once did you raise the fact that the picture is nothing like the description you had been given. Why?'

'I don't know, I'm sorry sir. Now that you've spoken, said it aloud, I realise how stupid I have been. I honestly don't know what to say. I have made a very grave error.'

Isaac raised his hand and with it, indicated for Anne to leave him alone. He followed her out of the room but went into the kitchen to make himself a coffee and then went back into his office for twenty minutes or so.

The team watched as their DCI drained his cup and then headed out of his room and over to the crime board.

'Everyone over here please,' Isaac was clearly not happy. 'Right, we have a new direction in this case.' He went on to tell them of the outcome of the interview with Lewis and the new developments concerning the clown. 'Can anyone tell me what this all means to our investigation?'

Anne kept quiet at the back of the group and Emily allowed her junior DCs time to think. After a few moments, Jian spoke.

'Sir, we had whittled the suspects down to Rebecca Firth and Lewis

Mayhew. If Lewis is ruled out that would mean Rebecca is our most likely killer, but those thoughts and eliminations were based on the sightings and dates of the clown. If there are now two of them and Lewis' clown was what we based our investigations on, then now we must bring all of our eliminated suspects back into the equation.'

Isaac nodded at his DC and then looked at the rest of his team.

'Jian is perfectly correct. Lewis did not kill Philip, therefore we need to re-question everybody again. Find out where they were at approximately 1:00am and 7:00pm-9:00pm on 8th December. I believe we are near to finding our killer and therefore this setback is just that. Let's not look back on errors made and concentrate on bringing an end to this case and catching Philip Oakes's killer.'

The detectives started to chat amongst themselves as their DCI went back into his office to make a few phone calls. After about half an hour he emerged with his coat on.

'Jian with me, I want us to visit Ethan. Emily take Hamish and go and visit Rebecca in the hospital and see if she is in a better state to answer some questions. Anne and Faisal, can you both go over everything we know, or thought we knew and see if we have missed anything.'

11:00am

There was silence in the car as they drew up outside Ethan's house. Isaac still had his throbbing headache and was feeling somewhat nauseated as well. Jian was driving and picked up on the fact that his boss wasn't in the mood for talking just yet. Despite it only being 11:00am, there was a gloomy, dark cloud above them that created an atmospheric scene, both in mood and in weather. As they both got out of the car, Isaac spoke.

'Did you hear me yelling at Anne?'

'Yes sir, we did. I know she screwed up but then again no one asked her for the description of the clown, we just took it for granted that it would look like a, well, a clown.'

'I know Jian, thanks for grounding me. Let's see what the Oakes family have to say.'

The front door opened tentatively and Adam Oakes stood in the doorway. No words were uttered as the teenager stepped aside to let them in. Ethan and Emma came to see who was at the door and on seeing the detectives ushered them into the lounge where everyone sat down. Isaac was shocked to see how ill Ethan was. Since he had last seen him, Ethan had lost a lot of weight and was drained of all colour. His eyes squinted and his mobility was that of a much older person.

'I need to ask where you all were on 8th December 1:00am and 7:00pm-9:00pm,' Isaac said.

'Why?' Adam said. 'I told you my dad wasn't the stupid clown because the dates didn't make sense.' The young man was clearly annoyed with the two men who had just entered his home.

'New evidence has come to our attention and therefore we need to re-ask questions of you all. So, Ethan can you tell me where you were at the times I have just stated?' Asked Isaac.

Ethan looked into space as if trying to recollect his movements from a few weeks ago. Emma put her hand on her husband's leg and gently rubbed. Upstairs, Isaac and Jian could hear movement.

'Saul is playing with Max,' Emma said after seeing their faces.

'At 1am I was asleep. You already know that I went and confronted my brother about his actions at 4:00pm. I then got in my car and drove around. I can't tell you where, as my state of mind was very poor. I know this doesn't look good for me, but I really can't help any more than what I have just told you. I got home about 10:00pm.'

'You drove around for six hours Mr Oakes?' Jian questioned.

'I stopped at the side of the road for about an hour I think, then maybe fell asleep in a car park somewhere. I really don't know.'

'What was your relationship like with your brother?' Asked Isaac.

'I have already told you this before. It wasn't great, obviously, otherwise he would have given me his bloody cells. I wasn't a great brother to him growing up. We lost our mother when I was ten and Philip was four. I missed her and in some stupid way blamed him for what happened. I did horrible pranks on him over the years, but they were just silly things. Typical older brother stuff. I loved Philip and I do wish I'd been a better brother.' Ethan was shaking and visibly upset.

'Mr Oakes, your brother led you to believe that he was going to give you his stem cells if he was a match. However, when confirmation came that he was indeed a perfect match he refused to donate them to you. That must have made you question why and it must have made you very angry. Why Ethan? Why did he refuse you life?' Isaac said with force.

Emma stood up and offered to make everyone tea. She then left the room and Adam went and sat next to his father.

'Yes I was really angry with Philip,' Ethan grabbed his son's hand. 'I was a cruel brother, mean, nasty, bitter and at my worst, I was vindictive and brutal. They must be the reasons why he wouldn't give me his cells. I did change towards Philip when he was thirteen and tried to become a nicer person, but Philip refused to see that side of me. The damage had been done and for Philip there was no going back.'

'Why when he was thirteen?' Asked Jian. 'Why did you change then?'

Ethan took in several deep breaths and shrugged his shoulders. 'I grew up I guess, saw how unhappy I made him. I don't hate Philip, well, didn't hate him. I truly loved him and if I am completely honest with myself, I didn't blame him for refusing me his stem cells.'

'Ethan,' Isaac said, 'did you kill your brother?'

'No I didn't,' was the reply.

Emma came back into the room and handed out the cups of tea. She had obviously been crying in the kitchen as her makeup was smudged where she had tried to repair it.

'Adam, where were you for the said times?'

The young man was shocked that he was being asked the same questions as his father.

'I told you, I got out of the car and ran off upset. I wandered around for a while and then went and saw two films, oh and at 1am I was asleep.'

'That's not the whole truth is it Adam?' said Isaac.

Adam's parents looked at their son and then back to the detectives.

'What do you mean?' Adam asked.

'Well you told us you went to see the new Jumanji film and a film called Kingsman. We checked and Kingsman was out in September and wasn't showing at the cinema you went to in December.'

'OK,' Adam said, feeling beaten. 'I did see the first film but then left and went and sat in our office at work. We all have a set of keys, so I stayed there until I felt less stressed.'

'Why didn't you tell us this before?'

'Didn't think you'd believe me.'

The tense atmosphere was broken when Isaac's phone rang. It was Emily.

'Sir, no go re Rebecca, she is still not in a great way. There is a slight improvement so the nurse has suggested coming back after the weekend as she might be in a better condition.'

Isaac thanked his DS and ended the call.

'My turn then is it?' Asked Emma.

Isaac looked up from his phone and nodded.

'As I told you before, I was staying at my mother's with Saul and Max. Saul wasn't coping well with his dad's health, so I took him away with me for a few days to help him relax a little. 1am I was obviously asleep. 7:00pm-9:00pm I was watching the television with my mother as both kids were in bed.'

The conversations had now ceased and an uncomfortable tense feeling had descended on the room. The two detectives watched the dishevelled family in front of them.

'Do any of you have any idea who might have killed Philip?' Isaac knew it was a futile question, but he was desperate.

'No,' was the answer from all three people.

52:

2nd January 2018

Arjun

09:00am

The New Year had come and gone. Little progress had been made over the past few days since Ethan's interview and the news of Rebecca's failing physical health. Isaac looked at the blurred clown picture again and was feeling frustrated that something was so familiar.

As he stood by the crime board he was aware he was now surrounded by his team.

'Nothing new to tell you at the moment,' he said. 'The hospital have said we can visit Rebecca tomorrow, so today Emily and myself will go and talk again with Mr Singh and then this afternoon we will be talking again to Mr Spencer.'

10:30am

The noises in the step-down unit were just as overwhelming as intensive care. Rohit was now off the critical list but still needed close observation. Arjun continued to sit by his brother's bed for the majority of the day. He only went home to shower and change his clothes and then he was straight back at his brother's side.

'Cup of tea luv?' Asked the hospital volunteer.

Arjun turned around and saw an elderly lady, blue rinse through her hair, about four stone heavier than she should be and huge swollen, red hands.

'No thanks, I'm good.'

'Doing alright is he?' She asked out of routine. 'I can see he's no more than a baby.'

'He's sixteen, not a baby,' Arjun's response was curt and dismissive.

'Only bloody asking,' was her response as she moved to the next bed. 'Cup of tea luv?'

Rohit slightly opened his eyes and saw his brother. He reached out and gently touched Arjun's hand. The painkillers were still potent enough to keep the young lad feeling dazed.

'Hey Arjun,' he said in a weak voice.

'Hey, how you feeling?'

'Does Rajan hate me?' Rohit asked.

Arjun pulled a face as he thought this was a strange question for Rohit to ask.

'Of course not, if anything he hates me. Stop worrying about things like that, get yourself strong again and come home. I miss you.' Arjun squeezed his brother's hand.

'How's mum?'

'She's worried about you. She is here every day and just goes home to freshen up.'

'Arjun,' Rohit sounded feeble. 'How are you? That was a terrible argument that happened.'

Arjun stood up and kissed his brother on the cheek. Tears were forming in his eyes.

'Don't you be worrying about me.'

Rohit closed his eyes again.

Arjun got up from his seat and moved over to the window. From here he could see into the visitor's car park. The step-down unit was only on level one, so Arjun had a clear view of the comings and goings. The clouds were grey and ominous and it looked like a storm might be brewing. He glanced all around the car park, mainly out of boredom, when he suddenly saw DCI Davidson and his DS. Arjun made a deep and loud sigh.

'What do they want now?' He asked himself.

Arjun didn't want to have a conversation near Rohit, so he left the ward and went over to the lifts and waited. Within a few moments the lift doors opened and the detectives walked out.

'I saw you arriving,' Arjun said in an exasperated voice. 'Let's go to the canteen and get a coffee.'

'Fine with us,' volunteered Emily.

As they walked Isaac noticed how dreadful Arjun appeared. The once strikingly handsome man was now gaunt and exhausted. There were dark marks under his eyes and a real sadness in his face.

Arjun went over to the hot drinks machine after he had offered to get the detectives a drink. Once they had been dispensed, he approached the man at the till and paid. Both Isaac and Emily thanked him for the drinks.

'Why are you here?' He asked in an exhausted voice.

'New evidence has come to our attention Mr Singh and therefore we need to ask you more questions,' Isaac said with an air of trepidation.

'Whatever, ask away.'

'Where were you at 1am on 8th Dec and then at 7:00pm-9:00pm same day?'

Arjun raised his coffee to his lips and took a few slow sips.

'I went to see...' Arjun still couldn't say his name, 'him' at about 5:00pm. We rowed on his doorstep until I walked away and yes I know I threatened him.'

'And where did you go after that?' Asked Emily.

'I don't remember, I was angry and needed time to myself. I wandered for a couple of hours and then headed back to the hospital. Can I go now please?'

'Last time you said you went home to shower and change,' said Emily.

'Well then, that's what I did. I don't remember the exact things, I was in distress because of my brother.'

Isaac drained the last few drops of his coffee before addressing the young man in front of him. He liked Arjun but there were still questions to be answered.

'Where were you at 1am on the 8th? You told us that you got an Uber at midnight, but you didn't get home until about 1:40am when your brother was hit by a car at approximately 1:50am.'

Arjun stood up and glared hard at the DCI. His head was pounding and he just wanted this all to be over with. He said nothing.

'Mr Singh, you left the pub at midnight and didn't get home until about 1:40am. This means you have about an hour unaccounted for. You could have gone to a twenty-four-hour supermarket, got a cheap clown's costume and made your first visit in Philip's garden at 1:00am and still got home by 1:40am.' Isaac knew he was sounding very frustrated.

'Clown? You know I'm not the clown, we have already discussed this.'

'New evidence has come to light Mr Singh, where were you between midnight and getting to your home at 1:40am?'

Arjun was now pacing up and down in the canteen and was showing signs of fury.

'Yes, OK. I got an Uber over to his house. I wanted to confront him for his vile behaviour, but when I got there I chickened out. I walked the streets for a while and then got another Uber to my house.'

'Mr Singh, do you have witnesses to back this up for you?' Isaac said.

'No, I don't.'

53:

2nd January 2018

Jacob

3:00pm

The noise coming from the house on the corner was bringing the curtain twitchers to their windows and on to their doorsteps. The rain was falling hard as well as a strong wind, but this wasn't putting off the on-lookers seeing the argument between a husband and his wife.

Jacob was yelling at Tanvi and getting himself extremely worked up with rage.

'They are my kids too Tanvi! You can't stop me seeing them. That really isn't fair. I love the boys and I miss them so much. I haven't seen them since you kicked me out. Have a heart and let me see MY kids.'

Tanvi glared at her husband and felt nothing but anger and hate. The hurt this man had caused her ran deep and wasn't going to get better anytime soon.

'You brought this on yourself Jacob, you were the one who felt the need to shag around. I was getting over having a second baby and needed time to recover and feel like a woman again. To feel like I was attractive, but you wouldn't wait for that. Your testosterone obviously went into overdrive. You make me sick and I don't want to see you again.'

Jacob lowered his head as he recognised his own wrongdoing in his nightmare. He knew he had broken Tanvi's heart and he was truly sorry for this and knew he'd blown any chance of getting back with her, so now it was vital he at least got to see his children.

'Please Tanvi, I know you hate me and I deserve that, but don't deny me my boys or them seeing me. I need them, never more than now. Please don't take them away from me.'

There was a true sadness in his voice that resonated with his wife, but not to the extent she would cave and bow to his wishes.

'The boys aren't here, I have sent them away,' she said with pure venom in her tone.

'What do you mean? You have no right to do something like that!'

Jacob made a step forward to gain access to the house, but his wife blocked him. The people in the street continued to gawk.

'Answer me! What do you mean you have sent them away?' Jacob's voice was full of hatred.

'They are in India with my parents for a few weeks. I am seeing a solicitor tomorrow morning to discuss divorce proceedings. I want you out of my life and the sooner the better!'

Jacob felt like his world was falling to pieces. Philip had completely destroyed his life and wasn't here to see the consequences of his actions. Jacob wasn't sure where his hate was really aimed, at Philip or his soon-to-be ex-wife.

'Tanvi, come on, let's not go there. Please, I made a very stupid mistake and I'm so sorry. I don't know what to say.'

Tanvi stood and looked at what she thought was a pitiful excuse for a man in front of her. 'It wasn't one mistake Jacob, it was many mistakes. I'm seriously done with you. I don't want you around my children. They need a man in their lives that they can grow to respect. You're even being questioned for murder! Did you kill Philip?'

Jacob ran his hand through his hair and breathed in deeply before he spoke.

'I want access to my children and I will go to any lengths for this to happen. I swear to God that I will make this happen.'

'Did you murder Philip?' Tanvi asked for a second time.

'I'm living in a tiny room in the hospital, the smells from the toilet and kitchen are disgusting and I am going out of my mind with fury and frustration. I want to see my children. I love my boys. Please!'

'Did you kill your best friend for sending me that video or because of the money you owed him?'

'I'm not talking to you about that. You have broken my heart and I am devastated,' said Jacob.

Still standing on the doorstep, he looked longingly at his wife and hoped his eyes told her how desperately sorry he was for everything he had done. She glared back at him and then slowly closed the door in his face.

4:00pm

Jacob sat on his bed wearing just a pair of striped briefs and a white t-shirt. The bed linen hadn't been washed the whole time he had had to live in the hospital room in the residences. The room echoed what was going on in his mind, a total mess. The smell of something made with fish was seeping under his door and was making him feel nauseated. Jacob reached over to his bedside cabinet and grabbed a half-filled glass of neat Vodka. He took a gulp and then sat back against the headboard. The bottle by his glass was already nearly half empty but Jacob somehow wasn't feeling any effects from the amount consumed so far. Images of Rory and Adrian kept coming into his head and caused tears to well-up in his eyes.

A loud bang on his door jolted Jacob back to reality and also caused him to spill some of his drink down his t-shirt.

'Go away,' he yelled at the door.

'Mr Spencer, it's DCI Davidson and DS Morgans, can you open the door please.'

'Go away, I've told you all I know, now leave me alone.'

There was total silence on the other side of the door and the detectives were getting annoyed. Jacob was sitting on his bed hugging his knees and wishing they would go away. The argument with Tanvi had depleted him of all emotions and he wasn't ready to talk to anyone else. However, he knew the DCI wasn't going to go away. He picked up his glass and drained the rest of the fluid, wiped his mouth with the back of his hand and went over to the door. Once he had opened it, he saw two people wet through and not looking happy. Inside he was smirking to himself at the sight of them as he stepped aside to let them in.

'Sorry for the mess but it's the maid's day off.' The sarcasm went unnoticed.

Both detectives surveyed the room in which they were stood and wondered about the mental state of the man standing in front of them.

'Would you like to put some trousers on Jacob?' Asked Isaac.

'Nope,' was the quick reply. 'Ask what you need to and then go. I don't mean to be rude, but it has already been a shitty day and all I want to do is drink the rest of that bottle of vodka on my bedside table, get into my bed and then pass out drunk to the world.'

'How much have you had already?' Questioned Emily.

'My business, now ask your bloody questions and leave me alone.'

Isaac saw how distressed and upset Jacob was. He half considered saying they would come back but got the impression that he would be like this on each and every visit.

'Jacob, we know that you went to Philip's house the day he was murdered.'

'What of it?'

'It means that you could've stayed within the area, come back later and confronted Philip, something happened and Philip was killed.'

'You're guessing now,' smirked Jacob at Isaac. 'I went to Philip's house, yes, but he wasn't in and I left.'

'Where did you go?' Asked Emily.

'Can't remember.'

Isaac was getting very frustrated with Jacob. It was obvious that the vodka was kicking in.

'Come on, work with us. Where did you go?'

'Drinking, it's what I do most days now. Anyhow, I thought you ruled me out as I was with Philip when the clown was seen on 1st November.'

'Big news Jacob,' there was definite tension in the DCI's voice. 'There are two clowns which means you're back in the running! Now, where were you between 1am and 7:00pm-9:00pm on 8th December?'

'Well blow me, two clowns, now that's funny. I don't remember where I was, but I believe I went drinking somewhere, got wasted and slept in my car. I honestly can't help you any more than that.'

'Jacob, did you kill Philip?' Asked Isaac.

'Me? No.'

'Do you know of anyone who you think could have?'

Jacob scratched himself through his briefs making the detectives uncomfortable.

'The drunk from the pub. Rebecca something. She was abnormally obsessed with him. I'd say her.'

The detectives thanked Jacob for his time and left. Once back in the cold car Emily looked over at her boss.

'Do you think he did it sir? Did he kill Philip?'

Isaac looked straight ahead and sighed.

'Maybe, he had motive and opportunity. In fact Emily, he had two very clear and plausible motives to kill Mr Philip Oakes. I think we are close to finding our killer. We need to visit the hospital tomorrow and see if we are able to speak with Rebecca. She rambled on about Philip needing to be punished and we need to try to find out what that was all about. We can start off at the office and update everyone on today's events with Jacob and Arjun and then head over to see Mrs Firth.'

54:

3rd January 2018

Rebecca

11:00am

Isaac had briefed his team with the outcomes of yesterday's interviews and now he was in the hospital car park with Emily, heading towards the main entrance. Parking had been difficult today and they had had to drive around four times before a space became available. The weather was being kinder to them today and although cold, the rain was at least holding off.

Rebecca was on Damson ward which was on the third floor. They both headed to the lifts despite knowing that the stairs were the healthier option, especially as the DCIs ankle was much improved. Isaac yawned hard and brought water to his eyes.

'Late night sir?' Asked Emily.

Isaac laughed and shook his head.

'No not really. I cooked dinner and then we watched a Poirot on the TV.'

Emily inwardly smiled as she knew the 'we' referred to his brother. She had never dared ask if her boss dated or had a girlfriend or a boyfriend. He never mentioned anyone romantically, just his brother who Emily realised was remarkably close to him.

'Which one?' She asked him.

'Which one?' Queried Isaac as if he hadn't understood.

'Poirot?'

'Oh,' laughed the DCI, 'Cards on the table and I guessed the killer.' They both sniggered.

The lift reached the designated floor and they stepped out and headed to Damson ward. Emily pushed the intercom and once the door was released they went on to the ward and over to the nurse's station where they introduced themselves.

'You can only really stay a few minutes,' the charge nurse said. 'She is very slightly more rousable today, but she is still a very sick woman.'

The detectives thanked the nurse, who had a strangely large nose on a small face and hair that may have been a wig. They headed over to her side room and went in. To their surprise there was a young man sitting next to her. Isaac thought he recognised him.

'Hey, I'm Liam, we have met before.'

They both recognised the nurse but wondered why he was sitting with Rebecca.

'We both work in the hospital and I'm often down at pharmacy getting medications for my patients and we struck up a friendship. I can't believe she has ended up like this. It's dreadful.'

'Has she said anything since you've been with her?' Probed Emily.

'She mentions that arsehole!'

Isaac looked at his DS and then back at Liam.

'Care to expand?' He asked.

'Philip, Philip Oakes. Refuses his brother his stem cells which would potentially save his life and also messes with Rebecca's feelings. I actually hate the man if you can hate the dead.'

'Hate is a strong word Liam,' Emily said.

'Look, I have been a nurse for many years and I have never seen the evil facial expression that man had when he walked out of the room after telling us he wouldn't help his brother. Then he gets Rebecca pregnant and doesn't stand by her. She texted me and told me all about it.'

'Things aren't always as they seem and people have ways of bending the truth,' explained Emily.

'I saw the aftermath of his actions on that day he denied his brother potential life. His son was inconsolable and his wife was in utter shock. Our consultant had never known such an outcome. That man was pure evil.'

Isaac walked over to the bed and saw that Rebecca's eyes were closed. He was extremely shocked at what he saw. Her cheek bones were protruding through her skin and her eyes were sunken. She had a tube in her nose that was connected to a feeding tube which was in turn connected to a small pump that was making a whirring noise. Liam made his excuses and left, but not before kissing Rebecca lightly on her head.

Both detectives stood on either side of her and Emily felt tremendously sorry for the poor woman.

'Mrs Firth, Rebecca,' Isaac spoke very softly.

'I think you are going to have to raise your voice sir.'

Isaac looked uncomfortable but realised his first attempt wasn't successful.

'Rebecca,' he said a lot louder.

Emily gently stroked her cheek and called her name.

The emaciated woman lying in the bed opened her eyes. The hospital gown she had on looked about four sizes too big.

'Philip?' she said in nothing more than a hiss.

The DCI put Rebecca right by introducing himself and his DS.

'Rebecca, I need to ask you some questions,' he said gently. 'Why did you need to punish Philip?'

He knew he needed to ask direct questions as time was a premium, however he wasn't holding out much hope.

'Rebecca,' he said again.

'My love?' she said.

'Rebecca, why did you need to punish Philip?' He asked again.

Rebecca was silent again. She had her eyes open and looked about the room. She made no acknowledgement that two other people were in the room with her but continued to whisper Philip's name.

'Sir,' Emily said. 'Stay with me, as this may sound odd. Tell her you're Philip and you're asking why you needed to be punished. I know it's not by the book, but we only have a small window of opportunity to get any answers from her.'

Isaac felt incredibly uncomfortable with the idea and said no.

'Rebecca, it's DCI Davidson,' saying this caused Isaac to feel very awkward as it was clear she wasn't well.

'My love, is it you?'

'No, it's not Philip. Rebecca, why did you need to punish him? What did you do?'

Rebecca turned her head and looked at Isaac. Her face lit up and smiled. She feebly reached out and touched his face. Isaac slightly shook at her touch as it made him feel extremely uneasy.

'I'm sorry Philip.'

'Tell me why you are sorry Rebecca. What did you do?' Enquired the DCI.

At that moment, the alarm went off on the feeding pump causing both detectives to jump. The tension had been building up and the noise came at a very inconvenient time. The door opened and a nurse came in with a new bag of feed.

'Everything OK?' He asked.

'Yes thank you,' they both said in unison.

After the nurse had left, Isaac tried again.

'Rebecca, how did you punish Philip?' The DCI thought he sounded like a broken record.

'Because of the barman, Arjun, that's why I needed to punish Philip,' Rebecca's voice was nearly inaudible.

'Go on Rebecca, what did you do to Philip?' Isaac had his ear close to her mouth. Her breath wasn't at all pleasant.

The silence had returned much to the frustration of the detectives. Rebecca's sunken eyes remained open but were staring at the wall opposite. A small smile appeared on her face and she raised her arm and then pointed at the wall. Isaac and Emily looked to where she was pointing but saw nothing.

'I needed Philip to be mine and that Asian lad had taken him from me. I needed to get 'my love' back from him, but to do that Philip would need to be punished.' Rebecca spoke in a clear voice for the first time since they arrived.

'How did you do that? What did you do?' There was now a tense edge to Isaac's voice.

'I killed the barman, I drove my car into him. That was my punishment for Philip. To deny him the bartender. With him out of the way, Philip would come back to me and our baby.'

Rebecca's face started to become distorted and she was becoming very agitated. Emily glanced over at her boss and an expression of concern spread across her face. Rebecca opened her mouth wide as if she were screaming but no sounds were coming out. She then started frantically looking from side to side as her agitation got worse. She began banging her head with her hands and in the process ripped out the drip in the back of her hand. Emily pulled the nurse call bell just as Rebecca pulled out the tube in her nose. The silent scream was now beginning to find sound. It was a screeching noise that penetrated their ears. Rebecca was trying to say something.

The door flung open and three nurses and a doctor came rushing in as they had heard the commotion. Rebecca was now screaming very loudly as she continued to scan the room.

'My baby,' she shrieked, 'where is my baby? Where is Philip? I want my baby!'

The detectives at this point were ushered quickly out of the room. They were both startled and swiftly left the ward and headed back to the car park and into their car.

'Now that wasn't nice to witness,' said Emily.

'Agreed,' said Isaac. 'It actually scared the crap out of me when she started screaming.'

'She believes she has had the baby, hers and Philip's.'

'It certainly sounded that way didn't it?' said Isaac. 'So, she didn't kill Philip, she thinks she killed Arjun and has no idea that she nearly killed Rohit instead.'

Emily nodded as her boss spoke.

'Let's go back to the office and write this interview up. We can let the rest of the team know that Rebecca isn't our killer.' Isaac let out a long sigh. 'Before we knew of the second clown, we were down to just Lewis or Rebecca being our murderer and now they are the two we have ruled out. This case is beginning to do my head in!'

55:

1993

Philip aged Twelve

The two boys were sitting in the lounge watching a Christmas film. They both had a sofa to themselves and made sure they stretched out. The fire was roaring away and producing lots of comforting heat. The Christmas tree lights were twinkling and the pine smell was evident in the room. It was thanks to Mrs Temple that the tree was put up. If it had been left to Mr Oakes, Christmas would go by unnoticed.

Through the wall they could hear their father and aunt chatting, or at least hear mumbling not actual words. The boys had been excused from the table so they could go and watch the television. Their aunt was a slender, wispy looking woman, with thin lips and a sneering face. The boys liked the fact that she pretended she didn't like alcohol, but Ethan had found four bottles of red wine hidden in her wardrobe.

Philip picked up his drink and gazed at Ethan for the longest moment.

'Why do you hate me?' He asked his brother.

Ethan slowly turned in Philip's direction and took in a deep breath.

'I don't hate you.'

'You're not nice to me.'

Ethan changed his position and sat up, putting his feet firmly on the ground. He picked up his drink of coke and took a swig, he then wiped his lips with the back of his hand.

'It's complicated Philip, but I don't hate you,' he seemed embarrassed.

'You really scared me when you dressed as that clown.'

Ethan had to hold in a smirk as he had thought that prank was one of his best.

'Philip, it's my job as your older brother to prank you and basically make your life miserable. It's part of life, part of growing up, plus we are a

complicated family.' Ethan lay down again.

The clock in the room chimed four times but it went unheard by the brothers. There were louder mumbles coming through the wall. Philip studied his brother and contemplated what he had just been told.

'I agree, we are a complex family. I have spent most of my life wondering why I was ever born. I suppose mum and dad must have been happy. I have no memories of her, but I expect you do Ethan. I don't for one moment pretend to know how you felt when we were told of her death, as you will have recollections of her that I don't have.'

Philip sighed and looked out of the window and watched the snow as it started to softly fall.

'I just feel that you have never liked me. You have done some really horrible things to me over the years and I don't think I ever did anything to you to deserve such unkindness. I'll never forget what you did to my Star Wars puzzle. Not the actual act of cutting it up, but the hatefulness behind the action. Dad is useless and always has been. I can hear him laughing in the dining room with auntie, but when else have you ever heard any emotional response from him? My whole life I have felt nothing but sadness and loneliness. I used to have quite a few friends at school, but since I was never allowed to go to their houses or for them to come here, most of them don't bother with me anymore. Thank god for Jacob, at least he has stood by me.'

Philip reached for his lemonade and took a long but slow drink.

'Ethan, I feel so isolated and desperate, that over the last few months I have felt an urge to hurt myself and this has really scared me. I reached for the scissors last week and nearly cut myself with them. I thought that somehow if I caused physical pain it would take away the sorrow that I feel in my heart every day. I know we are never going to be friends, but I would like it if we could be better brothers. What do you think? Can that happen?' Tears were beginning to fall onto Philip's cheeks. 'Ethan! Did you hear me?'

Philip looked over to the other sofa and saw that Ethan was asleep.

56:

4th January 2018

Isaac

04:00am

Isaac lay in his bed in that horrid state of not being asleep yet wanting to be and deciding whether he should give up on sleep and make a hot drink instead. He was tossing and turning. One moment his legs were under the covers and then the next moment they were on top. Isaac bashed his pillow to try to plump it up and turned onto his left side. Within a few seconds he was on his right side and then on his back. His eyes felt heavy and his limbs were aching, but sleep was not going to come. He put on his bedside lamp on dim mode and lay there looking up at the ceiling. A small spider was walking slowly across it and then came down the wall and went out of sight.

After half an hour of getting frustrated with himself he got up and went into the kitchen to make himself a cup of strong coffee. The case was going around in his head and causing him no end of exasperation. He believed they were close to the end but the last few pieces of the puzzle were still missing and right now he wasn't even sure what those were. Lewis and Rebecca had now been eliminated as suspects which helped but who was the second clown?.

'If only that bloody picture wasn't so blurred,' he thought to himself, 'and how can I be trying to solve a murder with two of the damn things!'

As the kettle was boiling the water, Isaac was suddenly aware that he was feeling exceptionally cold. He then saw his reflection in the kitchen door's windows which showed that he wasn't wearing any clothes. His head was so muddled that he didn't know if he was coming or going. He left the kettle to boil and went back into his bedroom and put on some loungewear trousers and a thick black hand-knitted jumper. He then went over to his bedroom window and stared out onto the garden. For a brief moment he worried that he might see a grotesque figure looking back at him, smiling or waving.

He left his bedroom to head back to the kitchen. As he passed Alan's room he briefly listened at the door and could hear light snoring. He was pleased he hadn't woken up his brother. Five minutes later he was sitting back in his bed with a large cup of coffee and found himself mulling over the clown.

By 5:00am Isaac was in the shower and by half past was in his car and heading to work. He had left Alan a note by the kettle.

'Sorry if you had breakfast planned but couldn't sleep, so have left for work. Have a good day.'

At 6:00am he was sitting at his desk going through the file notes with a fine toothcomb. He was sure they had missed something.

'Why did Philip hate his brother so much that he refused to at least try to save him?' he was thinking aloud. 'Why did Philip start to self-harm as a teenager and is this relevant?'

The main light in the room went on which startled Isaac as he was in his office with only the desk light on. He looked up and saw the cleaner had arrived to start his daily routine.

Isaac got up and went to make himself a hot drink and acknowledged him.

'Morning Glenn, how are you?'

'Sciatica is playing up something dreadful this morning, painkillers don't work and now my bloody shoulder is giving me shocking problems. Also last week, doctor started me on diabetic medications. I'm falling to pieces DCI Davidson.'

'Would a hot cup of tea help?' Isaac asked.

'It might,' sniggered Glenn.

Back at his desk Isaac continued to wade through the information gathered. Everyone seemed to be potentially in the area near the time of the murder, or able to get there within the timescale. He took a mouthful of his drink and went back into the central office area and over to the crime board.

'Any closer to solving it?' Glenn asked, as he cleaned the kitchen area.

'Not far, hopefully very soon,' was the reply.

Isaac took the blurred picture off the board and studied it hard. From what he could make out the frame of the person could match all his remaining suspects, which wasn't at all helpful.

'What is it that I've seen before?' he mumbled to himself.

From his office he could hear his phone vibrating on his desk. He went through to answer it.

'Hey, are you OK? I have just seen your note.' It was his brother.

'Yeah, hope I didn't wake you. Couldn't sleep and was getting irritated, so headed into work. I keep reviewing this damned picture and just know I'm looking at what I need to identify who our murderer is, but it just won't come to me and it's driving me demented.'

'It'll come to you when you least expect it to. Is it the surroundings in the picture, the shape of the figure, what it's wearing?' Enquired Alan.

'What it's wearing I think,' was Isaac's reply. 'You go back to sleep and I'll check in with you later and thanks for calling.'

The office was once again quiet and in darkness apart from the light in the DCI's room. Glenn had finished his work and had moved on to another part of the building. Isaac continued to look through all the case reports. The lack of sleep was telling as his eyes felt sore and words on the papers were blurring and giving him a headache. Although it was only 7:00am, he grabbed his coat and headed off in the direction of a local coffee shop. Isaac disapproved of large companies and preferred to give his money to small independent coffee shops, something he tried to instil in his co-workers but with little success, especially with DC Michaels.

Whilst sitting at a small table in the corner of the shop, he was drinking his Americano and eating a cheese and ham panini when DS Morgans came in. She ordered a take-out tea, then turned and saw her boss sitting on his own. She went over and sat with him.

'You look bloody awful,' she said.

'I'm so pleased you chose to sit here,' he said sarcastically. 'I've been awake since 4:00am. Emily, what are we missing? The answer is in that picture.'

'Let's finish our drinks and head back to the office. Get the team together and all brainstorm.'

'Good idea,' he replied.

4:00pm

Despite a day of all getting together, scrutinising the evidence, and surveying the picture nothing new had developed. There was a feeling of despondency within the team and morale was a little low. The landline phone rang in Isaac's office.

'Get that Hamish.'

DC Potter did as he was told by his boss and went to answer the phone. After two minutes he was back again.

'Sir, that was the hospital.'

Everyone stopped what they were doing and all looked over at the DC.

'Rebecca Firth died at around 3:00pm today. They thought we should know.'

The room was silent for a minute or two. Although she had been a suspect, the team and especially Emily had felt deeply sorry for her.

'They said her body just shut down and she went into a cardiac arrest. They were unable to get her back. The family have been informed,' DC Potter continued.

'That's very sad, but at least we were able to clear her name before she died,' was DCI Davidson's pragmatic response.

'What about the Singh's? They won't get their justice now,' uttered DC Asher.

The team all went back to their desks and continued with their work. The office was almost silent. Isaac took himself back over to the crime board. He removed Rebecca's and Lewis' photographs. This should have happened already but hadn't. He once again picked up the blurred photo and scanned it. Emily came across and leaned over his shoulder.

'Anything?' She asked.

'There is something here that I can't get and it's obvious. Alan asked what it was about this picture that made me think I knew something and I said the clothes, what it was wearing.'

The two of them looked together, surveying every inch of the image.

'Sir, what do you...'

'Ssh Emily,' Isaac interrupted.

The DS noticed that her boss' eyes had widened and his breathing was becoming more rapid.

'Emily, look! Look at the boots.'

The DS did as she was told and looked at the boots.

'Now see what it is wearing. It seems to be a white overall and black boots. Look at the boots, what is on the boots?' Isaac was talking loudly so the other members of the team joined them.

'Black boots with white spots I guess. Is that right?' She seemed confused.

'White overall and black boots covered in splodges of white paint! Oh God, why didn't I see it before?'

The whole team were staring at each other, each as confused as the other.

'Sir?' Emily said.

'Emily, think back to the day we first interviewed Ethan Oakes. Who came flying into the room wearing a white overall and black boots covered in paint? Whose boots did I trip over in the Oakes' hallway when I sprained my ankle?'

'Adam Oakes, It's Adam. He's our second clown!'

The office was now in an uproar and commotion. Smiles were coming from everybody. Isaac sat slumped in a chair with his head between his legs and his breathing fast but steady.

'It has been staring at us for ages. Why didn't we see it?'

'Sir, you look exhausted. Go home, shower, eat and rest. I will go and arrest and caution Adam on suspicion of the murder of Philip Oakes. I'll bring the overalls and boots in for forensics to do what they do. I will call Alex and ask him to stay late and get us some answers. Come back this evening and we can question him together.'

Isaac grinned at Emily as she sounded like the boss at the moment, but he recognised that what she was saying was sensible, as he was fatigued and hungry.

'That sounds like an incredibly good plan. Excellent work team.'

Isaac went into his office, grabbed his coat, and left his DS to go and make the arrest.

'Adam Oakes!' he said to himself.

As he left the building it was starting to rain and get very windy. The clouds looked dark and moody.

57:

4th January 2018

A Murderer is Revealed

7:45pm

Isaac opened the door and straight away saw the frightened figure sitting in the chair next to someone from legal aid. On the table sat a voice recorder. Isaac walked into the room in a commanding way and sat down in front of the shaking individual. DS Morgans sat next to her boss and turned on the recorder. This station was still very backwards when it came to technology. After announcing all those who were present in the room, the DCI looked directly into the eyes of the person sitting directly in front of him.

'So, let's start at the beginning with you telling me what led to the murder of Philip Oakes!'

Adam looked stunned and frightened. His hands were clasped together and sweat trickled down his forehead and on to his cheeks. He was too petrified to try to wipe it away. Emily went over to the side table, poured him out a glass of water and handed it to him.

'Thank you,' he said in a jerky voice.

'Adam, can you please tell us what happened to your uncle?' Asked the DCI.

The frightened young man just sat and eventually burst into tears. His whole body was shaking. The detectives couldn't help but feel sorry for him.

'Adam, I know you are scared but you need to tell us what happened. Did you kill your uncle? Did you kill Philip Oakes?'

There was no response.

'Adam, we have sent your overalls and boots off to the forensics late this afternoon. They said there was a small amount of blood on the bottom of the right boot and they are running a DNA profile on it. Did you kill Philip?' Isaac's tone was now sterner than before.

'Yes,' said a meek and anxious voice, 'I killed uncle Philip. I'm so sorry. It's his blood on the boot.'

The detectives glanced at each other and then back at Adam. His face was a blotchy red colour and his eyes were bloodshot and sore. The young man was rocking back and forth in his chair.

'I'm sorry, I'm sorry, I'm sorry,' was all he could say as he hid his face in his hands.

'Have you eaten? Do you want a sandwich and a hot drink before we continue?' Asked Isaac.

'Yes please,' he quietly said without looking up.

The interview was suspended until Adam had eaten and had calmed down enough to carry on.

When enough time had lapsed, the DCI continued.

'Why did you kill your uncle?'

Adam took a long deep breath and looked across the table at the detectives. He then turned to his legal aid. The clock on the wall was making a loud ticking noise, but apart from that there was a deathly silence in the room. Isaac looked closely at Adam and wondered when or even if the young man was going to speak. The atmosphere in the interview room was tense and suffocating. Finally, Adam started to speak, although slowly at first and constantly staring at the table.

'I love my dad. I know most eighteen-year-olds don't tend to say that sort of thing, but I truly do love him. He has always been the kindest of men and the best of fathers. When I was growing up,' Adam paused, 'he always made me feel very special. He valued spending time with me and making sure I was his number one priority. I think even mum was annoyed at times. When I talked about him to my friends, they all wished their dads showed them the same amount of love and gave them the time that mine gave to me. When Saul and Max came along, I was worried that I'd lose him in some way, but I didn't. I always knew I was, am, his favourite. I know parents aren't supposed to have them, but I was definitely my dad's. I don't mean that he doesn't love my brothers because he absolutely does, but I have the slight edge.' Adam let out a long and pitiful sigh. 'Dad has told us since the investigation started that he bullied Philip and wasn't the kindest of brothers, but people change, don't they?' The young man banged his fist on the table. 'They shouldn't be judged by past actions. Dad has told us that he was sorry for the way he treated Philip and had tried on many occasions over the years to try to make amends. Uncle Philip was always invited for Christmas, Easter, our birthdays, his birthday and often invited for Sunday roasts, but he never came, not once. When dad became ill, it was the worst thing ever. I know I didn't cope very well and was probably a real idiot in the way I acted, but I was, am so scared of losing him. I can't even begin to think about life without him, although I know that is going to be a reality very soon.'

Tears started to well up in Adam's eyes again, but he did the best he could to stifle them. Emily offered him some water which he gratefully took and drained the glass. He wiped his mouth with the cuff of his hoodie. Neither detective said anything.

'Uncle Philip said he was happy to have his blood tested and hoped he would be a match and then donate his stem cells. When he was a match, he appeared so pleased. We were all so ecstatic It turned out, as he told us when we went around to see him, that he wanted to get my dad's hopes up so when he refused to help, it would have a more devastating consequence. When dad asked why he would do such a thing, all uncle Philip said was something like, *"you know why"* and dad said he had apologised for that. I never found out what they meant by that. I saw how much pain and sadness there was on my dad's face. I had never seen him so broken, so destroyed. I made up my mind at the moment that I would come back later that evening and kill him. If my dad can't live, then I thought that uncle Philip shouldn't either.

Adam rested himself back in his chair and clasped his hands together on the table in front of him. Isaac thought that he looked like a wrecked young man. He felt an air of sadness for him.

'Did you kill your uncle as a form of revenge for what he had put your dad and your family through?'

Adam nodded sluggishly.

'Please say out loud your response Adam,' requested the DCI.

'Yes,' said Adam, 'I killed for revenge.'

The next part of the interview would be to get Adam to talk through the process of the murder. Isaac recognised the exhaustion in the young's face and contemplated giving him a rest for a period of time but decided to press on with the interview.

'Can you now talk us through what happened the evening of the murder?' Enquired Isaac.

Adam shifted himself in the chair and gently nodded. However, he didn't speak. His face was making some strange movements as if he were thinking what to say.

'Erm...I stabbed him,' was all he said.

'Can you expand on that Adam?' Asked the DCI.

'What else do you need to know? I stabbed him and he died.'

'That was reported in the papers, I need you to tell me exactly what happened. Tell me about the lead up to the death and how it happened.'

Adam looked confused and angry. As far as he was concerned, he had said all he needed to say and wanted the interview to finish.

'What happened?' Isaac asked again.

The young man started to get agitated and restless in his seat. He could feel the sweat trickling down his back and the chair felt uncomfortable.

'I told you that I killed him with a knife.'

'I need you to talk through the whole event,' persisted Isaac.

'I arrived at about 7:00pm,' Adam faltered again. 'He was a naturist so was naked when I arrived. I was used to this, so it didn't bother me.'

Both detectives glanced at each other with some suspicion at what had just been said.

'Go on,' encouraged Isaac.

'We obviously argued about what he had put my dad through and it all got very heated and nasty. He pushed me to try to get me out of the house, but I pushed him back. We ended up in the kitchen and continued to yell and push each other.'

'What was in the kitchen Adam? On the worktops?' questioned

Emily.

'There wasn't anything as he was a compulsive cleaner and hated things left on his kitchen work surfaces.' Adam was now smiling at himself. 'I got really angry with him and grabbed a knife from the knife block and ran at him. He tried to get away from me, but I stood in his way and violently stabbed him. He fell on the floor and I left.'

'Where was he lying when you left?' Probed Isaac.

Adam looked extremely nervous and bewildered, both Isaac and Emily picked up on this.

'Where you found him,' was the stuttered answer.

'Tell me where?' Asked Isaac again.

'He was over by the fridge in the corner.'

Isaac was now smiling and glanced over at his DS. Adam stared at the faces of the detectives and was also feeling pleased with himself. That impression didn't last long.

'You didn't kill Philip, as you know nothing of the crime scene.' Isaac glared directly at the young man. 'I can arrest you for wasting police time.'

'I did kill him. I was confused and can't remember all the details.'

'Adam, are you covering up for your father? He could have gone back after you, jumped out of the car the afternoon you went to see Philip and collected your work uniform and went back and killed his brother.'

The young man sitting opposite the DCI became hysterical and started to get extremely frantic.

'Please let me take the blame. My father is close to dying and I don't want people to think of him, I mean remember him, as a murderer. Please charge me instead.'

'We can't do that Adam. Do you know for sure that your father killed Philip?' Questioned Isaac.

'When we were in the car after confronting uncle Philip, he kept saying that he would kill him. He said it over and over again.' Adam was distraught.

There was a knock on the interview room door and Jian came in. Isaac held up a hand to stop his approach.

'Adam, do you know for sure that your father killed his brother?'

‘No,’ Adam said through sobs.

‘Sir,’ Jian said as he stepped forward. ‘Someone is outside and they have confessed to killing Philip Oakes.’

Isaac and Emily’s eyes widened as they gazed upon the DC standing in front of them. Adam also looked stunned.

Isaac stood up and followed Jian out of the room.

‘I’ve put the person in the interview room two sir,’ said DC Wong.

‘Who is it Jian?’ Asked Isaac.

‘It’s Emma Oakes sir.’

58:

4th January 2018

Confession of a Murderer

10:30pm

Adam had been moved to another room within the building with Jian keeping him company and Emma was now in interview room one. She had legal aid representation but hadn't really wanted one. Both Isaac and Emily were present and about to start questioning Mrs Oakes.

DCI Davidson sat opposite Emma and was hoping this wasn't another attempt to cover up and protect Ethan Oakes, but somehow knew that it wasn't. Emma sat in a very rigid and regal way, she also had an air of elegance about her.

'I have been at the hospital with Ethan as he was re-admitted today with another episode of sepsis. I came home and my mother told me that you had arrested Adam and also taken his uniform in for analysis.'

'What have the hospital said about your husband Mrs Oakes?' Asked Emily, genuinely concerned.

'They have said that his body can't take much more of this and they don't give him longer than about one month.'

'We are both deeply sorry to hear that, but we do need to start this interview. I am sure you are aware Mrs Oakes that your eldest son has already confessed to the murder of his uncle?' said Isaac.

Emma merely nodded, as her mother had told her of the arrest when she had got home and this had been the reason she had come in.

'He would do that. I assume Adam thinks Ethan killed his uncle?' She asked as a question.

'Yes, he said he didn't want people thinking of his father as a killer and therefore wanted to save him that extra pain and worry before he dies.'

'Adam didn't kill Philip,' Emma said with assertiveness in her steady voice, 'I did.'

'We know your son was lying as he didn't have a clue about the crime scene. Can you tell us about it?' Asked Isaac.

Emma shifted in her seat and spoke with assurance.

'Philip was wearing his dressing gown. On the kitchen worktop there was a wallet and an expensive looking watch. There was a pizza from Tony's Authentic Pizzas and one slice had been removed. Philip was lying on the floor with his gown open. He was on his front and his feet that were covered in cuts were closest to the back door. The kitchen was spotless in every other way. Blood was beginning to seep from underneath him. If you check with Sky, then I am sure they can tell you that on 8th December at the time of Philip's death, the film The Green Mile was playing. I heard it coming from the lounge. There was nothing that forensics would have got from any other rooms in the house as the whole scene took place in the kitchen and outside in his garden. Philip ran out into the street screaming and yelling and that's how he cut his feet as he had no shoes on. I hid behind his shed as he was in the street and nipped back into the house to confront him.' Emma stopped and glanced at the detectives. 'I assume you believe me and want me to continue?'

Isaac and Emily had both been absorbed with what they were being told that they hadn't realised Emma had stopped talking.

'Oh, sorry, yes Mrs Oakes we believe you, please continue,' said Isaac.

'Philip came back inside, oh dear, I forgot to tell you what made him come outside in the first place. Let me go back to the evening before. As you know I was staying with my mother and Saul and Max. Ever since Philip came around to ours screaming that Ethan was the clown, I had been fascinated by the idea. I saw how petrified he was and couldn't help but think how wonderful it would be if there were two clowns torturing him. I loved the idea. If he could feel the persecution and pain we were going through as a family for just a few moments then I wanted to be the one to do it. I sneaked home at midnight and dressed up in Adam's uniform and used my makeup to make some sort of clown face. Ethan and Adam were both asleep as I could hear snoring coming from their rooms. I went around to Philip's house and waited for him to come home. I knew he was out as Ethan had told me so. When I saw his bedroom light go on I stood in the garden and hoped he would look out and he did. I jumped up and down and tried to seem menacing and frightening.'

Isaac now realised why the picture was so blurred if she had been jumping about. Emma was now appearing quite relaxed as she told her confession.

'The next evening I put the boys to bed. I made sure we had a very busy day at London Zoo so that both children and my mother would be tired. Max was asleep by 6:15pm, Saul was reading in his room, but I knew he'd stay there. My mother was dozing in her armchair by the fire but would soon be fully asleep. I told her I was going to my room and didn't want to be disturbed. I waited until 6:45pm and then went out to the car. I drove over to Philip's house and got dressed up as the clown again in the car. I waited for a while and then saw a lad arrive delivering a pizza. Philip stood there with his gown open and the poor young lad appeared quite upset by it. I waited for him to leave on his motorbike and then crept around into Philip's garden and waited. I didn't have to wait long before he came into the kitchen. He took out a knife to cut up the pizza when he looked up and saw me through his kitchen window. He was obviously frightened to death and I won't lie, I was really enjoying seeing it. However, it was then that it all started to go wrong. I thought he'd run into his lounge and I'd leave. That was going to be my last appearance as the clown, as all I had intended to do was scare him enough to have a slight idea about how my wonderful husband was feeling. Unfortunately, he didn't turn and run but came dashing towards me. I ran and hid as I just told you and then re-entered the kitchen. Philip eventually came back in and saw me. I had taken off the wig by then and had placed it on the worktop near the pizza. Philip started yelling at me. To my utter surprise, he ran at me. I was now the scared one and as a matter of self-protection I grabbed the first thing I saw, which regrettably for both of us was the knife he had got out to cut his food. Philip ran into me and the knife went straight into his heart or so I believe. I was so shocked about what happened, I guess I was stunned, that I just left out the backdoor. I took the overalls and boots back to the house so they wouldn't be missed if Adam decided to go back to work. I then went back to my mother's house and found everyone asleep. If I'd known this was all going to end the way it did, I would never have used Adam's uniform.'

The detectives had listened to every single word that Emma had spoken. She sat as if she had said everything that she needed to.

'So your intention was never to go to Philip's house and kill him?' Asked Isaac to clarify.

'No,' Emma said, 'I went to scare him and then confront him about the way he had made Ethan feel and what he had done to us as a family. Him running at me changed everything. I never meant to kill him and that you must believe.'

'Why did you take a slice of the pizza? We know Philip didn't eat it as forensics have proved that,' said Emily.

'Oh I don't know, dramatic effect, maybe I was hungry or maybe I just did it for something to do.' Emma looked crushed.

Isaac stood up and read Emma her rights and then asked Emily to stay with her as he went to find Adam, who was in the room next door.

'Hey Adam, I'm not going to press charges on you for wasting police time as I understand your good intentions behind what you did. However, we do know that you didn't kill your uncle and although I can't go into more detail with you at this moment, I can tell you that your dad did not kill his brother.'

Adam started to cry again with happiness and Isaac hadn't the heart to tell him the final truth.

'A police constable is going to come and take you home. Look after yourself Adam, you are a real credit to your mother and father.'

Adam smiled and thanked Isaac.

'Sir,' he called out just as Isaac had opened the door to leave. 'Why did my uncle hate my father so much? Why was he prepared to let him die without even trying to help?'

Isaac looked pitifully at the young man in front of him.

'I'm sorry Adam, I don't know. We never found out.'

59:

1994

Philip aged Thirteen

Philip sat alone quietly on the beige sofa in the lounge and was watching the television. He was used to being on his own in the house, especially since Ethan had turned eighteen last year and took himself out nearly every night. Tonight wasn't anything unusual. Philip had made himself a cheese, tomato and salad cream sandwich and had this with a packet of salt and vinegar crisps and a coke. His dad wasn't in and in truth he was never at home, well, hardly ever, maybe enough to keep the social workers away. Mrs Temple rarely came anymore, but that was a blessing as she had become too intense and bossy during the past year and Philip felt he was too old to need her fussing over him.

In truth, Mrs Temple loved Philip like he was her own son and had been pushing him to become something in this world. She recognised the hardships he had gone through and wanted him to be able to see how special he was, but at thirteen Philip only saw this as an interference.

Ethan had spent ages getting himself ready for tonight. He had been about forty minutes in the shower and about the same amount of time on his hair judging by the number of times he kept running down the stairs and asking Philip,

'Does this look alright?'

Ethan had bragged to his brother that he was out seeing a new girl tonight and he was hoping to have sex with her. To be honest Philip was just pleased to be by himself and finally able to watch what he wanted on the television.

His brother who was now nineteen, was as unpleasant as he had always been. Philip often thought back to all the horrible things Ethan had said and done to him over the years since their mother had died. The worst had been dressing up as a clown and jumping out of his wardrobe.

Their father had disengaged himself from his two sons the day his wife died and when he was in the house he rarely spoke. He chose to stay in his study either reading or working. However, that wasn't an issue because Philip liked his own company. He couldn't be let down or hurt by himself. He had taught himself to be happy and jovial at school. In fact, whenever anyone was around, Philip pretended to be a normal happy teenager as he didn't want anyone coming over to him and have them seeing how desperately sad and lonely he was. That would be too awful.

After a few hours of being on his own and enjoying his snacks and television, Philip heard the front door slam shut. He could tell that his brother was not happy and therefore dreaded Ethan coming into the lounge.

'The bitch!' Ethan screamed from the hallway.

Philip cringed as he sat on the sofa and heard Ethan swearing in the hall.

'The fucking bitch!'

Ethan flung open the lounge door and glared hard at Philip.

'I said, the fucking bitch!'

'I heard you,' said a nervous Philip.

He hated it when his brother had been drinking. Ethan wasn't a nice drunk, but equally Ethan wasn't nice when sober. Last week he had slapped Philip around the face, hard! Philip couldn't understand why as there seemed to be no reason.

Ethan dropped himself onto the sofa next to his brother. Philip pulled his legs underneath himself.

'She led me on,' Ethan ranted. 'She knew what she was doing and fucking led me on.'

Philip stood and went to move off the sofa.

'SIT DOWN PHILIP!' screamed Ethan, 'I am telling you about my evening.'

Philip sat back down, but he sat as far into the corner of the sofa as he could get and watched his brother closely.

'She let me pay for everything tonight, before going back to her place.' Ethan said. 'Then as we started to kiss and get horny, she backed off and

said her parents would be home soon.'

Philip could see the anger in his eyes and could sense that his brother's fury was building and he started to panic inside. He didn't want to get slapped again.

'She knew I was hard, I'd taken it out for her to see,' continued Ethan.

Philip was now very worried about where this evening was heading and what it meant for him.

Ethan had no idea about the level of concern his brother was feeling.

'She bloody touched my dick and knew I was horny.' Ethan continued to scream.

Philip started to move again, but Ethan yelled at him to sit down. Philip was petrified.

Ethan then stood up and started to pace around the room. Screaming and shouting and getting himself worked up. The drink inside him wasn't helping the situation.

'BITCH!' he yelled as loud as he could.

'Why wasn't dad at home?' thought Philip in sheer panic.

He watched his brother getting increasingly wound up.

'What are you looking at?' Ethan yelled at Philip.

'Nothing Ethan, I promise. Can I go to bed please?' Philip was pleading.

'No, you FUCKING can't!' was the terrifying answer.

Ethan now seemed to lose any sense of control. He flung himself at Philip and started to slap him repeatedly around the head. Philip was screeching, crying, and trying to protect himself, but Ethan wasn't stopping.

'BITCH!' screamed Ethan, 'she knew I wanted it, bitch!'

The next thing Philip was aware of, was being hauled up by Ethan who was shrieking in his face. Philip had never felt panic and terror like it before. He'd never seen Ethan like this, not this angry, not this violent and not this out of control.

Ethan punched Philip in the face and Philip fell to the floor. He missed hitting his head on the coffee table by only an inch or two.

'Ethan STOP!' pleaded Philip, 'please stop, you're really hurting me, please stop.'

These words went unheard by the man who was now so totally out of control. Philip's sobbing and pleading were going unnoticed.

Philip then felt Ethan's hands grabbing at his belt and he started pulling off his trousers, his underwear was coming off too.

'Oh God! No, please, Ethan please, STOP! DON'T!' Philip shrieked.

There was no turning back now for Ethan. Philip felt the spit from his brother's mouth land onto his anus. Then came the stabbing pain, pain like nothing Philip had ever experienced as Ethan pushed his penis as far into Philip as he could get it. Ethan was too strong. Philip's strength had gone. He just lay there, silently sobbing as his brother thrust inside of him. It seemed to go on forever. He could hear Ethan panting heavily, at the same time grabbing Philip's hips so he could rape harder and deeper. The pain was shooting through Philip and Ethan was continuously shouting about his failed conquest this evening.

After what felt like hours, the thrusts started slowing down and then came five short, but deep thrusting movements. It was over at last. 'Bitch!' Ethan said, but this time softly and full of regret.

He pulled himself out of his brother and stood up and looked at Philip lying on the floor, crying. He saw blood on his own penis and knew he'd made Philip bleed. As he stood there, many thoughts were running through his head. He wasn't sure he was able to comprehend what he had just done to his brother.

An overwhelming panic filled Ethan's body and he started to shake and feel nauseated. He looked all about him but saw nothing for a few moments, but it felt like hours. Ethan then stepped over the weeping boy and headed for the lounge door. He saw Philip's trousers and underwear where he had thrown them after he had ripped them off of the struggling lad. As he got to the door, he stopped. He stood there for a few moments and then, without turning around and with a trembling voice, he said,

'I'm sorry Philip, I shouldn't have done that.'

He walked into the hall and went quietly up the stairs and into his bedroom.

Philip just lay there for what seemed like a lifetime. His tears were slowing up, but inside he felt numb. Lying there on the floor he felt cold and shivery, despite the fact that the heating was on. He very slowly stood up and looked around himself. He was searching for his underwear, but not able to focus on anything. Eventually he saw them over by the television and walked over to get them. The pain was terrible. He stopped and knew the tears had started again and was also aware of the feeling that he had fluid running down the back of his leg. He touched the liquid and then looked at it. Blood and he was sure there was also his brother's semen. He retched and ran as best as he could into the kitchen and threw up in the sink, all over the cups and plates that had been left there since breakfast.

Once he had been sick, he raised his head and caught sight of his reflection in the window. He looked like he'd aged. He collapsed onto the kitchen floor and as he cried, he pulled himself into the foetal position and sobbed. His tears were falling down his cheeks and his whole body was shaking.

Upstairs in his dark unlit bedroom, Ethan lay in his bed and started to cry uncontrollably into his pillow. His whole body was quivering and he was mortified at what he had just done to his younger, helpless brother. He reflected that over the years, since their mother had died, he had been a cruel person, especially to Philip. Her death was the fault of a man speeding in his car and not his brother's. Ethan regretted all the terrible things he had done to Philip. He knew he should have been protecting him and not bullying him.

'Things need to change, things have to change,' he said to himself through the crying.

As he lay in his bed, in the distance he could hear his brother sobbing.

'I'm so sorry Philip,' he said under his breath, 'I promise I'll start looking after you and make you happy again.'

Ethan then put his head under his pillow and cried himself to sleep.

With no idea of how long he'd been on the kitchen floor, Philip started to slowly get up. Almost immediately he was aware of the pain that was still present. He felt bruised. Philip also knew that he needed to wash. His bottom and the tops of his legs felt sticky.

Walking into the lounge he saw his trousers and underwear by the television. He bent to pick them up and straight away felt the sticky hairs at the back pulling at his skin. Philip walked out of the lounge and slowly headed upstairs, taking each step as slowly as he could.

When he eventually got to the top, he stopped outside his brother's room and he could hear Ethan snoring. He felt nothing and walked into his bedroom and took off his t-shirt and socks and grabbed his towel, went into the bathroom, and locked the door.

He then turned on the shower to allow the water to warm up and stared at himself in the mirror. He grimaced and sadly he was shocked. What he saw was his face streaked with his tears and his eyes were swollen and red.

'I hate childhood!' he said quietly to himself.

Philip just stood for what felt like hours and continued to stare at himself in the mirror. He tried to understand what had happened tonight and why it had happened.

'Was it my fault?' He asked his reflection in the mirror.

The bathroom was steaming up with the hot water from the shower and he started to lose his reflection in the mirror. Philip wiped the glass with his towel and opened the bathroom cabinet and took out a pair of scissors. He gazed at them for a few moments, then re-wiped the mirror so he could see himself in it again. He opened them up and cut into his shoulder. It wasn't a large cut, but the skin bled. It felt good to cut!

He dropped the scissors into the sink and stepped into the shower, allowing the water to cover his still shaking body. He looked down and saw the red streaks of blood being washed away. It made him feel as if he wanted to be sick again.

This evening changed Philip forever, and robbed the world of a kind and gentle soul.

As the hot water pounded his back, Philip had just one thought.

'I will get you back Ethan!'

About the Author

Gavin Maynard-Wyatt is in his early 50s and this is his debut book. For as long as he can remember he has had a love for murder mystery whodunnits. At 11 years old he read his Grandad's copy of Agatha Christie's *At Bertram's Hotel*, and his passion for whodunnits was started. Following years of self-doubt, Gavin finally put fingers to keyboard and *The Murder of Philip Oakes* was born. Formulating this story was an exhilarating experience that has helped Gavin's confidence as a writer grow. He is currently writing his second book which will also feature DCI Isaac Davidson and his team of detectives.

Gavin works as a cancer nurse for young people, has one child and lives in West Sussex. He enjoys going for long walks in the countryside, cooking, reading and has a love for elephants!

Printed in Great Britain
by Amazon

34834225R00202